ONE KISS

"Just be as quiet as you can."

"I thought you said there was no danger," she whispered in return, her voice telling of her fear.

"There's no need to take chances either."

Abigail stepped into the coldest water imaginable. The water, even at its deepest, came only to her knees and Abigail forced herself, with a muffled groan, to sit. Already her legs were growing numb, but not numb enough. She felt a tickle. Without thinking Abigail reached down and picked up a small snake, or at least what she thought was a small snake. She forgot all about being quiet.

Hawk jumped to his feet at the scream. It took only four leaping strides before they met at the water's edge. He pulled her against him and lifted her from the water.

Abigail grew slowly aware of the fact that she was in his arms, naked with her chest pressed against his.

His hand ran over her back, never stopping until it smoothed over her thighs and then returned to the lushness of her backside. "Just let me kiss you once, and I'll stop." Abigail forgot her thoughts, forgot the fact that she was standing naked in this man's arms. Forgot everything but the feel of his mouth upon hers. One kiss was quite enough.

Taylor—made Romance From Zebra Books

PATRICIA PELLICANE

NIGHTS of PASSION

ZEBRA BOOKS
KENSINGTON PUBLISHING CORP.

To Kathleen Drymon;
The Best of Friends

ZEBRA BOOKS are published by

Kensington Publishing Corp.
475 Park Avenue South
New York, NY 10016

First Printing: April, 1994

Printed in the United States of America

Chapter One

Abigail Pennyworth sat on her veranda, protected from the sun's harsh light by its overhanging roof, fluttering an ivory fan before her face, desperate for a stirring of air that was so thick, she swore it was as easy to swallow as to breathe. It was hot, breathlessly so. The sun's glare was exaggerated tenfold behind a white overcast sky. In the distance came an occasional rumble of thunder, along with dark brooding clouds that promised rain.

The worst of it was, should it rain, it wasn't likely to improve her discomfort. Rain never brought relief. Rain only made everything wetter, hotter, and infinitely more uncomfortable.

She should ride out to the lake, she thought. On a day like this, nothing eased the miserable discomforting heat like a dip in its cool clear waters. Just the thought of her chemise, wet and icy cold, clinging to her body brought a smile.

"Lord, I don't know where that girl takes herself off to. I've searched everywhere."

Abigail turned as her aunt Elizabeth came from

the big white house. Aunt Elizabeth had been called Betty Jo in her youth, but her youth as well as her prime had been gone for some time. Now, fast approaching seventy, the woman exhibited brief moments of reality liberally interspersed with what Abigail charitably called forgetfulness.

The truth was, Aunt Elizabeth lived mostly in her own private world. A world that was more than thirty years dead, where the South had never fallen, where Atlanta had not burned, where she was eternally young, hopeful, and delighted with the thought of her most recent beau. Her conversations centered around nothing more important than the choice of said beau and the gown she planned to wear to the next cotillion. She never seemed to notice that the intended cotillion never came about.

Years ago something had happened to her mind. Perhaps it was the horror of the war itself or the ravages suffered in its aftermath. Somehow she had managed the impossible. For her, time had come to a permanent stop. Now thirty-odd years after the war, she thought herself still a young woman awaiting a special man's return, planning a glorious homecoming. Abigail didn't mind her aunt's often incoherent babblings. They were better by far than the days when she couldn't bring herself from her bed.

From as far back as Abigail could remember, Aunt Elizabeth had lived with them. Long ago her odd actions had become the norm, and at twenty-four, Abigail had never known her aunt any other way.

Abigail had explained innumerable times that Amanda had gone off with Thomas Hill. And yet it seemed to make no difference how many times she repeated the fact. Abigail was of a mind to believe that her aunt simply chose not to remember.

In the distance came a small cloud of dust. Abigail rose from the white cane rocker as Billy Henderson turned from the road. His horsemanship was, to say the least, greatly in need, for Abigail had never seen a more awkward ungainly seating. She watched as the horse strode up the long drive, holding her breath, expecting at any second to see him flung from the saddle. His feet actually came from the stirrups, and Abigail believed he held his wobbly seat only by the grace of God, for his legs flapped about as wild and free as did his long blond hair.

Somehow he managed, and Abigail had no notion how, to pull the horse to a stop at the steps to the veranda. The problem was, the horse came to a sudden stop. Billy's body did not. It continued on for some dangerous inches, nearly over the horse's head. It shouldn't have, for they had seen this gangly performance on more than one occasion; still, a gasp of fear was torn from both women. Even though he was no longer moving fast, hardly moving at all in fact, he almost fell again. Abigail frowned at the clumsy display. The boy would obviously never be a horseman and should seriously consider the purchase of a buggy.

Billy worked for his father, in Chelsy, a half hour ride from her home. Mr. Henderson owned and operated the telegraph office, and Billy was apprenticing to one day take over the business.

Billy flashed her a friendly crooked-toothed smile, his freckles brighter than usual, no doubt due to the day's heat. He came from the horse at last and

7

handed her a thin white envelope. Even if he'd been another, Abigail would have recognized that envelope as a wire. No other seemed so white.

Her heart began to race, knowing this was news at last. Abigail's sister Amanda had been gone for almost a year, and she had almost given up hope.

Her fingers fairly itched to tear the envelope open, but she forced a calm she was far from feeling. "If you wait a moment, I'll get you something for your trouble, Billy."

Billy shook his head. "A drink from your well would do me fine, Miss Pennyworth. The weather is already turning. Can't imagine what it will be like in August." He nodded toward the older lady. "Mornin', Miss Pennyworth."

"Are you Abigail's new beau?"

Billy had been to the house on more than one occasion and was not ignorant of the older woman's idiosyncracies. He smiled. "Just a friend, ma'am."

Abigail watched as her aunt fluttered her fan in what could only be called a coquettish fashion. On a woman approaching seventy, the action looked out of place and oddly sad.

Abigail sighed, her soft cheeks coloring with embarrassment. Aunt Elizabeth was aware of the fact that Abigail was planning to marry Robert the moment Amanda was found. Aunt Elizabeth knew it and yet never failed to ask every man who came to the house the same question. Abigail's smile was weak at best as she tried to think of something to say, something that might ease the discomfort of the moment.

She glanced at the boy again and then realized by

8

his glances toward the corner of the house that he had already forgotten the old woman's comment. He appeared to be looking for someone. And then she remembered Becky. Becky, the daughter of her tenant, worked three days a week in the kitchen out back helping Mrs. Charlie, their cook.

"Why don't you walk on back to the kitchen, Billy? I know for a fact that Becky has a pitcher of lemonade just wastin' away in the icehouse."

"Why don't you ring for Maggie, Abigail? I'm feeling a mite thirsty myself."

Despite the fact that there was no Maggie, that Maggie had been Aunt Elizabeth's maid, in fact, slave, some fifty years ago, Abigail nodded as she walked into the house. She stopped in the shadowy hall. The moment she was alone, she tore open the message and then almost swooned at the news. Amanda was safe. Amanda had been seen only last week in New Orleans with a man who professed to be her husband.

Abigail was bothered by the word "professed." Apparently her worst fears had proven true, and there was no proof of the marriage, or Mr. Pinkerton would not have worded the message in that exact fashion.

Her lips tightened, and her cheeks colored with the mortifying thought. If she ever got her hands on Thomas Hill, she was going to kill him for doing this to her sister.

Poor Amanda. The girl didn't know her own mind. She wasn't responsible for the depravity of others. Abigail could only imagine what the girl must have gone through. Despite the heat Abigail shivered at the thought. She was never going to forgive Hill for taking advantage of Amanda. Never!

It took only a second to clear away the indecision. She was going to New Orleans. If there was a chance of finding Amanda, there was no way she would sit here and wait.

Robert Stacey rolled to his back, his breathing harsh and irregular, his arm flung over his eyes. A smile teased his handsome, if slightly too full, mouth as the lady's hand immediately reached for his limp member and began to fondle him. God, he couldn't remember knowing a woman more insatiable. No sooner had he reached the peak of release than she wanted it again.

"Easy, baby. Give me a minute."

Molly snuggled herself, along with her huge breasts, against his side and curved her lips into a pretty pout of disappointment. The action was wasted on the man. His eyes were closed. "I want you again, baby." Molly was experienced enough with men and their sensitive egos to know that telling the truth in this situation was totally out of the question. Robert was a selfish lover. Like many he imagined himself quite good in the art of loving, believing a woman to be thrilled, if simply the recipient of his tool. The truth of it was, he had no idea what the hell he was doing. He was fast. Much too fast, if a woman was looking for satisfaction. Molly knew from personal experience that with this man it always took two or three times before she found release.

Robert grinned as he watched her raise herself to

her elbow and rub those huge breasts against his chest. She was hot for him all right. Hot and sexy and obviously delighted, if her moans meant anything, every time he plunged into that sweet wet heat. He'd have another go at her in a minute. But for now he was content just to watch her play.

"Sit on me," he said and smiled as she willingly, no anxiously, did his bidding.

Robert couldn't think of anything more delightful than to watch a bouncing pair of tits, especially a pair like hers. It didn't matter that he was getting married, if and when Abigail's half-wit sister was ever found. The fact was, he was set to enjoy Molly and her sweet body for a long time to come.

Besides, a man was expected to keep a mistress. It was an accepted fact of life. He grinned at the thought of all that money. Once he was married and could well afford it, he might consider keeping Molly and her friend Kit. Robert felt his sex thicken at the thought. Damn, if he wasn't the luckiest bastard. His future wife was rich, and once he got his hands on her money, he could afford to keep two, possibly even three women at a time in his bed.

A knock sounded at his door.

"What is it, Jakes?"

"Miss Pennyworth is here to see you, sir."

Robert sighed. "Damn." Just before he realized that Abigail had never, no matter how he had tried to coerce her, come to his rooms before. If she were here now, it had to be something important. "Sorry, baby. We'll have to finish this later."

Molly sighed with disappointment as she watched him dress. "Should I wait?"

11

Robert, his thoughts elsewhere, had forgotten the woman's very existence. Maybe the Pinkertons had found Abigail's sister. God, he hoped so. Lately bill collectors had been pounding at his door every day. He needed to get his hands on that money.

"Should I?"

Robert glanced at the naked woman, a frown creasing his handsome forehead. "What?"

"Should I wait?"

"I don't know how long I'll be."

"It doesn't matter," she said. "I haven't anything else to do." She then continued in silence, except maybe to take care of some business you neglected to finish.

Robert quickly dressed in trousers and boots. He splashed an abundance of cologne over his face and chest (it wouldn't do to have Abigail detect Molly's perfume) before sliding his arms into a hip-length silk jacket. His chest was bare beneath the material. Abigail would imagine he had been relaxing in his rooms.

Even though it was mercifully swift, Abigail felt almost smothered in his embrace. Lord, but the man wore the most god-awful scent. It had a woodsy flavor, and yet as now, she often detected the heavy cloying scent of roses. How odd. Once they were married, she'd see to it that he used something quite a bit lighter.

"Is everything all right?"

"Everything is wonderful."

Robert knew what that meant. He could feel the relief washing over him. "Where is she?"

"In New Orleans."

He took her in his arms again, pushed aside the

ridiculous feather in her wide-brimmed hat, and buried his face in her soft, sweetly scented neck. "Thank God."

"I'm leaving tonight."

"What?" He pulled back, his smooth forehead marred with a puzzled frown. "Where are you going?"

"To New Orleans. I have to find her."

"But you said—"

"Mr. Pinkerton's wire said she had been seen in New Orleans."

"You mean he doesn't have her in custody?"

For a fraction of a second, her eyes hardened at his remark, which touched on sounding callous. "She's not a criminal, Robert."

"I know. What I meant was—"

With slender fingers, Abigail waved aside the attempted explanation. She knew what he meant, and she hadn't the time right now to listen to another bout of flowery dialogue. She came immediately to the point. "It seems Thomas Hill had a confrontation with one of Pinkerton's men. By the time the man came again to his senses, the rooms my sister and Hill had occupied were empty."

"If they left the city, why are you going?"

Abigail shrugged. "Others have seen them since. Mr. Pinkerton believes they are still there.

"I have to hurry. I've a great deal of packing to do." Abigail reached up on her toes and placed a light kiss on his lips. "I don't know when I'll be back, but I'll wire you . . ."

"You're not going alone, or worse yet, with your aunt?"

She shook her head. "I'll take Jessie with me." And at his worried look continued with, "I'll be fine, and Mr. Carver promised to look in on Aunt Elizabeth."

Mr. Carver had been the family's solicitor for about a hundred years. Robert figured his looking in on the peculiar old woman would be as effective as finding piss in a stream. He didn't care. All he cared about was Abigail and, of course, what her money could do for him.

He wasn't about to let her travel alone. Suppose something happened? Suppose she never came back. What the hell would happen to him? If trouble should arise, Jessie, her maid, would be of no use. Robert came to an instant decision. "I'm going with you."

"But, Robert, your businesses. You can't just leave everything."

The fact of the matter was, whatever businesses he had inherited from his father were in the past tense. He had long ago gone through most of the monies they had allotted him. Last year the little that had been left had been claimed by his creditors. Robert was virtually penniless and during the last year had fallen deeply in debt. Nothing was keeping him here, nothing but her promise of marriage. "I'll take care of everything. Don't worry."

She smiled as he held her against him again, relaxed, feeling safe and secure in his arms. She hadn't wanted to ask him to go with her, to leave his businesses in the hands of another, and was terribly grateful that he had made the offer. Abigail was a strong woman, but aware that even a strong woman traveling without a man's protection could easily become a target of criminal intent.

"I've got to pack. The last stage leaves for Charlotte at eight. Even then I'm cutting it close if I want to make the train to Charleston and my connection south."

Robert couldn't help but think of the lady still in his bed. If he knew Abigail, and he did, he wouldn't have a chance to enjoy another female for some time. It was ridiculous, to his way of thinking, to waste the night away in an uncomfortable coach, while Molly lay in his bed, available and willing. "Why not wait until morning."

Abigail shook her head. "I can't. We're so close."

Robert nodded, hiding well his disappointment. "All right, I'll meet you at the station at eight."

"Don't be late," she said as she hurried toward his door.

"Wait," he said, the word stopping her in midstride. Her hand was on the doorknob. It was more than obvious that she was anxious to be about her business. "People might talk if we travel together. Why not get married before we leave?" Robert thought his suggestion absolutely brilliant. If he could get her to agree, he could feign a problem at the last minute, with one of his supposed businesses and wouldn't have to go at all. If he could get her to agree, he could spend his marriage night, his whole honeymoon, in fact, in the arms of his favorite bed partner instead of with this cold stick of a woman.

"We haven't the time."

"I could take care of the details. The ceremony would take only a few minutes."

"Robert, please. I can't think about marriage now. I'm so close to finding her."

"Of course, dear," he said, this time unable to disguise his disappointment with his usual devastating smile.

It was perhaps the only thing she didn't like about the man, this tendency he had to sulk whenever he didn't get his way. Still, no one was perfect, and Abigail supposed it not all that difficult to overlook one minor fault. "I promise we'll marry the minute I find her."

Robert grinned, knowing he'd wipe away her small frown at his next words. "It's just that I love you so much."

Lord, but the man was beautiful. It was no wonder that she loved him. "I know, sweetheart. Don't forget, eight o'clock."

Robert nodded. "Do me a favor? When you buy your ticket, pick up one for me. I might not have the time to . . ." His hands searched through his pockets as if he expected to find money there. Only he knew his pockets, all of his pockets, in fact, had been empty for some time.

Abigail smiled. "Of course."

Robert watched the door close behind her and then glanced up the long flight of stairs, knowing Molly was still in bed awaiting his return. It was almost five. What with packing and getting to the stage on time, that left him only two hours to enjoy her and, damn it, he was going to do just that.

* * *

He was late. The stage was already packed and the travelers boarding by the time his carriage pulled into the depot. It was Molly's fault, of course. He had kept her in bed until the last minute, and then she had given him a special treat, something to remember her by, she'd said, just before he pulled his trousers into place. Damn, but that had been good. It had taken him almost a full five minutes to recover from her expertise. Even now, thoroughly drained, his sex threatened to thicken again at the thought of what she would do for him when he returned.

Robert handed his two cases to the driver to join the others already tied atop the coach and quickly stepped inside.

"I thought you were going to miss it," Abigail said, obviously relieved at his appearance.

"It took a bit longer than I expected to get everything settled."

She smiled and made room for him. When she moved, her hip touched against a silent man sitting at the opposite end of the same seat.

Jeremiah Hawk took in the occupants of the late night stage, in particular and with some speculation, the lady who had moved to accommodate the last passenger.

He had been mildly surprised to find the passenger, her companion, was a man. He had thought perhaps she was awaiting the arrival of her maid, or an older woman, for it was a well-known fact that it was hardly safe for a woman to travel alone. Since she wore no gloves, he hadn't missed the fact that she was not married. Hawk frowned. It wasn't any of his business, of course, but a lady never traveled with a

17

man who was not her husband—unless, of course, she wasn't a lady after all. Hawk couldn't credit the possibility. No, she was a lady all right. He was experienced enough with women to know when one was a lady and when one was not.

Hawk wasn't the least bit sorry that her moving had brought their hips into contact. The ride to Charlotte was bound to be long and uncomfortable. The night was hot, damp, heavy with the promise of rain, the coach crowded. But he didn't mind the discomfort half so much with this woman pressed against his side. She was pretty—Well, perhaps pretty was a less than accurate description. She was beautiful. Jeremiah couldn't remember when he'd seen a woman quite so beautiful before.

She wore a simple but obviously expensive dark blue traveling suit, the cuffs and collar trimmed in black. Beneath the short tight jacket, her blouse buttoned high upon a slender throat. An inch of white lace peeked from her cuffs. Her hair was blonde, sort of streaked with gold and silver, and Hawk presumed quite long, for it was piled high upon her head into some sort of fancy twist. She wore a matching fedora hat with a long blue veil. It came to her chin and was pulled back and tied into a knot at the top of her hat. The hat itself was simple enough (thank God, no stuffed birds), with the exception of an ostrich plume that promised to give Hawk some trouble. Every time she turned her head, the feather hit him in the face.

Next to her sat a dandy. It was the only word to describe him, for the man was perfectly attired as well

18

as exquisitely groomed, fingernails spotless, not a blond hair out of place.

Across from him sat a preacher accompanied by, what the man believed it necessary to proclaim as, his two innocent daughters. Hawk knew some real conviction to the truth in their father's out-of-place announcement. One glance in their direction and Hawk figured they probably came close to rivaling the Virgin Mary in their current state of purity, for he couldn't imagine any man considering either of the ugly twosome as candidates for his bed.

Both had skin the color of paste; scrawny, almost emaciated bodies; and long pointy noses and receding chins. Accompanied by crooked teeth they were a sad sight to be sure. Hawk had already learned from the talkative preacher that he had been visiting with relatives, and once the stage reached Charlotte, would continue his journey south and west by train, back to his little flock in Texas. His two daughters were to be wed upon returning. Hawk could only imagine the men in Texas to be desperate.

All he knew about the woman at his side was that she was traveling to New Orleans. He didn't know why and figured asking might be considered a bit too forward and might give her the impression that he was interested. He knew even less about the man traveling with her, except for the fact that he didn't like him on sight. If pressed, Hawk couldn't have explained why. He just didn't.

The driver called out and the stage lurched forward, almost flinging the small woman at his side (her name was Miss Pennyworth, if he wasn't mistaken) to the floor. Only Hawk and his quick reflexes saved her from an awkward fall. The fact that his arm brushed against her breasts when he reached for her seemed to go unnoticed. Unnoticed at least by the lady. Hawk couldn't claim the same sense of ignorance.

One of the women across from him, each being almost as small but much less shapely, than the lady at his side, should probably have sat one on each side of the coach, thereby allowing the others some much needed space. Only they hadn't. One sat to the right, the other to the left of her father, which forced Hawk, Abigail, and Robert to squeeze into an area that was hardly large enough for two.

"I'm sorry," she said for something like the tenth time when the jostling coach caused her to brush against him.

The woman was soft and felt damn good against his side. She smelled good, too. Too good. Clean with just a trace of perfume, French perfume. The scent and feel of her were doing strange things to his body. Things he didn't want to think about. Not here and definitely not now. Thank God it was growing dark. Still, he crossed his legs, for he'd know some real embarrassment should his body's unwanted reaction be noticed.

"Lord, it's hot, isn't it?" Abigail said to no one in particular. If she had known that the coach was going to be this crowded, she would have waited until morning. Too late, she realized she should have done just that. The fact of the matter was, a few hours would have made no real difference.

Her voice was soft, sweet, almost husky, undeniably and deliciously intriguing. Hawk figured the man next to her was a damn lucky bastard. She waved her fan before her face again, bringing her scent to Hawk's nostrils. He would have liked to tell her to stop, for the scent of her only exaggerated his body's unwanted response, but what excuse could he possibly give?

To his relief, after a few minutes, Abigail did stop. The fact was, the three sitting opposite her—the preacher and his two daughters—believed it ungodly and definitely a temptation of the devil to disrobe and bathe more than what was necessary. Necessary being once a month, if the weather held, and their closeness left Abigail nearly panting for clean air.

"Do you mind if we lift the canvas?" she asked with a note of desperation.

"Oh, no," replied one of the ladies. "I'll look a fright if windblown."

Hawk bit his lip, trying to hold back a grin. He figured being windblown could only be an improvement.

Abigail moved closer to Robert, at least her head did; her hips were wedged between him and the man to her right. Only Robert offered her no relief. He was again wearing that woodsy scent that, impossible though it might be, reminded her of roses. If it weren't unseemly, Abigail would have begged to ride atop the coach. There, at least, she'd be able to breathe.

"Do you ladies mind if I smoke?" Hawk asked as a matter of form, his intent to do so no matter what their preferences. He, too, had noticed the distasteful scents emanating from across the way and thought to cover the disagreeable body odor with rich tobacco.

Abigail almost groaned at the thought but made no reply. This was all she needed.

Hawk, although slightly restricted due to lack of room, managed to roll a cigarette and light up.

To Abigail's surprise, the scent was not at all repugnant. The fact was, most of the smoke left by way of a canvas-covered window, and the wispy remnants went far toward disguising the odious aromas within. Abigail breathed a sigh of relief, believing the man's smoke highly preferable to what she had so far been forced to breathe.

She spoke to Robert. "Did you manage to get everything finished?"

Robert grinned into the dimness, knowing he did that and more. He patted her hand. "Everything. Don't worry."

"I expect we'll make the eight o'clock train tomorrow morning for Charleston."

"Good. The sooner we get this business done, the sooner we'll be married."

"Married? You mean you're traveling together, while not united in the holy state?" The preacher was clearly aghast.

Abigail felt her cheeks warm with embarrassment. How had he managed, with one question, to make her feel guilty when there was nothing to be guilty about?

"Miss Pennyworth has promised to be my wife the moment we return," Robert stated proudly.

"I'm afraid that will not do. You cannot travel together unmarried."

Had she been a woman of less determination, Abigail might have acceded to the man's righteous indignation. But the fact was, Abigail had no intention of doing anything wrong. And the fact that he clearly believed she would gave rise to her own indignation. "Reverend . . ."

"I'm afraid I cannot allow such happenings. My innocent daughters—"

Abigail was angry now. How dare he assume the worst? And how dare he voice those assumptions? "Could use a bit of loosening up, if the truth be told." The last of her words were lost in Hawk's laughter, turned instantly into a loud cough. "Along with a bath, I suspect."

"How dare you try to influence the mind of an innocent?"

Abigail sighed, knowing she had gone too far. She never could control the tendency she had to speak her mind. "The truth is, sir, my betrothed and I intend to do no wrong. And it is hardly your business if I do."

"Not my business, you say?"

Was she mistaken? Inside the coach it was getting darker by the minute, especially since the canvas flaps were not allowed to be raised and the setting sun's brilliance was lost on the travelers. She couldn't be sure, but it appeared as if a maniacal gleam had entered the preacher's eyes. "It most certainly is my business. I am a man of God, and God knows a Jezebel when he sees one."

"Robert." She hit the man at her side in the ribs with her elbow. The dolt just sat there allowing this deranged man to say whatever he wished. "Are you going to allow . . . ?"

"Sweetheart, it might be better for all if we permit him to say the words." Robert figured it wouldn't hurt none to allow the preacher to put a bit of pressure on her. He was beginning to believe the marriage might never come about any other way.

"It would not be better. Robert, you know my feelings on this. I've told you again and again, we will marry after we find—" She looked quickly around the interior of the coach, realizing almost too late that she had been about to blurt out a most scandalous family secret. "I mean after we return home."

Robert sighed. "Yes, dear."

Hawk grinned. The man was a weakling. This little spitfire of a woman was going to walk all over him every chance she got. From what he'd heard so far, the man hadn't the strength to go up against her. Hawk figured what she needed was a man, a real man. Someone who would put her in her place. His gaze slid to his left. Beneath the protective brim of his hat, it lingered upon her shapely form. Judging by that body, the best place for this one would be between the sheets of a bed. It just might be the only way to quiet the woman. For just a second Hawk allowed himself the luxury of imagining the pleasure of putting her there himself.

His imaginings were interrupted by the sound of the preacher's moan. The man sounded as if he physically struggled with the devil himself. A moment later he began to pray aloud for her soul. "Lord, come to this woman, relieve her of the devil's temptation. Bring not . . ."

It was more than Abigail could take. How dare he? Her hiss was just slightly louder than his muttered words, but filled with angry promise. "I suggest, Reverend," her blue eyes were hard, icy with determina-

24

tion, "that you pray a bit more quietly, lest the fornication you so greatly fear your daughters to witness not be delayed until a more seemly moment."

Hawk strangled on his laugh and wondered exactly what she might have done if the man had continued praying for her soul. He grunted in satisfaction as the inhabitants of the coach entered an uneasy silence.

Abigail couldn't remember when she had last been so insulted. The fact was she could hardly contain her anger and that fool of a so-called godly man wasn't the only recipient of the emotion. She would have liked to rail at Robert for not coming to her defense, but instead he had weakly sided with that madman. Granted he was anxious for their marriage, but anxious or no he should have first defended her honor.

She moved as far from his side as space allowed and didn't care a whit that the movement only brought her hip into tighter contact with the stranger sitting beside her. If it hadn't been almost dark outside, she would have called for the driver to stop. Anything—even walking the entire distance to Charlotte—would have been more suitable than this horrible coach and the horrible people in it.

Hour after hour went by, engulfing her and the other occupants in the monotonous, mind-stealing sounds of horses hooves, creaking wood, squeaking axles, and the ache of wheels upon hard, unforgiving, rutted roads. It was dark. Had it not been for the constant jostling, she might have slept. Still, the movement hadn't prevented others from doing as much. Robert groaned every so often as his relaxed form, most especially his head, hit against the side of the coach, while the man on the opposite side of her, with his chin upon his chest, snored ever so gently. Too bad she couldn't say as much for the three across the way. As if the bouncing hadn't been enough, the grunts, groans, and snorting sounds they made while asleep did an excellent job of keeping her awake. Abigail sighed as she closed her eyes, knowing there was no chance she'd find sleep.

Only she did. Once it began to rain, a heavy summer downpour that would last an hour or so, and the hard road grew soft with mud, she slid into a deep dreamless sleep.

Chapter Two

Hawk wrinkled his nose against the tickling. He didn't have to open his eyes to remember where he was. It had been raining. The ride was a bit smoother, telling of some slippery progress upon a muddy road, and he could smell the damp clean air. Inside it was dark, the moon and stars above them lending only occasional flashes of soft light as the canvas window covers flapped in the breeze. But for the usual groanings of the coach and the snores and gruntings of those within, all was quiet.

Hawk took all this in within seconds. What he couldn't take in, nor understand, was what the hell was cutting into his throat and at the same time tickling his nose? It took only a second or two for his eyes to adjust to the mostly black interior. It was then that he realized the woman's hat was in his face, while her head rested comfortably upon his chest.

He grinned, imagining another confrontation with the preacher and her resulting anger if the man had been witness to what would no doubt appear to him as a moment of intimacy.

27

Hawk shifted. The movement was not so much to safeguard her reputation but to find himself a bit more comfort. It did no good. He raised his chin. Her hat only dug deeper into his throat. He reached for the crown of her head and felt for the pin holding the hat in place. Why the hell women wore these things was beyond his imagination. Next he unknotted the veil. A moment later the hat rested upon his lap, the veil draping to the floor. Knowing no eye would bear witness, Hawk couldn't resist the temptation to bury his face in her lustrous sweet-smelling hair.

They had been on the road for hours, and yet the scent of her was as clean and sweet as when she had first climbed aboard. Hawk had enough experience to know that most women, and men for that matter, often doused themselves in rose water, or the like, rather than give in to the need to bathe as often as necessity demanded. The three across the way being prime examples of the distasteful aftermath.

Hawk was pleased to realize that this woman was different from most and delightfully so. Besides her obvious cleanliness, he liked the softness of her against him, but most of all he liked the way she had earlier stood up for herself. In general men appeared to like submissive women, but not Jeremiah Hawk. If there was one thing he couldn't stand it was a whimpering fool, be it male or female. And the man traveling with her was that and more. Had she been under his protection, no Bible-spouting buffoon would have insulted her without knowing instant and probably brutal retribution.

He moved his arm, encircling her in its strength as he shifted his hips forward into a slightly more reclining position. The movement had been a mistake. He knew it the moment her hand fell to his lap, knocking her hat to the floor.

His entire body broke into an instant sweat at the weight of that hand against him. Damn, if he didn't know better, he would have sworn she was purposely trying to tempt him to madness. Maybe he did know better. Maybe that was exactly her intent.

Get a hold of yourself, man! The woman is sleeping. She doesn't know where her hand rests.

Hawk knew his silently spoken words to be the truth. She had given him no reason to believe anything else. No seductive looks, no purposeful leaning into him, rubbing herself against him as if by "accident," no come-hither smiles. She was a lady, undoubtedly, and would be more than a little embarrassed if she realized the discomfort she had brought him.

He took a deep breath, reached for her hand, and placed it upon his thigh, away from the throbbing ache she had unwittingly caused, only to groan when a moment later her head snuggled deeper into his chest and her hand returned to its original position.

Jesus! Could he have been mistaken? Could it be that this woman wanted what she touched but simply thought it unseemly to come right out and ask for it? The thought made his mind swim. He felt himself growing thicker, hotter. Not here! Not now! he silently swore and yet couldn't stop his body from pushing into her limp hand.

Limp was the word. Her hand was limp. Christ, get some control over yourself. She has no idea what's happening. He felt her breasts rise and fall against his side in a slow steady rhythm. She was sleeping all right. Now all he had to do was make his body believe it.

A fact far easier to say than do. A man's body didn't always do what a man's mind asked of it. And it didn't help any that the movement of the coach caused her hand to bounce gently and then rub against him.

She murmured a muffled sound of displeasure as the coach hit something, probably a large rock, and bounced back to the rutted road with a hard jolt. Her head moved lower and then up as if trying to find a more comfortable spot.

To allow her comfort, Hawk shifted just enough so she might lean more fully against his chest. Neither was twisted now, and she breathed a sleepy sigh of obvious contentment as she nestled her face into his neck. Her leg sprawled unconsciously over his. Her hand stayed in place.

There was no hope for it. She was totally relaxed and sleeping soundly. He couldn't move her away without seeing her fall to the floor at the next bump or swerve of the vehicle. All he could do was settle back and, God help him, enjoy every minute of the pain. Hawk figured after a few hours of this he'd be a candidate for an asylum. At the moment he didn't give one good damn.

It took a while for his heart to steady itself, but after maybe an hour he finally dozed.

Sleeping was definitely a mistake. Sleep let down a man's guard. Sleep allowed things a man could normally control.

She smelled so good. Damn but she did, this soft

pretty woman with the silky golden hair. His lips touched her cheek, her neck. She moved her head just a bit to allow him easier access and then breathed a delighted sigh.

He was hard, pulsing with the need of her when his lips finally found the sweetness of her mouth. God, she tasted as good as she felt, as good as she smelled.

She didn't seem to want him to kiss her at first, but his mouth soon persuaded hers to open, to relax, to accept the thrust of a hot tongue. She allowed him a sample of her delicious sweetness, and yet acted like she didn't know what to do next. Hawk chuckled a low honey-coated sound as she finally, tentatively at first, met his tongue with her own.

Damn women and their teasing.

Her hand cradled his stiffness as Hawk pushed himself harder against her. His hand reached for a soft lushly curved breast.

And then, amid cursing, screams, and cries of fear, the world tipped wildly out of control. Hawk thought at first it was part of the dream until he realized he was laying on his back, with the lady of this particular dream pressed hard against him.

Abigail grunted a sound of pain as Robert's elbow dug deeply into her back. He scrambled about a most confining space, while emitting the most vile curses. Luckily the ladies present were too much in shock to hear, even had they understood. Robert sat, careless of the woman he professed to love, his hands desperately searching for a means of escape. He felt as if he were in a coffin. He couldn't stand it.

It was blacker than black, and he was in a box that had no opening. He'd never known this kind of terror. He had to get out. He'd die if he didn't.

"Let me out," he screamed madly, clawing at the wood, the already ripped upholstery, and then followed that scream with another bout of odious curses.

"Take it easy, man," Hawk said. "Reach above you for the door."

"Oh, God," Abigail groaned as Robert knelt, his body bent in half, his back pressing against the wall behind him, his knees into her back. A moment later the door opened and he stood. By now he was mostly outside the coach. His present position should have relieved most of his anxiety. It didn't come close. Careless of his intended's welfare, he lifted himself outside, actually jumping off Abigail's back. He never thought to reach inside to assist his supposed love in her escape, but instead instantly jumped to the ground.

Abigail knew only untold relief as Robert raised himself out the door. The breath had been knocked from her lungs. She couldn't do much of anything but desperately gulp for air.

Hawk cursed the man and his inconsideration. Being at the bottom of the three, he knew well enough Robert's every shift of weight. But it was the man's jump for freedom that particularly riled. Didn't he know he was stepping on a lady? Didn't he care? When he got out of here—when he got his hands on the idiot—he was going to show the man exactly what it felt like to be under a pair of boots.

"Are you all right?" Hawk said, his mouth just

32

above her head. He groaned as a woman's booted toe smashed against his cheek. Apparently those at the opposite end of the coach were leaving in much the same manner as had Robert. Quickly he reached around the woman against him, guarding her back from further injury.

"I think so."

Someone else stood on her but was suddenly thrown off. "Watch where you're standing. You're hurting her."

A mumbled apology cut into the grunts and groans of those still trapped inside.

"Everyone all right in there?" It was the driver. Hawk recognized the deep rough voice.

"Yeah. What the hell happened?"

"We lost a wheel. When we went down, the team broke free and ran off. Could have been worse, I reckon. The ground's all soft from the rain.

"Can you get out by yourselves? I've got to find the horses."

"We'll manage," Hawk returned and listened to the sounds of the driver's grumbling as he started off into the darkness in search of the four unhitched horses.

"Robert," Hawk called, having no knowledge of the man's last name.

"What?" The voice came from outside. Hawk realized that the damn coward had swung himself over the side and was already on the ground.

"Help the ladies out."

"I can't. I fell off. It's too slippery. I can't get back on." Robert trembled at the very thought. There was

33

no way that he was going back. He might slip and fall in. He wasn't about to take the chance.

He had managed to get out. There was no reason why the rest couldn't do the same.

Hawk cursed again as another of the women, or perhaps the same woman, made an attempt to reach the door, only to use his forehead as a step.

It was time, more than time in fact, to take control of the situation. If he didn't, someone was likely to get hurt, and it was probably going to be him. "All right. Everybody listen to me. Stay where you are, and I'll get you out."

"Can you move?" he asked the lady who still lay upon him.

Abigail nodded. "I think so." It was only then, when she tried to move, that she realized her hand was trapped between herself and the man she had fallen against.

Trapped in a very unusual position, and an even more unusual place, trapped against something that she had first imagined to be very hard, but now appeared soft. She frowned at the thought, knowing she had to be mistaken. It was probably his belt her fingers pressed against. It was probably the buckle of that belt she had first noticed.

Hawk lifted her into a sitting position and forced back a groan as her derriere, a very fine derriere, if he wasn't mistaken (and he probably wasn't since he had some experience along those lines) came into direct contact with his groin. "Damn," he muttered.

"Watch your language, sir. There are ladies present."

It was because there were ladies present, one particular lady, in fact, that he had cursed in the first place. Hawk deliberated over allowing the preacher to remain where he was, perhaps forever.

"Move over," he said as he guided her, as best he could, down his legs. God, it wasn't easy to help a woman in the dark, especially when every time he touched her it was where he shouldn't be touching her. He said "Sorry" something like five times before he actually got his legs free.

"Are you all right?" he asked again.

"Fine," Abigail said, knowing she wasn't half so confused, frightened, or dizzy as she had been at first. Well, perhaps she was dizzy, but she wasn't frightened at all. The stars above them glittered upon a black velvet sky. The open door allowed fresh air to relieve the small stale enclosure. She breathed a sigh of relief, knowing all she had to do was wait and this man would soon have her out of here.

He helped the others first, since they seemed closest to panic and the most anxious. It didn't take more than a minute or two and he was reaching for her. "Come on, miss. Your turn."

Abigail stood. Her chin came even with the opening. She smiled, suddenly imagining the silly sight of the two of them, heads exposed, just as if they were turtles, ready to hide once more should danger spring upon them, back into the protection of their shells. She couldn't stop the sudden laugh.

Robert heard it. It was only then that he realized he had left her behind. What if Abigail had been hurt? What if she had been seriously injured or killed? Where would that have left him?

"Abigail, are you all right?" he called out.

"Now he asks," Hawk muttered to himself, but not out of Abigail's hearing. She felt a sudden wave of embarrassment for her fiancé and his selfish actions.

"He didn't mean . . . I mean, he didn't realize . . . I . . ."

"I know," Hawk said as he reached for her waist and lifted her into a sitting position. "Don't worry about it."

In lifting her through the small enclosure, her body brushed scandalously against his. The odd thing was, she didn't just brush against him. It appeared he had momentarily forgotten his intent and held her still as he looked into her face.

It probably took only a few seconds longer than it should have, but to Abigail it felt as if an eternity had gone by where gazes caught, and hearts grew to thunder, while flesh tingled in awareness. She almost breathed a sigh of relief to find herself in a sitting position at last, her legs dangling inside the coach. She couldn't explain the wild beating of her heart, except to say that the erratic pounding was probably caused by a delayed reaction to the accident. Of course, she silently reasoned. That's all it was.

"Thank you," she whispered in a shaken voice, after taking huge gulps of cleansing air. The stench inside the coach had been an awful thing, but the smell of this man was even worse. Worse because it was so good. As he raised her to the opening, Abigail had almost given in to the need to reach for him, press herself more firmly against him. How odd. What could she be thinking?

She was hysterical, that was it. She'd never been in

an accident before and hoped to God she never would be again. Her back was sore, her ribs ached from where Robert had stood upon her, and used her body as a springboard. Her neck also hurt as if she'd been thrown about like a rag doll. She needed a few minutes to compose herself.

Although she appeared quite in control, nothing could have been further from the truth. And the truth being, Abigail suffered from a mild case of shock along with a touch of hysteria. She couldn't be blamed if she acted just a bit out of character.

Her skin, which had earlier held a creamy healthy hue, now appeared ghostly white and pasty in the moonlight. Hawk studied her for a moment and then asked, "You're not going to faint, are you?"

Abigail almost laughed at the question. "I never faint, and I'm not about to start now." At least she wouldn't have, had she any control of the matter.

Hawk blinked in surprise as she, still in a sitting position, fell suddenly against him. Damn, was he forever destined to find this woman soft and pliable in his arms? How the hell much was a man to bear before giving in to temptation?

"Abby . . ." he said against the side of her throat, his face pressed into the soft silky hair that had fallen free of their combs and pins. The name Abby fit her far better than the longer version. If she were his, he would always call her that. He ran his hand over her pale cheek. "Abby, can you hear me?"

"Let me sleep, Jesse." Her own words brought her suddenly awake into a dizzying world where everything appeared to be moving. She knew in an instant that what she had vowed would never happen, just had. "Oh, dear. I fainted, I think."

Hawk grinned. "You're probably not as fine as you think you are. Does anything hurt?"

He ran his hands over her neck, testing for soreness, her shoulders, her chest. "Does this feel all right?"

Abigail closed her eyes, her head tilted back, her face toward the stars. She breathed a sigh of pure delight. "It feels lovely."

Hawk grinned at her response and then shook his head. Something was wrong with her. Hysteria or perhaps shock, or maybe a little of both. "Here, let me see," he muttered as he reached for her midriff, checking for a bruised or cracked rib.

"What are you doing?" she asked in a tone that was almost childlike in its innocence.

"I'm looking for an injury. Does anything hurt?"

"My neck is a little sore."

Hawk nodded at the information.

"Are you a doctor?"

"Deputy marshal," Hawk informed.

"You should have been a doctor, you know. You have a very nice way of . . ." She seemed to lose her train of thought, as she appeared to suddenly realize, "You're an Indian, aren't you?"

Had she looked directly at him just once during the entire ride, she might have instantly concluded that obvious fact. But a woman would be considered forward in the extreme if she looked directly into a man's eyes. Abigail came to the decision that she had been missing something by constantly keeping her gaze to a low, diverted, and ladylike manner. She vowed not to make that mistake again.

As if fascinated she took in the sight of eyes as black as the sky above them, high cheekbones, thin nose and lips, hollow cheeks, a hard jaw that spoke of probable stubbornness, and black, shoulder-length hair that had been held back with a piece of rawhide. Now that his hat was gone and the rawhide loosened, his hair had fallen forward, framing a star-tlingly handsome face.

"Yes, ma'am."

Abigail giggled. "I'm not a ma'am. I'm old enough to be a ma'am, but I'm not married."

"I know." Hawk couldn't take his eyes from her. She was just about the most beautiful woman he'd ever seen.

"Most people think I'm an old maid. I guess I am, or would have been if I hadn't met Robert. We're going to be married."

"I know."

"I had to wait, you know. I had to find someone perfect. After all, there is Amanda to consider. The others didn't want to get involved when they realized I had to take care of her."

She was babbling. Hawk knew something was wrong.

"How come all Indians don't look like you?"

"What do you mean?"

"I don't know." She shrugged, apparently losing her train of thought again. "You know, I've lived close to the Smoky Mountains since I was a child, and I never saw a man like you before." There was an entire Cherokee community upon those mountains. Hawk's father owned a small ranch there.

"I lived there when I was a boy. I've just come from seeing my father." Hawk had stayed only a day. After finishing up a job that had taken him all the way to Virginia, he had stopped by for a quick visit before returning to New Orleans.

"We're neighbors." Somehow that struck her as being a particularly delightful situation. "You're tickling me."

"Sorry."

"That's all right."

Hawk didn't respond. The woman was clearly out of her head. He pulled his hands back from the temptation. If he took advantage of the situation, as he was greatly tempted to do, she'd probably shoot him when her senses returned.

"I don't think anything is broken."

"Thank you," she said as if he had performed the miracle with his own hands.

"But I think you should rest for a while."

"Don't worry." She patted his chest in a consoling gesture, as if he were the one who had sustained injury, while trying desperately to ignore the wave of dizziness her nodding caused. "I'm fine."

Hawk couldn't hold back his smile. "Are you always this stubborn?"

"Always," she said matter-of-factly. "It's a family trait."

"That must make for some real harmony in your house."

Abigail laughed, forgetting she was leaning up against a stranger, talking to him with only inches separating their mouths, as if they were the best of friends, or lovers. Forgetting the overturned coach, forgetting her fiancé waiting below, she bit her lip and teased as if she'd known this man forever. "In my house I allow everyone to enjoy my opinion."

Hawk laughed and thought he rather liked this feisty woman with the somehow slightly wicked sense of humor. Idly he wondered if she realized how delightful she had become, all soft and deliciously teasing. "Are you always so generous?"

She nodded, only remembering when she did what the movement did to her equilibrium. "Stubborn and generous." She laughed softly at her teasing.

Robert heard the sound. "Abigail? Where are you?"

"I'm here, Robert," she said, while never taking her gaze from the man she leaned against. She never noticed that her arms had somehow found their way around his neck. She never noticed that her fingers played with his blue-black hair.

She shivered, and Hawk knew she suffered from the effects of the accident. "You're trembling. Are you cold?"

The night air was cool and damp, but Abigail didn't feel chilled. She couldn't imagine why she was trembling. "No," she said, while frowning just a bit. Hawk knew she didn't understand what was happening.

"You really are a very good-looking man. Do you know that?"

The only thing Hawk knew for sure was that this adorable woman was obviously suffering from some form of shock. What he had to do was get her down

41

from here, wrapped into a blanket, and settled before a fire.

It wouldn't hurt none if he could get a bit of whiskey into her as well. "Let's go," he said as he pulled himself from the coach and eased her off its side into waiting arms.

Hawk felt his lips twist into a sneer of disgust at her fiancé's fawning. Too bad the man hadn't shown a fraction of this sudden regard when it was most needed. Now he cooed and coddled the woman as if she meant the world to him. Now . . . after he'd stepped on her. Hawk figured if he had done as much, he wouldn't have been able to face her again.

"Are you all right, darling?" Robert asked for at least the tenth time.

And as if she hadn't heard the same question asked of her again and again, she smiled once more and replied, "I'm fine."

"Here." Hawk extended his hand, offering her an almost flat, silver bottle that he had taken from his bag.

She smiled her gratitude. Amazing that he knew she was thirsty. What a nice man. Abigail brought the bottle to her lips and took two greedy swallows. It wasn't until she swallowed the second gulp that she realized something was terribly wrong. Some of the liquid dribbled to her chin when she quickly removed the bottle from her lips. And then . . . nothing happened. Nothing at all. She neither breathed in nor out but simply sat there, her eyes wide with shock, her lips parted, her body frozen in place.

Except the inside of her was as far from frozen as it was likely to get. She'd never before felt a rush of such blazing heat, never known a chest and stomach could hold such fire without displaying a single flame. She glanced at herself just to be sure. No, not even a hint of smoke.

Abigail needed help. Didn't anyone notice she wasn't breathing? Her eyes widened further and then further still. Tears blurred her already dizzy vision, and the people around her merely spoke of the coach and the problems they expected in righting it.

And then as suddenly as it was shut off, her ability to breathe returned with a loud, harsh, desperate intake of air. All looked in her direction, only Hawk aware of the reason behind the gasp.

"What's the matter?"

"I—" She gasped again, not at all sure she wouldn't continue to do the same for the remainder of her life. "I thought it was water." She gasped once more as tears ran freely over rounded cheeks and down her face.

"It's whiskey," Hawk informed her a good two minutes too late. She shot him a hard glance, but not nearly as hard as the one she shot the good reverend at his dramatic reaction.

"Whiskey! Lord, have mercy. A woman drinking the devil's own brew." He turned the two ugly women with him away. "Don't look, daughters."

Up until that moment Abigail had completely forgotten the preacher's earlier abuse. Suddenly she felt an unusual sense of freedom which allowed her to say exactly what she pleased. And she pleased to say plenty.

Abigail had had just about all she was going to take from this most disagreeable man. As far as she

43

was concerned, she'd just received her last insult. And if his two homely offspring shot her just one more of their uppity glances, she wouldn't be held responsible for her actions. Again Robert remained silent. She shot an expectant look in his direction, waiting for him to come to her defense. Nothing. Fine. If Robert wasn't going to do anything, say anything, she'd just have to take care of the matter herself. With a determined glare she raised the bottle as if in salute and then brought it to her lips again. She mimicked the father: "That's right, don't look, daughters." And then finished with, "I'm about to do something you only wish you could."

She ignored their gasps of horror. And then not nearly as low as she imagined, for she thought she spoke beneath her breath, she finished with, "Don't worry, sweetlings, the devil isn't interested in something as ugly as the two of you."

Hawk pressed his lips together, stifling a laugh as Abigail downed another two hefty swallows, each gulp doubling her first tasting. Hawk figured she'd just about finished off half the flask. She gave the bottle a puzzled glance as she brought it from her lips. Amazingly enough the fiery liquid hadn't burned nearly so badly this time. And best of all it hadn't stolen her breath either. What it did, in fact, was make her feel all warm and cozy inside, a feeling Abigail thought she rather liked.

She had been about to take yet another sample when Hawk reached for the flask. "Easy," he said, "too much of a good thing can get you in trouble."

Abigail, feeling very comfortable indeed, especially since her belly and chest were deliciously warm and

44

her trembling had miraculously eased, didn't argue the point. She smiled instead. "Thank you, sir. It was very good."

The last of her remark was obviously meant for the preacher and his family. Hawk only grinned.

"I've had just about enough of this. Fornicating, drunkenness; what other vices will we have to witness . . . before—?"

"And I've had just about enough of you." Hawk walked toward the man, towering a good eight inches above him. If he wasn't afraid, he damn well should have been. Hawk used his finger to poke the skinny little preacher hard on a shrunken chest. "This trip is long and tiring, the coach crowded, and now we've lost a wheel. Your whining complaints aren't helping matters any." He poked him again. "For the remainder of the trip, keep your sermons and preaching to yourself." His voice lowered to a whispered threat, "Or find you and your daughters walking the rest of the way to Charlotte."

Abigail was impressed. The feeling slightly exaggerated in her partially inebriated state. A man had come to her rescue, a knight in shining armor, sort of, but his armor wasn't all that shining, was it? She frowned. No, it wasn't shiny at all. As a matter of fact, she couldn't find a shiny spot on him. That was a relief, she thought, and then a moment later wondered what she was relieved about.

She wasn't thinking clearly but at the moment never realized that fact.

It didn't lessen any the effects of her injury, the fact that she had downed four hefty swallows of whiskey. A drink far too strong for an unsuspecting young woman who had never before partaken of the brew. What it did was to make her more dizzy than ever. But with that dizziness came an odd sense of right and comfort. Abigail felt good, very good indeed.

Thankfully, in the morning, she wouldn't remember just how good, for Abigail suddenly decided the night was far too quiet. She started singing a little tune that no proper young lady had any business knowing, and if she knew would never repeat. It pertained, in fact, to a certain young woman with tempting charms, and the men who wanted to get to know her just a little bit better.

The preacher was clearly aghast at the suggestive song. Her fiancé tried to stop her, his embarrassment obvious, but Hawk knew only delight. She was delicious. "Come on, let's everybody sing," she said while beginning again another tavern ditty.

Three men and three women sat on their luggage, the ground being wet still from the rains. They grouped around a small fire, greedy for its warmth against the damp night air, awaiting the driver's return. The coach had not as yet been righted. After several tries it was agreed that the team of horses were a necessary accompaniment toward accomplishing that feat.

Hawk sat across from her, watching her sleep in Robert's arms, knowing an odd sense of unreasonable anger. He knew what holding her felt like. When had a woman last felt so good? Hawk frowned at the odd question and the confusing anger that assailed. He wasn't jealous or anything. It was just that she didn't belong with that one. Odd that she couldn't see what appeared so obvious.

She was a strong woman, a woman who needed a stronger man. A man to care for her, look after her, and hold her in his deepest regard and yet take no nonsense for his efforts.

The man who supposedly loved her hadn't once come to her defense but had left that task to a stranger. That one had actually stood upon her, careless of the damage caused, in his attempts to reach his own freedom. No, he wasn't for her. Hawk figured someone ought to point out that fact. Not him, of course. He wouldn't be the one. She was a beautiful woman, but beautiful or no, it was hardly any of his concern.

It was almost morning by the time the driver returned with four horses in tow. The four men, with the aid of a fallen tree and straining horses, finally righted the coach. The team was hitched to the coach, and all again found their seats.

Abigail couldn't understand why everyone was looking at her so oddly, when they looked at her at all, that is. Even Robert acted strangely, most always averting his gaze. Everyone did, in fact, except for Mr. Hawk. What was the matter with the rest?

She might have cared, if she hadn't felt so terribly ill. Her stomach growled in a most unladylike fashion. She tried to disguise the sound with a cough but soon stopped trying. The forced coughing only added to her headache.

The thought of food nearly emptied her stomach on the spot, but Abigail knew the lack of it was the reason why she felt as she did. In her hurry to pack and make the stage, she had missed her dinner last night. Except for downing a slice of bread and a cup of tea, she hadn't eaten since yesterday afternoon.

The moment she reached Charlotte, she was going to find a place to eat. And if after that she didn't feel measurably better, she'd look up the first pharmacist she came across. She couldn't travel the rest of the way to New Orleans like this.

Chapter Three

The man was a fool. Hung over indeed. The last she'd heard, one needed to be intoxicated in order to be hung over the following morning—and Abigail had never in her life partaken of strong spirits. The most a lady allowed herself was a sip of sherry, and that was only when company came for dinner.

Abigail frowned as she reluctantly opened her purse. It galled her to pay for a misdiagnosis. After all, the charlatan was hardly deserving of a fee when suggesting she might consider moderation in the future. Utter gibberish.

Still, if only to avoid a fuss and the resulting delay a fuss would cause, she pulled a bill from her purse, placed it upon his desk, and left his office, upset enough to ignore his parting word of good day.

Robert was waiting for her outside. He took her arm as she winced against the strong afternoon sunlight. "What did he say? What's the matter?"

"He doesn't know for sure. Probably something I ate." Abigail felt not a moment's qualm at the lie.

The man certainly didn't know for sure. And it had to be something she ate.

"Darling, you look terribly ill. Perhaps we should wait until tomorrow before we go on."

It took an effort, especially since the sun was so terribly bright. Lord, couldn't you have granted me just one overcast day? Abigail wondered mutely. She shot her betrothed a sharp look. It was obvious to her that he wanted to stay in Charlotte, at least for the remainder of the day. Hadn't he suggested during breakfast, more than once, in fact, that they put off their departure until the following morning? "I'll be fine, Robert."

"Are you sure, sweetheart?" From the corner of his eye, Robert caught the flash of a red petticoat and a trim, black silk–clad ankle as a lady prepared to step into a waiting carriage. He turned his full attention on said lady and felt an instant stirring as his gaze moved up the length of her. It didn't help matters any when his gaze reached her pretty face, and she smiled in his direction. Damn, there were enough women in this town to satisfy any sweet tooth. Robert felt like he'd stepped into paradise and was practically panting to have a go at one or two of the delicious confections he had so far observed. And he'd do just that, if only he could convince Abigail to stay for the night. "I don't think it would hurt any if you took the afternoon to rest. We could start again in the morning. Bright and early."

Abigail did not miss the fact that she barely held Robert's attention. Amazingly enough she felt no annoyance in the realization. Shouldn't she feel something? Abigail shrugged aside the question. Men were known to have roving eyes. It meant nothing. "I'll rest on the train," she insisted.

Robert's sigh only caused Abigail's headache to grow in strength. She didn't want to face another of his sulks. "All right, Robert, if you insist, then stay. We'll meet in New Orleans."

The fact of the matter was, Robert couldn't stay. Paying for their breakfast had left him with three coins in his pocket . . . the last of all he owned but for the clothes he carried with him. Three coins were not nearly enough for a hotel room, never mind the women he wanted to entertain there.

"All right, my dear. If you're sure you feel up to it, we'll go. Shall I get the tickets?"

Abigail nodded and sighed with relief as she found an empty chair outside the little ticket office. Shade, thank God. The sun was terribly bright. She kept her eyes closed against its glare, lest the pain in her head never cease. A moment later Robert returned to her side and announced, "I've been robbed."

"Surely not," she gasped and then groaned as she squinted into the bright light in order to see him more clearly. Lord, would this headache never go away? "In broad daylight?"

"No, last night probably. That Indian, most likely. They're all a sneaky bunch of bastards. Sorry, dear. I don't know why we put up with—"

"Robert! What are you talking about? What Indian?"

"The one in the stagecoach, of course. The one who kept staring at you all night." Robert figured he'd found a perfect patsy. They'd probably never see the man again, and if they did and something came of his accusation, a white man was sure to be believed over an Indian. "His name was Hawk, wasn't it?"

Abigail blinked in confusion. She couldn't remember an Indian. Not only didn't she remember an Indian, she had absolutely no recollection of the few moments shared with that fellow traveler. She wouldn't remember for some time the short but decidedly intimate conversation that passed between them.

Abigail tried to think. It was an effort, for the headache she suffered was a horror. The only other man in the coach, besides a preacher and Robert, had been the man sitting to her right, and he hadn't been an Indian. Robert had to be mistaken.

"Perhaps you lost the money." Last night was little more than a vague blend of movement and discomfort in her mind. Abigail didn't remember much, but she was aware that there had been an accident. Surely it was a possibility that his purse had fallen unnoticed during the mishap.

"Yeah, and perhaps we can fly to New Orleans," he said obviously dismissing the plausibility. "What am I going to do now? I'd wire the bank in Chelsy, but we haven't got the time." Robert knew how to work a woman to get the best out of her, especially this woman. He had no accounts in Chelsy or anywhere else for that matter, but it was necessary that he pretend he did, for a time at least.

"Wire the bank, anyway. Have them transfer a sum to the bank in New Orleans." She opened her purse and handed him enough for two fares. "Here, buy our tickets."

"I feel terrible about this. Are you sure?"

"Don't be silly. You can pay me back later."

Robert took the money, turned from her, and grinned. Pay her back? he said in silent ridicule. What reason would there be to pay her back when she was going to be his wife, and the minute she said the words, all her luscious money would be his?

He bought the tickets. A few minutes later they entered the waiting, noisy, smoking train. Their luggage filled the seat behind them. Abigail sat opposite Robert in a car that smelled almost as awful as the coach last night. The stale air did little to relieve her discomfort. Abigail asked Robert to open a window, only to find the three closest to them jammed. She sighed her despair.

A moment later she gasped.

"What's the matter now?" Robert turned to see what had brought about the sound.

The man looked familiar, but last night she'd rarely glanced in his direction and couldn't be sure. "Is he the man who stole your purse?"

Hawk had entered the train and sat himself across from them some four seats back. Robert shook his head, having no choice but to follow through on his earlier accusation. It didn't really matter if his allegation ruined a life. An Indian should have known better than to associate, no matter how briefly, with decent folks. "Brazen bastard. He just smiled at us."

Robert didn't like the interest in the man's eyes as his gaze swept over Abigail. He had looked at her the same way last night, as if they shared some intimate secret. No, he didn't like it at all. He'd be happy to put this one in his place. "If I had the time, I'd notify the sheriff."

Hawk touched the brim of his hat as his gaze touched upon Robert Stacey and then moved to Abigail. Her eyes were big and wide as if she suffered some sort of shock. He almost laughed. If the tint of green in a complexion that had, on first sight, appeared luminous, and the slight pinching around her mouth meant anything, the woman wasn't feeling quite herself.

"He doesn't look like a thief, does he?" she asked in what sounded like breathless amazement. Abigail wasn't sure what she expected a thief to look like. Granted, he had a certain mysterious or dangerous air about him, but a thief? She couldn't fathom the thought. Perhaps because he dressed so well. A brocade vest covered most of a dazzling white shirt as it peeked from beneath a perfectly tailored coat. His trousers were a bit tight, but obviously, like his coat, well made. As he watched her, he removed his Stetson. It rested now in the empty seat at his side. The hat was well worn but apparently cared for. Abigail realized his manner of dress to be somber, not anything out of the norm; still, it told of excellent if subdued taste. She shook her head, not at all sure why, but she simply couldn't believe this man was a thief.

"Don't look at him," Robert said.

She forced her attention back to Robert. Oddly enough not so easy a chore. Abigail had not had the pleasure of an exacting observation last night. No lady would be bold enough to closely examine a fellow traveling companion, especially if that fellow traveler were sitting at her side. She frowned. "Are you sure he's the one?"

54

"Of course, I'm sure."

"How much time do we have?"

"Before we leave?"

He nodded and Abigail glanced at the small watch pinned to the bodice of her dark blue traveling suit. Before she got a chance to reply, the train's whistle sounded twice. An instant later it began to move slowly out of the station.

Robert sighed. "When we stop again, I'll notify the sheriff."

"Robert, I don't think—"

"Don't worry about it. I'll take care of everything."

Robert had told her not to look at the man, but Abigail found her gaze returning again and again to the man in question. And each time her eyes met his, she felt oddly unsettled. It was impossible to relax. Robert had to be mistaken. This man with his direct look, perhaps too direct a look, couldn't be a thief.

To Abigail's annoyance, Robert began to doze off. He had slept most of the ride to Charlotte. Could he never stay awake? She glanced again at the stranger only to find the man's dark gaze moving over her. She could almost feel its touch. She squirmed uncomfortably. It wasn't easy to sit here and watch him watch her.

Abigail's hat had been ruined in the accident last night. She hadn't another with her, at least none that matched her suit, so she went without. The problem of going without was she couldn't hide beneath its large brim. Abigail had never been a woman to hide from anything, but with the way this man looked at her, she thought she never needed hiding more.

An hour went by and the train continued its slow chugging journey east to Charleston, where she'd make the connection south. The constant rattle and less than smooth ride left her stomach in a sorry state indeed, and her head fared no better.

She tried to rest, but closing her eyes only caused her stomach to churn violently and the feeling of dizziness to increase to an alarming degree.

Compounding her fatigue and illness was the fact that the dark man across the way had yet to direct his attention elsewhere. Strangely enough she was feeling less uncomfortable as each mile slipped by. The fact was, the more he looked at her, the more a strange sense of excitement came upon her. No, not excitement exactly. What she felt was nervous. That was it; she almost nodded as she came to understand. His dark searching gaze made her nervous. Now all she had to do was figure out why. Abigail had been looked at before, even stared at upon occasion, but a man's attention had never caused her heart to race, nor prompted this odd sense of unease. And then she realized what was at the root of her feelings. She wasn't at all well. No doubt her imagined feelings were due to that fact.

She glanced his way again, her blue eyes narrowing as she tried to understand the peculiar sense of camaraderie that was slowly making itself known. She frowned at the thought. It couldn't be, and yet she felt as if they had shared some private moment. They hadn't, of course. Suddenly a picture of him smiling at her in the dark flashed through her mind, and she remembered a small portion of a blurred night when he had helped her from the overturned coach. That was it, of course. He had been kind, even sympathetic toward her. That was why she felt as she did. That was why she couldn't imagine Robert's accusations to be true.

Still, she'd never known Robert to lie. It had to be true. Abigail came to a decision. She owed the man for his consideration and care. She couldn't let him suffer because of one mistake. She had to warn him.

Hawk watched the woman across the way. He had thought her a beauty last night, but it didn't compare with what she looked like in the full light of day. He felt like a kid, unable to tear his gaze from her. Hawk couldn't remember a time when a woman had so captivated. Even obviously ill, she was the loveliest thing he'd ever set his eyes on.

He watched in amused delight as she tried not to glance his way. At first she appeared somewhat annoyed. Then she set out to ignore him, and then finally she returned his gaze, once or twice even offering a smile along with it.

Hawk felt his heartbeat quicken as she came to her feet. Was she coming to him? Was she actually going to leave her traveling companion and keep him company for a spell? Hawk couldn't believe his luck.

Once Abigail was seated across from him, she suddenly realized there was no way that she could broach the subject without causing each of them a great deal of embarrassment. Still, there was no help for it. She knew by his actions last night that the man was basically kind and caring. For his own good she had to bring up the subject. He deserved a second chance.

Abigail had found through the years that the best

way to approach a distasteful subject was to forge ahead. There was no sense in delaying the inevitable. Still, she thought it wouldn't hurt to start with a thank you. She owed him at least that much.

"I wanted to thank you for what you did for me last night."

His grin sent shivers down her back and caused her stomach the oddest sensation. It was most peculiar indeed. "It wasn't that much."

"It was," Abigail corrected and then went immediately to the reason she was here. "Now I'm afraid you'll have to give it back." Abigail realized she was being terribly blunt, but she couldn't figure any other way.

Hawk frowned, unable to comprehend. He hadn't expected her to come to him in the first place, and when she had, he certainly hadn't expected her to say something totally out of context.

"Excuse me?"

"I said, you'll have to give it back."

"Give what back?"

Abigail frowned. "Don't act like you don't know what I'm talking about."

She glared at him and Hawk felt his lips curving into a smile. He'd been the recipient of one or two of those glares last night and realized he loved the way her big eyes could narrow in warning as if she possessed the physical strength to force him to do her bidding. She looked so adorable while doing it, he found he had to concentrate just to keep his hands to himself. Hawk decided it wouldn't hurt any to go along with her for a minute. She was sure to eventually make herself clear. "All right."

She held out her hand, only to find it remained empty, while the man across from her sat watching with a puzzled and slightly blank expression. "So do it."

What the hell was she talking about? It was obvious she wanted him to give her something. Only Hawk couldn't imagine what she had in mind. "Lady, ah . . . Miss Pennyworth, I'd be happy to do as you ask, but . . ."

"Have you already spent it?" At his continued blank look, she went on with, "Oh, Lord," seeming to direct the conversation inward as if she were talking to herself. "Now what to do?" Her gaze fell to his hand and for some unknown reason, more of last night, in bits and pieces, came to mind. How he held her so gently, how he'd touched her face, how they had spoken, how she had leaned against him. Her cheeks colored at the intimate memory, and she squirmed uncomfortably.

She shook away the discomfort. He knew she'd been hurt. There was no reason to be upset. Still her mind couldn't let go. She remembered most clearly his gentle treatment. Abigail nodded, more determined than ever to see him not suffer for his mistake.

"How much was in it?"

"In what?"

"The purse, of course."

"Of course." Hawk tried to concentrate, but all the concentrating in the world couldn't give him a clue as to what she was talking about.

"How much have you spent? A hundred dollars? Two?"

Hawk shook his head. This was getting more confusing by the minute. He didn't have a notion. "Lady, I . . ."

"Mr. Hawk, that is your name, isn't it?"

He nodded.

"I don't want you to go to jail."

"Thank you." He crossed one leg over the other, his booted right foot resting on his left knee. He leaned back a bit, enjoying very much this lady and the oddest conversation he'd ever had in his life. "And you think I might?"

"When my fiancé wakes up . . ." She shook her head. "Rather, when we reach our next stop, Robert intends to tell the sheriff what happened."

"Does he?"

"Yes, and if you don't give the money back, I may not be able to stop him from pressing charges."

Hawk finally got the picture. Apparently she believed, thanks to her sleepy friend, that he was the culprit behind some missing money. Hawk's jaw hardened at the thought and he said tightly, "Lady, I didn't take any money."

"All right," she tried to pacify. It was obvious her comment had caused him some annoyance. "Let's say you didn't. Robert thinks you did. And I don't want you to get into trouble."

"Why?"

"Because I think you are a very nice man."

"I'm not."

"But you are," she exclaimed. "Last night—"

"Was nothing," he finished for her, uncomfortable with the fact that her mind seemed to have exaggerated the little he had done. "Don't worry about it."

"I certainly will worry about it."

Hawk felt an odd sense of satisfaction that this woman appeared to be on his side. Funny that he should so appreciate that fact. Funny that he should so enjoy her loyalty. "Why don't we let the sheriff straighten out the problem?"

"No! I don't want . . . No." She shook her head and then moaned at the pain it caused. Putting aside the discomfort for a moment, she went on. "This is what we'll do. I'll give you the money, and you give it to Robert."

"No."

"Yes," she instantly countered. "Just say you found it."

"No," Hawk repeated with some force.

"Why not?" she asked with real exasperation, which was followed by a weary sigh, "Please, Mr. Hawk, don't be difficult."

Hawk might have smiled at being spoken to as if he were a child. Might have, that is, had she not asked him to admit to something he did not do. Admit it not with words perhaps, but with his actions. "Lady, I've already told you. I didn't take the money."

She watched for a long moment before she took a deep breath. She released it into a sigh. "There's no need to give me dark scowls, Mr. Hawk. If you say you didn't take it, I believe you." And she did. She should have known the man hadn't taken Robert's wallet. It had been lost, just as she first suspected. There was no way that she could deny that fact after one look into those dark eyes.

"But you think others won't?"

Abigail didn't answer the question. She wasn't unaware of the prejudice many held against Indians. She hadn't a doubt the man realized the same, but pride kept him from seeing things her way. "Fine," she said after a moment of thought. "If you won't give it to him, I shall, and I'll tell him you gave it to me while he was sleeping."

"You'll be wasting your money, if you do."

"Why?"

"Just take my word for it."

"I'm afraid I'll need more than your word, Mr. Hawk. What do you mean?"

"Fact is, I was in the telegraph office when he sent a wire to his bank." Hawk shrugged. "After he left an answer came."

"So?" Abigail began to feel an inkling of something being terribly wrong. She had felt it before, in regard to Robert, but it had never been anything quite this strong. She straightened her spine and found every muscle in her body tightening as she awaited his next words.

"So I was standing at the counter. I couldn't help but see the answer."

"And it said?"

"It said his accounts have been closed for almost a year."

Abigail felt a wave of relief, unable to understand why she had been so tense. What was it she dreaded? What deep dark thought had lurked at the back of her mind? She forced a smile. "There's been a mistake, of course."

"I don't think so. I think the man is broke and is only making out like he has money."

"That's a ridiculous thing to say. Why would he do that?"

"So you'll marry him."

Abigail frowned. "I don't want him for his money."

There was no doubt in Hawk's mind that this woman came from money. Those who did had a certain air about them. It came through in the way they talked, the way the walked, the way they dressed. And she had it, all right. "Maybe he wants you for yours."

Her mouth tightened into a straight thin line of censure. "How complimentary. Thank you," she said stiffly, as she came to her feet.

Hawk realized he'd been far too blunt. "I didn't mean to insult you. I meant the man ain't worth shi—" He shook his head. "I mean . . ."

"I understand what you mean, Mr. Hawk." It was one thing to warn the man of impending trouble, but quite another to stand here listening to him insult the man she was going to marry. "Good day to you, sir."

"Couldn't we do this somewhere else?" They were standing on the wide platform beside a waiting train. Abigail saw the people boarding the train shooting the four of them some inquisitive looks.

"We could go to my office, ma'am," the elderly sheriff offered, understanding her distress.

"We'll miss the train," Robert said with a touch of disgust. And then as if he couldn't have cared less that his accusation was about to ruin a man, he snapped, "Just arrest him, will you?"

"I'm afraid I can't do that, Mr. Stacey. Not without some proof."

"You want to search me?" Hawk offered.

The sheriff looked as if he were about to agree with the suggestion when Hawk finished with, "That's fine with me, only I want you to search him as well."

"That's ridiculous. Why should I be searched? You're the one who stole my purse." Robert turned a rusty color as his own words caused him to remember that his purse was still in the inside pocket of his coat. It was empty, but it was definitely still there. And he had just reported it stolen.

Hawk emptied his pockets into the sheriff's hands and then raised his arms above his head.

"Oh, please," Abigail said at what she considered a most exaggerated and unnecessary action, while wondering if her face had ever felt so hot. People were watching from the train, from the platform, even from the street.

The sheriff couldn't help but notice the lady's misery. "Put your hands down."

Hawk obeyed with a grin.

Abigail felt some annoyance, for the man seemed to think this affair was somehow amusing.

The sheriff grunted as he opened a wallet. "Deputy marshal?! What the hell? Why didn't you tell me?"

"I figured it'd be better if you saw it yourself."

The sheriff turned to Robert. "I'm sorry, Mr. Stacey, but someone else must have . . ." He shook his head. "You've made a mistake."

"I don't think so. You've never heard of a crooked lawman before?"

It was obvious to all that the sheriff hardly took

kindly to the man's accusation. Abigail knew it was a foolhardy thing to say. One did not accuse lawmen of being less than exemplary, while speaking to one of their kind.

"Go ahead. Finish," Hawk said, the laughter in his eyes replaced by a dark narrowed look of scorn.

"What do you mean, finish?"

He spoke to the sheriff, but nodded toward Robert. "Search him."

"Deputy, I don't think—"

"I do," Hawk said as he suddenly reached inside Robert's coat and pulled out what was supposed to be the lost purse.

Abigail gasped, her eyes widened in shock. How had he known the purse was there all along? And why hadn't Robert checked before making allegations against an obviously innocent man? "How . . . ?"

"Most men keep their wallets there," Hawk explained to her astounded look.

Robert shook his head. "It doesn't mean anything."

"I think it does," Hawk returned. He'd been a lawman long enough to know when he was being lied to. And he'd rarely seen a man do as bad a job of it as this one. "I could have you arrested for false—"

"I didn't mean that the purse was stolen. I meant that the money in it was stolen. I had five hundred dollars."

The sheriff scowled. "Five hundred dollars that just jumped out of your wallet?"

"No, someone—"

"—took it," Hawk finished for him, his voice drip-

65

ping sarcasm as he added, "and then somehow put your wallet back."

"He must have." He glared in Hawk's direction. It was obvious that Robert had not given up on the claim that Hawk had to be behind the incident.

"You must have lost it. Perhaps when you paid for breakfast," Abigail offered, hoping the excuse to be reasonable enough to convince and then wondered why she should feel the need to supply him with an excuse at all?

His first impulse was to deny the possibility. He'd really wanted to put the blame on this bastard. It would have been the least he could have done for the accusing silence he'd had to endure last night. But Robert was far from a fool. He knew an out when he saw one. "That's it. I must have dropped the money when I paid for breakfast."

Abigail frowned. She thought the words came too eagerly and with an odd mingling of exhilaration and relief, as if he were suddenly delighted, despite the loss. She looked from one man to the other. It was obvious to her that neither man was convinced. Abigail wanted to give Robert the benefit of the doubt but felt again that strange sense of something being wrong. She dismissed the notion even as she wondered why Robert had been so shaken and then so obviously relieved? If he hadn't lied, why would he act so strangely? She knew like most men, and some women, herself included, he hated to be proven wrong. That might account for his odd behavior.

She knew some real annoyance at the knowing, almost gloating look Hawk shot in her direction. The man was obviously satisfied, apparently believing his ridiculous suspicions to be true. Only she could have told him they weren't true. Robert didn't love her for her money. Robert had more than enough money of his own. Hadn't she seen for herself his lifestyle? Didn't he wear the best of clothes? Didn't he own . . . ?

Abigail shook aside her thoughts. The deputy's mind seemed to be set, and any explanations or justifications she might impart would no doubt fall upon deaf ears. Abigail wondered why she felt it suddenly so important to straighten out this mess, to make him believe what she knew to be the truth.

Annoyed at herself for feeling the need to try, she dismissed the thought. What difference did it make what he believed? Her private life was hardly any of his concern.

She gave a soft weary sigh. Right now all she wanted was to put this embarrassing ordeal behind her forever. The train's whistle blew. Abigail's luggage was still on board. Her eyes widened with alarm at the thought of her clothes being lost forever. "The train. Please, we have to hurry."

Chapter Four

Now that she had reached her destination at last, now that she sat across from the marshal, Abigail wondered how she was going to manage? Certainly he was a kind and courteous man. Still, it was going to take every ounce of what meager courage she possessed to tell him.

She pressed a lacy handkerchief to her forehead and throat, dabbing at the moisture. It was unbearably hot. Granted the summers in North Carolina were far from pleasant, but summer was still some months away, and Abigail could only imagine the discomfort, if one were to spend that season in this southern city.

As his dark gaze moved to hers, Abigail knew he waited for her to begin. Lord, how was she to speak of the unspeakable? Abigail bit her bottom lip. How could she explain? How could she tell the scandalous story without ruining Amanda's reputation and possibly her own as well?

Abigail put aside her reluctance. There was no help for it. If she wanted his assistance, and she desperately did, she'd have to ignore any feelings of embarrassment and tell the whole of it. She forced the words from a tight dry throat. "Marshal, I . . ." Lord, she hadn't said anything yet, and she could already feel the heat creeping up her throat to set her cheeks ablaze. "My sister has run off with a . . . man."

She said the last word very softly, and Cole Brackston felt a stab of sympathy for her plight. She was obviously embarrassed to speak of it, and yet in her love for her sister, she had forced herself to do what was necessary.

He felt the need to console but knew that wasn't what she wanted or needed from him. Cole asked in a most businesslike fashion, "And you think she might be in New Orleans?"

"Mr. Pinkerton said as much."

Cole nodded, not unaware of the detective and his agency. He had once or twice had an opportunity to see them at work. That this woman had gone to the Pinkertons, rather than the law, spoke most clearly of her need for privacy. "How old is she?" It was one thing for a woman of lawful age to run off with a man (no crime in that, no matter how unsavory the thought to some) and quite another if the woman was still a young girl.

"Sixteen."

A sigh whispered between Cole's clenched teeth. "And her guardian? Why has he sent you in his place?"

"I'm her guardian."

Cole's gaze narrowed as a frown creased his forehead. "That's a bit unusual, isn't it?" He'd never heard of a woman, a lady, in fact (and she was a lady, if ever he saw one), to take the role of guardian.

"Perhaps, but I'm of age, and there wasn't anyone else. We only have each other, Mr. . . . Marshal."

"Cole," he said, trying to bring a measure of ease to her obvious discomfort. "Everyone calls me Cole."

Abigail nodded.

"The man she is with—has he married her?"

"I don't know for sure." Her throat closed up, and she had to force the rest. "But I think not." At that statement Abigail's cheeks grew as red as fire.

She raised pleading blue eyes to his. "I know most young girls are already married at sixteen, but Amanda isn't like the usual sixteen-year-old. She's . . . she's a bit immature for her age. Thomas Hill took advantage of her."

Cole nodded again, understanding more than ever this woman's concern. "There are laws against men taking advantage of children."

"Oh, no, please," she said, clearly aghast at the thought of anyone else being privilege to this most unfortunate incident. "I don't want any . . ." Cheeks that had finally returned to their normal color were once again bright red. "All I want is your help in finding her. I want to take her home."

"If she's still in the city, we'll find her," he said in all confidence. "Have you a picture of her?"

"Yes," Abigail said as she searched through her oversized bag. "I have it in here somewhere."

Behind her, the door was nearly wrenched from its hinges as a man slammed it against the wall. It took only two steps and he stood before the marshal's desk. "There's another fight over on Lafayette. A man's been shot!"

Cole muttered a curse beneath his breath as he came quickly to his feet and reached for a rifle that hung on the wall behind his desk. "Stay here. I'll be back as soon as I can." An instant later his hat was shoved upon his head and he was running out the door.

Almost oblivious to Cole's leaving, Abigail worriedly continued rummaging through her large bag. She at last pulled out one of the two pictures she'd brought with her. She placed it on the desk, her gaze studying the small face, the innocent blue eyes. A very good likeness, she thought. It had been taken a year ago on Amanda's fifteenth birthday, two days before she disappeared. A year ago. Lord how things had changed in only a year's time.

Her mouth tightened as she remembered Thomas Hill. The man had been charming in the extreme. Even now, a year after the happening, Abigail could find no fault in his gentlemanly and most proper behavior. An artist of some standing in the community, he gave lessons to many of the young girls. Abigail had not the slightest inkling that his interest in Amanda went beyond her drawing abilities, until Amanda had suddenly turned up missing, leaving behind only a short note telling her sister not to worry.

Abigail remembered again that awful day and the fear and horror that had nearly driven her to the pits of despair.

Damn him to hell for convincing Amanda to run away with him. Damn him to hell for a year's worth

71

of worry and fear. Only the worry and fear were nearly at an end. She was close, far closer than he knew.

She would have dearly loved to put the man where he belonged. She would have enjoyed seeing him rotting behind bars for the rest of his life. But in order to accomplish that, the story would have to be told. No. She wouldn't risk Amanda and her reputation for all the revenge in the world.

Abigail shook her head. All she wanted was her sister back. She didn't care if Thomas Hill rotted in hell after that.

Anxious to get this interview done with, she began to pace as she awaited the marshal's return. A moment later Abigail noticed a button had come undone on her boot. She was bent in half seeing to the matter, when the door opened behind her. She heard a man's voice say, "Is that for me?" just as he ran a hand over her in a most intimate and shockingly familiar manner. It brought her instantly to an upright position—popped her straight up might be a more accurate telling—and propelled her about, her blue eyes glaring contempt and outrage at the villain who had dared to touch her.

Hawk stepped inside the office and grinned at the woman waiting for him. He had stopped off at her rooms, only to learn from her maid that she had gone out early this morning. He'd been gone for weeks. No doubt she was as anxious to see him as he was to see her. And when he saw her waiting in his office, he couldn't resist, especially since that tempting little bustle beckoned so prettily above what he knew to be a very nicely rounded derriere. He gave her bottom a most satisfying caress. A second later he blinked in astonishment as he heard her yelp of surprise. She snapped up and spun about to face him. Surprise mingled equally with amusement when he realized the woman was not his lady friend, Lydia, but an outraged little blonde he had never thought to see again. Abigail Pennyworth glared at him with murder in her eyes.

Hawk grinned at the misunderstanding.

Abigail wouldn't see the humor of it for some time to come.

"I thought you were someone else," he explained.

The fact that he had not offered an instant apology was not lost on a fuming Abigail. "And that is your usual way of greeting a woman?"

"Some women."

"How nice for you," she said tightly. Her disdain couldn't have been more obvious.

Hawk laughed and sat a hip on the desk. The movement brought him much too close to where she stood. Abigail thought better of standing her ground, of refusing to allow this man to intimidate. She hadn't a doubt that she was in some danger—that this man, with his quiet ways, his subdued strength, his oddly graceful masculine manner, might be the most dangerous she had ever come across. She returned to her seat.

"I didn't expect to see you again."

"Nor I, you." Her comment told clearly enough her disappointment that things had not worked out as planned. Hawk only smiled.

"What are you doing here?"

"Waiting for the marshal." She tried to ignore his

presence, looking at everything in the room but the man who silently commanded her attention.

"Can I help you?"

"No."

Her short abrupt response only caused Hawk further interest. He raised one black brow as he crossed his arms over his chest. "I'm the deputy, you know."

"I know," she returned. She'd known, of course, that he was a deputy marshal, but she hadn't known that he was based in New Orleans. She hadn't seen him after that awful incident at the train station. And at this moment she could only wish never to see him again.

The worst of it was, for some ridiculous reason, his presence was causing her some real distress. She couldn't name the exact reason why, but she felt suddenly jittery and nervous, so much so that she couldn't sit still. Abigail came again to her feet and once more began to pace.

"So telling me your problem would be the same as telling the marshal."

She stopped walking and shot him a hard look. "Who said I had a problem?"

"Are you a relative of Cole's?"

"No."

"He's married."

Abigail frowned in some confusion. The man was talking gibberish. "What are you talking about?"

"I'm talking about the marshal and the fact that he is not only married but loves his wife."

Abigail's look told clearly of her suspicions, those being that the marshal's deputy might not be in full possession of his wits. "When I see him again, I'll remember to offer my congratulations," she said, her voice heavy with derision, and then asked quite simply, "What has his marital status to do with me?"

For some unknown reason Hawk felt something like relief. He knew for a fact that no man could love a woman more than Cole loved Emy, and he hadn't imagined, until Miss Pennyworth grew so obviously secretive, that she might be that kind of woman, but . . . He shrugged aside his thoughts, anxious to know more about this woman and whatever problem she might be facing.

"You wouldn't be here if something weren't wrong." Perhaps Robert was missing or dead. Hawk couldn't deny the sudden rise in his spirit at the thought.

"That's ridiculous. Of course, I would."

"Yeah? Name one reason."

She couldn't meet his dark gaze. "I could be looking for my . . . friend." She almost said "sister" but realized at the last second the near slip. The fewer people who knew about her sister and that miserable Thomas Hill, the better.

Hawk didn't miss the hesitation. He knew she was lying, but had every confidence he'd soon know the truth. "Is your friend a man or woman?"

"A man."

Hawk frowned. She was lying again or at least telling only part of it. He grew suddenly annoyed with her half-truths. His mouth thinned into a forbidding line. "You might as well know, I have the marshal's confidence."

She shook her head. "I've asked him not to tell anyone."

"Why?" Hawk frowned again. What in the world could a woman like her be hiding behind all this secrecy?

"Because it's personal."

"Don't you think it would be a smart move on your part if more than one man helped?"

Abigail bit her lips together as her gaze fastened to the toe of his boot. He might be right. He was a lawman, after all. It did make sense if two were aware of her problem, if they were both willing to help.

"All right. I've come to find my sister."

"Do you have her address?"

Abigail shot him a look of annoyance. She raised one brow as she said with some ridicule, "Of course I have her address. That's why I'm standing here." A moment later she breathed a weary sigh. "If I knew where she was, I wouldn't have to find her, would I?"

Hawk shook his head. "You're in New Orleans. You must have chosen this city for a reason."

"She was reported . . . was seen here."

"Where exactly?"

"It doesn't matter. I've already been there. There's no trace of them. They've gone."

"They?"

She gave a vigorous shake of her head. "I mean she."

"All right, so she's with someone, probably a man."

Abigail's eyes widened. "How did . . . ?"

"If she was with a woman, you wouldn't be so elusive in your answers. I take it they're not married."

Despite the fact that it was most probably the

truth, Abigail knew a flash of annoyance that he should take it upon himself to so conclude. "Well, you take it wrong."

"So they *are* married?" he asked in some surprise.

"I don't know if they are or not." Amazingly enough she felt no embarrassment this time. What she felt, in fact, was anger.

Hawk's mouth curved into a smile. He couldn't help it. She was adorable. The way she held her head high, despite her chagrin, the way her back stiffened at his remark, the spark of fire in her eyes as she protected was just about the most . . .

"And you can wipe that grin off your face this minute, or I'll wipe it off for you." Abigail almost moaned as she realized what she'd just said. Would there ever come a day when she'd think before speaking? Instantly contrite, she bit her bottom lip and lowered her horrified gaze to the floor.

Hawk's chuckle was low, honey coated, smooth. It did strange things to her stomach. Abigail frowned. Had she heard that sound before? "It's against the law to threaten a lawman, did you know that?"

He pushed himself to his feet. Abigail took a step back. "I didn't . . ." For one ridiculous moment she felt the need to run. Her gaze moved quickly around the room, searching for the most expedient exit.

"Just for my own information, how would you wipe it off?" His voice was silkier than ever, and Abigail didn't like it one bit.

If she hadn't known better, she would have thought he was teasing her. He wasn't, of course. He couldn't be. Still, instinct told her, the wisest course of action would be to change the subject. Abigail wasted no time in doing just that. "Are you going to help me?"

At her question Hawk came to the sudden realization that things had been about to get out of hand. He nodded and again leaned a hip upon the desk, suddenly all business. He picked up a pen and leaned over the desk, reaching for a piece of paper. "What was her last address?"

"I told you, I looked already. She wasn't there."

"Give it to me anyway. I might be able to find something."

Abigail did as he asked. He wrote the address down. She knew a moment's confusion when he asked, "Where's your friend?"

"My friend— Oh, you mean Robert?"

"Yeah, Robert," Hawk returned with some disgust.

"He had an appointment." Abigail couldn't meet his eyes again. The reason being, she wasn't sure where Robert had taken himself off to. He could be in any number of places, since she knew him to have quite a few business interests in New Orleans. Still, the fact that he was not with her was annoying. They had made plans before retiring last night to meet for breakfast, and when he hadn't shown up, she had gone to his room. Knocking had brought only silence for an answer. No doubt he had slept his fill and gone off to the bank early. Apparently he had been delayed.

Hawk shot her a look of disbelief.

"What was that for?" Abigail hadn't missed his glance nor the silent message behind it.

"An appointment?" he asked with some obvious doubt.

"Robert has quite a few business interests in New Orleans."

"Right, and I'm the Mayor of London."

"Mr. Hawk, I can understand why you might not like him, but there is no reason for snide comments."

"Oh, you can understand that, can you? Then you should know I have every reason."

"It was a mistake," she said, obviously referring to Robert's accusation.

"I don't think so."

"What do you mean, you don't think so?"

"I mean he was lying, lady."

"He couldn't have been. What reason would he have to . . . ?"

"I'm an Indian. If I didn't happen to also be a deputy marshal, which of us would have been believed?"

"I believed you and I didn't know."

"Which one would the sheriff have believed?" he insisted.

Abigail refused to answer the question. Instead she asked one of her own. "Why pick on you? What purpose would it . . . ?"

"It would be a good excuse, don't you think, to explain why he doesn't have any money?"

Abigail made a disparaging sound. "Are you going to start that again? I told you it's not true. He has his own money. Lots of it."

"Yeah, you said that before."

"I can't tell you how complimentary it is to tell a woman a man wants her only for her money."

"He'd have to be a damn fool, wouldn't he? Especially if the woman was you." Hawk breathed a sigh, knowing the man was that and more, never realizing the lavish compliment. He never thought how flattering his remark. He was simply stating the truth. "I know it isn't pleasant to hear, but sometimes the truth is hard to take."

Abigail felt a moment's surprise at the soft, smoothly spoken compliment. She didn't know what to say, how to answer words that were spoken as if a fact. She didn't think anyone had ever said anything quite so astonishing before.

But then she remembered the rest and felt again the need to defend. For just a second she wondered why. Could it be she simply couldn't admit to making a mistake? No. She felt the need to defend because none of what he said was true. She knew for a fact that Robert had his own money. All right, so sometimes she had an occasional moment of doubt about the man and their relationship. Most likely that had something to do with why she delayed their marriage. But she did not doubt the fact that he had money.

She breathed a sigh, knowing nothing she could say would sway the man from his beliefs. The fact was, it didn't matter in the least what he believed. She couldn't have cared less. "And some people wouldn't know the truth if it hit them over the head."

At that very moment, in a brightly lit loft above Madame Plachette's Perfumery, Thomas Hill eyed the woman he had absconded with nearly a year ago. His full lips twisted into what had, for the last six months or so, become a perpetual sulk. "Wire her again."

Amanda's blue eyes widened with a pleading note at the order, and a slight frown marred her pretty forehead. "Tommy, I wired her three days in a row. She doesn't answer. Maybe she's gone away."

"You'd better hope she hasn't. Look—" he emptied his pocket upon a scarred low table, "we have exactly twenty-one dollars left. How much longer do you think we can pay the rent and eat on that?"

"I'm working, maybe if you . . ."

"Yeah, and you make what?" Amanda had taken a job sewing for a young woman who owned a dress shop over on Canal Street. "Four dollars in a good week? How the hell can we live on that?"

"Madame Marie said she knows where you could find work. She said her friend Jacques could use you in his restaurant kitchen. And he's willing to pay ten dollars a week."

"Doing what? I can't cook."

"You could learn."

"What the hell are you talking about? I'm an artist. I want to paint, I need to paint." He waved an arm toward the end of the room. On the floor in the far corner were a number of canvas paintings, each abandoned in varying stages of completion. Thomas Hill believed himself an artist of some quality, but the truth of the matter was, the talent he possessed was just a shade above mediocre. Granted he sold a painting to an unsuspecting client now and then, but he would never become the master of the art he imagined himself to be.

"I know, but couldn't you, just for a little while . . ."

"No, I couldn't." Amanda looked as if she were about to cry again, and Thomas breathed a sigh of disgust. "For crissake, don't start that again. I'm sick to death of watching you cry. Lately all you do is cry."

The fact that Amanda only cried when her feelings were hurt, and that her feelings were hurt only when Thomas yelled at her, was easily dismissed. He had more important things to worry about than Amanda's delicate feelings.

"Your sister has the Pinkertons on us. How much longer do you think it will be before they find us again? If we don't get our hands on some money and get out of here . . ."

Amanda's blue eyes grew dark with misery at the thought of that nice detective so horribly battered. Amanda was a very gentle soul. Granted she might have been lacking some in wisdom and easily swayed by bogus charm, but she wasn't so terribly slow as to be worthy of the names Thomas often labeled her with. The fact was she simply could not stand the thought of violence. She'd never seen it before leaving home, never knew men actually hit one another simply because their thoughts might differ, and still couldn't understand why that should be. "I don't know why you had to hit the man. He didn't do anything but ask me some questions."

Thomas sneered his disgust. God, but she was stupid. He'd hit the man more than a week ago, and the woman wouldn't stop nagging about it. "For crissake, let it go, will you? I did it, all right? I don't want to hear any more about it."

He watched her blue eyes fill again with tears of hurt. Damn her to hell. What Amanda saw as a most handsome mouth twisted into an ugly sneer. He couldn't imagine what he'd ever seen in her. She was nothing but a weight around his shoulders. She might as well have been a ball and chain. For the last six months, he'd felt like he was suffocating. He couldn't go anywhere, do anything without her at his side. He was sick of it, sick of it all.

Back home everyone knew she was a bit slow, but Thomas Hill had never imagined just how slow. She was a simpleton, there was no other word that fit so well. He hadn't minded so much in the beginning. In the beginning, because he was smart enough to have convinced her to take her jewelry with her, they had had money. Things were good then, so good in fact that he could overlook her simple childish ways. Now the money was gone, and he regretted ever taking her with him in the first place. But once she contacted her sister and he got his hands on more, things would be good again. Especially good since he had every intention of getting the hell out of here, alone.

Amanda watched in silence, pleading only with her eyes, as he stormed out of the small room. She wondered for maybe the hundredth time how things had become so difficult. Tommy had been so sweet, so kind in the beginning. Now he almost never had a kind word to say to her. Even when she worked a twelve-hour day and cheerfully handed over all she'd earned sewing until she could hardly see each stitch, he only took her money with a grunt, shoving it into his pocket, while shooting her a look of disgust.

She wished she were smarter. If she were, maybe she could think of something. Something that would make everything better.

She hadn't told Tommy yet, but she was going to have a baby. The thought scared her. She didn't know how to do it or how she'd manage when the time came.

She wished she could talk to Abigail. Abigail knew everything, but Abigail was home, hundreds of miles away. She should go home, she thought. Abigail would tell her what to do. Abigail could make everything all right again.

Only she couldn't. Not now. They were going to have a baby. They were going to be a real family. Amanda smiled at the thought. She'd tell him tonight. A baby would make everything better.

Robert came slowly awake from a short nap and smiled as he realized one hand cupped a soft warm breast, while the other lay upon a nicely rounded rear. The woman's hands were between their bodies, fondling, bringing his limp member to a delightful hardness. He'd had his share of whores but thought the French just might be better, more giving than most.

Robert feigned sleep, knowing she was hungry for more of him, delightfully anticipating her next move. He smiled as she continued to gently caress. The best of it was, when her efforts brought about no immediate response, she merely took another route. He didn't have to push her head or anything. To his delight, her mouth, of its own accord, started moving down his neck, his chest, his belly. She found no resistance as she pushed him to lie more fully upon his back, and Robert finally gave up all pretense of sleep as he raised his hips to her hungry mouth.

Damn, but it was a good thing he'd taken the money from Abigail's purse when he'd had the chance. Without it he'd never have known this pleasure.

She'd knocked on his door a while back, knocked and softly called his name. At the time he'd been deep inside the whore he'd spent the night with. It hadn't been easy, but he'd forced his body to grow instantly still, making sure the bedsprings gave not even the slightest hint that he was there.

Silently he congratulated himself on his control. He smiled at the memory, for the whore (he'd forgotten her name . . . was it Susy?) took that very moment to climax, her muscles squeezing at his sex, drawing him deeper into the madness, driving him wild as his body of its own accord jerked uncontrollably forward. He had no doubt that it was the danger of being caught that had accentuated the pleasure. The thought of his fiancée standing just outside his door, coupled with the fact that he hadn't been able to utter a sound, had turned out to be one of the best moments in his life.

Robert came to a decision as the whore took him deep into her mouth. He was going to convince Abigail to marry him and do it today. He had to get his hands on her money, if he wanted more of this. And Robert knew, if he wanted anything it was definitely more of this.

Chapter Five

The desk clerk relayed the message, and Abigail moved toward the hotel's restaurant. "Where were you?" she asked as she sat across from Robert at a small table near the door.

Robert offered her his most charming smile. "I'm sorry, sweetheart. I didn't realize I'd be delayed. I thought I'd have a quick meeting with the firm that handles my business interests down here." The lie came easily, naturally, and best of all, so convincingly that Robert almost believed the words himself. The thought occurred that he just might be wasting some real talent. Perhaps once married, he should entertain the idea of going on the stage. No, he reconsidered. The man behind the scene, the man with the money, employed the most power of all. Now that thought held some enticement. Where else could a man find so many eager young ladies, all able and more than willing to do his bidding at the mere mention of work?

Robert cut short the enticing picture, lest the anticipated pleasure make itself known and bring about some questions. "And then I went to the bank. The fools . . ." He shook his head, his expression one of utter disdain at the incompetence he'd been forced to contend with.

"What happened?" she asked as she placed both her bag and umbrella on the empty chair between them.

"They can't seem to get anything straight."

"What did they say?"

"There's been some kind of mix-up. All they keep saying is my accounts are closed." He breathed a disgusted sigh and said, "When I get my hands on—"

"What about your local accounts? Surely because of your business interests here, you can take what you need from them."

"All my accounts are in Chelsy, dear. Profits from all over the country are wired directly into my account there."

Abigail thought that particularly odd. Her father had left her and Amanda a few business interests in both New York and San Francisco. She knew it was expedient to establish accounts wherever businesses were located. Strange that Robert didn't see the wisdom in that fact. "If you have accounts only in Chelsy, how does your manager pay your workers?"

"He doesn't." Abigail's blue eyes widened with surprise at his answer. "I've found it simpler if vouchers are sent in, and I or my man of business issue the checks. One set of books brings about a minimum of confusion, dear," he explained and then patted her hand in a condescending fashion, as if speaking to a child. It was a stupid mistake, for Robert should have known the woman opposite him oversaw a tiny empire of her own and would hardly agree with his operating techniques.

Abigail wasn't the least bit pleased with his patronizing manner. Upon reaching her twenty-first birthday, three years ago, she had worked for a time with Mr. Carver, the family's solicitor and had since, almost single-handedly, overseen the running of her plantation, its tenants and crops, as well as the few business interests her father had left them. She had even found herself welcome, after a slightly uncomfortable beginning perhaps, sitting in her father's place on the board of directors for Chelsy's bank. She knew business and knew it well.

It boggled the mind to imagine the forced delays if all payments to personnel had to be sent from her office. Why, people might wait up to a month for a week's salary at that rate.

Abigail imagined the management of Robert's businesses in dire need of a complete overhaul. If he had *any* businesses, that is. Abigail almost gasped aloud at the wayward thought. Of course, he had businesses. She was allowing Mr. Hawk's suggestions to influence her thinking. It was more than obvious the man did not like Robert. Abigail knew it only fair to put aside as prejudiced any remarks on the deputy's part. Still . . .

"Don't worry your sweet little head about it, dear," Robert said unwisely at her frown.

"Robert, you're mistaken if you think I have a sweet little head." She shot him a sharp look. "And I'm not in the least worried about your businesses. I've quite enough to worry about with my own, thank you."

"Sweetheart, I didn't mean . . ."

Abigail breathed a sigh, knowing she'd done it again. Would the day ever come when she'd be able to control this impulsive, unfeminine, and most unattractive need to speak her mind? "I'm sorry, Robert. I know what you meant." She offered him a weak smile, knowing she not only didn't know what he meant but truthfully didn't care. She accepted a menu from a hovering waiter.

"I'll have coffee and an order of shrimp." She smiled over the large menu at her dining companion. "I've heard the seafood in New Orleans is not to be equaled."

Robert wasn't the least bit pleased that she had taken it upon herself to order. A lady was supposed to allow the man that privilege. Damn, but this one was just a bit too independent for his tastes. She was going to learn a thing or two the minute he put a ring on her finger. Robert bit his lip, trying to hold back a smile. After he got her to buy the ring, of course.

Robert gave his order and the minute the waiter was out of hearing, he began what had become a crusade. "I've been thinking."

Abigail raised her gaze to her dining companion, waiting for him to go on.

"I'll have to go back and straighten out this mix-up."

"Why not have your man of business take care of it? Surely he could wire you the needed funds until you are able to see to the matter yourself."

Robert shook his head. "Impossible. Mr. Standings is out of the country."

Abigail's eyes widened at the name. If Mr. Standings was Robert's man of business, wiring any amount of money would certainly be impossible, for Mr. Standings was more than just out of the country. "Mr. Standings has been dead for two years, Robert. I personally paid my respects to his widow."

God damn it! He'd forgotten. This woman was no fool. He'd have to be more careful in the future. "I don't mean the old man. I meant his son."

"His son-in-law?" Abigail asked, knowing the man to have left behind only daughters.

"His son-in-law," Robert eagerly conceded. "The fact is, I haven't a choice. I have to go back."

Abigail didn't take kindly to the notion. Granted the man had hardly been of much help, having slept most of the journey and then disappearing this morning, leaving her to face the marshal and his deputy alone. Still, he was someone she knew in a city of strangers, and she was loath to see him leave. "Why don't I advance you, say, two hundred dollars?"

"Abigail, you've already paid for our tickets, the hotel room." And the whore last night and the one I plan on having tonight, he mentally went on. He shook his head. "I can't take any more from you."

"Nonsense." Abigail opened her purse and took out a roll of bills. "You can pay me back when we return home."

"I won't take it. Taking money from a woman is simply not done."

"Oh, Robert, don't be ridiculous. We are going to be married, aren't we?"

"Of course, but we're not married yet." He breathed a long sigh, knowing it portrayed all the distress he was supposed to feel. "No, I'm afraid I'll

90

have to go back." He allowed a moment to pass before he said, "Unless . . ."

"Unless what?"

"Unless we get married today."

Abigail shook her head. "I can't. Not yet. I . . ."

"That's all you ever say. If it's not one problem, it's another."

"That's not true, Robert. I have only one problem. You know how important it is that I find Amanda."

"I understand your worries for her, but what about us? When are we going to have a life?" It damn well had better be soon. He couldn't take the pressure of living on the edge of financial ruin much longer.

"As soon as I find her."

"Promise you will marry me then. The moment she is found."

"I promise," Abigail said as she slid a roll of bills across the table. "Now take this."

Robert placed his hand over the bills, but not before a certain deputy marshal stepped into the room and glanced at their table, immediately taking in the exchange of bills. Hawk shot Abigail a knowing glance as he passed them, his hand at the narrow of a woman's back as he escorted her to a waiting table.

Abigail felt the most unreasonable urge to jump from her chair and follow the couple, to explain, to tell him she had had to force Robert to take the money. A moment later came a seething outrage. How did he dare pass judgment on another and do it with that silent but superior glance? He didn't know Robert. He didn't know the problems that had besieged since the beginning of this trip.

That wasn't exactly true. He did know but simply chose not to believe.

Abigail sighed unhappily. The man had positioned himself so that their gazes met every time she looked up from the table. She wondered if he'd done it on purpose. She didn't want to feel that dark gaze moving over her. She didn't want to see the condemnation in its depth.

Hawk smiled at his companion. "Excuse me for a minute, will you, Lydia? I need to talk with someone."

Abigail saw the movement from the corner of her eye. He was coming to his feet. Please, Lord, not toward her! Why couldn't he simply leave her in peace?

He was standing at her table. Wasting no time with proper greetings, or civility of any kind, he plunged right into what was on his mind. "Cole tells me you have a mind to search out your sister yourself."

Abigail didn't take kindly to the sharp edge in his tone. It had been a long time since she sat in a schoolroom. Longer still since anyone of authority dared to address her as if she were a wayward child. Her blue eyes narrowed to a sparkling glare. "And if I did, how is it any of your concern?"

"It's my concern if I have to report the finding of your body in some alley."

Abigail frowned. What in the world was the man talking about? "Do you believe you're making sense?"

"I believe you're not as stupid as you'd like to make out."

"Mr. Hawk—"

"Deputy," he interrupted.

Abigail breathed a sigh that told of some real effort as she strove for patience. "Deputy, I'm afraid I haven't a notion as to what you are talking about."

"What I'm talking about, lady, is the fact that you don't know what the hell you're doing."

"Now see here," Robert said as he came to his feet. "I won't have you talking to—"

Hawk shot him a killing glare and said simply and perhaps a bit too softly, so softly, in fact, the words were almost a hissing threat, "Sit down."

Robert instantly obeyed. Abigail scowled at his lack of fortitude. She knew she wouldn't have given in so easily. There wasn't a man alive who could cower her into instant obedience with two words spoken from the side of his mouth.

She would have stood herself, if it weren't for the fact that her standing would no doubt create something of a scene. Instead she sneered the words, "Exactly what is it you want?"

"I want you to sit tight. Stay at the hotel and mind your own business. The law will take care of finding your sister."

"And I see you are working very hard on it." She shot the back of his companion a glance. "Very hard, indeed." Her voice was heavy with sarcasm when she raised her gaze to his again. "Just for my own information, exactly how many dinners do you suppose it will take before you find her?"

Hawk grinned, and Abigail gave a silent curse that his smile should cause her this most peculiar fluttering in her stomach. Instantly she discounted the notion. It hadn't, of course. She was just hungry. His smile had absolutely no effect on her whatsoever.

"I'm off duty."

"How nice for you, Mr. Hawk. Now, if you don't mind, Robert and I were just about to enjoy our own dinner."

"It's Deputy Hawk," he reminded again, knowing she called him Mister, instead of his rightful title, just to get a rise out of him. Too bad it didn't work. Well, it almost didn't work. "And you didn't answer me."

"I didn't answer you because, as far as I can remember, you didn't ask me a question."

"Are you going to stay out of it?"

"Certainly not," she said, her tone telling clearly of the absurdity of the notion. "She is my sister and I intend to do everything I can to see—"

"I could arrest you."

Abigail laughed in disbelief. "For what?"

"For interfering with the law."

Her lips thinned, and her eyes glared a threat. "Really? Why don't you try it?"

"If you get in my way, you can count on it, lady. A few hours in jail should go a long way toward gaining some respect for the law."

"Why wait?" Even as she said the words, she knew she was going too far. Still, she couldn't seem to stop them from coming. "So far you haven't shown me a thing worthy of respect."

Robert gasped.

Abigail ignored him and went on. "I have every intention of getting in your way." She didn't, of course. She wouldn't even know how to go about getting in his way. But Abigail never took kindly to

94

a threat, and a threat from this man rankled most of all.

Hawk's eyes narrowed; his lips tightened.

Robert could see disaster looming upon the horizon if he didn't bring some calm to this moment. "Wait a minute," he said as he came again to his feet. "You can't arrest her for looking for her sister. She hasn't broken any laws."

Hawk knew Robert was right. All she'd done so far was mouth off to him, and he couldn't arrest her for that. That wasn't a crime, although he wished to hell it was. He couldn't imagine anything that would bring him more satisfaction than to take this little smart-mouthed bundle of fury off to jail. No, she hadn't broken any laws. How the hell had the moment gotten so out of hand? How had he allowed her to cause him this loss of control?

Hawk shot her his most menacing glare and knew a moment of dismay, for it brought about none of the desired effects. He'd seen hardened criminals quake at one of his looks, but this woman was either too stupid, or braver than she had any right to be, for she only glared her own anger in return. "Any way you want it, lady. It wouldn't bother me any to put you where you belong." He almost wished she'd ask exactly where he thought she belonged. He would have enjoyed her shock. The fact that her fiancé stood next to him wouldn't have stopped him from saying, "In my bed."

That same night and all of three blocks from Abigail's hotel, Amanda listened as the key turned in the lock. She smiled, knowing only happiness as he came into the room. It was late. And as always, when he was late, he smelled of whiskey. Amanda didn't mind. A man had every right to a drink now and then, if that was his preference.

She listened as he stumbled a bit, taking off his clothes in the dark, and she almost came from the bed to help him, but Thomas never appreciated her help when he was like this. Wisely she remained where she was and waited for him to join her. Waited for his arms to circle her small body and bring her close to his comforting warmth. Waited for just the right moment to tell him.

She loved him. She really did. If only Abigail would have permitted her to have a beau, to be like other young girls, to eventually allow her to marry. Then she and Tommy wouldn't have had to run off. Things would have been so different, so much better.

He sat on the bed with a hard bounce, in total disregard for the woman sleeping there. The truth was, Tommy couldn't have cared less if he woke her up. If she had any complaints about his drinking, he vowed she'd be sorry. He almost wished she would say something. He'd had a rage building up inside him for months. Lately he'd hardly been able to keep that rage under control. He could hardly wait for the moment when she got what she deserved.

He lay down at her side, only he didn't reach for her. The girls at Madame Blanche's knew—better than this fool—what most pleased a man. All he wanted was a few hours of sleep. In the morning she'd try to contact her sister again. And if the bitch knew what was good for her, she'd answer this time.

Amanda waited for his cuddling and knew a deep sense of disappointment when his deep breathing turn into a gentle snore. But Amanda, always giving and forgiving, shrugged aside the emotion, knowing he had worked hard today and was obviously exhausted. She turned to him. A few moments later she, too, slept—warm and happy in her lover's arms.

Dawn was just creeping over the horizon when Amanda stretched, sighed sleepily, and then smiled. Today was the day. Today she was going to tell Tommy the good news. By evening they would probably be married. Once married, Amanda knew Tommy would insist on going back home. And once they were home, everything would be wonderful again.

No longer would they have to worry about money. Tommy could paint to his heart's content, and she could have their babies.

She glanced at her lover's face, never seeing the lines of debauchery etched from nose to mouth that would deepen even more upon awakening. She didn't notice the florid complexion, the added flesh softening a once hard jaw. She saw instead what was in her own mind. A handsome man—who loved her more than anything in the world—and would love her even more when he heard they were about to have a baby.

Amanda dressed hurriedly and in silence. She wanted everything to be ready when he awoke. She wanted everything to be perfect.

Twenty minutes later she juggled a bag of delicious flaky pastry and a loaf of French bread as she let herself back into their room. Amanda smiled at seeing him still asleep. Thomas always asked for strong coffee upon awakening. Amanda hurried to put up a pot, knowing the aroma would soon bring him awake.

It did.

She sat at the small table set with a steaming pot of coffee, delicate cups, heavy cream, pastries, and bread. He grunted a sleepy sound, rolled to his side, and then came slowly into a sitting position. His bare feet were on the floor, his head held in his hands.

Pain sliced through his skull, and with squinting eyes he shot her a baleful look of scorn. How the hell did she do it? Every morning. Every goddamn morning for almost a year, she woke up cheerful and happy to see another day. Christ, he could hardly get himself out of bed before she danced her merry way into the fucking kitchen. Something was wrong with people like that. Something was wrong with her. He knew that for a fact.

She watched from the corner of her eye as he came naked from the bed, stretched, and walked toward the table. He knew she didn't like it when he didn't get dressed right away in the mornings, and he took some pleasure, no matter how scant, that his sex hovered over their breakfast, that she turned her gaze from his body to the steaming cup before her.

"No cream this morning," he said as she was about to prepare his cup.

Thomas sat opposite her, reached for the offered coffee, and cursed as it burned his lip.

Amanda was anxious to get on with the telling but took a moment to console. "Are you all right?"

"Just dandy," he said sarcastically.

Amanda bit her lip. He was in one of his nasty

moods. It didn't matter. Once she told him her news, he would be in the best mood imaginable. Once he found out he was going to be a father, he'd be happier than he'd ever known. "I have some good news."

"Your sister sent the money?" he asked, knowing that bit of news just might be the only thing that would get him out of this foul mood. The thought of money might even take his headache away and ease his queasy stomach.

"Not yet."

Thomas sighed, knowing he wasn't interested in anything else. Still, the woman seemed ready to burst, and he didn't have much choice but to hear her out. "What then?"

"We're going to have a baby."

Thomas breathed a sigh of disgust, careful not to allow too much of the emotion to show. He couldn't alienate her now, not when they were close to another windfall. "I know, as soon as we get married. And we'll get married as soon as your sister sends—"

"No, I mean, I'm going to have a baby. I'm already . . ." Amanda blushed and allowed her gaze to return to the table.

It took a moment, but her exact meaning finally dawned through the haze of pain. "What? Now? You're pregnant?"

Amanda's cheeks grew warm again, and she knew some embarrassment that he should be so blunt. Still, even though she had yet to find the courage to meet his gaze, she nodded.

A smile touched the corners of her mouth as she awaited his burst of exuberance. Only it didn't come.

Instead she heard a vile curse and then a sneering, "Get rid of it."

Amanda knew no sense of disappointment. The fact was she'd been so sure of his reaction that she suffered only mild confusion as he cursed again. She blinked, obviously puzzled, not understanding half his muttered words.

"Get rid of it? What do you mean?"

"I mean go to a midwife and have her take care of it. We can't have a baby now. We haven't got enough for two, never mind another mouth to feed."

"But Thomas, I can't do that. It's our baby."

"You can't? You can't?" he taunted and then breathed a deep sigh, trying to hold back this need to strike out. Yes, he had hit her before, but that was nothing compared with what he wanted to do now. He had to wait, wait until her sister sent the money. He finally managed, "You can, Amanda, and you will. Having a baby now is impossible."

"You don't mean that." She shook her head, her eyes huge and filled with disappointment.

"Don't I? I've never meant anything more in my life."

"Thomas. I thought you'd be happy. I thought we'd get married and everything would be . . ."

Did this stupid bitch really believe that he would father a child by her? Who the hell would want a simpleton as the mother of his child? Suppose the baby suffered the same affliction. Thomas shivered at the thought. "And we will," he lied. "Once your sister sends the money, we will."

"I won't kill our baby," she said simply, her blue eyes hardening with determination. "I love him."

100

"More than you love me?"

"No, but—"

"Then do as I say."

"I won't."

"First you can't. Now you won't." Damn it to hell, but he'd had enough of this. "If you want the baby so much, go ahead and have it, but I'm leaving." Thomas knew that threat would do the trick. He waited for her to plead with him to stay, to promise to do as he said. Only she didn't. Instead she sat there, saying nothing, the corners of her mouth drooping in a childish pout.

He snarled his disgust. To hell with her sister and her money. He didn't give a damn if he were forced into the streets. It was preferable to spending another minute in this one's company. He couldn't stand the sight of her.

"I thought you loved me. I thought you wanted to marry me."

"Wanted to marry you?" He laughed wildly at the thought. "Want to be tied down to a simpleton? Want to call an idiot my wife?"

"What?" Her eyes rounded in shock. Thomas had, on occasion, been cruel in the past, but nothing like this.

"You heard me. You're not that far gone. You know what it means to be stupid, don't you, Amanda?" he jeered. "You know what it means when people make fun of you because you're so stupid that you don't know anything."

Blue eyes widened with pain. "Thomas, please."

"Tears again, Amanda? Sweet stupid Amanda and her tears. Christ, you make me sick."

Amanda sat there, the object of his scorn, unable to do anything to stop the barrage of insults and curses that flowed from his cruel twisted lips. And then it appeared that curses no longer satisfied. Suddenly, he couldn't hold back any longer. He struck her with a tightly balled fist, the blow knocking her slight form from the chair. She cried out more in surprise than pain to find herself suddenly upon the floor, but the pain wasn't far from coming.

He stood then, hovering over her prone form, and the fear in her eyes brought him a sense of power, so damn good it rivaled sex. His face contorted with the fury he had kept at bay for all these long months. His eyes gleamed with insanity and ultimately satisfaction as he leaned low and swung his fists into her face, her neck, her chest, hitting her because she was stupid. Hitting her because he had thought the money would have lasted longer; because her nature—sweet, beguiling, almost childlike—had been a delightful diversion at first and had become boring after only a month's time; because Mrs. Masterson had refused to pay him for the picture of her son, which had taken more than three weeks to finish; because the red-headed whore last night had been busy and he'd had to settle for the blonde; because he was sick of this damn city; because the coffee had burnt his lip. . . .

His second blow split her lip and loosened a tooth. She tasted blood. Stars flashed behind tightly closed eyes. But she couldn't worry about the damage he caused her face. Not now. Her first concern would always be to protect the baby. Nothing could happen to this baby.

She spread her hands over her abdomen and pulled her knees almost to her chin, curling herself into a tight ball, protecting herself, as best she could, from this brutal attack. He kicked her, aiming for her abdomen, but it was her leg that took the blow. He kicked her again, this time in her back. Later she would thank God he wasn't wearing his boots.

Still, the force of every blow brought a guttural grunt. She didn't recognize the sound of her voice, for it reminded her of a dying animal. Blackness swam around the edges of her consciousness. She could see it like the framing of a picture and welcomed the beckoning promise of comfort closer, closer. She was going to die. Amanda knew she was going to die. She felt an almost overwhelming sense of sadness at the thought, for her dying meant her baby would die as well.

No! She couldn't let that happen. She couldn't allow anything to happen to her baby.

She screamed, but her screams went unnoticed as the blows continued to come. And then she fought back, like a cornered animal, kicking and screaming, and kicking some more. It took a long moment before she realized he no longer stood over her, that the blows had ceased at last. It took longer still before she noticed, from eyes already swelling shut, his naked body sprawled upon the floor at her feet.

Amanda had no way of knowing that she had kicked him, quite by accident, in fact, in a most sensitive place, sending agony spiraling up his body to crash into his brain. The pain had been so sudden, so unexpected, and so terribly intense that it momentarily stole his breath. He found it impossible to keep his balance. He staggered a bit, but it was no use. And then the bitch had kicked him again, and he thought he would surely die. With his hands cupping his groin, his knees gave out beneath him, and he fell backward into the table, hitting his head upon the hard edge, unconscious before he hit the floor.

Amanda could hear nothing in the suddenly silent room, nothing but the pounding of her own heart and the soft murmurs of her own pain. He was dead. Fresh tears for a lost love came as sobs tore at her chest. She wanted to go to him, but she couldn't bring herself to touch his lifeless body. What had gone wrong? What had happened?

She sat there for a long moment watching his chest. It wasn't moving. The sense of doom was nearly suffocating. She had killed the father of her baby.

She took a trembling breath, trying for a measure of calm, and wiped the blood as it trickled down her chin. She'd go to prison for this, she thought dully. Maybe she'd even hang. Again came thoughts of her baby. No, they wouldn't hang her, at least not right away. They'd wait until the baby came.

Amanda knew almost debilitating panic at the thought. She couldn't allow them to take her baby. No one could love it like she would. No. She wouldn't allow anyone to take her baby.

It took some effort, but she managed to get to her feet. It wasn't easy to think. The room swam around her head, and she had to hold on to a chair lest she fall again to the floor.

What to do? What to do? God, if only she could think. And then it suddenly came to her, and she knew what she had to do. She had to get away. And she had to hurry before someone came, before someone found the body.

Her hands, her entire body shook as she threw a few articles into a carpet bag. Her shawl, underthings, an extra dress. She had to hurry. Oh, God—please help me to hurry.

A small mirror hung over the dry sink. Amanda gasped as she stood before it and saw the damage done. Blood was everywhere. It streamed from her nose, from her mouth, from the cut below one eye. Trembling fingers washed it all away. She licked her lip as more came to the surface and pressed a cool cloth to her nose to stop the trickle of blood. The cool cloth felt wonderful, but she didn't have the time to indulge in the comfort. The moment she got the bleeding to stop, she stripped away her dress and pulled another over her head.

She took a deep breath and forced shaking fingers to rework the knot in her hair. Her hat didn't match her dress, but it was the only one she had with a veil. She arranged the dark material over her face, hiding the evidence of what she'd just gone through.

She was at the door. One last glance at the man she'd loved beyond family, friends, and morals, beyond anything in her life brought a fresh bout of sorrowful tears. She hesitated and then returned to empty Thomas's pockets of eighteen dollars. In a flash she was gone, running away from what she had done, running toward safety, home, and Abigail, never hearing his low moan of pain, just after she closed the door.

Somewhere behind the blinding pain, Thomas Hill listened as the door closed and then came the sound of running footsteps on the stairs. He cursed as he rolled to his stomach, his hand cupping the pulsating agony between his legs. He was going to kill the bitch. If he ever saw her again, she'd wish she had finished what she'd started.

Chapter Six

"Excuse me, sir, have you seen this girl?" Abigail asked of the attractive man who leaned a shoulder against one of the many gaslight posts that dotted the busy waterfront. Abigail realized, of course, that it was most inappropriate for a lone woman to accost a man who was unknown to her. But what choice did she truly have? Early this morning Robert had once again gone off to God only knew where. She wasn't about to sit idly by and await his return. Who knew when he would return?

No, it didn't matter if Robert was in attendance or not. Abigail had to be about the business of finding her sister. And this man looked pleasant enough, especially when he smiled. One would have to leap to some wild conclusions, having the strangest mind imaginable, to suppose her in need of anything but an answer to her straight-spoken question.

Besides, they were hardly alone. To her right stood a number of shops, many taverns, and a few boardinghouses. The cobblestone and wooden wharf was filled almost to overflowing with a wide assortment of humanity. Black men, shirtless backs moist with sweat, straining beneath their burdens, unloaded cargo from the boats as they sang a hauntingly sad yet melodious tune. Wide-eyed visitors, looking every which way but where they headed, stumbled along the uneven cobblestones. Hawkers sold their wares directly from crates taken from the boats, which had only moments before ended their journey downriver, while ladies of every fashion strolled, all in the company of a gentlemen or maid, and street urchins darted to and fro snatching what they could from carts filled with fruits and vegetables.

Among the throng of busy activity, she never noticed the young boy who had been watching since she left her hotel.

To her left the Mississippi flowed gently beyond the grass-covered levy toward the salty waters of the Gulf of Mexico. Four paddleboats sat moored, while clouds of steam puffed from their tall chimneys, two just docked, two awaiting departure at the captain's command.

Despite Abigail's business capabilities and reasonable common sense, she was an innocent at heart, a trusting sort, who knew nothing of the seedier segment of society. Therefore Abigail never imagined that the man she approached was one of New Orleans's most notorious pimps.

Mike Hennesey smiled as he glanced at the picture. He only wished he had seen this little piece. A girl like that could bring him a fortune. Still, the one standing before him, although a bit long in the tooth (his dark gaze moved with calculated interest over her small neat frame, accurately estimating her age to be about twenty-four), had some real possibilities. A smart woman would take the few years she had left and use them to her best advantage. Mike wondered if he could convince this one to his way of thinking.

"Ma'am," he said as he touched the brim of his hat and allowed his most devastating smile. "I might have, but I can't be sure."

Abigail's heart quickened with hope. After hours of asking everyone she'd come across, could it be that she'd finally found someone who could help? Abigail was not unaware that New Orleans was a good-sized city, but it wasn't so large as to allow a girl to completely disappear. Someone among its citizenry had to have seen her.

"Are you sure she's in the city?"

"Very sure."

"Why don't you let me take the picture. There's a friend of mine who would know for sure."

"Oh, I couldn't." Abigail shook her head. "It's the only one I've got left."

Mike nodded. Experienced in the art of seduction, he gently laid his trap. "I understand, of course. Too bad though. Is she a relative of yours?"

"My sister."

His smile was as pure and gentle as any she'd ever seen. "Wait here. I'll try to describe her to my friend. Perhaps he knows something."

It was easy enough to see that this man was trying to help. But describing Amanda to someone would hardly be as effective as if one saw the photograph for himself. Again she shook her head. "I'll go with you. This way I could show him her picture."

"Are you sure?"

A lady would have to be either a fool or no lady at all to disregard propriety and go off with a stranger. Abigail was desperate enough not to care. Desperate enough, in fact, not to realize the man could have brought his friend to her.

"It doesn't matter. If there's a chance . . ."

Hennesey grinned and extended his arm in a most gentlemanly fashion. The moment she took his arm, he pressed his hand over hers and led her toward the best of his three bordellos.

Amanda, her face hidden behind a dark veil, stepped aboard the paddleboat, *Princess,* just as Abigail allowed the man to guide her away from the docks. Her heart beat happily within her chest. The long weary hours had paid off. She was on the verge of finding her sister.

Silently she gloated, imagining Hawk's disapproval. She didn't care a whit what that puffed-up arrogant oaf said. Did he honestly expect her to sit idly by and do what—eat bonbons while awaiting word of her sister? She grinned as she imagined his anger at finding out she had ignored his order. She laughed a soft happy sound, knowing she'd been right and through her efforts alone Amanda would be found. And if a certain deputy marshal didn't like it, well, he could just go to hell.

The man introduced himself as Mike Hennesey. Abigail returned the courtesy, stating her own name.

They walked down one alley and up the next. He guided her around the next corner, turning her suddenly behind the privacy of tall gates into a courtyard, and then into a two-story silent building. The

110

foyer was dark, the air thick with the cloying scent of heavy perfume.

He guided her into a sitting room and inquired of her preferences for tea or coffee while they waited. Abigail smiled, said, "Coffee, please," and was left alone.

Abigail blinked as she tried to accustom her eyes to the dimness. A wall of tall windows were covered with red velvet draperies. Abigail wondered at the oddity. She might have thought that windows this far south would have been dressed in the lightest of fabrics, for the heavy material disallowed even a breath of air into a room that was badly in need of that commodity.

She fidgeted nervously upon the hard settee, smoothing her skirt, resting her umbrella and bag beside her, while mentally hurrying the gentleman along. She was close, so close she could almost feel it.

Ricky stood before the deputy and watched his deep scowl. "Are you sure?"

"Yes, sir." He'd run all the way and was still a bit breathless.

Hawk nodded. "All right. I won't need you anymore today." He flipped the boy a coin, never seeing the brilliant smile, nor hearing the promise to watch the lady again whenever he was asked. Hawk came to his feet and left the office. He was going to strangle her with his bare hands. The goddamn fool! What the hell did she think she was doing?

* * *

It was the worst coffee Abigail had ever tasted. Unbelievably bitter. She took only one sip, restrained the shiver that threatened and then smiled. "Will your friend be along shortly?"

"I've sent a boy to his lodgings. I expect him any minute."

Abigail smiled again. She thought she caught an intensity in Mr. Hennesey's look and then put the mistaken image to a trick of lighting or the lack thereof. Why didn't he open a curtain? Why didn't he allow some air into the room? She glanced his way again. No, the man hadn't looked at her any differently than he had from the first. Nothing but kindness was in his dark eyes.

Still, a sort of stiffness filled her and her smile grew forced as the tall clock in the foyer ticked away the minutes, her gaze moving around the still dim room.

"Please, ma'am, finish your coffee."

"Thank you, but I've had enough."

"You mean it's unpalatable?" Mr. Hennesey looked terribly disappointed. "My kitchen help is off this morning. I've been trying so hard . . ."

His need to please was so obvious that Abigail found herself lying straight out. "No, no, it's fine, perfect in fact."

"Then please . . ." he said, and smiled behind his cup as she lifted hers and finished the contents in one shuddering gulp.

She smiled weakly as she replaced both cup and saucer upon the small table, while hoping her shiver had not been too obvious. The man had been so kind, so anxious to help. Pretending to like his coffee was the least she could do.

In the silence that followed, she began to question what she had done. If she hadn't feared so for Amanda, hadn't worried so desperately for her welfare, she'd never have found herself sitting in a strange man's home, awaiting the arrival of yet another man.

It occurred quite suddenly that no one knew where she was, but after a second or two of something close to panic, Abigail pushed that discomforting thought aside. She had no cause to fear. Mr. Hennesey had been a perfect gentleman. Why then did Hawk and his condemning expression come to mind? Odd that she should suddenly think of the man and his disapproval. Well, he would be wrong in this case. She couldn't have asked for kinder, a more gentlemanly soul.

She blinked and found herself having to force her eyes to open again. Lord, how had she grown so suddenly tired? She felt the almost overpowering need to yawn. It was the lack of air, she knew. "Do you think you could open a window, Mr. Hennesey?"

"Of course. Are you warm?"

"Perhaps just a bit."

"You might open your dress, ma'am. It would make you more comfortable, and I promise I wouldn't mind."

Abigail blinked in confusion. Had she heard him correctly? Certainly not. "Excuse me?"

Mr. Hennesey grinned and then leaned suddenly and scandalously close. "Too tired, my dear?"

Abigail felt his breath slither against her skin but

113

merely blinked in bewilderment as he said, "Very well, my dear, I'll do it for you."

Abigail watched his fingers move over the buttons of her high-necked dress. She knew what he was doing and yet amazingly enough simply sat there and watched. What was happening to her? Why couldn't she raise her hands from her lap? Why couldn't she utter a word to stop this?

Hennesey smiled at her confusion as the last of the buttons came undone. She watched as he gently lowered the neckline of her chemise and shot her an evil grin of hungry appreciation as her breasts filled both hands. "Lovely."

Her head fell back. Her eyes closed, but not before Abigail's mind finally understood that she had been drugged. Understood as well that she had made the worst mistake of her life.

The door slammed against the wall as it was flung open. Heavy footsteps sounded in the foyer, but before Hennesey could come to his feet, to see to the untimely interruption, a man stood before him and the nearly naked woman who reclined half upon him and his sofa.

"What . . . ?"

Hawk's gaze took in the scene with one glance. She was unconscious, probably drugged, naked but for her frilly drawers and silk stockings, and this snake's hand was playing with a breast. "Hennesey," came the hissing sound of rage, "you bastard."

Hennesey shoved her limp form aside and stood, but it was already too late. He never saw it coming.

All he knew was one moment he was coming to his feet and the next lights flashed again and again behind his closing eyes. He forgot his intentions, his arousal. He forgot the lovely half-naked woman and the enjoyment he was about to know. All his mind seemed capable of understanding was pain and blinding light that mercifully lasted but a few seconds. And then as his body slumped to the floor, he knew only delicious safe blackness.

Hawk ripped one of the musty drapes from a window and wrapped her inside its heavy folds, making sure that her face was covered as well. Next he walked outside and hailed a cabby, ordering him to wait. And then Abigail was in his arms and he was inside the cab, yelling orders for the driver to take them to his rooms.

Hawk had no choice. He knew where she was staying. But knew as well that he couldn't take her to her hotel without irrefutable harm being done to her reputation.

Hawk jumped from the coach, flipped the driver a coin, and making sure that her face was covered, quickly entered the building. Inside he met no one as he carried Abigail to his rooms.

He breathed a sigh of relief as the door closed behind him at last. Only his relief wasn't to last for long. She was still out cold. Hawk wondered for how long.

He placed her on his bed and flung the dusty red material to the floor. It was then that he realized he'd made a serious mistake. She wore only her drawers and stockings. Hawk's mouth went dry. He knew he shouldn't look, but God help him, he couldn't tear his gaze away. She was breathtakingly beautiful, lying there as if a wanton. He felt his loins tighten and pulse with instant throbbing desire.

Christ Almighty! Get a hold of yourself, man! This woman needs your help, not gawking.

Hawk moved to his armoire and retrieved a fresh shirt. He was pushing her arms into it when she suddenly asked without a trace of sleepiness, "What are you doing?"

Hawk glanced at her, surprised to find her fully awake, readying himself in an intant for the cascade of insults that were sure to fall upon his ears. "I'm trying to cover you."

"Why?" She shook the shirt from her arm and giggled when he tried again to put her arm through the sleeve. "Stop. I don't want it on." She glanced at her body, surprisingly enough, not at all shocked, but knowing a mild sense of confusion at finding herself clothed in only her drawers and stockings. She gave a slight frown. It seemed most peculiar to be wearing her drawers and almost nothing else. Oddly enough she knew no embarrassment at that fact and suddenly decided the best course of action would be to dispose of them as well. She had but one purpose of mind and that was to get them off. "Where am I?"

"In my rooms." He watched as her hand moved to pull down her drawers. He gasped and pulled her hand back. "Stay still."

Hawk figured he was living some kind of nightmare. Nothing short of the most sensuous dream could account for the fact that her breasts jiggled enticingly with her every movement. Nothing short of a nightmare could account for the fact that he didn't dare touch her. That she was bare to the hip, that instead of touching her, as he wanted more than anything to do, he was trying to stop her from pulling the rest of her things off, that he was trying to put the shirt on. She was laughing at his efforts, managing to foil one attempt after another.

Her drawers were at her knees now. Amid their wrestling, she managed to kick them off. Hawk only groaned. He couldn't look or he'd be forever lost.

What the hell was he fighting her for? He rolled from a kneeling position at her side to pin her beneath him, holding her hands over her head, only to hear her laugh again as she shifted, raising her hips just enough, her body telling him clearly what it wanted. Jesus!

"Abby," he breathed, terrified to move, for her breast was barely an inch from his mouth. God, please, he silently prayed, not at all sure what it was he prayed for. All he knew for a fact was if she arched her back just a fraction he would be done for. "Listen to me."

"What?" Laughter lit up her blue eyes, and a grin tugged at her lips. She forgot she'd just asked him a question and said, "Take off your shirt. I want to feel you against me."

"You don't know what you're saying." Hawk wondered if what he said was true. She sure acted like she knew what she was saying. Her body seemed to know what she was saying. Maybe . . .

No. She was drugged. She didn't know, and if he took advantage of her now, he'd be no better than Hennesey. "Abby, listen," he said, releasing one hand to hold her face, her gaze on his. "You've been drugged."

But releasing her hand had been a mistake. Her fingers reached immediately between them, fumbling for a minute with his belt, giving up and going on to further discoveries. And then her eyes widened with intrigue as her hand palmed his arousal. He cursed his body and its unwanted reaction. "I want you to make love to me."

"No, you don't."

"Yes, I do. Don't you want me?"

Hawk figured it best not to respond to that question. "Abby, Hennesey drugged you. You were supposed to want him."

"I wouldn't want him," she declared honestly. "I hardly know the man. It's you I want."

"I'm going to get up."

"Don't." Her hand slid inside his trousers. Hawk froze. His heart pounded like he'd run miles. What the hell was he supposed to do? How much could a man take?

It took a long moment, but Hawk finally found the strength to mutter painfully, "I'm getting up, and I want you to stay here."

Abigail smiled. "To get undressed?"

"Yes. I'll get undressed. Wait right here."

She nodded.

Hawk came slowly from the bed and inched himself toward the door. In a flash he was outside, turning the key, locking her in, knowing he'd never be sorrier for anything in his life as he was at that moment.

"Hawk," she said, standing suddenly on the opposite side of the door, the wrong side of the door. No, he was on the wrong side. "What are you doing?"

"Go back to bed." He took a deep breath, trying to shake aside the need, the longing. "I have to get something."

"You'll be right back?"

"Yes, I'll be right back."

He heard her laughter as she moved away from the door and returned to his bed.

Two hours later Hawk believed he was once again in control of his feelings. He believed it, that is, until he unlocked his door and entered his room only to find a naked lady sprawled upon his bed. Her blond hair curled like a halo of light around her sweet face. And her face in sleep was even more lovely than when awake. No, it wasn't, he silently reconsidered. In sleep she couldn't shoot him glares, nor smile and show that adorable dimple. Still, sleep had some advantages.

His gaze moved slowly, luxuriously, over her form. He'd allow himself one look, he swore. Just one look and he'd bring the covers over her. Her breasts were large, but he'd known they would be. The fashion of the day was very tight and form-fitting bodices. What he hadn't known though was the fact that they would be milky white, with one soft blue vein running from chest to nipple on the inside of each. He couldn't have known that the tips would be a lovely shade of pink, so lovely in fact that he found his mouth watering for just a small taste.

Her midriff was flat, her waist minuscule above

flaring softly rounded hips and the treasure that was hidden behind a fluff of pale blond curls.

His body trembled at the silent call, a siren's call for his touch. Hawk cursed, for it took only this one long look to bring every wicked thought and need crashing back into his body. He might not have left at all for all the good it had done.

His hand reached for the sheet. He held it, ready to bring it over her, when she stirred, moaned a soft sleepy sound.

Abigail awakened from a deliciously wicked dream where she and Hawk, of all people, frolicked like carefree naked children. She'd wanted him to make love to her. She'd been laughing gaily, dancing shamelessly around him while he watched and teased with a gentle smile and those dark lovely eyes. She couldn't believe it. She'd never dreamed of anything so erotic before. A dream had never left her so empty with such an odd feeling of need.

Her eyes blinked open. The accusation in their blue depths momentarily froze him in place. Hawk cursed the fact that he hadn't covered her thirty seconds sooner. Now it was too late.

"What are you doing in my room?" If possible, her eyes grew colder and harder than ever. And Hawk wondered how he was going to convince her of the truth of things. "Answer me."

"I'm not in your room. You're in mine."

Abigail glanced around the room, noting for the first time that she wasn't in her room. Was he telling her the truth? Was she in his? If so, how had she gotten here and why?

Abigail's gaze moved over the strange room and its

unfamiliar furnishings. It came to a stop at the bed. She gasped as she realized at last that she was lying here naked before him, and the beast—the unscrupulous beast—hadn't said a word about it. She tore the sheet from his grasp, believing he had lifted it and like a sneak had looked his fill.

Hawk felt a wave of unwanted and unwarranted guilt. He knew he was blushing. Him? Blushing? Why, he hadn't known embarrassment since he was a little kid.

He hadn't done anything except try to help her, but he might as well have if the look in her eye meant anything. "I know what you're thinking. It's not true."

"You didn't look at me?"

He hesitated a moment. There was no sense in denying the truth. "Well, yes, I looked but . . ."

Abigail shivered at the thought. Her face flamed. God, she'd never been so embarrassed in her entire life. And then it came to her that she didn't have anything to be embarrassed about. He was the culprit behind this debauchery. "You beast. You depraved, perverted, degenerate."

"Wait a minute."

She tore the sheet back, enraged that he could have taken such advantage. She had nothing to hide. It was his black soul at fault here. She shoved him back and came to her feet. Her hands on her hips, she glared her hatred. "You want to look? Go ahead. Enjoy yourself."

Hawk simply stood where she had pushed him. He had expected anger, yes—perhaps cowering and maybe a few tears. He hadn't expected this. He couldn't say anything. He didn't know where to begin. The worst of it wasn't that he couldn't answer her. The worst of it was he couldn't tear his gaze away.

The next thing he knew his cheek was burning like hell from her slap. He figured he deserved that, for the few lust-filled moments he'd enjoyed just before she awoke.

A second later she was wrapping the sheet around herself.

The slap had done two things. It had shaken him from an almost paralyzed state and at the same time loosened his tongue. "Are you calmed down yet?"

"Calmed down?" She snickered an evil laugh. "Putting a bullet between your eyes would be the only thing that could calm me down."

Hawk couldn't help the grin. He couldn't remember ever knowing a woman with this kind of spirit, with so fiery a temper. She wasn't the least bit afraid. She'd awakened to find a man leaning over her naked form and yet knew only anger.

"Sit down, we have to talk."

"Drop dead."

Hawk laughed. "You're adorable." He blinked in surprise. He shouldn't have said that. He hadn't meant to say that. It had just sort of slipped out.

"See how adorable you find this," she said as she lunged for the dry sink and the bowl that held his morning water.

Hawk rushed to take it from her hands, but it sloshed over them both. She cried out and swung at him again. He ducked the coming blow and tackled her, none too gently, to the bed. With his legs on each side of her hips, he sat on her, and leaned forward, holding her hands over her head.

"Maybe I deserved the first one," he said as he struggled to hold her in place without inflicting too much harm. "Maybe," he reiterated with a hard shake as she bared her teeth, trying to bite his arm. She glared into his hard eyes. "But if you hit me again, don't be surprised if you get hit back."

"I hate you. I'll see you dead for what you've done."

"Exactly what the hell do you think I've done?"

"You took advantage of me."

"Right," he ridiculed. "And I did it in my room and then waited for you to come to your senses so you could attack me.

"It was Hennesey who took advantage of you."

She struggled against his strength, baring her teeth again. "I thought you were a man of honor."

Hawk knew a sense of disappointment that she should now believe otherwise. For some insane reason he wanted to shine in her eyes. "Think, lady. Think of where you were, of what you were doing before he drugged you."

"Drugged?" She laughed in disbelief. "Someone drugged me?"

He shook her again, this time gently as if the movement would stir some distant memory. "In the whorehouse. Remember?"

Abigail slipped one hand from his grasp and almost contacted a blow to his jaw. He grabbed her hand just inches from delivery as she began to fight him again. "You beast, you pervert. I've never in my life—"

123

He captured her hands again, easily subduing her with his strength and weight. Hawk laughed at her shock, knowing she had no idea that she'd been sitting in a whorehouse when he'd come to her rescue. He took his bottom lip between his teeth, unable to stop the teasing words. "You can thank me now for saving you from a fate worse than death."

"I'll thank you all right," she grunted as she tried to throw him off. "Right after I stab you in the heart."

Hawk couldn't help it. He couldn't remember when a woman had so appealed.

"The second you let me go, I'm going to kill you."

"Maybe I'll never let you go."

Her struggling instantly ceased, and they looked at each other for a long moment before she asked, "What do you mean?"

Hawk frowned at the inadvertently spoken remark. What the hell *did* he mean? Of course, he'd let her go. He didn't want her. Well, maybe his body did, but that was all. He wasn't interested in a woman like her. Uppity, spoiled, nasty-mouthed brat who thought because of her money that she was too good for anyone, even her boyfriend. No, he could never be interested in a woman like her.

Hawk knew his thoughts a lie, even as they made themselves known. She wasn't spoiled, she wasn't uppity at all. And her nasty mouth was only in evidence when he riled her. The fact that he enjoyed riling her was instantly dismissed.

Hawk shrugged aside his thoughts. The important thing to do was to get her out of here and do it as soon as possible.

"Look, we have to talk. If I get up, will you promise not to throw anything else?"

Abigail refused to answer but simply glared her hatred. She was going to get him for this. Somehow, someway, she would make him suffer.

Her struggles had loosened the sheet tucked above her breasts, and she instantly pulled the fabric over herself again, but not before Hawk caught a flash of milk-white and soft pink naked flesh. He ignored the things it did to his body and moved to an easy chair in the far corner of the room.

Abigail wrapped herself as best as she could. A moment later, in a demure fashion, as if clothed in the most elaborate of ball gowns, she sat on the bed.

"This is what happened. The boy I sent to watch you . . ." Hawk hesitated a moment at her gasp of surprise. "His name is Ricky. Ricky saw you go off with Hennesey. He followed. After you went into the whorehouse, Ricky thought he should come for me. Which is exactly what he did."

Abigail shook her head. Now that the worst of her anger had subsided, now that her emotions had calmed some, she was beginning to remember something. Only it was a vague blurred picture of a young attractive man. She couldn't place him. What did it mean? She raised confused eyes in an appeal that almost brought Hawk to her side again. "I can't remember."

"It's the drug. He must have gotten you to drink something. Maybe you'll remember later."

Abigail wondered if it might not be better if she forgot everything that had happened to her today. She suddenly knew she didn't want to remember.

"How did I get here?"

"I called a cab."

"Where are my clothes?"

"Most of them are still at the whorehouse."

"Will you please stop saying that? I've never in my life visited such an establishment. You are obviously mistaken."

"All right. Your clothes are still at Hennesey's place."

"You mean you brought me here, in a cab, *naked!?*" Her cheeks grew dark, burning at the very thought.

"You were wrapped in this." Hawk pointed with the toe of his boot toward the discarded drapery. "Do you remember what happened when I got you back here?"

"No. Why? Should I?"

"No. I was just wondering."

"Something happened, didn't it?" She took a deep breath as if steeling herself for the worst. "What was it?"

Before Hawk had a chance to deny again her question, she gasped, "My purse! Amanda's picture! Oh God, I had six hundred dollars in it."

Hawk scowled. "Son of a bitch! Didn't I tell you to stay in your room and wait? Didn't I tell you that you were heading for trouble?" He came to his feet and moved toward the door.

"Where are you going?"

"To get the purse back. And maybe kill the son of a bitch if he says he doesn't have it." He didn't know why, for sure, but he'd never felt more in a killing mood.

Chapter Seven

"Excuse me, sir," a tall black man said, coming at once to see to the disturbance as the door smashed against the wall. "But the ladies won't be ready for another hour or more."

"Where is Hennesey?"

"Mr. Hennesey is indisposed."

Hawk smiled at the polite word. "I'll just bet he is." He glanced a the black man. "Exactly where does he conduct these indispositions?"

"Excuse me?"

"Where is he, man?"

Mr. Clay might have been a man of some standing and authority in this small organization, but he knew better than to thwart this man. The glare aimed his way left not a doubt that he too would know some similar indisposition, if he did not immediately cooperate. "Upstairs. The first room on your right."

Hawk mounted the stairs two at a time. Again he felt no need to knock but simply entered the heavily draped, dim room. "I told you to leave me in peace, Clay. Take care of whatever—"

"It's not Clay."

Hawk took some delight in the instant terror displayed. He figured the man warranted terror and more for the dastardly act he'd thought to perform on Abby, and he was perfectly willing to see to it that this one got everything he deserved.

Hennesey was not so terribly hurt that he could not manage to scramble from the bed. Still, it would be days yet before he would fully recuperate from the brutal punishment received a few hours ago. So it was with some loss of equilibrium that he stood cowering, naked beside his bed. An instant later noticing—as best as a man could with eyes that would open only a quarter of the way—no mercy in the man standing opposite him, he lunged to his side, hoping to reach safety in the next room with a locked door between them. He didn't come near to making it. Off balance, he fell instead upon a low table. Potpourri, crystal decanter, glasses, and expensive whiskey went crashing to the floor, with Hennesey's naked form immediately upon the clutter.

"Where is it?" Hawk saw no point in delaying his questions.

Hennesey cried in horror as blood gushed from a wound on his thigh. Jesus, a little higher and he might have been ruined for life! He never heard the question.

Hawk took a pillow cover and threw it at the man. "Answer me, Hennesey, or I'll finish what I started."

"What?"

"I said, where is it?"

"On my thigh. Christ, I almost cut my cock off."

Hawk glanced toward the man and the gushing

128

wound he gently dabbed at. Too bad, he thought to himself. This one deserved that and more. "The purse, where is it?"

"Call Clay for me. I need a doctor."

"You're going to need a damn undertaker if you don't answer me."

"What? Why?"

"Where is her purse?"

"What purse?" Hennesey had no notion of what the man was talking about. The fact was, immediately after he had awakened from that brutal and merciless beating, he had managed, with the last of his strength, to get himself upstairs. He hadn't seen a purse. He didn't know anything about a purse.

"I don't know. I didn't see it."

Hawk thought the man might be telling him the truth. He probably didn't know where it was, but Mr. Clay would know.

Hawk walked out of the room, slamming the door behind him, just as Hennesey called out, "Tell Clay I need—"

Hawk met Clay at the bottom of the stairs. "Mr. Hennesey tells me he found a purse this morning. The owner is anxious to see to its return."

"There was a purse in the sitting room when I came in this morning."

Hawk nodded. "Let's see it."

Hawk returned to his rooms with her purse, umbrella, dress, petticoat, and high-buttoned boots. Her chemise was nowhere to be found.

Abigail had been pacing as she awaited his return and glanced with surprise at the articles he had brought with him.

A sheet was still wrapped around her slender form, but beneath that sheet she wore her drawers and stockings. The sight of a silk-clad ankle caused Hawk a frown. Hawk hadn't expected her to remain naked, had he? Then why did he feel this surge of disappointment?

She had brushed her hair and repinned it to the back of her head. Hawk didn't like it any better than he did the fact that she was half dressed. Why hadn't she left her hair down? What the hell was she so anxious about?

"I didn't find your hat," he said as she wordlessly took the articles from him.

Abigail nodded, knowing that a lost hat was the least of her problems. Hawk had managed to extricate her from a particularly nasty and dangerous situation. She knew she had to thank him, but she couldn't actually bring herself to say the words. Abigail didn't doubt that the moment she began he'd remind her again of his orders to stay put, to leave in his and Cole's hands the finding of her sister. He'd throw it in her face, the fact that she had acted foolishly. No doubt he'd again ask her where Robert had taken himself off to.

She didn't want him to ask. She didn't want to have to defend the man again. Abigail grumbled a nasty word, only half beneath her breath.

Hawk lifted one corner of his mouth in what might have been mistaken for a smile. "Oh, you're very welcome."

She threw the articles on the bed and glared in his direction, knowing she had no choice in the matter. "Thank you, Mr. Hawk."

Hawk took a deep breath, apparently ready to rile her every action, when she interrupted with, "There's no need for you to start. I know I acted the fool. Can we just leave it at that?"

"And what? Wait for the next time, when you'll no doubt do something equally as stupid?" Hawk couldn't help the rage that flooded his being. His mind went on to the most dastardly and sinister conclusions. Conclusions that almost took his breath away. He wondered why he should feel such terror. What the hell did he care what happened to this little uppity, nasty-mouthed brat. He didn't care, at least no more than he would have cared for any citizen of this city. Still, the thought of what Hennesey had in mind refused to leave him. All he could remember was watching the man's hands on her breasts.

"The fact is," she said in her defense, "if you had done your job, I wouldn't have had to do it, would I?"

"Too bad you don't know what the hell you're talking about, lady." Hawk shook his head. "When I got to Hennesey's, his hands were all over you. You were lying across his lap. If I had been two minutes later, his hand would have been inside your drawers, his fingers in your—"

Abigail gasped at the very thought. That this man should speak to her in so bold a fashion brought her cheeks to a cherry-red state. A moment later she decided he was merely trying to scare her. "You're disgusting, and I don't believe you for a minute. No one would do something so awful. You're trying to scare me. Why?"

"You're right about that, lady. I am trying to scare

you into showing some intelligence. And you're wrong if you think the world isn't full of evil. God, you're as innocent as a babe fresh from her cradle. Just the thought of you out there alone scares the shit out of me."

"There's no need to be crude, Mr. Hawk."

"I've told you a dozen times, lady, it's Deputy Hawk." There was a moment of silence between them when he finally asked, "Isn't there a man who could see to you? Don't you have . . . ?" And then he apparently remembered her fiancé. His voice was nothing less than thunder. "Where the hell is Robert?"

Abigail felt a surge of annoyance at the bellowed question. It didn't seem to matter that she'd asked much the same thing all morning. God, but she was sick of looking for the man. "First of all, I don't know. Seeing to business, probably.

"And second, I'm a full-grown woman and don't need anyone to look after me." She ignored his snort of disbelief. She was a full-grown woman, all right. That was half the problem.

"And third, how is any of this your business?"

Hawk glared his anger. How was this his business? He only wished to hell it wasn't. He wished to hell he could just walk out of here and never see her again. "Oh, no need to thank me, lady. I just saved your ass, is all."

"I've asked you not to be crude, Mr. . . . ." And at his hard threatening glare, she corrected, "Deputy."

How the hell did she do that? The woman was standing there with a sheet around her, for God's sake. How did she manage to look so damn uppity?

132

"Thank you," she said unable to hide the disgust she knew at being forced into thanking a man she couldn't stand. "Now get out so I can dress."

"Lady, nothing could please me more than your getting dressed and out of my room, out of my life."

Hawk remained pleased for all of two days.

He sold three paintings, each for little more than the cost of canvas and paint. And every time he sold one, he cursed the bitch. It was all her fault. Her and her simple childish ways. How was a man supposed to work when he had a fool like her to care for? No wonder his paintings were worthless. No wonder he'd have to sell the lot of them just for enough to get him out of this city.

Thomas Hill sneered his disgust as he downed another whiskey. One of these days, he swore to himself, he'd find a benefactor. One day soon the whole world would recognize his talent. She'd be sorry then. The bitch would be sorry she hadn't listened to him and done for him as a woman should.

He'd find himself a new woman. Someone who knew how to please a man in bed. God, but he was sick of a little sweet thing who didn't know the first thing about pleasing a man. Yeah, he'd find himself a woman, all right. A woman who wouldn't be so stupid as to get herself pregnant.

He'd go to New York. He'd take the Mississippi as far as Memphis, or maybe even farther north and then a train to New York. He'd never been to the big city. He couldn't wait to see it, taste it. He'd be able to paint there. He'd be able to live again in that kind of bustling excitement.

Through the mirror over the bar he eyed the red-headed whore. She was the one he'd wanted last night. Thomas thought about the five dollars he had in his pocket. He'd have to sell more of his paintings tomorrow, but first . . .

"I think you're right."

Robert blinked at the statement. They were looking over their menus at the hotel's restaurant, this being the only place and time they were together each day. Since he hadn't asked a question, it was beyond his ability to imagine what she was talking about. "What do you mean, dear? Right about what?"

"About going back and seeing to your businesses."

Robert, thanks to the money Abigail had pushed upon him had, for the last few days, been like a kid in a candy store. He'd spent all of each day and most of every night in bed with one lovely or another. Today there had been two of them. Robert had never so enjoyed himself and had no intentions of leaving. Not now. "Abigail, sweetheart. I couldn't leave you alone. There will be time enough to clear all this mess up after we return home."

Abigail hadn't mentioned what had happened yesterday. Robert had no knowledge of the catastrophe that had nearly befallen her. "Robert, just in case you haven't noticed, you have left me alone every day since our arrival. I see you only at dinner. As a matter of fact, because of this need you have to sleep, you've left me alone the entire trip down here."

"I promise to make it up to you, dear. Tomorrow, bright and early, I'll be at your side, ready to search every nook and cranny of this city.

"As a matter of fact, I've spoken to a number of people about Amanda and—"

Abigail gasped. "You didn't tell them who she was?"

"No, of course not. All I did was ask if any of my business acquaintances had seen a young blond girl about sixteen years old.

"I don't mind telling you they gave me some odd looks."

Abigail, having no knowledge of his acquaintances, couldn't imagine why that should be and she didn't ask. What she did instead was prompt him with "And?"

"Well, one of my friends said she had seen someone who looked like her over on . . ."

"She? You have friends in New Orleans?"

"No, no." He shook his head. "Did I say she? I meant he, of course," Robert corrected without missing a beat. "He said he knew of a young lady living over on Canal Street." Robert smiled at her stunned expression. "I thought I would surprise you by waiting until this evening. Perhaps you'd like to see for yourself, after dinner, if it is Amanda."

"After dinner!? Do you imagine that I could sit here and eat, while it is possible that Amanda is within reach?" she asked as she came instantly to her feet. "Let's go."

They were out of the hotel on their way before she asked, "When did you find out about her?"

"This morning. Right after one of my meetings."

"And you didn't say anything until now? Robert, she might already be gone."

"She's not gone, my dear. Don't worry."

But Abigail did worry. There was no way she could not worry.

She worried enough, in fact, not to notice the beauty that surrounded her. The streets were dark but for gas lamps lit at each corner, allowing them some meager visibility. Above the narrow cobblestone sidewalks, iron-railed terraces jutted from the second floor of nearly every building. Flowers were in abundance, whether hidden behind the protective gates of some lush courtyard or potted in open display upon a doorstep or terrace, their delicate scents pervading the warm night air.

They stopped before number 16. Robert knocked. No answer. Both Abigail and Robert noticed the door was slightly ajar. Abigail knew she shouldn't, but she couldn't resist. Her heart hammered in her throat as she pushed the door wider and entered. Was she almost there? Was Amanda within her grasp? Please, God, she prayed that it was so.

The hallway was dark, shadowy, but for a glimmer of light, candlelight, in fact, flickering from a room down the hall. Abigail and Robert moved quietly toward the light.

Hawk cursed. What the hell was the matter with him tonight? He couldn't remember the last time he'd felt so restless, so . . . What? What the hell was gnawing at him? What the hell did he want? The picture of Abby came suddenly to mind. Hawk cursed and tried without much hope to rid himself of her memory. All right, so she appealed. More than appealed, if the truth be told. He wanted her like hell, but the woman, despite her obvious attributes—and Hawk couldn't remember when he'd last seen attributes quite so ripe and lovely—wasn't for him.

God, why couldn't he stop thinking of what she looked like without her clothes? Why couldn't he stop remembering how she had squirmed deliciously beneath him? He cursed again and shook himself from her spell. What the hell did he think he was doing, mooning over a woman when a dozen and more were easy enough to come by?

She was still searching the city. Ricky had kept him informed of her every move. In a day or so she'd realize her sister was gone, he thought. In a day or so she would be gone as well.

He couldn't wait. And in the meantime there was a pretty young woman who would welcome him with open arms.

Hawk let himself into her apartment and grinned as he listened to her singing. He shut the door very gently, so as not to disturb her. Lydia had a lovely voice, one she used five nights a week at the local theater. He smiled as she reached a particularly high note, her voice sweet, clear, and delightful.

He moved down the hall and stepped into her bedroom. He smiled as she finished the song. He bit his bottom lip as his gaze took in the skimpiness of her garment. Lydia, now that he thought on it, had quite a bit more than a lovely voice. He could easily, even

137

in this light, see through the silk chemise. She wore nothing beneath it. Damn, but she had a beautiful backside.

Hawk felt his body stir. He needed this badly. Nothing else could better free a man's mind of one woman than to take another to bed. "You're in fine voice tonight, Lydia."

Lydia spun around and laughed at his sudden appearance. "So you've finally decided to show yourself?" It had been three days since she saw him last.

Now that she faced him, Hawk's eyes darkened with interest as his gaze moved down the length of her and back. "I see you've decided as much."

Lydia chuckled a low sexy sound as she followed the direction of his gaze. She knew the garment was thin enough for him to see everything and delighted in the growing hunger he didn't bother to hide.

"I was hoping you might drop by, so I wore this. Does it please you?"

"Exceptionally," he said as he took a step toward her.

"It's too quiet," Abigail whispered as they moved down the hall. "Maybe she's already gone."

"She's probably sleeping."

Abigail turned the corner of the room and gasped. Two lovers stood in the center of the room. A tall dark man held a lady in his arms, a beautiful tall blond lady. The strap to her chemise had fallen down her arm, allowing the exposure of one gleaming and, Abigail thought, quite beautiful breast. The fact that his mouth was firmly fastened to the tip of that breast

138

caused Abigail's cheeks to burn. Not for what they were doing, well, not exactly, but for the fact that she had stumbled upon them by accident.

Apparently she made some sort of sound, for Hawk spun from what he'd been about, pushed the woman roughly behind him, and suddenly (and Abigail thought quite miraculously) produced a pistol as he did so. He aimed the gun at Abigail's heart. She stared in shock, wondering at first where it had come from. It took her a second before she realized he had pulled it from the holster tied to his thigh.

There was an awful moment of silence before Abigail stuttered, "I . . . I'm s–sorry, I thought—"

"What?" Hawk cursed, hard and vile. "Do you realize I could have killed you?"

She held up her hand. Obviously far from her usual poised self, she could only continue on with, "No. I . . . I didn't mean—"

"What the hell are you doing here?" He placed his gun in his holster.

"Robert got word that Amanda might be here."

The woman behind Hawk reached for a wrap and pulled it around her nearly naked body, much to Robert's dismay. He made an obvious sound of disappointment; Abigail noticed it and frowned. They had, actually he had, almost gotten them killed, and all he was interested in was what he could see of a certain lady.

Abigail felt a surge of anger, only she couldn't for a moment figure out why. Was she upset because Robert seemed to find the lady interesting? She gave a mental shake as she discounted the thought. No. Oddly enough she couldn't find it within herself to care a whit what or who Robert found fascinating. Then why was she upset? It certainly couldn't be because she had found Hawk kissing a woman's breast? Impossible. Why, the thought was ludicrous. What did she care? All she could think was her delight that it wasn't her breast he'd been kissing. At the thought Abigail felt a oddest sensation tighten her chest. Oh, God, Abigail, get ahold of yourself, she thought. She tried, but it took her longer than she might have liked, for she couldn't stop or even understand the sensations that were careening throughout her body. Her breasts felt suddenly fuller than usual, as if for some unknown reason they were swelling. They tingled. Why, she couldn't have said.

"I want to talk to you." Hawk ignored Robert's presence, not that Robert minded being left alone with this beauty. Hawk took Abigail's hand and dragged her down the hall into another room. At least this wasn't a bedroom. Abigail shuddered at the thought. It was a sitting room, a very fancy, pretty sitting room, she thought, having the opportunity of only a glance.

He backed her up against the wall the second they entered the room, effectively blocking from her view all but his wide shoulders. "What the hell are you doing here?"

"I told you, Robert heard that Amanda might be here."

"And you just walked in?"

"I knocked." She shot him a look of scorn. "Apparently you were busy."

"Damn it, Abby," he said as his body moved slightly closer, almost closing the small distance that separated them. "I could have shot you." He shuddered, horrified at the thought. "Jesus, I could wring your neck for putting yourself in danger."

"You could what?" Her blue eyes grew frigid at his threat.

"You heard me."

"Who do you think you're talking to?"

"An uppity brat, if you have to know."

"Me? Uppity? Take a good look in a mirror, Mr. Hawk. I've never met a man more . . . more . . ."

"More what?" He grinned, his anger momentarily forgotten as hers grew. "Handsome?" Hawk didn't know why exactly, but he was suddenly filled with delight at the prospect of standing here arguing with this little spitfire. Perhaps it was simply relief he felt. Relief that he'd thought fast enough. That she wasn't lying dead on Lydia's bedroom floor. He nodded. That was it, of course.

"More aggravating, more arrogant, more thickheaded, more mean spirited. If you would cease, just for a time, your debauchery, perhaps you just might get some work done. You might even find my sister."

"Debauchery?" He grinned at her condemnation. Was there a thread of jealousy in her voice? Oddly enough, and he couldn't say why exactly, but he hoped there was.

"Yes, debauchery. I never see you but with a woman at your side."

"I had no woman with me when you were in my rooms." Hawk seemed to think on his words a moment and then corrected, "Oh, yes, wait a minute. I seem to remember a particularly delightful little piece. She was naked in my bed, if I'm not mistaken."

"You beast!"

"As a matter of fact, it was all I could do to stop her from seducing me." Hawk wondered if she'd ever remember how she had, despite their wrestling, pulled away the last of her clothing and pressed her sweet body to his.

"Liar!" Her hand came up and rendered a stinging slap to his cheek. She knew she had gone too far. She felt herself tremble at the dark look of menace in his eyes.

His voice was low, filled with promise. "I told you once before that if you hit me again, expect to be hit back."

Abigail wasn't afraid of him. Still, she couldn't stop her body from stiffening with the coming retaliation. She closed her eyes and waited. Waited in vain as it turned out.

Hawk watched her for a long frustrating moment before he cursed. She stood there as brave as any man, believing that he was about to hit her. Damn her. Damn her to hell. "Lady, I could . . . ," he said as he reached suddenly for her shoulders and brought her feet from the floor. His body pressed hers against the wall, holding her helplessly in place. And then with a groan that told of his inability to resist, and another "Damn you" as if it were all her fault, his mouth was on hers.

Abigail froze in amazement. She had expected a slap, she'd been promised a slap and couldn't get her mind to understand this most peculiar happening. She couldn't believe it. It had to be her imagination, of course. Hawk wasn't kissing her. Even a man as rough and crude as Hawk wouldn't dare touch her.

Wouldn't dare kiss her without first asking her permission.

Oddly enough Abigail was so stunned, it never occurred to her to fight him. She was so amazed that she couldn't think beyond this most astounding happening. One minute he'd been yelling at her. Well, perhaps not yelling exactly. Their faces had been close together, their words soft, despite the anger each knew, and the next minute she was in his arms being kissed as if two strangers kissing were the most natural thing in the world.

She tried to turn her face away, but he caught her chin, holding her still as he muttered "No" against her lips.

Abigail felt a surge of dizziness. A strange unbidden thought came suddenly to mind that she rather liked the idea of talking against one's mouth. She'd never experienced anything quite so unusual before. And it did some most peculiar things to her stomach. At least she would have liked it, she thought, if she'd wanted this kiss. She didn't, of course. She didn't want it at all. She hadn't imagined ever being kissed by this man. Well, not consciously, at least. She had dreamt about it once or twice but never had she actually . . .

Abigail realized she was babbling. Mentally babbling. Was there such a thing? She supposed there must be, for she seemed to be doing an excellent job of it.

The thing was, she could have easily gone on in this stunned and babbling state if he hadn't suddenly gentled the kiss. He'd been angry and rough at first, but that roughness had lasted all of three seconds.

Almost from the instant their mouths had come together. No, she corrected, almost from the instant he had covered her mouth with his, to be precise, his mouth had gentled.

Abigail tried desperately not to allow that gentleness to affect her. She tried. She really did, but for some unexplained reason, control of this moment seemed just beyond her reach. How odd, she thought. Never in her life had she been in anything but total control.

His mouth touched briefly, softly against hers, again, again, and again until the world tilted just off its center, until she felt herself oddly floating, until her lips parted and grew softer, eager for more of this teasing of her senses.

"Sweet, oh, God, so sweet," he said against her mouth, and Abigail heard a soft whimper. Vaguely she wondered who had uttered the sound. Was someone in pain? And then she forgot the question as his lips coaxed hers further apart.

Now this was something, wasn't it? she thought dreamily, never realizing her thoughts weren't as clear and lucid as always. How had he ever thought of such a thing? Abigail had never imagined that a man could kiss like this. That a tongue rubbed gently and just inside a bottom lip could cause her heart this most delightful fluttering.

Her mouth grew softer, her body as well.

His tongue slid into her mouth. Abigail thought that act most amazing. Her lips parted further, oddly craving more of this delightful investigation and Hawk took the opportunity offered to learn every inch of her mouth.

Abigail's brow creased with confusion. She'd been kissed before. So how was it that this kiss should prove so different? Exactly how had he known to do these extraordinary things with his lips and tongue? Where had he learned it? How had he realized the pleasure gained by prying her lips apart? How did he dare to discover her mouth with the gentle sweeping of his tongue?

Her thoughts began to drift. He smelled so good. She hadn't realized that he would smell and taste so good, so clean, like a man, like a distant sip of whiskey, like the faint scent of rich tobacco, like leather, like a man. Did all men taste like this? She didn't know. The few kisses she'd shared with others had never . . . never . . . He pulled her tighter to him, all hard yearning muscle against her softness and Abigail forgot all but the taste and feel of this man.

Hawk groaned at the feel of her against him. God Almighty, she was soft. Soft and warm and delicious. His mind swam with the need to discover that softness, to touch and kiss every inch of it. And he would. He vowed he would.

She touched him, and he thought it might be more than he could bear. She wanted him. God, yes, she wanted him. She might not know it, but her body did.

Abigail's hands had somehow found their way around his neck. She hadn't a notion as to how that had happened. But she was suddenly more than pleased that it had, for her fingers were threading through long dark hair, disturbing the thick black silk as the rawhide string fell away. She'd never felt anything so erotic as a hard man and soft silky hair. It reached to his shoulders and framed an astoundingly handsome face. Abigail couldn't get enough of touching it, of touching him.

His face was smooth, hard, beautifully chiseled, the bones beneath the taut skin prominent. Her hands framed his face for a moment. His cheeks were hollow, and growing more so as he sucked at her lips, her tongue, greedy to know the secrets of her mouth.

Abigail never knew a man's lips could feel so soft against hers. Never knew that those soft lips could create a world of pleasure and cause her the most unsettling need. She squirmed against him, instinctively knowing there was more. Anxious to know, to experience it all.

He raised her higher, and she gasped her delight as his mouth fastened on her breast. The world swam out of focus. She couldn't think. She never wondered how her dress had come undone. How he had so easily brushed aside her chemise, all without her notice. All she knew was that his mouth was a furnace of heat and the sensations he caused her were mind-boggling. Every time he sucked, she felt a strange pulling just below her stomach. An ache, a pulling, an empty hollow of need.

Abigail felt every bit of her restraint gone, her mind a cloud of passion, her needs bubbling urgently to the surface. My God, it felt good. So very, very . . . Abigail stiffened in horror, her thoughts never so clear. This was what she had walked in on. This was exactly how she had found him, only moments ago with another woman! No. Lord, no! What could she be thinking to allow herself to become just another of his trollops?

"No," she said, as she struggled in earnest against

him. "Hawk, stop it!" She shoved against him until his mouth eased itself from her, until he lowered her again to the floor.

"What? What the hell is the matter?" he asked as his hand reached to assist her to gain her balance. He leaned over her, his arms against the wall bracing his body, his breath hot and moist against her face, exhibiting none of his usual control. "What's the matter with you? Why did you stop me?"

She couldn't seem to get her breath, and her fingers trembled as she forced them to adjust her clothing and rebutton her dress. She willed her heart to beat again its normal rhythm. She forced her brain to clear, her voice to steady itself. "Why did I stop you? Let's see." Abigail strove for ridicule, but her voice trembled and wavered breathlessly despite her best efforts. "Could it be because we are in your lady's home? I assume this home belongs to the pretty lady. Or could it be because my fiancé and the lady are in the next room?" She glared her contempt that he should have brought about such a lapse in her usual control. That she should have allowed this . . . oh so familiar and disgraceful treatment. "Perhaps, Mr. Hawk, I stopped you because I found you kissing your lady only a few minutes ago, just as you were kissing me."

Hawk grinned. He hadn't thought of that. In his mind one act had nothing at all to do with the other. He'd kissed Lydia because the woman was lovely, and it was obviously expected of him. He'd touched and kissed Abigail because he couldn't stop himself. Because he'd never wanted to touch and kiss a woman so badly in his entire life. To his way of

147

thinking, there was quite a bit of difference in the two.

She touched shaken fingers to her hair, making sure it was still in place, and then she was gone before Hawk dared to reply.

Hawk listened to them leave. Sighed with relief as the door closed, firmly this time, behind them. And wondered what the hell he was going to do.

Hawk knew the truth of it. Despite his constant denials, there wasn't a thing he could do to stop the need he felt for her. He wanted her more than he'd ever wanted another. His body still pulsed with that need.

"Damn little witch," he groaned. He'd tried to ignore the things he felt for her, the things he wanted from her. In the attempt he'd kept his distance and been more abrupt than he might have been at their every meeting. The problem was, the more he saw her, the more he wanted. Tonight, trying to get her from his mind he'd had every intention of taking Lydia to bed. And the little thorn in his side had gone and ruined even that.

A half hour later Hawk sat in Lydia's parlor, a glass of whiskey in his hand.

"Would you rather forget about it, darling?" Lydia asked, knowing the man, by his dark silent brooding and heavy drinking, was obviously no longer in the mood. "We could have a late supper and make an early night of it."

Hawk raised his gaze from the glass in his hand, raining all manner of curses upon his stupidity and one particularly aggravating and frustrating woman. Here was a beautiful woman, a beautiful willing woman, and he sat like some sort of idiot—drinking when he could right now be enjoying her as her body was meant to be enjoyed.

He smiled into her gentle gaze. "Forgive me, Lydia, but there is nothing I'd like more than to make an early night of it." He came to his feet and smiled as he took her hand in his. "Why don't we start right now?"

An hour later Hawk gave a silent curse as he rolled from her body. It had taken forever and even upon reaching release, he had not found half the delight he usually knew in this woman's arms. It was all her fault, of course. Damn that little witch. Damn her blue eyes and nasty mouth. Damn her soft sweet body and hardheaded determination.

He almost groaned aloud a desperate prayer: "God, please, make her go home."

Chapter Eight

Amid the lush growth atop the Smoky Mountains, a small farm stood in the predawn hours, mostly silent and still, as if readying itself for reawakening. Swirling morning mist had yet to rise from surrounding dense underbrush and trees so thick they appeared to form a living barrier against an ever-encroaching world.

Not ten feet into that forest, four men dismounted weary horses and watched a lone chicken cross the open space between house and barn, pecking occasionally at the ground with her sharp beak as she moved with a jerky uneven gait.

Smoke rose from the chimney, and each man felt his stomach growl at the thought of hot food and coffee. Only food wasn't the only thing on their minds.

After that bank job they had ridden hard for almost a week, knowing the law was hot on their trail. Yesterday Willie had hung back and finished off the bastard. Now all four were almost giddy with the promise of freedom. Their pockets were nicely filled with money. All they needed now was food and a woman. And if hot food was being prepared inside that little house, a woman was no doubt at the chore. Once their bellies were full, she'd be at yet another, more pleasing chore. The men looked from one to another, their thoughts in unison, as they imagined the use of her body. Dirty, unshaven, an evil grin twisted their mouths.

A man wiped his hands on a large red handkerchief hooked into his belt as he left his barn. At his side a dog ambled along and, after years of watching, had somehow managed to match his master's graceful gait. Joseph Hawk, his darkly tanned face lined with life's hardships and disappointments, glanced at his little house and knew yet again, as he had every day of the last five years, an intense longing for his wife. Mary had loved their little farm. And Joseph had loved only Mary.

Every day she had awakened, delight dancing in her dark eyes, as if life's commonplace chores were but a new and fascinating discovery. Her one sorrow had been the fact that she had conceived only once. Mary had longed for a large family, and as the years slid by her sweet smile was often tempered by a gentle sadness.

He'd missed her terribly after she'd gone. Even now, five years after her passing, he could still remember her touch, her scent, her laughter, her rare moments of sadness. Idly he wondered how much longer he'd have to wait before seeing her again.

His son was gone off to New Orleans, to make a life of his own working for the law. Joseph figured that was as it should be, believing every man had a right to chose what he wanted from life. Still, he missed the boy and anxiously awaited his next visit.

Joseph breathed deeply of the early morning cool air and glanced toward the sky, listening as the world awakened. He grunted a sound of satisfaction, for he had finished with many of the morning chores. He'd have another cup of coffee, he thought, before finishing the rest.

To the east came growing rays of yellow gold that would soon cast the sky into brilliant, almost blinding color. To his left the darkness of night held as if daring the sun to do its worst.

Joseph Hawk glanced at his old lazy dog. "I have stew left from last night. I guess you'll be wanting some. Not that you deserve it. I've never seen a lazier dog." And again he repeated the same phrase as he had for the last fifteen years. "As soon as I can find someone to take you off my hands, I'm getting rid of you."

Rusty glanced to his left and whined.

"What, another bitch?" Joseph asked, a smile touching one corner of his still handsome mouth. "Don't you know you're too old for that sort of thing?"

The dog's whine turned into a low menacing growl and Joseph frowned at the oddity. His expression cleared a moment later. "Probably that skunk again," he said with a nod. His expression hardened as he warned, "I swear, if you bother with that thing, you'll spend the next few days in the barn."

The four men crouched among the underbrush. Willie, the leader of the gang, snickered a soft sound of appreciation as his gaze took in the tall man with the long black hair and dark complexion. Indians. He hadn't realized it until now, but they were in the Smoky Mountains and the Cherokee Reservation.

Willie figured he could do just about anything he wanted here. No one cared what happened to Indians. And he'd heard that squaws were the best little whores of all. He figured the one in that house would service them all and beg for more.

He pulled the rifle from his saddle, crouched once more, and took aim.

The dog's growl deepened and grew in intensity. Joseph glanced again toward the forest surrounding his farm. It was at that moment that he heard the shot, but the sound had no time to register, for an instant, massive, and punishing blow crashed into his skull, sending pieces of splintered bone, gray matter, and blood to stain the hard brown dirt behind him. Despite the fact that Joseph was a big man, the force lifted him into the air and carried him backward two feet.

He knew no pain, just a moment of total blackness, and then Joseph Hawk smiled, his heart swelling with joy at his wife's low gentle laughter. A young woman again, she gathered her skirt in one hand and ran to him in welcome. His arms reached out, closing greedily around her warmth. He buried his face in her hair. He'd waited so long, so incredibly long.

Amanda left the paddleboat at Memphis and walked through the busy streets toward the train station. She knew a sense of trepidation, alone in a dark city, but put the emotion aside. She'd be home soon. Soon she'd know again warmth and comfort and, best of all, safety. There was no need to be afraid, she reasoned. Once she got home, Abigail would help her. Abigail would make everything right.

Max Dallas lit a cigarette as he watched the passengers disembark. His eyes widened with interest as the young woman walked down the gangplank. She was alone. He grinned. Easy pickings. Damn, but he couldn't lose tonight. He'd won big at the tables. Two hundred dollars lined the inside of his left boot. And now this. He pushed away from the light post and followed her down the street.

Amanda waited her turn and then sighed with disappointment when the clerk glanced from the money in her hand to her blue eyes and shook his head. She didn't have enough. The paddleboat and the two dinners she'd eaten aboard had taken one-third of her money. She needed more, much more to get home. What was she going to do? "How far will this take me?" Amanda asked as she shoved all she had left toward the ticket clerk.

The clerk eyed the few bills and then asked, "Which direction?"

"Toward Charlotte. I want to go to Charlotte."

The man consulted his list of fares and shook his head. "Two hundred miles from here. A town called Summer."

"Summer?" Amanda repeated. "Is that far from Charlotte?"

The man didn't answer her question. "You want a ticket or not, lady?" the clerk asked, his eyes hard, his voice a study of indifference.

"I don't know. I have to think."

"Yeah, well, think over there." He nodded to his right and the two chairs that sat unoccupied in the small office. "You're holding up the line."

Amanda did as she was told. She sat in the chair and wondered what should she do. Should she try again to wire Abigail? Would her sister send the needed cash for her return trip? Or would Abigail ignore the wire as she had the last three?

Amanda shook her head. No. Abigail wouldn't ignore her pleas for help. She hadn't been at home. There was no other explanation.

Her thoughts were interrupted by a low male voice, a voice filled with concern. "Are you all right, miss?"

Amanda glanced to her left and smiled at the handsome man who leaned down just a bit to speak to her. "I'm fine, thank you, sir."

"Are you in need of some assistance?"

"Well, I . . ." Amanda hesitated. Abigail had told her innumerable times that a lady did not speak to a man, even if that man was obviously a gentleman, without proper introductions. Amanda figured she'd had enough problems because of her foolish mistakes. She wasn't about to look for another. She came to the only answer possible. She'd go to the sheriff. He would help her, she was sure.

And then she remembered Tommy's lifeless body and the fact that she had killed him. No. She couldn't ask the sheriff for help. She was probably wanted. Was that the word they used? Amanda figured she didn't have much choice in the matter. It was either accept this kind man's help or . . . or . . . She simply did not know what else to do. "I do have a problem, sir. I haven't the needed fare for my trip back home."

The man gave a gentle if flippant sort of laugh. "Money? Is that all? How much do you need?"

Amanda blinked in surprise. "Do you mean you'd be willing to help? Oh, I'd be ever so grateful. Just give me your name and address, and I'll have my sister return it the minute I get home."

"Your sister? What about your father?"

Amanda shook her head for an answer.

"Is there no man to care for you?"

Amanda smiled, and never realizing in her innocence the sinister reason behind the question, answered honestly. "Abigail is all I have left." Abigail and the baby, she thought to herself.

He almost laughed out loud. No man, not even an elderly father to consider. Dallas thought he must be doing something right. Absolutely everything was working for him today. "How much do you need?"

Amanda glanced toward the chart on the wall and bit her lip in anxiety. She named the price.

Dallas smiled. "No problem. I'll have it for you in the morning. The minute the banks open."

"Oh, thank you, sir. It's so kind of you."

Dallas wasn't sure if this was all an act or if the girl really was the innocent she portrayed. He figured it was probably an act. Innocent young girls did not travel alone. Still, it didn't really matter which. All he knew for sure was she would be decorating his bed tonight. And if it took a little sweet talking on his part, he figured it would be well worth the effort. He allowed her his most gentle smile. "What are you going to do tonight? You can't stay here."

"Can't I? Why?"

"The office closes in an hour."

Amanda never realized the lie. "Oh, dear."

"I know of a boardinghouse that takes only the best clientele."

"But I have only . . ."

"Don't fret, miss. I know the lady. She'll wait for payment."

Amanda smiled as she took the man's offered arm and allowed him to lead her out of the small building.

They were on the sidewalk before he said, "My name is Max Dallas, and you are?"

"Amanda Pennyworth."

"Well, Miss Pennyworth, come along now and I'll soon see you set for the night." Dallas almost laughed at that statement. He'd see her set all right. He couldn't wait.

"I don't know how I'll ever thank you."

"No need to worry about that, Miss Pennyworth. I have a sister about your age," he lied. "I would hope some gentleman would see to her care if she were ever in need."

Amanda smiled. She had never met a man so kind, so generous. She'd never be able to thank him enough.

Two blocks from the ticket office, Dallas ushered Amanda into a dark building that smelled strongly of boiled cabbage. She wrinkled her nose at the scent but said nothing as he guided her up a flight of stairs. A lone lamp was lit at the landing, allowing only a minimum of light.

"This way," he said as he walked toward a door that stood just opposite the landing. It opened at his touch. "Just let me light a lamp for you, and I'll be on my way."

Amanda stood in the doorway and waited. But not for long.

She gasped as his arms were suddenly around her waist, dragging her into the room. For a long moment Amanda couldn't fathom the truth of it. What was happening? What in the world was he doing?

And then his mouth was on hers, his lips open, his tongue forcing hers to part and she knew what he was doing. Tommy did this to her when he was drunk. On those nights he didn't seem to care if he hurt her or not.

Amanda's thoughts returned instantly to the present as his hand reached for her breast. He made a small sound of pleasure as he roughly twisted the tip. She shivered in disgust as he then ran his hand down her body to grab her just above her thighs.

Dallas grunted in satisfaction. She hadn't fought him at all. So the little bitch knew what this was about after all. Good. With a piece that looked as good as this one, a man didn't like taking it slow.

Suddenly he pushed her back. Off balance, she almost fell. The lamp in the hall lent just enough light to enable her to see his shadowy form. She watched in horror as he moved to shut the door.

"Nooo," Amanda cried as she lunged forward. She couldn't let him lock the door. She couldn't let him do this to her. Amanda crashed into him. The movement caught him off guard. He stumbled forward almost to the landing. Amanda right behind him shoved, desperate to get away, and then watched in horrified shock as his momentum intensified and he went flying forward, over the railing, and down the flight of stairs.

As it turned out, today wasn't Dallas's lucky day after all.

She stood there for a long moment before she dared to breathe, before she dared to look. Would she find him creeping back? Would she see him crawling toward her, his once kind expression replaced now with the promise of vengeance?

Amanda trembled with fear as she glanced over the railing and brought her hand to her mouth to stifle a cry. He was dead. No one could lie with their head so twisted and not be dead.

Vaguely she wondered why no one had come. He had cried out as he fell, but not one door along the hall had opened to see to the problem. Amanda walked quickly down the stairs, carefully stepping around his body.

A moment later she was on the street again, shivering with shock, heading for the ticket office once again.

"A ticket to Summer," she said.

The clerk issued the ticket and went on to the next in line. He never noticed the lady's dress was torn at her throat, that bruises were already forming around the tear. It didn't register that her hat was missing, that her gaze was more than a bit glassy, that she appeared to have sustained some kind of shock.

Amanda boarded the train and found a seat next to a window in the back of the car. She wished she could make herself smaller, wished she could disappear, in fact. A man looked at her and smiled. She looked away and shivered, feeling very much like a cornered animal, knowing if he came near her she was going to scream.

To say they were disappointed was to put it mildly. They thought maybe she was hiding at first, but realized after the house was in shambles that there wasn't a woman anywhere within miles of the place. Maybe worse than having no woman was the fact that Hank couldn't cook worth a shit.

"I thought you said you did some cooking a while back?"

"I did. In the army."

"Well, you didn't do enough of it."

"He probably killed off the whole damn company," Josh said as he spat the last of the cold greasy stew on the floor.

"What are we doing here? Hank is trying to poison us, and I'm itchin' for a woman, bad."

Willie grinned at Mike's comment. They were all itching for women. It had been a while. More than a while, in fact.

"Let's head out. I heard that Natchez has . . ."

"Not Natchez." Willie shook his head.

"Why not? The town is known for a good time. Nobody is going to bother us there."

"I thought that's where you came from?"

The fact of the matter was Willie had come from Natchez, at least a small farm just outside of the city. And that was exactly why he never wanted to see the place again. When he thought of it, he could still feel the stinging blows of the whip. Willie figured his father had gone crazy when his wife died. Blamed

160

him for his mother's death. Said he'd still have his Millie if it weren't for him.

Christ, he hated that place and the drunken bastard who had beat him every day of his life while growing up there.

Willie shook his head. He didn't want to think about it. He didn't want to remember what it had been like. The last thing he remembered about the farm and his father was the smell of fire. He almost smiled at the thought. He'd been just a kid, but he'd given the old bastard what he'd deserved.

He'd been only sixteen, but after years of whippings he'd finally taken enough. That last night he'd waited for the old man's snores. He'd been drunk again, as always.

Willie figured he never smelled the kerosene nor the smoke as the flames took hold. Not until it was too late.

Willie had watched the place go up in flames while sitting astride his horse. Only he hadn't expected the door to be suddenly flung open and a walking torch to come flying toward him. Sometimes the screams still haunted his dreams. He remembered the staggering gait, the hand reaching for him, the stench of burning flesh, the opened mouth filled with fire, the flames that all but blinded and still he came.

The horse was wild with fear and almost threw him.

Willie had shoved the burning old man back with his foot, but it hadn't helped. His father had come for him again, knowing he was dying, and in a last desperate act of hate, wanting his son to join him in his grave.

Willie shuddered at the memory. He'd thought the old man might never go down. But he did, and Willie had never known to this day a pleasure half so great.

"Forget Natchez, I'm going south. Maybe Baton Rouge and then maybe west."

They left the next day.

Compared with other mountain ranges, the Smokies were considered small, but when riding through the lush thick forests that coated every slope and incline, the mountains appeared endless.

They had ridden two days and were still deep within the range. It was on the evening of the second day when they came across the two laughing women at the river's edge. They had been washing, so both were nearly naked. Each of the four men figured that was just as well. It would save them some time.

It took almost no effort at all to catch them, for they ran without thought directly into the water, rather than the surrounding woods, and even less effort to tear away their thin undergarments. Two men per girl. One to hold her down, one to do the dirty deed. And when they were finished, they switched positions and then switched again and again.

The women suffered badly at first, but were soon so stunned with the viciousness of the rapings and the many punches and slaps delivered that they never realized their suffering was nearly at an end. They felt no fear when they saw the knife. Each, if they thought at all, wanted only the blessing of forgetful darkness. Each got what they wanted.

* * *

"You know her?" Abigail felt her heart leap with a burst of excitement as her gaze moved from Amanda's picture to the lady holding it. "Are you sure?"

"Of course I'm sure, madam. I know her, all right. She comes in here almost every morning. My husband makes the flakiest pastry in the city. She loves them." The woman smiled proudly and then shrugged. "I haven't seen her in a couple of days though."

"Do you know where she lives?"

"She said she had rooms over Madame Plachette's Perfumery."

"Where is . . . ?"

The woman behind the counter gestured to her left. "Three houses, that way."

Madame Plachette's Perfumery, no matter its French connotations, was in fact owned by an Irish lady by the name of O'Connell. Despite her desperate need to find Amanda, Abigail couldn't help but smile at a woman so small, with features so pointed, she might have passed for one of her country's infamous leprechauns. Abigail had never thought of herself as anything but average in height, but when faced with this minute creature, she felt positively enormous. "She was here."

It took a long moment before Abigail's brain absorbed the sentence. The past tense sentence. She'd come so close. She'd waited so long. It couldn't be that she'd missed her. Oh, please, God, it couldn't be.

Her voice was weak, as if unwilling to voice a question that must be asked. "You mean she's gone?"

The woman nodded. "Left three days ago, maybe."

Abigail reached out for the wall. Her entire body trembled as if palsied. She needed something to support her, lest she find herself crumbled to the floor. "Do you know where she went?"

The old woman shook her head. "Heard them fighting again. A few minutes after everything quieted down, the little girl was running down the stairs, she was." The woman shrugged. "I haven't seen her since."

"What about Thomas Hill. Did he . . . ?"

The woman scowled. "He left two days later. Cheated me out of a week's rent, he did. He's no good, that one. She was such a little thing, you know . . . delicate, like you." The woman shook her head sadly. "I told my Charlie, but he said stay out of it. A lot of men beat their wives."

"Beat!" Abigail couldn't have been more shocked, nor could she have known a greater burst of rage. "You mean he hit her?"

"Well, he did more than just hit her, if you ask me. I would hear her crying and then a bump here and there. Last time the furniture got knocked about some." The woman shook her head. "He was no good."

Abigail appeared calm as she replaced Amanda's picture in her bag. She said nothing more than thank you before she nodded and left the building. One more strike against Thomas Hill. Abigail swore somehow, someway, he was going to get what he deserved. She was going to personally see to it.

She walked directly to the marshal's office. Hawk was sitting behind the desk as she smashed the door against the wall and glared her hatred for all things male. She walked directly toward him, stopping only when the desk prevented further movement.

It took only a glance at her white face to bring Hawk instantly from his chair. "What the hell happened now?"

Abigail spoke through lips that barely moved. "Until three days ago she was living above the perfumery on Lafayette. Right under your nose and you couldn't leave your lady friends long enough to find her."

Hawk ignored the last part of her statement and moved to her side. "I know. I found out last night."

"Oh? You mean you managed to get out of bed long enough for . . ."

Hawk breathed a sigh. It wasn't true of course. She might not believe it, but he hadn't had a woman in bed, or otherwise, since that disastrous night with Lydia. Hawk had since come to the less than happy conclusion that to try again would only bring about the same results. The fact was, he had no wish to touch another. For some absurd reason, he couldn't look at a woman without comparing her with this small, feisty, usually aggravating little morsel. "Abby, calm down."

"Calm down? He was beating her!" She grabbed a handful of his shirt as if she had the strength to throttle him. Hawk towered over her and yet, in her anger, size seemed of no consequence. It was at that

165

exact moment Hawk realized he was in love. "Damn you, I could kill him, and I could kill you for—"

Her words were suddenly cut off as tears tightened her throat. She blinked, swallowed, and tried again. Nothing. Abigail shook her head. She couldn't talk. All she could do was stare into dark eyes, darker still with sympathy. It was the sympathy that did it. Abigail never resorted to tears. Why, she hadn't cried in years. She couldn't even remember the last time she had allowed the weakness.

And yet here she was. She who never cried was unable to stop the tears from flowing freely down her cheeks, while a tortured sob threatened to burst free of her chest.

Hawk felt a twisting around his heart. God, she was so adorable, so brave, so strong. His arms slid around her waist, pulling her against him, for he'd never in his life known a need so great to cuddle, to soothe, to babble incoherent nonsense in an effort to console. He knew her to be strong, at times as strong as any man, and yet at this moment, she was soft and sweet, never more in need of another's comforting strength. "Abby, sweetheart. She's all right. Don't cry."

Abigail was on the verge of hysterics. Perhaps more than simply on the verge. In her distress she never realized the most intimate embrace. All she could think of was her sister and the fear the young girl had to know at being bruised, battered, and now somewhere, God help her, alone. He pressed her face to his neck and she breathed of his warmth, his clean scent, while his mouth moved to her hairline, and

Abigail only tipped her head a bit, allowing him the opportunity to nuzzle.

"She boarded a paddleboat a few days ago," he whispered. "I promise you, she's all right."

It took a moment for that information to penetrate her extreme emotions. When it did, Abigail stiffened and pulled back. She wiped away her tears with an offered handkerchief, never realizing his arms moved around her again, that their hips were pressed tightly together, that their faces were inches apart as they spoke. "She did? Are you sure?"

"Positive."

"Where did she go?"

"I don't know that yet. I'll hear something soon."

"What do you mean?"

"I sent two men north. They'll talk to the hands on board. Someone will remember her. We'll find her."

It was then that Abigail realized their intimate position. She pulled out of his arms and began to pace. "Where could she have gone?" she said more to herself than to the man watching her. "What could she be thinking?"

Abigail came to a sudden stop, apparently having made some decision. Without a word spoken, she walked toward the still opened door.

Hawk reached for her arm, bringing her to a stop, spinning her back to face him. "Where are you going?"

"I don't know."

"Don't lie to me, Abby. What are you going to do?"

"I'm taking the next boat north."

"Abby, you won't know where to get off. You won't know until—"

"I'm not waiting. I have to find her."

"I told you she was all right. As soon as I hear anything, I'll . . ."

Abigail shook her head and repeated, "I'm not waiting."

Hawk cursed in helpless frustration as he watched her walk out of the office.

Son of a bitch! She'd almost left him behind. It was a good thing he'd finished earlier than usual with the whore. It was a good thing he'd been lying in bed and not deeply asleep, exhausted from the afternoon's activities, and heard the soft tapping at his door.

She'd had a note in her hand, ready to slip it beneath his door. Robert shuddered as he realized just how close he'd come to being stranded in a city with no more than twenty dollars between him and starvation. What the hell would he have done? How would he have gotten back? How would he have found her again?

He shot her a dark menacing scowl as she hurried forward, with baggage in hand, up the narrow gangplank to the waiting paddleboat. Silently he vowed that she would pay for this. The minute he placed the ring upon her finger, she was going to know who was master here.

* * *

She had been gone for three days and Hawk had yet to put aside the constant need that seemed to forever twist at his guts. There was no sense going home. All he managed to do there was pace every night away.

Cole had asked him to join Emy and himself at her father's restaurant. Hawk thought he just might do that. Perhaps a night spent in Emy's lively company would take his mind from another. Maybe if he was lucky enough, he might even forget, at least for a little while, what it felt like to hold her against him.

At one time the thought of her leaving would have made him delirious with happiness. It hadn't exactly worked out that way. He'd once been so anxious to see her gone, and yet now he knew only an empty void, a void he had no idea how to fill.

Through the large open window, Cole saw Hawk's approach. He cursed softly beneath his breath. The curse brought a compassionate look from his wife. "He's coming."

Emy placed her hand on her husband's arm. "Don't wait, Cole. Tell him outside."

Cole nodded, knowing Emy was right. A man would be at a disadvantage gaining this kind of news in a public place. He brought the telegram from his pocket and headed for the door.

Hawk would have had to be blind not to know something was wrong. Cole couldn't have looked more upset, more unhappy. "What's the matter?" His chest twisted with pain. He didn't wait for an answer before he went on with, "Is she all right?"

There was no need to mention names. Both men knew of whom Hawk spoke.

Cole shook his head as he moved around the building, heading for privacy in the alley. "No. It's your father."

Hawk sucked in a lung full of air and froze as terror gripped his heart. Cole couldn't seem to force himself to go on, but in truth there was no need. Hawk knew, by his hesitation, by the suffering in his eyes. "He died."

"I'm sorry."

Hawk nodded. It was easy enough to see that his friend truly was sorry. The problem was, it didn't matter how sorry anyone felt. Nothing was apt to ease the searing pain in Hawk's gut. It twisted at his chest and stole his breath, crushing its weight upon his body as if to rob him of his very life. He reached out to the wall for support, lest he crumble in this agony before another's eyes.

"How? When?"

"A few days ago. Four men were seen riding through the reservation." Cole handed him the wire that had been brought to the office that afternoon. "It was quick," he offered, knowing it would bring no real relief from the pain. "Over in an instant."

It was only then that Hawk realized the whole of it. His father hadn't simply and suddenly just died. *"Murdered?"* The word came out as a croak. Hawk didn't recognize his own voice.

Cole nodded. "Shot through the head."

Hawk staggered. "Jesus Christ!"

"Two women were found dead the day after your father."

Hawk digested this information. The bastard must have sneaked up on his father. Joseph Hawk wouldn't have given any man an easy time of it.

170

All manner of curses slid from his lips, and Hawk never realized any one of them. "You'll have to get someone to take my place. I've got to go."

"There's nothing you can do."

Hawk almost laughed at the statement. "If it were Emy, would you say that?"

Cole knew he was right. If something like this had happened to his wife, he wouldn't have rested until the men responsible were dead. "It might take months to track them down."

"It doesn't matter if it takes years."

Cole nodded. "I'll see you when you get back." The two men shook hands, and Hawk walked off into a night as dark as his soul.

Chapter Nine

"You're not serious!"

Abigail glanced at Robert's shocked expression, unconcerned at his obvious distress. "As I've said before, she could be anywhere. If we take the train, we might easily pass her and never know it."

"So what do you expect to do? Ride all over this country?"

Abigail might not have known it, but the fact was, he didn't have much of an alternative but to do her bidding. He didn't have an alternative at all. At least for the moment. Still, Robert couldn't resist one last try. "Abigail, we have businesses in need of our care. Suppose something happens? Suppose Amanda returns? We'll never know."

"I've left my businesses in capable hands as I'm sure you have, and I'll wire Mr. Carver every few days or so. He'll know if Amanda has returned home."

"Jesus, I don't believe this."

"It's very simple, Robert. If you feel so strongly about it, don't come."

"Easy enough to say, Abigail, but I can't leave you to fend for yourself. I have to go."

Abigail ignored his continued mutterings. She didn't care if he liked it or not. There was no way that she was going home without Amanda. Her sister had vanished in Memphis. There hadn't been a trace of her since she stepped off the paddleboat. Abigail knew she was close. She'd find her, she swore. She'd find her if it was the last thing she ever did.

Early the next morning, dressed in trousers, a shirt, and vest, she mounted her newly bought horse, with a reluctant Robert at her side. Saddlebags were packed with a week's worth of supplies, and Abigail knew she was ready to face whatever lay in store. She turned her horse east.

Two days later Hawk reached his father's home. Elizabeth Rogers, a longtime friend of both his mother and father, was there. The house was warm, the scents of freshly baked bread and chicken made Hawk's stomach growl with hunger. It was only then that he remembered he hadn't eaten in days.

Elizabeth's eyes mirrored Hawk's barely suppressed emotion. She thought what this man needed most was a woman to take him in her arms and bring him a measure of comfort, but she knew as well she wasn't that woman. One look told her he suffered terribly but would bear the pain alone. Jeremiah Hawk was a man of intense emotions. It was commonly known that father and son had respected and loved each other deeply. Perhaps someday another could bring him comfort, but even that would have to wait until justice was done.

He didn't ask why he found her here. He didn't do anything but look at her with eyes so filled with pain they were difficult to meet.

Elizabeth looked away from the dark misery. "I was waiting for you."

Hawk said nothing. A moment later he turned and left her to her cooking. She knew it was time for him to mourn. Time to allow the heart-rending sorrow of goodbyes, and he could only do that alone.

Two hours later Hawk returned from the two small plots beneath the large oak, on a hill just north of the house, to find Elizabeth gone. He grunted in approval. This wasn't the time for making conversation. He needed no company.

His dinner was warm in the oven. He might be hungry, but he couldn't eat. All he could think about was his father and the short, one-day visit they had had a month back.

He shouldn't have left. Damn it, why hadn't he stayed here? His father might be alive right now, if he had. Hawk left the table, his food nearly untouched; he stepped outside.

He walked to the empty barn, wishing he could call out and hear his father's voice just one more time. Joseph Hawk had wanted him to farm, to take over this particular farm one day, but had offered no objection when his son had decided on another route.

He leaned against the open doorway and sighed.

"They found him there," Elizabeth said, suddenly appearing from around the side of the barn, her horse in tow. Hawk had thought she'd gone. He didn't want to talk to neighbors, even good neighbors like Elizabeth. He didn't want to talk to anyone. He didn't want to do anything but think.

She pointed to the ground at Hawk's feet. Hawk found himself shifting, somehow unable to stand in the exact spot. "The dog was at his side. The preacher wasn't too happy about it, but we buried them together. Everyone knew how much he loved that old ugly dog."

Hawk had forgotten about Rusty. Why hadn't the dog given an alarm? Had the end been so sudden? Hawk figured it to be so, or both his father and his faithful dog would have fought back.

"They dragged him inside." She nodded toward the barn's floor. "Probably stayed on awhile. A day, maybe more, by the looks of the house."

Hawk said nothing.

Reading correctly his thoughts she said, "You couldn't have done anything."

Hawk raised his gaze to hers. Elizabeth thought she'd never seen pain quite so stark.

"Nothing but get killed along with him."

Again he said nothing.

"There were four of them. They raped and murdered Ben Stuart's girls, over on the next ridge. I guess that means they're heading west, at least for now."

Hawk glanced up at a darkening sky and nodded. "I'll leave in the morning." He was a Cherokee Indian, and before he could ride he'd learned to track. Hawk knew there would be no problem finding the men who did this. The only problem he could envision was which one he was going to kill first.

"Eat before you go," Elizabeth said as she mounted her horse. "I've packed you a few things to take along. Don't forget to eat.

"Jeremiah . . . " she said as she pushed her foot securely into the stirrup.

"Yeah?"

"Ben Stuart wants them dead."

Hawk's mouth tightened, his eyes harder, colder than any she'd ever seen. His entire body looked as if it were carved from cold stone. She knew he'd forgotten that he represented the law. She knew he was going to revert back to ancient ways. A man with that much rage had no choice. So she wasn't surprised when she heard him say, "Tell Ben he can count on it."

A man of awesome power and strength mounted his horse early the next morning. A man who held little resemblance to the deputy marshal from New Orleans. This man wore only soft moccasins, buckskin trousers, and matching vest. A plain rawhide band circled his head, holding shoulder-length black hair from his face. His dark eyes glittered with purpose, holding not a shred of gentleness. A man might quake beneath that black stare, knowing the terror of unmerciful death, for all Hawk could feel was the need for vengeance. He faced his horse west.

Amanda left the train and began to walk. Careful to stay hidden, just off the road lest someone, lest a man (she shivered at the thought) accost her. God, she couldn't bear it if another tried to hurt her. She

176

thought she might go insane if she were forced to kill again.

Someone had told her once that the sun rose in the east. So she watched that she faced the light in the morning, knowing her home and Abigail were out there somewhere, awaiting her return. She didn't know how far she was from home, but she'd get there. Nothing was going to stop her.

It was the evening of the second day when she came across the inn. The Hungry Boar. Amanda smiled and thought the name most befitting. She was at least as hungry as a boar. Amanda had no money, so taking a room was out of the question. But she did have two hands and feet, as well as a strong back. She thought she'd ask for work. If nothing more, it might earn her a good meal. She needed food to keep up her strength, and she just might need all of her strength to get home.

William Cassidy watched the young girl enter the tavern room. She was about ten years younger than him, he thought, sixteen if he judged rightly. She looked to be in some trouble, if he wasn't mistaken. Her hair hadn't been brushed in some time. Her dress was of poor quality, ripped and dirty, she looked like a homeless waif.

William tried, but he couldn't stop looking at her. For a long minute he couldn't understand why. And then it dawned on him. Her eyes. Her eyes were as blue as the sky on a summer day. And the more he looked, the more sure he became that they were filled with fear. William could only wonder why. What had happened that had made her so afraid?

"Yes, miss?" he said as she came at last to the counter.

"Excuse me, sir, but I'm looking for work. Would you need any help?"

William might have asked the same of her, but decided whatever her problems were they were her own business. He eyed her slender form, her delicate frame. "My serving girl left two weeks ago. Have you served tables before?"

Amanda bit her bottom lip and wondered if she should tell the truth. She couldn't imagine serving tables to be all that difficult an undertaking. And if she claimed inexperience, she just might lose her chance to work. She nodded.

"Where?"

Lord. This was exactly why she never lied, for one lie only seemed to grow into two and then two into three. "In Charlotte."

"Where, The Prince?"

Amanda had never heard of The Prince, but she couldn't remember the name of the place where she and Abigail had eaten on her one visit to the city, so she nodded again.

"Is Davy still there?"

Amanda shrugged. "I haven't been there in a while."

She was lying and William knew it. A girl like this one wouldn't last five minutes in that place, with its rough crowd. And there was no Davy. A man named Harry, who was dirtier, rougher, and meaner than the worst of his clientele owned and ran the place.

"I've got two rooms on the third floor, empty. Pick one." William eyed her closely, wondering if he wasn't making a mistake. To hire on a girl who lied probably wasn't the wisest move he'd ever made. Still, there was something about this one. Something that caused a man to want to reach out to protect.

William shook aside the ridiculous thought, knowing it to be nonsense. She was a young girl in need of work and had probably lied because she was inexperienced. There was nothing more to it.

"You'll find aprons in the kitchen." He nodded to his right and the long hall that led to the back of the building.

Amanda smiled. "Is it all right if I clean up before I start?"

William nodded again. "Just don't be long about it." He withdrew his watch from his pocket, gave it a glance, and remarked, "The stage is due within the hour.

"You hungry?"

Amanda nodded. "A little." She almost laughed aloud at that understatement.

"Tell Mrs. Washington to give you a bowl of stew."

Amanda walked into the kitchen and found a black woman working at the stove. "Mrs. Washington?"

Sarah Washington turned to find a young, very dirty girl standing in her kitchen. She frowned at the oddity. Bill didn't allow homeless waifs in his tavern room. He would have told her to go to the back door if she wanted a handout. "You want something, honey?"

"The man . . ." Amanda bit her bottom lip. She'd forgotten to ask his name.

179

"Mr. Cassidy?" Sarah offered.

Amanda was unsure if she should agree or not and merely shrugged. "He said to get something to eat before I start."

"Start what?"

"Serving tables."

Sarah nodded. It wasn't any of her business who Bill hired on. She was only pleased that he had finally found someone to take Sally's place. It was almost impossible for her to cook, clean, and do the serving as well.

After she downed two bowls of stew and a huge chunk of bread, Amanda was reaching for an apron when her gaze fell upon the washtub in the kitchen corner. She promised herself later, after she was finished with her chores, she was going to sit in that tub until her skin wrinkled.

There were two roads that led east from Memphis. Abigail took the more northern trail, never knowing that had she taken the southern route, her search might have been over in a few short days. With an ever-complaining Robert at her side, she pushed her horse from dawn to dusk, stopping every coach and rider she met on the way, stopping at every farmhouse and inn, to inquire of her sister, a girl no one had seen.

She wasn't about to give up. They had been on the road more than a week when they stopped for the night.

Abigail built a fire, leaned back as the flames took hold, and smiled. She was getting rather good at this, she thought. When she began this journey, starting a fire had been a monumental task that often took hours, for neither she nor Robert had any experience along those lines. Now it took only a few minutes before the warmth came to stall off the evening chill.

Robert reached into the saddlebags and took out a bottle. He uncorked it and drank deeply. When he tipped the bottle away from his mouth, he wiped at the moisture left behind with his sleeve and sighed. "Christ, I'm tired of this."

Abigail wasn't sure exactly how many days they'd been traveling, for one seemed to blend into another, and she had somehow lost count. What she did know was she was tired of hearing Robert's constant sighs, moans, and grunts of discontent. The truth of it was, she hadn't asked him to come along. And though it might have been a foolhardy and no doubt dangerous journey for a woman to attempt on her own, Abigail would have much enjoyed doing without his uncooperative company.

"What is it now, Robert?"

"My ass hurts. Is that all right with you?"

Abigail stiffened in surprise. She'd never heard him use that particular tone before, nor words half so crass. "There's no need to . . ."

"I'm sorry, darling." Robert instantly joined her before the fire, his arm reaching around her waist. "I didn't mean to take it out on you. I know you're . . ."

"It's all right," she said, nodding as she pulled from his embrace. Abigail couldn't understand it. She'd never before felt so ill at ease at his every touch. Actually there was a time when she'd felt quite comfortable with his arm around her. Not excited perhaps, but comfortable. But that had been before Hawk.

She stiffened again at the wayward thought. Good Lord, what in the world could she be thinking? It certainly did not matter that the man had once held her against him, that his hard lips had sought hers out, demanding from her a passion she hadn't dreamed possible to give.

Her thoughts were becoming more ridiculous daily, for it suddenly occurred to her that as each day passed, she thought more and more of Hawk. She shook her head in denial. Impossible. It hadn't mattered then, and it certainly didn't matter now that she had allowed those kisses. She'd never see the stubborn, insensitive, arrogant beast again, and for that she could only thank the Almighty.

Her stomach rumbled with hunger, but more than food, she longed to be clean. God, how long had it been since she'd last bathed? Tonight they had stopped by a small lake. She promised herself that after supper, when it was completely dark, she was going to bathe. She couldn't wait.

The scent of coffee drifted a good distance downwind. Willie Parker's mouth began to water.

Mike grumbled unhappily. "We should have taken supplies yesterday. Damn, what the hell were we thinking about?"

The three men laughed at that question, each knowing exactly what they were thinking at the time. The girl had been young and tighter than an old maid's ass, and they had been about to sample her one more time before finishing her off as they had her father, when the hands had starting coming in from the fields. Not one of the four professed to be brave— well, perhaps they did—but it was one thing to be brave and another to act the fool. They could, especially when together, kill a lone man, but to face eight men, all bigger and stronger than a goddamn mountain would have been suicide.

Yeah, they should have taken supplies from the last place they had stopped, but they had been too busy saving their necks to think about food. Now they were out of everything. And Willie, along with the rest, was starving.

"I think I'll have myself a taste of that coffee."

Hank, Mike, and Josh all grinned as they mounted their horses, following their leader.

Ten minutes later, with their horses tied behind them, they watched, through the thick underbrush, two men sitting at a fire. Suddenly one of them leaned up, reaching for the pot of coffee. Willie Parker grabbed Hank's arm as he leveled his rifle at the man and shook his head. "It's a woman."

Hank shot his partner a look of disbelief. "You're seeing things."

"You think I don't know a woman's ass when I see one?"

"How can you see anything? She's sitting on it."

"She wasn't a minute ago."

"I never saw a woman in pants before." Mike's eyes were likely to pop from his head, his interest obvious. He couldn't tear his gaze away. "Maybe it's only a boy."

183

Willie ignored his men's mutterings. He knew a woman when he saw one. It didn't matter that she was dressed like a man. "Kill the other one," he ordered Mike.

"Which? The big one?"

"I'll do it," Willie said in some disgust. He didn't want anything to happen to the woman. At least not just yet. He pulled his gun from its holster.

"I have only four bullets left," Robert said as he bit into a meat pie bought from an inn, where they had earlier that day stopped to inquire about Amanda.

"Does it matter?" Abigail inquired. "We haven't eaten anything so far that wasn't bought."

"Meaning I'm an awful shot."

Abigail glanced at his contrite expression. Apparently the man suffered some humiliation at the failing. The fact was, he couldn't have hit a standing wall three feet away. Abigail figured she'd never seen a man who could shoot worse. "Meaning you excel in other things," she said, pampering a deflated ego. "We aren't living in the Wild West. A businessman isn't expected to be good with a gun."

"And thank God for that."

Robert bit again into the pie. His teeth had just closed over a succulent piece of meat when a sudden impossibly hard thwack against his back propelled him forward, almost to the fire's edge. He never heard the gunshot, but turned to look, wondering what in the world could have hit him.

Abigail watched in astonishment as a thick spurt of blood suddenly surged from a hole just below his collarbone. What in the world? She sat in place, unable at first to comprehend the happenings until the next shot snapped Robert's hand, and the pie he'd been eating went flying into the night, along with his pinky finger.

It took the sound of the second shot, and the destruction it caused, for her to realize someone was actually shooting at them. She cried out and unlike her companion, rolled from the fire, crawling on her stomach to the edge of the woods, where she wouldn't be so obvious a target.

Robert didn't have the sense nor the presence of mind to do as much. The fact was, he was so stunned by the damage done that he could only fall to his back and lie there, moaning in his agony.

Abigail cursed her stupidity. They were under attack by some unknown and unseen villain, and she had no weapon save for the rifle that was still attached to her saddle, and God help her, the saddle sat at the opposite end of the clearing.

She had to get to that rifle. Abigail had no doubt that to do anything less would mean her life.

She dragged herself forward, hugging the ground as best she could, toward the thick foliage and the promise of safety in its dark covering, her heart thundering, her breathing almost nonexistent. She had to get into the underbrush. She had to lose herself among its dark heavy growth.

She gave a silent sigh as she rolled at last into the dark moist refuge. Her body trembled as if palsied, but she couldn't take the time right now to allow the relief. She had to get to the rifle. Perhaps she could never boast of being the best, but Abigail had often practiced shooting in the woods behind her home.

185

She could, she knew, at the very least, defend herself from this unknown foe.

Abigail carefully and silently circled the clearing, until she was just opposite the saddle. Slowly, silently, she crept forward, hardly daring to breathe in her terror. At last she lay half in and out of the clearing, protected from view behind the saddle. Her hand slowly pulled the rifle to her side. Somewhere in the dark came muttered curses and the shuffling of underbrush. Her stomach sank with despair. There was more than one. More than two if she wasn't mistaken.

She tensed awaiting the coming final attack, knowing it was the end, for she could never win out against odds so great. A silent prayer whispered from stiff terrified lips.

"Where the hell did she go?" a man asked, obviously upset, if his tone of voice meant anything.

"How should I know?" another returned as footsteps beat the surrounding brush.

Abigail would later realize that she should have waited for all to enter the clearing. To do so would have possibly ensured her survival, but in her terror it was beyond her ability to think rationally. The moment one man cleared the brush and stumbled forward, freed at last of clinging vines and heavy branches, her finger tightened on the trigger and a shot roared into their mutterings.

"Christ!" someone yelled as the first man collapsed in a wave of startled agony. He was rolling from side to side, clutching at his thigh, his curses filling what had suddenly become a silent night.

The others fell back, leaving their comrade to his

fate, while a man screamed his rage. "Kill the bitch!"

"Where the fuck is she?"

An instant later a barrage of bullets pounded into the brush. They hadn't seen her, for the dim light of the campfire did not reach behind the saddle. They imagined she was hiding somewhere in the foliage.

Abigail lay flat upon the ground, knowing only terror, helpless to do more than pray.

A few moments passed, and the silence that came again was broken by a man's voice. "Did anyone get her?"

"I don't know," another answered.

"Josh? Did you?"

"I don't know where she is." Abigail started, for the voice came from no more than ten feet to her left. In an instant she rolled to her back and swung the rifle before her. The blast was deafening, the resulting cry of pain a shriek of torment.

"She got me. The bitch got me!" the man screamed as he stumbled back into the brush. "Jesus, she almost tore my arm off."

"She's behind the saddle," yelled another. "Get her!"

She couldn't move. There was no way that she could move. To do so would be to enter a hail of deadly bullets. To do so would only hasten their promise of death.

Abigail knew she was going to die. Her last thought before the bullet crashed into her skull was of Amanda. Who would take care of her sister?

* * *

Hawk had no doubt that he was heading in the right direction. He'd not only followed a trail that a child could have picked up but had come across the destruction the murderous gang had carelessly left in their wake. A young couple lay dead in their farmhouse. A girl had been abused in another. Her father shot through the head.

He was close. He knew it, for he had slept and rested his horse only when both man and beast were pushed to their limit. He had ridden with the wind, while the four ahead—knowing nothing of the pain and torment that would soon descend—had been in no great hurry, stopping to pillage, rape, and murder as they pleased. Yes, he was close, perhaps no more than an hour behind them when he stopped for the night.

Hawk made no fire, ever mindful of possible danger. There was a chance that any one of the four might suspect they were being followed. In that case one or all four might circle back. Hawk knew the chance to be remote, still it did exist. He sat on the hard damp ground, his horse beside him, both man and beast hidden in a maze of thick trees and bush, to await the sun's rising. Tomorrow he'd finish with this chore. Tomorrow, he'd know his revenge. Perhaps then he would know peace, perhaps then he could sleep.

He heard the sounds of gunfire and hurried his horse forward, coming to a stop some ten yards from a clearing. He couldn't see much, little more than a clearing in which a small fire burned and two men lay injured.

From the corner of his eye, he noticed some slight

188

movement. A man, or more likely judging by his size, a boy lay hiding behind a saddle. Hawk wasn't sure, of course, *who* was right or wrong. All he did know for a fact was bullets were flying at the boy from at least two directions and, pinned down, there wasn't a chance he could defend himself.

Hawk instantly took in the situation. To his way of thinking, the odds were hardly fair, especially when the injured man in the clearing rolled to an elbow and added his gun to the melee of flying bullets. Without thought, Hawk brought his gun from its holster. It was dark. He hadn't meant to do more than unarm the man, but the bullet went just a bit farther to his left than originally planned and smashed into the man's ribs.

An instant later Hank gave a sound of dismay as he watched blood and air gurgle from a wound in his chest. He was done for. It took only one glance to know it. Still, his hand came instinctively to the wound as if trying to stop the flow. It happened so fast he hardly had a second to realize his fate. He never got a chance to know fear. A second later the blackness came and he rolled over, his face hitting hard against the unforgiving earth.

Willie cursed, the words softly muttered, for he was not unaware of an intruder in their midst. An intruder with amazingly accurate aim. Someone was out there. Someone hidden in the darkness. It was enough to give a man the creeps.

Willie never took into consideration that he had done as much. That he had stood in the shadows, more than once in fact, to stalk a victim. All he could think about was getting out of here before the next bullet ended up in his chest.

"Let's go," he yelled, uncaring of the fact that the sounds of gunfire obliterated most of what he said. The truth was, he didn't care if Mike and Josh heard him or not. All he cared about was saving his own skin.

He was on his horse, racing from the danger before either man realized he had gone. A moment later both Josh and Mike found their horses and followed.

Hawk listened to the sounds of men and animals riding through the forest. Listened until nothing could be heard but endless nocturnal sounds. A frog croaked from somewhere nearby. An owl made itself known. Crickets and cicadas, silent during the fracas, now joined the harmony. An animal scurried from its hiding place, no doubt to safer quarters.

Hawk felt a heavy weight settle itself around his heart. He shook his head in disgust. By all rights he should be on his horse, racing after the killers, but knew finding them would have to wait. He couldn't leave these injured men to their own fate. Someone had to see to their care.

With a weary sigh he moved into the clearing, positive all three villains had fled. With the tip of his boot, he shoved at the shoulder of the man he'd shot. Nothing. Not even a grunt of pain. The man was dead. Hawk knelt at his side, placing his hand on a still throat, just to be sure. Nevertheless, as was his habit, he kicked aside the gun that had fallen from the dead man's grasp.

Next he moved to the other man, lying injured,

bleeding, whimpering his stark terror as he watched the Indian approach.

It was only then—when Hawk looked into Robert's terrified face—that he realized the boy hiding behind the saddle was no boy at all. Forgetting Robert and his serious injuries, he ran to her side, unable to think, unable to breathe as he rolled her to her back. Blood covered her face, disguising her features, but he would have known her anywhere by that golden halo of hair.

Curses mingled crazily with prayers as he leaned forward. She couldn't be dead. No, he wouldn't believe that she was dead. "Jesus, no. Please, God, no!"

Hawk pressed his ear to her chest. Was it his own pounding heart he heard? Was it? "Don't die, Abby, please. Damn you, you can't be dead." He lifted her limp upper body into his arms and gave her a violent shake. "I won't let you die!"

Again his ear was upon her chest and still he heard nothing but the pounding of his own heart. Why couldn't he hear? God, please. And then he suddenly did. A faint yet steady rhythm sounded between every harsh throb of his own heart. She was alive! Hawk felt tears sting the backs of his eyes and grumbled out yet another long stream of curses, his terror easing as rage came to fill his entire being. How could she have put herself in this kind of danger? How did she dare do this to herself?

"I'd appreciate it, Mr. Hawk, if you could keep a civil tongue in your mouth," came her voice, soft perhaps, but as clear as if she'd sustained no injury at all.

Abigail never questioned the amazing fact that he

was there. She didn't know how he'd managed it, but like a guardian angel, he had saved her once again. What she did question, however, was the fact that he was obviously angry. Abigail couldn't for the moment understand why.

Hawk sneered into a face all but masked with blood and dirt. If she wasn't already injured, he would have liked nothing less than to put his hands around her throat and . . . No, what she deserved was a good shaking. Better yet, came the tantalizing thought of putting her over his knee.

"You're lucky you're hurt, lady, or I'd . . ."

Abigail knew an instant flooding of anger. The emotion cleared quite efficiently a muddled brain. "You'd what?" she asked as she wiped at the blood that coated more than half her face and struggled into a sitting position. Abigail ignored the debilitating weakness, the dizziness that threatened to topple her over, and managed her own sneer. "Beat me?" she asked, reading correctly the dark menacing threat in his eyes. "Is that what a big brave man would do to someone half his size?"

"Someone should have beat you, lady. Someone should have beat some sense into you a long time ago."

"Right," she said with no little sarcasm. "And I imagine you think you're the one to do it?"

"Shut up and sit still, you're bleeding all over the place."

"Well, I'm not bleeding on you, so what do you care?"

Hawk watched her for a long moment. Her hair was a mess, covered with blood, dirt, and dead grass.

192

Her face possessed much the same properties, and yet to him she'd never looked better simply because she was alive. Hawk wanted to crush her against him and never let her go, nasty mouth and all. "Am I ever going to get the last word in?"

"Not as long as I'm alive," she swore.

Hawk figured he'd settle for that. He didn't care that she'd always answer him back. He didn't even care that her responses were usually nasty. He didn't care about anything as long as she was alive.

He breathed a sigh that, oddly enough, mingled despair with relief and left her then to return to his horse and the supplies in his bags. Hardly a moment went by before he was kneeling at her side again.

He soaked a clean rag with something poured from a bottle and pressed it to her head. Abigail cried out at the sudden blinding, searing pain. It wasn't until a moment ago that she'd felt the injury at all, and he had gone and worsened it tenfold. "You bastard! You did that on purpose."

Hawk chuckled a low sound of amusement even as he ducked a coming punch. A second later she was pressed up against his chest, her arms pinned at her sides, his low rumble of laughter echoing in her ears.

"I'm going to get you for that," she promised.

"I'm only trying to help you, you little witch." Hawk waited a long moment before he felt her soften against him and reasoned she had calmed enough to let her arms go. He leaned her away from him and squinted into her face. "Come over to the fire so I can see what I'm doing."

Abigail pulled herself from his arms and deliberately refused his offer of assistance. "I can walk."

Only she couldn't.

No sooner had she gotten to her feet than Abigail saw the ground rushing up to meet her. She made a small sound of surprise and then knew only blackness.

She awoke moments later, cradled in Hawk's arms, half reclining before the fire as he wrapped a bandage around her head. The moment she opened her eyes she heard, "Don't say another word. I haven't got all night to argue with a spoiled little brat. Your fiancé is in bad shape."

"Robert?" she said weakly, only then remembering the blood gushing from his chest. "Is he . . . ?"

"He's bleeding bad." Hawk finished the bandaging and just before he left her said, "Now stay still."

Abigail swore she stayed in place only because at the moment she felt as weak as a kitten. Her supposed obedience didn't have a thing to do with his order. As far as she was concerned, he could order her from now until forever and she would have done just as she pleased.

"Is he all right?" she called across the few feet that separated them.

"He will be. Lost some blood though." Hawk didn't mention that it was fever they had to worry about—fever, they both had to worry about.

Abigail wasn't sure exactly how long Hawk worked over Robert. All she did know for a fact was he was smiling with some real satisfaction when he returned to her side. It took his next comment before she realized why.

"So I see you've finally decided to obey me."

"I only look like I'm obeying you," she gritted out

between powerful shudders, unwilling to give him even that little satisfaction. Abigail frowned as she shuddered again. Why couldn't she stop this shaking? "It would take you and an army to stop me once I've set my mind to . . ." Now her voice started to tremble. She shot him a helpless look that held more than a touch of fear. "What's the matter with me? Why can't I stop shaking?"

"You'll be all right," he said as he pulled a blanket around her shoulders and then checked beneath her bandage. It looked as if she'd already stopped bleeding. No doubt the wound hadn't been half as bad as he first feared, although she'd have to fashion her hair into a style that would hide the resulting half-inch scar. He gave silent thanks.

"Oh, good answer," she sneered. "Could you be a bit more vague?"

"Fact is, little smart mouth, you're probably suffering some sort of shock." He couldn't resist adding, "People usually feel cold just before they're about to die."

Hawk heard her soft gasp and forced aside his smile. He had no doubt that she was as far from dying as one was likely to get, but it wasn't beyond him to try to scare her a little. He figured it was the least he could do after the terror he'd known upon finding her half unconscious, with blood covering her face. Suddenly he couldn't hold back, and a low wicked chuckle escaped his throat.

"You bastard," she said again, allowing her anger to give her the needed strength. "I knew you were lying." She hadn't known, of course, but she wasn't about to let him know that.

Hawk grinned. "That's the second time you called me that. For your information my mother and father were married three years before I was born."

"Shut up."

Hawk only grinned again. "All right darlin'," he said as he came to his feet again. "If we're finished with all this love talk, it's time to get going."

"Going? Where are we going?"

"There's a chance his friends might come back." Hawk nodded toward the dead man occupying their circle of light. "And if they do, I want some cover."

"So where are we going?" she repeated.

Hawk was packing up as he spoke. "Away from here."

"My, my, aren't we informative." Her voice dripped sarcasm. "I can't tell you how you've eased my mind."

He saddled both horses and as gently as possible slung Robert's unconscious body over one. Hoping the movement wouldn't start his wound bleeding again, he then tied him as best he could to the saddle.

He doused the fire. Next he retrieved his own horse and placed Abigail upon the saddle. A moment later, with the reins of both animals in his hands, plus those of his own horse, he pulled himself up behind her.

The horse moved out of the clearing with only a gentle squeeze of powerful thighs.

Chapter Ten

She wouldn't at first lean against him but held her back stiff, her weight slightly forward. She was exhausted and didn't feel all that well; still, she'd die before uttering a word of complaint. There wouldn't come a day when this arrogant brute would see her soft and helpless. Abigail dismissed the fact that he had already seen her softer and more helpless than a newborn babe, a number of times, in fact.

Hawk only shook his head at her stubbornness. Idly he wondered why he felt so intrigued by so disagreeable a woman. Surely he could have found another who was just as pretty—all right, just as beautiful. There had to be a hundred, probably a thousand, who had forms as lush. So why was it he found this one to shine above all others? Hawk couldn't figure it out.

"Abby," he said softly, almost lovingly, but with a hint of amusement.

"What?" she asked in great suspicion. He was up to something, she was sure, for he never spoke so gently.

"You can thank me now for saving your ass again."

Abigail opened her mouth ready to bombard him with a flurry of insults, liberally interspersed with every curse word she could think of. At the last minute she changed her mind and said, "Thank you for saving my ass, Mr. Hawk."

Hawk grinned and wondered why this woman refused to address him by his proper title. "You have a nasty mouth, lady."

"One couldn't possibly say the same of you, of course."

Hawk laughed.

Abigail sat up straighter than ever.

"Lean against me."

"No."

"Why? I've felt more than your back against me before. As a matter of fact, I've felt just about . . ."

Abigail knew he was talking about the intimacy they had shared. Her cheeks flamed at the mention, and she interrupted him with, "Only a beast would remind a lady of an indiscretion."

"Tell me you didn't like being in my arms."

"Like it? I loathed every minute of it."

"That's not how I remember it."

"No?" she said in great sarcasm. "Are you saying you actually remember me from all the rest?"

"Is that what's crawling up your ass? Are you jealous?"

"Good God, are you insane? What would I have to be jealous about?"

"I haven't had a woman in weeks," he said flatly.

"Why?" she asked. Forgetting her pledge to keep her distance, she turned and leaned against him.

"Damned if I know." He did know, of course. The fact was, he couldn't find any interest in another woman, what with the memory of this one's taste, scent, and feel. She was the one he wanted. She was the one he loved. Only he wasn't about to give her another weapon to use against him. He'd already said too much. "Look, we might as well get something straight. We're going to be together for some time, so it might be best if we could—"

"What does that mean, together for some time?"

"It means I can't leave you to fend for yourself, so you'll have to come with me."

"You're being ridiculous. Of course I can fend for myself."

"Yeah, you looked like you were doing a mighty fine job of it back there."

"They snuck up on us," she said in her defense.

"And what? They won't sneak up on you again?"

"I'll take precautions the next time."

"There won't be a next time. You're coming with me."

"Damn you, Hawk. Just who do you think you are? I don't have to listen to you."

A moment of silence passed before he asked, "What are you doing out here?"

"Following my sister, of course."

"Of course," he repeated almost dully.

"And what is that supposed to mean?"

"It means, little fool, you could have gotten yourself killed."

"Don't call me a fool. I shot two of them," she stated proudly.

"Right, but you didn't kill either one, and there were two others. What do you think would have happened if I hadn't heard those shots?"

Abigail knew well enough what would have befallen her if he hadn't happened along. She didn't want to think about that now. The scenario that repeated itself in her mind's eye was too terrifying to speak aloud. So she changed the subject. Asking what she'd longed to ask almost from the first moment he had magically appeared. "Why are you out here? Why aren't you in New Orleans? And why are you dressed like this?" Despite her injuries, it hadn't gone unnoticed that Hawk wore only buckskin trousers and a vest, that his chest was bare, that dark thick arms wrapped around her.

"I'm trailing someone."

"Who?"

"The men who murdered my father," he said flatly.

Abigail couldn't have been more shocked. She gasped. "Oh, my God! I'm so sorry."

Hawk did not respond. The truth was, he wasn't sure he could trust his voice, for he'd never been closer to tears than when faced with her sympathy. He would have given anything, . . . anything if she would have wrapped her arms around him, if he could have buried his face in her neck and given in to the need to empty himself of the pain.

"Men? You mean there was more than one?"

Again he did not respond but left her to draw her own conclusions.

"The men who attacked us, were they the men you were—?"

"Yes."

"Why didn't you go after them?"

"I will, once you're better."

"Once I'm better? What do I have to do with it?"

"I told you before, you're coming with me."

"Mr. Hawk, I have no intention of going anywhere with you. I have to find my sister."

Hawk grinned. "We'll find her together, after I—"

She cut him off with, "You're being ridiculous. I hardly know you, and I certainly will not traipse all over this country in your company."

"I figure by the time I find them again, we'll know one another a bit." His hand snaked around her waist and pulled her close against him.

She didn't fight him. In truth she didn't have the strength. She had been trying to ignore her weakness, the dizziness that refused to abate, but now her stomach was giving her some trouble. "I don't feel at all well," she said as her body gave in to his insistence and collapsed weakly against his.

"Why? What's the matter?" Hawk asked in obvious concern.

"I don't know. I just don't feel—" She gagged and Hawk knew she was about to vomit. Quickly he brought his horse to a stop and lowered her to the ground, where he held her until the violent waves of nausea finally eased.

Abigail might have known some real humiliation here, were it not for the fact that she felt so wretchedly ill. "What's the matter with me?" Abigail asked

as he wiped her mouth with a handkerchief damp-
ened from his canteen.

"You took a blow to your head, sweetheart. This
happens sometimes."

"Will I be all right?"

"You'll be better than all right, Abby. Don't
worry. All you need is a few days of rest."

"Do we have to ride much farther?"

"We're almost there."

Apparently *there* was a mountain. The ride could
have taken fifteen minutes, but at the slow rate Hawk
moved through the forest, it took more than an hour
before he pulled his horse to a stop at the base of it
and dismounted. Gently he brought a sleeping Abigail into his arms and started up the sharp incline.
Moments later he pushed aside what appeared to be
thick undergrowth but was, in fact, a number of
branches cut and placed at the mouth of a cave.

Hawk frowned. He'd been afraid of this. During
the ride here, he had tried to deny the fact that Abigail was a bit warm. He couldn't deny it any longer.
He hadn't a doubt that by morning a fever would
rage. Robert would eventually suffer the same, but
Hawk didn't care about Robert. All he cared about
was seeing Abby through this danger.

His patients lay sleeping on the blankets brought
from their saddles, one on each side of a small fire.
Neatly stacked against the cave wall sat a coffee pot,
a frying pan, and the supplies taken from their saddlebags. Nearby a cold brook emptied into a small
pond. There was enough wood for a fire, water to
drink, and game to hunt. Hawk nodded in satisfac-

tion. Abby would soon be well, but in the meantime, they would not lack for the necessities.

Hawk left them to bed the horses down for the night.

He returned with the healing herbs of a root, which he boiled into a tea meant to ease her fever. After allowing the tea to cool, he forced the liquid down Abigail's dry throat. Watching her carefully, Hawk knew some real satisfaction that she was able to keep it down.

Later Hawk prepared his own blankets at Abigail's side. Gently he gathered her sleeping form to cuddle against him and sighed at the luxurious feel of her. How long, he wondered, would he be forced to wait before she came to him of her own accord? Just before he fell asleep, Hawk vowed his waiting was almost at an end.

The next morning, after feeding and watering the horses, Hawk returned again to the forest floor, searching for the needed herbs that would hurry the healing of both Abby's and Robert's wounds. While boiling them, he tore his only shirt into strips, and then he dipped the clean rags into the healing liquid. Using the rags to apply the poultice, he settled down to wait.

The days passed in constant care. Hawk had never worked so hard in his life. Every night he fell into an exhausted sleep, only to awaken again the next morning to Abby's feverish moans.

It was during the third day that Hawk imagined

her fever too high. He had to get it down, and he had to do it now.

From the cold stream running down the side of the mountain, Hawk filled a pot with water. He searched through her saddlebags for a length of cotton and found it in her chemise and an extra shirt. After removing all but her drawers, and soaking both articles in the water, he spread them over her back and chest.

Abigail cried out at the shock of the cold water, but Hawk quickly pulled a blanket around her and hugged her tightly against him. She shivered horribly, and Hawk could only pray he was doing the right thing. Perhaps he was making her worse? No, he reasoned. This was the only way. She wasn't going to die, not if he had anything to say about it. "Abby, don't fuss, sweetheart. I know it hurts," he said as he brushed her hair back and looked into her tight face, her eyes glazed with fever. "It will help you, I promise," he said softly, murmuring into the blazing heat of her neck. It didn't take more than a few seconds for the cold material to turn hot, almost dry again, and Hawk repeated the procedure, over and over, for the next few hours.

By the next morning, Abby was considerably better. Her fever wasn't gone, but Hawk knew he'd see the last of it before the end of the day. The thing was, Hawk had devoted all of his time and care to Abigail, and Robert had grown decidedly worse. Hawk had expected that. No one could take a bullet to his chest and not suffer some serious consequences.

The wounds, thanks to the poultice, were not festering, which was a good sign; still, they were not healing as they should. Hawk couldn't understand why. It was only a day later, when he was helping Robert to relieve himself, that he understood.

Robert had been leaning heavily against him—for in his weakened condition, it wouldn't have taken more than a soft breeze to knock him off his feet—when Hawk had chanced to glanced down. He made a sound of surprise and instantly pulled away, the movement almost sending Robert to his grave, for they stood at the edge of the cave.

Hawk didn't know much about doctoring, or disease, but for the herbal remedies his mother had used. Still, he figured he knew what that sore meant. Considering where it was located, he supposed it could mean only one thing.

As far as he knew there was no cure for it. Robert was a dead man, whether he survived his wounds or not.

He'd known from the first that the man was no good. In New Orleans he'd made discreet inquires. There were no businesses. It didn't take him long to discover that Robert had spent most of every day and all of every night in the arms of one prostitute or another. Apparently Robert had had the disease for some time and was sure to have given it to every woman he slept with. Hawk shook his head at the thought and cursed. The city would be rampant with disease before long.

He glanced at a sleeping Abby and gave a prayer of thanks that she had not married him, that they had not been lovers. And he knew for a fact that they had not. He remembered that kiss in Lydia's parlor. It had been wonderful, more so for the innocence he felt in her response. A woman who had lain with a man would have known how to kiss, would have understood the need that raged within her own body.

Despite her anger that night, Hawk had seen the confusion in her eyes and knew the truth of it.

Later, lying with her cuddled to his side again, Hawk fell asleep amid endless prayers of gratitude.

The fire simmered to glowing embers, allowing the small cave almost no light. He pressed his hand against her forehead and smiled at the cool dry flesh encountered. She was better. A lot better. She'd be in need of rest today, but perhaps she'd be able to talk to him for a few minutes. Hawk couldn't believe how desperately he missed their conversations. Even a snide comment promised to soothe this aching need.

Hawk glanced at the sky and figured it to be an hour or so before dawn. He should get up, he knew. He should see to the fire, but the feel of her against him was too good to move. He smiled as he felt her stir. She moved her head on his shoulder as if to find a more comfortable position and breathed a sweet sigh as she drifted into deeper sleep.

At least he'd thought she was sleeping. Right now he couldn't be sure, for she was kissing his neck.

"Abby," he said, his body suddenly stiff with dread. It was bad enough to hold her against him, but to feel her mouth press light sweet kisses along his neck tested his endurance beyond imagining. "Abby, are you awake?"

Abigail muttered a soft incoherent sound and kissed him again, this time allowing her lips to part and her tongue to sample the taste of his skin. She rolled half upon his bare chest, the buttons of her blouse open more than usual, since he hadn't bothered completing the chore after replacing her shirt again.

She curled a leg, clad only in long drawers, over his and Hawk cursed his body's instant and powerful response. It took every ounce of his control to keep his hands at his sides, for he wanted nothing more than to pull her to lie fully upon him, to feel her nakedness against his.

Apparently she felt much the same need, for her blouse was suddenly completely open and her bare breasts rubbing against his chest.

God, it was too much. How many more times would he suffer in his need to touch her, to feel her, to lose himself in her soft giving body? This was the third time she'd squirmed against him. The first time she'd been asleep in the stagecoach, the second time drugged and completely naked. This time she was ill with a fever and had opened her blouse. Would there ever come a day when she would do this with all her senses about her?

"Abby, wake up," he said, knowing he hadn't the strength to leave her and yet he dared not linger in this delicious moment.

"No," she murmured, just as obstinate as ever.

Hawk smiled and tightened his hold. He knew she wouldn't understand . . . or remember. Perhaps that was why he dared to say, "I love you."

As if she did understand, Abby breathed a delighted sigh and snuggled closer than ever.

Hawk had seen her, held her half naked in his

arms, again and again over the last two days, but had not touched her. Not even once, well perhaps once, his fingers might have brushed upon her, but he hadn't allowed them to linger. Now it was beyond his power to resist. Just one touch, he swore. Just one glimpse of the paradise in store, one hint of the magic he'd one day know and he'd stop. Beneath the cover his hand moved to cup her fullness, to weigh in luxury her soft sweetness, to stir with his thumb the giving flesh to an aching hard bud.

Abigail moaned. She knew she was sleeping, but she never wanted to awaken from this dream.

She was the most soft, most beautiful woman, and Hawk knew he'd never get enough of touching her.

One second she floated in that special place that couldn't actually be called sleep and the next she was more fully awake than she'd ever been in her life. She lay there for a long moment before her dazed mind could grasp the horror of what was happening, of what this depraved beast was doing. "Lecher!" she gasped.

Hawk groaned in frustration as he heard the word and felt her stiffen against him.

"How dare you? How dare you touch me?"

So after three days of fever and hour upon hour of delirium, she'd finally decided to wake up, had she? Great, just great. Timing being just about everything in life, Abby couldn't have chosen a worse moment to come to her senses. Hawk breathed a weary sigh as she pulled from his arms. He suffered under no delusion that he'd be believed. Still, he couldn't allow that look of disgust and her condemning words without coming to his own defense. "Lady, you turned to me.

You opened your own blouse. What the hell did you expect me to do?"

She gasped in outrage. Were there no depths to which this man would not sink? "I didn't— I wouldn't— I'd *never* do such a thing. Leave it to a villain like you to say something so despicable."

"Right, lady, I'm a monster." Hawk came to a sitting position and ran his fingers through his long hair. He tied a piece of rawhide around his forehead to keep the dark strands in place. "You might as well know the truth of it. I kept you naked and had my way with you the whole time you suffered from the fever."

Abigail watched as he rolled from the blankets and frowned that his leaving the bed should cause her this odd sense of emptiness. She frowned at his words as well. She knew they weren't true. She didn't know how, but she knew it. She lay there for a long moment, after he left her side, the blanket held securely under her arms as she remembered, at first bits and pieces, and then just about everything of the last few days. She frowned at the memories, at the intimacies. She should be upset, she knew, but couldn't seem to feel anything but gratitude and something . . . something she couldn't quite name.

He had held her in his arms and whispered soft soothing words, pressed cold cloths to her face and neck and then larger pieces to her chest and back. He had forced her to drink one horrible brew after another, and then gently soothed the resulting shivers. She had trembled with fever, at once cold and hot, and he had held her to him. She remembered moments when she had been terribly ill. How he had wiped her face with his handkerchief after all had emptied from her stomach, and when she'd had to relieve herself, how he had carried her to the bushes. Her face grew warm at that thought, but she knew he hadn't had a choice and neither had she.

She remembered finding him at her side every time she'd awakened. No, he hadn't taken advantage of her. He hadn't done anything but help her.

Perhaps they had both been at fault this morning. Perhaps she had . . . Abigail bit her lip. It wasn't easy to face a wrongdoing, but she had no doubt that he spoke the truth. Well, almost no doubt. Despite what he said, she couldn't imagine doing something like that. Still, there was that dream. Was it truly a dream? Could she have forgotten, in her sleep, her usual modesty and turned to him, luxuriating in his touch, almost pleading for more?

His back was to her, stiff with anger, as he stirred and added to the fire. She looked at him for a long moment. She'd never seen a man's naked back before. She'd never realized that skin could look so smooth and yet so firm. She hadn't known that muscle rippling beneath dark, golden skin could appear so intriguing. "What's your name?"

Hawk breathed a sigh and then turned to face her. Was she again in the throes of fever? "My name is Hawk," he said as he reached out to touch his hand to her forehead. Hawk frowned. She wasn't hot. His puzzled gaze moved to hers.

"No, I mean your first name."

"Jeremiah."

"Really? How surprising." Abigail smiled. "I

210

would have thought it would be Flying, or Little, or Black." She giggled at the thought.

"Don't be funny," he warned, having a time of it keeping his own smile at bay.

"No, not Little. It would be ridiculous, wouldn't it, if you were called Little Hawk?" She nodded at her own thoughts. "Black is much more appropriate, I think."

"Abby," he warned.

She giggled again. "Do you know that when you are angry with me, your eyebrows almost come together?"

Hawk smiled. "No, I didn't know. How do you feel?"

"Better."

"Weak?"

She nodded. "Weak, but better." His hand rested on his thigh and for some insane reason, she couldn't resist touching it. They both watched as their fingers intertwined. "Thank you," she said when she raised her gaze to his again. "I never would have made it alone."

Hawk shook his head, happier than he could ever remember, just because she'd touched his hand, just because she'd said thank you. God, he felt like a little kid, unsure of what to say or do next.

"You need to rest. I'll get breakfast ready."

"How is he?" Abigail asked as she watched Hawk check Robert. He had just removed her bandage and pronounced the wound almost healed and in need of air to finish the job.

"He's better, but not healing like you."

Breakfast was almost ready. Abigail felt her stomach rumble at the smell of coffee and frying bacon. She came to a sitting position. "I have to . . . ah, I have to go outside for a minute."

"I'll help you."

"I can do it." Beneath the blanket, she pulled on her pants. It took more effort than she'd ever imagined. She was wet with sweat and shaking with weakness when she finished the chore and pushed aside the blanket.

"Abby, you're likely to kill yourself, and all my work will have been for nothing."

Abby came to her feet and reached out flying arms, trying for balance. Hawk was instantly at her side, his arm around her, cradling her against his strength. "All right, maybe I'll let you bring me down, but that's all. I can take care of the rest by myself."

Hawk smiled. "Yes, ma'am."

It took only a few more days, and Abby's strength returned fully.

Hawk was anxious to be gone, but he couldn't leave until Robert was better. The truth was, he didn't give a damn about the man, but a human being, no matter how much of a slime, was still a human being. Besides, Abby wasn't likely to think kindly of him if he gave in to this urge to leave the man to fend for himself.

Hawk came into the cave with two rabbits. He threw the pair on the floor, his dark eyes glinting with annoyance, for Abigail was leaning over Robert,

212

pressing a cool rag to his forehead. He found himself suddenly angry and almost barked, "Do you know how to skin these?"

Abigail jumped at his sudden appearance, for she hadn't heard his approach. She looked at the rabbits at his feet. "Well, actually . . ."

"You don't," he said in condemnation.

Abigail found herself making excuses. "I can't help it. I never had to—"

"Do a thing but lift a finger to get your every desire met."

"Is that my fault?"

"I never said it was." Hawk turned his back to her and started the skinning himself.

He watched her walk to the cave's edge and look out over the mountainside to the forest below. "Why are you wearing pants?"

Abby turned at his words and caught the scowl that again brought his brows together. "What's the matter with you? Why are you angry?"

Hawk could have told her he hated the idea of her touching Robert. Hated the idea of her touching any man, in fact, but said instead, "I'm not."

"No? You're giving a good impression of it. And what does wearing pants have to do with anything?"

"Nothing, if you don't mind every man you meet ogling your ass. You look like you're begging for a good toss."

Abigail stiffened at the crassness and sneered, "You're the only man who would dare think of such a thing."

"You don't know much about men if you believe that."

"I know enough about you to know that you're disgusting."

"Right lady, I'm disgusting. I'm every depraved, repulsive thing you can imagine, but it doesn't stop me from thinking when you prance around like that."

"If it bothers you so much, don't look. Better yet, leave."

Hawk watched her for a long moment before he said very softly, "When I leave, you'll be going with me."

Abigail laughed a low silky sound that turned Hawk's gut into a knot of unbearable need. It took all of his strength not to go to her, to take her into his arms and make her his now and forever. "I don't think so. Leaving with you is out of the question, and you know it."

"It doesn't matter much what you think. The fact is, I'm not leaving you alone."

"I won't be alone. I'll be with Robert."

"Right, a paragon of virtue."

Abigail frowned. She knew Hawk had never liked Robert, but she couldn't understand the man's sudden and obvious disgust. "What's gotten into you?"

"I want you to keep the hell away from him."

She frowned again. "Why?"

Hawk couldn't tell her why. He doubted that she'd understand even if he did. "It doesn't matter why. Just do it."

Abigail laughed. "You really have a nerve. Who do you think you're talking to? The man is my fiancé. We're going to be marr—"

He cut her off. "I don't think so."

"What?"

"You won't be marrying Robert."

"Won't I? And who is going to stop me?"

"The man is diseased." There. He'd said it. He'd gone and done exactly what he'd promised himself he wouldn't do.

"What does that mean? What kind of disease?"

"The kind a lady shouldn't know about. The kind a man gets when sleeping with waterfront whores. He'll die from it in a few years, and if you become his wife you'll die, too."

Abigail's mouth dropped open. She frowned as she realized she felt nothing but shock. So where was the pain? Where was the heartache she should have known? After all, she'd promised to marry him. Shouldn't she know a measure of sorrow? Perhaps he was wrong. Perhaps Hawk hated Robert enough to . . . "How do you know?" she asked very softly, suddenly knowing it was true, knowing she had been wise to feel some doubt. Could this be the reason Robert had made himself so scarce? Had he been with whores during their stay in New Orleans?

Abigail had never expected that her husband would be a virgin. She understood, at least she'd thought she did, that a man had certain needs. Needs that a woman could never know. It was not frowned upon for a man to take a mistress. Some even continued on with their relationships after their marriage.

But waterfront whores? Why? She shivered at the thought having seen one or two, on business trips. Even now she could remember the lank hair, the dull eyes, skin that looked decidedly less than healthy.

215

Would Robert end up like that? Would she have as well if she'd given in to his plea and married him? She shuddered at the very thought.

"He has a sore."

Hawk didn't have to tell her where. She could imagine some things. She never realized she was wiping her hands on her pants. Horror was written all over her face. "So? Does that have to mean . . . ?"

"As far as I know, it does."

"But you're not a doctor."

"Right, I'm not a doctor. Just stay away from him."

"Jeremiah! You've touched him!"

Hawk cursed at the sudden crash of emotion that squeezed at his chest. He wouldn't have believed that the simple saying of his name could have affected him so. It took a long moment before he could trust his voice. "I don't think I can get it from touching him. Besides, I didn't touch him there."

"But you told me not to touch him."

Hawk continued on with the skinning. "There's no need for you to take any chances."

A few minutes later she said, "I'm going to take a bath after we eat."

He smiled, imagining her revulsion, since she hadn't as yet stopped wiping her hands. "If you want a bath, we should go down to the water now."

Abigail shook her head. "When it's dark."

"Just be as quiet as you can."

"I thought you said there was no danger," she whispered in return, her voice telling of her fear.

Hawk knew there wasn't. He couldn't count the number of times he'd bathed in the forest at night. Still, he wouldn't frighten her with stories about animals coming to the water at night. The chances were slim that they would bother her, and he was here. "There's no need to take chances either."

Hawk sat upon a fallen tree, his rifle over his knees and tried not to listen to the sounds of her disrobing. He could feel his heart begin to race, knowing but for overhanging clouds he'd be able to see everything he'd ever wanted. He couldn't stop himself from trying. His eyes strained into the darkness, but all that was visible was a murky shadowy outline of her form. He could hardly breathe. Just knowing she was standing there, not ten feet from him and naked, was almost more than he could bear. Hawk wondered how long he'd have to wait before she'd come to him. How long before he'd feel her softness against him . . . ?

He heard her soft gasp and then, "God, it's cold."

He smiled.

Water splashed and he heard yet another gasp and then a soft, "Lord."

The night was warm, the air comfortable against her nakedness—spring being fully in evidence.

Abigail knew some awkwardness at disrobing before him. Even if he couldn't see a thing, she felt decidedly ill at ease. Still, circumstances demanded that she not come to the water alone. She tried to put from her mind the nocturnal animals that lurked in the brush. Of the possibility that they had been followed, that the men who had attacked them were out here somewhere. It had been days since she'd last washed. She couldn't stand the thought of waiting any longer. Being clean again was worth any discomfort and almost any danger.

Abigail stepped into the coldest water imaginable. She halfway expected chunks of ice to hit against her legs, but of course it wasn't that cold. It only felt like it was. The water, even at its deepest, came only to her knees and Abigail forced herself, with a muffled groan, to sit.

Her head ached as she dipped it beneath the moving water. Quickly she soaped her hair into a lather and rinsed. She wouldn't dally here. She had to wash and get out as quickly as possible. Hardly a minute went by and she was coming to her feet. The water was too cold to linger. Already her legs were growing numb, but not numb enough. She felt a tickle. Without thinking Abigail reached down and picked up a small snake, or at least what she thought was a small snake. Since she couldn't see, she couldn't be sure. She forgot all about being quiet.

Hawk jumped to his feet at the scream. It took only four leaping strides before they met at the water's edge. He pulled her against him and lifted her from the water. Abigail was hardly conscious of the fact that she was without clothes. The only thing she could think of at the moment was the slippery reptile she had unwittingly touched. "A snake! Oh, God. I just picked up a snake." Abigail shuddered uncontrollably, pressing her face against his chest, her body tightly to his length.

"Why did you pick it up?"

Abigail shuddered. "I don't know. I felt it . . ." She shuddered again. "I don't know."

"Did it bite you?" Hawk knew a sense of rage at his foolishness. He should have insisted that she bathe while it was light. Yes, there was always a chance that someone might come across them, but at least she would have been safe from this. If nothing else she would have been able to see what the water held.

"I don't think so."

"Does anything hurt?"

Abigail thought for a minute and then shook her head. "No." Nothing that is, if she didn't count her feet. The floor of the brook was lined with small sharp stones, every one of them giving her a reason to moan. Still, even knowing she suffered no harm, she couldn't shake the terror of actually holding a snake in her hands. It took a long time before her trembling eased.

Abigail grew slowly aware of the fact that she was in his arms, naked with her chest pressed against his. Only a vest separated their bodies, and since the vest was open, it wasn't doing much of a job of it. "You can put me down now," she said, feeling her cheeks growing warm. Lord, how embarrassing. This was the second time, no . . . the third that she'd found herself either naked, or close to it, in his arms. The fact that touching him wasn't the least bit disagreeable hardly mattered. It was shameful and wrong.

"Jeremiah," she whispered, only to hear a groan of response. "What?"

"You can put me down now."

He shook his head, the movement almost infinitesimal. "I can't."

Abigail frowned at his response. "Why?"

219

"You feel too good. And I've waited so long."

"For what?"

"To touch you, to love you."

Abigail took a short startled breath at this alarming bit of news. Granted, she had not been unaware of an occasional moment when something more than words passed between them. Sometimes a look came to his eyes, especially at night when she prepared for bed. But she hadn't fully understood the meaning behind those looks then. All she'd known for a fact was, she was safer to ignore them.

His hand settled on her derriere, and Abigail jumped at the shock of his touch. "Don't," she said, but amazingly enough without much force.

"Abby, don't be afraid of me. I promise I won't hurt you, just let me—"

"I can't. I've never . . ."

"I know." His arms tightened around her, and he pressed his hips forward into her softness. "God, I know."

Abigail might have been an innocent. Still, she had been kissed a number of times and knew that when a man was growing too excited, it was time to call a halt to the moment. Oddly enough it had never been so hard to stop a man before, and he hadn't even kissed her. She shivered. Well he hadn't except for the little bit of nuzzling and gentle bites he was placing along her shoulder. But one couldn't really count them as kisses.

"You have to stop." The words were muttered with a sort of a breathless quality into his neck.

"I know," he breathed. Hawk knew she was right. This wasn't what he wanted for their first time. There

220

were no blankets to lie upon, no light. And he had to see her, to watch as his hands moved over her, to watch the passion cloud her eyes. No, it couldn't happen yet. Not until they were alone. Alone and safe. His body trembled at the knowledge. It didn't matter. He'd wait forever if he had to. Still, nothing on earth was going to stop him from sampling a taste of what lay in store. He'd waited an eternity for that.

Besides, he had to show her, to tease her into wanting him as much as he wanted her. There was no other way. She had to remember, every time he stood near her, what it was like being in his arms. She had to know his kisses. Every time he said something and she looked at his mouth, she had to remember. Remember and want.

His hand ran over her back, never stopping until it smoothed over her thighs and then returned to the lushness of her backside. "Just let me kiss you once, and I'll stop."

"Just one kiss?" She breathed against his mouth, and Hawk knew one would never be enough. "Maybe two."

"Or three?" She thought she was being slightly amusing, but it came out sounding more like a breathless plea.

"All right. But that's all. Three kisses will have to be enough for you."

Abigail almost smiled. This man was dangerous. Very dangerous. She'd have to be . . . Abigail forgot her thoughts, forgot the fact that she was standing naked in this man's arms. Forgot everything but the feel of his mouth upon hers. One was quite enough. She hadn't remembered how good he was at this.

221

Well, perhaps she had remembered, but she'd desperately tried not to. For she knew how the touch of his mouth upon hers could rob her of her senses. Yes, one was really quite enough.

But two weren't. She shouldn't have allowed the first one, and now all she could think about was more. When she was able to think at all, that is.

Abigail breathed a sigh as he tore his mouth from hers. "How do you know how to do that?"

"What?" he asked as his mouth went on to discover the taste of her jaw, her throat, her chest.

Her head fell back as she allowed him the opportunity to really touch her with both his mouth and hands. Abigail thought she'd never known anything quite so lovely. "What?" she asked, losing her train of thought for a minute. "Oh yes, your lip, the way you move it."

"How?"

"Like this," and Abigail showed him just what she was talking about.

"That's very good," he said, and she moaned in agreement. "But you need more practice."

"I know. I haven't done this much."

"I'll let you practice whenever you like."

"That's very kind of you."

"It's easy to be kind to you."

Abigail couldn't believe that she was allowing this, and yet she felt no need to call a stop to the moment. She stood in his arms as he ran his hands, both his hands, over her, touching her everywhere and doing it again and again.

"You shouldn't touch me there." Abigail said the proper words but couldn't hold back her groan of pleasure as his hand slid between their bodies and settled at last just below her belly.

"Why not?"

"I don't know, but I'm sure you shouldn't."

His fingers dipped lower and she couldn't hold back a sharp gasp as he touched her. "Do you like it?"

A long moment of silence went by before she understood the question and found the courage to answer it. "I'm not sure. I think so."

"I love touching you there."

"Do you?"

"I wish we could lie down."

"It's probably better that we can't."

"I didn't feel you move," Abigail said as she realized for the first time that he was sitting and she was half reclining upon his lap.

"You haven't felt me at all," he gently reminded. "Put your hands on my chest."

Abigail never hesitated to obey and never knew such delight in obedience. "You feel so good."

"Not better than you."

"Your muscles are so big and your skin is smooth."

"Jesus."

"What's the matter?"

"Nothing. I just like this so much."

"Are you going to kiss me again?"

"There's one more to go, isn't there?"

"Yes."

"Do you want me to kiss you?"

"Yes."

"Do you want me to stop touching you?" His

hands were moving over the length of her, stopping only when her own searching fingers got in his way. He touched her everywhere, as if committing her body to memory.

"I don't think we should—" Abigail groaned and arched her back as he took the tip of her breast deep into a furnace of unbelievable heat. "Your mouth is so hot. I can't believe . . . Oh, God," she gasped as an ache, a terrible almost frightening ache, came to life just below her belly.

His fingers gently parted her flesh, easing just inside the soft folds of her body. Abigail not only allowed the intimacy but because his mouth still held her breast, found herself wanting to part her thighs so she might fully experience this lovely, remarkable moment. The gentle massage was more than she had ever expected. How was it possible that she had lived twenty-four years and never known that this could feel so good?

A heaviness settled across her abdomen, a heaviness that urged her to raise her hips toward his moving fingers. She made a soft whimpering sound that begged for more, that begged him to never stop.

The lower part of her body grew heavier, thicker, until it felt strangely disconnected from the rest of her. It seemed to throb with life, with some unnamed need. She strained toward his hand urging him to give her more, more, only she couldn't exactly say what it was she wanted.

Her belly grew tight, the tightness promising pain and she thought to back away, suddenly afraid of the unknown.

He felt her stiffen and knew she was pulling away.

224

MORE PASSION AND ADVENTURE AWAIT... YOUR TRIP TO A BIG ADVENTUROUS WORLD BEGINS WHEN YOU ACCEPT YOUR FIRST 4 NOVELS ABSOLUTELY *FREE* (AN $18.00 VALUE)

Accept your Free gift and start to experience more of the passion and adventure you like in a historical romance novel. Each Zebra novel is filled with proud men, spirited women and tempestuous love that you'll remember long after you turn the last page.

Zebra Historical Romances are the finest novels of their kind. They are written by authors who really know how to weave tales of romance and adventure in the historical settings you love. You'll feel like you've actually gone back in time with the thrilling stories that each Zebra novel offers.

GET YOUR FREE GIFT WITH THE START OF YOUR HOME SUBSCRIPTION

Our readers tell us that these books sell out very fast in book stores and often they miss the newest titles. So Zebra has made arrangements for you to receive the four newest novels published each month.

You'll be guaranteed that you'll never miss a title, and home delivery is so convenient. And to show you just how easy it is to get Zebra Historical Romances, we'll send you your first 4 books absolutely FREE! Our gift to you just for trying our home subscription service.

BIG SAVINGS AND FREE HOME DELIVERY

Each month, you'll receive the four newest titles as soon as they are published. You'll probably receive them even before the bookstores do. What's more, you may preview these exciting novels free for 10 days. If you like them as much as we think you will, just pay the low preferred subscriber's price of just $3.75 each. *You'll save $3.00 each month off the publisher's price.* AND, your savings are even greater because there are never any shipping, handling or other hidden charges—FREE Home Delivery. Of course you can return any shipment within 10 days for full credit, no questions asked. There is no minimum number of books you must buy.

4 FREE BOOKS

TO GET YOUR 4 FREE BOOKS WORTH $18.00 — MAIL IN THE FREE BOOK CERTIFICATE T O D A Y

Fill in the Free Book Certificate below, and we'll send your FREE BOOKS to you as soon as we receive it.

If the certificate is missing below, write to: Zebra Home Subscription Service, Inc., P.O. Box 5214, 120 Brighton Road, Clifton, New Jersey 07015-5214.

FREE BOOK CERTIFICATE
4 FREE BOOKS

ZEBRA HOME SUBSCRIPTION SERVICE, INC.

YES! Please start my subscription to Zebra Historical Romances and send me my first 4 books absolutely FREE. I understand that each month I may preview four new Zebra Historical Romances free for 10 days. If I'm not satisfied with them, I may return the four books within 10 days and owe nothing. Otherwise, I will pay the low preferred subscriber's price of just $3.75 each; a total of $15.00, *a savings off the publisher's price of $3.00.* I may return any shipment and I may cancel this subscription at any time. There is no obligation to buy any shipment and there are no shipping, handling or other hidden charges. Regardless of what I decide, the four free books are mine to keep.

NAME _____

ADDRESS _____ APT _____

CITY _____ STATE ____ ZIP _____

TELEPHONE ( ) _____

SIGNATURE _____
(if under 18, parent or guardian must sign)

Terms, offer and prices subject to change without notice. Subscription subject to acceptance by Zebra Books. Zebra Books reserves the right to reject any order or cancel any subscription.

ZB0494

GET
FOUR
FREE
BOOKS
(AN $18.00 VALUE)

ZEBRA HOME SUBSCRIPTION
SERVICE, INC.
120 BRIGHTON ROAD
P.O. Box 5214
CLIFTON, NEW JERSEY 07015-5214

He whispered against her flesh, "Let it come, sweetheart. Don't be afraid. I've got you."

His words might not have fully registered, but the low silkiness of his voice did. And it was exactly what was needed to relax her, to bring her to the edge of reason and over the side into a pit of madness. The waves of pleasure came then. One on top of another, so strong they hurt, and yet the hurting was better than anything she'd ever known.

Her body trembled. And as if it had a will of its own, it jerked forward and upward and she cried out at the unexpected blinding crash of ecstasy.

Her head fell back, over his arm and she breathed, "Oh Lord, Lord." And then once she was able to breathe normally again, "What was I saying?" she asked as his mouth released her, only to nibble on the tip of her breast and then to spread his tongue over the now slippery surface.

"That you love this."

"I think I do love it," she said, her surprise at her admittance obvious.

Hawk smiled and pulled her tightly against him, his face buried in her warm throat. "How do you feel?"

"Like I'm floating."

He chuckled a low very masculine and knowing sound. "I have to kiss you again."

"Yes."

"The next time, I'll have more than three."

"Yes," she said again.

He kissed her then, starting at first with a gentle brushing of lips and then a small sweet nibble and then more and more, he deepened the kiss until neither of them knew of time and place, but only of wanting. His lips parted, and she followed his lead and met them wider, wider, until her mouth was naught but an extension of his own and he breathed and tasted of her dark sweet magic like a man lost in his need for sustenance.

"Oh, Abby, my God," he said as he tore his mouth from hers. "I wish I could kiss you forever."

"I wouldn't mind just one more."

He groaned a sound of pain. "I can't."

"Why?"

"Because when I kiss you I come damn close to losing control, and I don't want this to go any further."

"Why?"

"Because, sweetheart, you're new at this." He breathed into her hair, knowing an unbearable ache at being unable to do more. "We have to go slow. Wait for the right time. I don't want to hurt you." What he meant was, he had to position her correctly for not only the most satisfying results but for the least amount of discomfort.

"I never thought I'd ever say this, but you'd better get dressed now."

Abigail felt a chill race down her back. In fact, she felt chilled all over and was suddenly struck with a sense of mortification that would not be soon nor easily matched. Not only had she allowed this man the free use of her body, she had actually asked for more. Nothing could have been more horrible, more catastrophic. What in the world could she have been thinking? And how had he managed to take advantage of a weak moment? How had he known she wouldn't resist?

"Let me up."

Hawk recognized the iciness in her tone and knew she was already having second thoughts. There was no way that he was going to allow her to leave him like this. His arms tightened around her.

"Don't be upset, sweetheart. What happened between us is only the first step. Soon you'll come to me and ask me to—"

"What?" she said loudly. If possible her body grew even more stiff. Hawk figured rightly that he'd been just a bit too honest. He hadn't meant to say it in exactly that fashion. He tried to defuse the moment, knowing even as he did, it was too late.

"All right, maybe that will take a little while, but . . ."

"Forever. It will take at least forever. I'd never ask a man to—"

"You don't think so?" he asked, annoyed at the fact that she could turn her emotions off and on so easily while he sat in the throes of this tormented and, thank you very much, unfulfilled need. "How much do you want to bet?"

Abigail scrambled her stiff form out of his arms and quickly searched out where she had dropped her clothes. She was pulling them on, faster than she'd ever dressed in her life, despite the fact that her entire body, including her fingers refused to stop trembling. Once again dressed she stood glaring her hatred at his shadowy form, never considering the fact that he could see no more clearly than she. "I hate you and would gladly die before I allow you to touch me again."

Having had little experience with virgins and the embarrassment they were bound to know after the moment of passion had passed (the ladies of his acquaintance being considerably more experienced), Hawk didn't understand what the hell her problem was. One minute she was hot, eager for his touch, the next hateful and colder than the Arctic. "Lady, you'll not only allow it, you'll beg for it."

"I wish you would die."

"A minute ago, you wished I would kiss you again."

"I never said that," she hotly denied. Well, she never said those words exactly. Had she? Abigail couldn't remember precisely.

"Get back to the cave."

"Drop dead."

"Do what I said." His voice was barely a low whisper of a threat. "Unless you're looking to see me finish what I started."

Abigail knew when to concede a point. She might not like the idea but was smart enough not to push him further. She figured she had gotten her message across anyway. There was no need to belabor the fact.

Chapter Eleven

"But you can't leave us here!"

Hawk looked across the fire at the still-weakened man and forced the sneer from his voice. "I can't wait any longer, and I'm taking her with me."

"What do you mean, *you're* taking her?"

Hawk's voice grew hard with determination. "I mean just what I said." There was no way that he was going to leave Abby behind, not with this sorry excuse of a man.

"She is my fiancée."

Hawk shook his head. "Understand this. She belongs to me." Hawk didn't bother to clarify that she didn't belong to him exactly, but he expected she soon would.

Robert sneered his disgust. "Abigail would never allow an Indian to touch—"

Hawk came to his feet and glared his own disgust. "I figure even an Indian is a better man than you."

Abigail chose just that moment to enter the cave. She'd made her decision while about her morning ablutions. There was no sense in waiting any longer.

229

She had her strength back and was anxious to see the last of this cave and the two men occupying it. She'd already lost quite a bit of time and figured she was almost two weeks behind Amanda now. Anything could have happened to her sister in two weeks. Nothing was going to stop her. She was leaving today.

Robert's voice as well as his gaze pleaded as she entered the cave. "Abigail, tell me it's not true. Tell me you're not leaving with him."

Abigail frowned. "Of course I'm not leaving with him," she said, and then at the look of gloating Robert shot toward Hawk, she finished with, "I'm not leaving with you either."

Hawk grinned. She might not think so, but she was. If he had to tie her to the horse, she was leaving with him.

"But darling. You can't—"

"I most certainly can, Robert. And I intend to do so this very morning."

"But what about us?"

"Us?" she asked with some drama. "I'm afraid there is no us."

"But darling," he whined in what Abigail supposed was a plea that should have melted any resolve.

"I'd appreciate it, Robert, if you could use my Christian name when addressing me. Darling is beginning to give me the shivers."

"What's the matter? Why are you acting like this? What have I done?"

"I think you know what you've done."

"What did he tell you?" Robert asked, while

230

shooting a grinning Hawk a look of venomous hate. "What lies has he . . ."

"If there is one thing I'm positive of, Robert, it's the fact that Mr. Hawk does not lie."

"Well, if he told you—"

"He didn't have to tell me that you were with one whore after another the entire time we spent in New Orleans, Robert. It took me a while, but I figured that out for myself."

"But how?" Robert couldn't believe this. He'd been discreet. There was no way that she could have known.

"Perhaps it's the fact that you've become diseased."

Robert's jaw dropped with shock. "That's a goddam lie."

Robert's eyes grew wide with shock, with horror at the very thought, even as his complexion paled some two or three shades. Abigail could see he hadn't known. She was sorry about blurting it out. She might not love this man, but she certainly didn't want to hurt him or, for that matter, see him dead. Still, the fact remained that if he had made her his wife, she would now be dying as well. The thought caused her an involuntary shudder. "The fact is, it's nothing less than a shame that anyone should die because of so insignificant an act."

Hawk only grinned. He knew she was directing the comment toward him and the fact that he'd told her she would come to him and ask for more. Apparently she had other ideas on the subject. Hawk figured he'd give her a while. The need would come upon her soon enough, now that she'd sampled a taste of what lay in store.

She hadn't spoken to him in two days. But he was a patient man and had every confidence that once she was over her snit, she'd be looking for more, and he was just about bursting to see her needs met.

"Who the hell is going to die? I don't care what this bastard told you. I am not diseased. Christ . . ." Robert frowned as he noticed what she was about. "What are you doing?"

Abigail reached into her saddlebags and produced her purse. Inside was a roll of bills. She peeled off a few, quite a few too many Hawk thought, and placed them at the foot of Robert's blanket. "I'm going to leave you with this. In a few days you should be strong enough to travel. This will help you get back."

"But what about . . . ?" Robert was about to say his creditors. He wished to hell that damn grinning Indian would leave them for a minute. He desperately needed to talk to her alone. "Do you mind?" he directed the question to Hawk.

"Not at all," Hawk returned, even as he leaned back against the cave wall and crossed his arms over his chest, ready and quite willing it seemed to hear even more.

"What I meant was, would you give us a moment of privacy?"

"Sure." Hawk shrugged. "Why not?" He moved to the edge of the cave and stepped outside. He came to a stop no more than three feet from the opening. There he crouched down, leaned against the mountain, and listened.

"Sweetheart . . ."

"Abigail," she reminded.

Robert breathed a sigh, shoved a hand, his uninjured hand, through his hair and began again. "Very well, Abigail, I swear it's not true."

"You have no sore?"

"Well, yes, as a matter of fact I do." He frowned, wondering how anyone could have known that. "But it's nothing. It always goes away."

"You mean it's reoccurring?"

"Now and then. I promise you, it's nothing."

"How long have you had it?"

"A few years." Robert shrugged as if it were of no matter.

"Have you seen a doctor?"

"Darl . . . I mean, Abigail, I promise you it's—"

Apparently he had not. Abigail shrugged. It was his life, after all, and if he refused medical care, who was she to insist? She cut off the last denial with, "Actually, Robert, it doesn't matter to me one way or the other. I don't want to see you die, of course, but I won't be marrying you in any case."

"But—"

"There's really no need to go on about it. You see, I've quite made up my mind."

Robert nodded at this bit of news and pressed his lips together as his mind sought out a solution to this dastardly turn of events. She was so cool, so calm. He could have dealt with tears, he thought, but this . . . Robert knew defeat when he faced it. Still, it was beyond his power to leave it go. He couldn't resist one last try. "You made some serious promises, you know."

"As did you. One of them, I think, was to remain faithful."

"And I had every intention to do just that once we were married," he lied.

Abigail nodded. She didn't know if he was telling the truth or not, and it didn't matter in the least. "The fact is, it's over. It would serve no purpose to press your cause."

"No, no. I understand, of course. If you no longer love me, why I couldn't expect you to . . ." His words dropped away. What the hell was he going to do now? How was he to return home and face his creditors? It was impossible.

"The fact is, Abigail, I was wondering if you could advance me a small loan."

"I just gave you—"

"I know, but I'm sorry to say I need more. Much more."

"Why?"

"I'll have to pay off a debt or two."

"How much?"

Robert named a figure, and Abigail gasped her shock. It was more than all her business interests combined brought in in a whole year.

She had to ask, "Was Hawk right? Have you no business interests? No income?"

There was no sense in propagating the lie. At this moment he had nothing to gain and much to lose. He hated to do it, but he had no choice but to throw himself on her mercy. God damn that dirty Indian. He nodded.

"How in the world did you spend so much?"

Robert shrugged. "I told them I was marrying you, and my credit became suddenly limitless."

"I'm glad I was good for something, at least. Certainly you showed me not a shred of respect with your flagrant whoring."

"Abigail, darling, men will be—"

She cut him off. "Actually, Robert, I don't care what men will be. I can't even figure out why God created them. I've never seen a more useless collection of egomaniacs." She leaned forward just a bit and asked, "Perhaps you could tell me, what exactly *are* you good for?"

Hawk chuckled just outside the cave's opening and silently promised the time was coming when he'd show her just how much good could be found in a man.

Abigail didn't miss the soft humorous sound. Good. It was time she thought, well past time, in fact, that he knew exactly what she thought of him.

Robert felt some real desperation. Right now he'd agree to just about anything. "Yes, well, I . . ."

"All right. I'll give you a thousand dollars. I'll have it ready for you at the bank, once I return home." Abigail saw that the amount didn't at all satisfy. A thousand dollars didn't come close to paying off his debts, but she felt no sympathy for his plight, no weakening of her resolve. After all, she owed him nothing and was giving only out of the kindness of her heart. She breathed a weary sigh. "That will have to do, I'm afraid."

"It will be at the bank waiting for me?" The shock of her breaking off their engagement was beginning to wane. Robert began to think again. With a thousand dollars, plus the sale of just about everything he had left, including horses and perhaps even some of his clothes, he could leave town. He could leave the country. Yes, that might be the way to go. Once away from his creditors, he could start again. Perhaps he could find another lady, maybe one even richer than Abigail.

Abigail nodded. "I'll make sure of it."

"You might have to wait on that for a bit," Hawk said coming inside the cave. "She won't be returning home for some time."

"Ignore him," Abigail said to Robert, while shooting Hawk a passing glance of irritation.

"I wouldn't," Hawk warned. And then he turned to Abigail and said, "Abby, I don't know how long we will be. If you feel you should give him something, give him whatever you've got on you. You won't be needing it. I have a few dollars with me."

Abigail only shot him another silent angry glare and began to pack up her things. She was rolling her blanket to tie it behind her saddle when Hawk came to stand upon it. "You're ignoring me," he pointed out gently.

"How astute of you."

Hawk laughed. "I think this is going to be mighty interesting."

"I suppose you're waiting for me to ask what?"

"I'll make it easy for you. It's going to be interesting watching you grow into an obedient—" He was going to say wife, but Abigail cut him off with a laugh. "You won't live long enough to see me obedient."

"I like you all feisty. It reminds me of the night—"

Abigail glanced at Robert and then realized she was shooting the wrong man a desperate look. She felt her cheeks grow red with embarrassment and hissed, "Shut up!"

But Hawk ignored her order and continued on with, "—you sat at the campfire singing tavern songs. A bit unsavory to some maybe, but I thought you were delightful."

Abigail frowned. She hadn't expected him to say that. The fact was, she never remembered her actions the night the stagecoach overturned, so she thought he was either mistaking her for another or making the whole thing up. "Get your ladies straight, Mr. Hawk."

"You don't remember?"

"Get out of my way." She meant to shove him aside, but all the pushing against him managed to do was to knock her backward. Her hands were on her hips as she glared. "Move off my blanket."

Hawk did as she ordered. "How did you learn them?"

"Learn what?" she asked as she finished with the blanket and glanced around the cave, making sure she left nothing behind.

"Tavern ditties. Ladies don't usually know them."

"Maybe I'm not a lady." Abigail grunted as she picked up her saddle, blanket, and saddlebags and looked at her former fiancé. "Goodbye, Robert."

A moment later she was outside the cave with Hawk rushing to get his things together and catch up.

"You didn't say goodbye to me," he said, finding her at her horse, in the midst of saddling the animal.

"That's because I'm ignoring you."

"I think you should kiss me goodbye. It's the least you could do."

"For what?" She shot him a look of astonishment, for kissing him was the very last thing on her lists of things to do. The truth of the matter was, it wasn't on her list at all.

Abigail mounted her horse and turned the animal toward the east and the rising sun. "Goodbye, Mr. Hawk."

"Just a minute," he said as he grabbed at her reins. "You're heading in the wrong direction."

Abigail wrenched the reins free of his grasp and dug her heels into the horse's sides. In a flash she was darting through heavy foliage, bent low over the saddle; her every movement spoke of confidence that she would make good her escape.

Abigail was an expert horsewoman, but even her expertise was no match for Hawk. He was behind her within seconds. She hurried the horse, allowing him more rein, even as her heels hit into his sides again.

And then suddenly she seemed to be propelled into the air. She'd thought at first that the horse had taken a spill, but no. A strong, inflexibly hard arm had grasped her tightly around her waist and swung her from one horse to another, as if she weighed little more than a feather. Only this time she was hanging over a saddle instead of sitting upon one.

Abigail screamed her fury. Even though her hair hung over her face, almost blinding her to everything but the quickly passing ground, she had no need to see. She knew who had so sorely abused her. "I'm going to kill you!"

"Calm down," he said, his hand flat but firmly upon her rear as she bounced along.

Abigail grunted with every jolting step of the animal beneath her belly. If he didn't stop soon, the beast would surely do her ribs some real damage.

Hawk slowed the horse at last. Abigail had no way of knowing he had gone after her own horse and now held the reins of both in his hand.

"I don't want to have to tie you, but—"

She bit his leg.

"Ow! You little—"

Before Hawk could stop her, she bit him again.

Hawk smacked her rear—*hard*.

Abigail screamed her rage and reached behind her. With a balled fist she caught him a respectable blow on the side of his waist.

Hawk shoved her off his horse.

Abigail sat on the ground, her hands behind her a bit for balance as she waited for the world to stop spinning.

"Don't bite me again."

Abigail swung her hair from her face and glared a silent promise for many more where that came from as an answer.

"Next time I'll give your ass more than one smack."

"If you touch me again, I'll put a bullet between your eyes."

Hawk thought she just might carry through on that threat, so he reached for her rifle and slid it inside his blanket, retying the rope to make sure it stayed in place. He knew she didn't have any other weapons. His gaze moved over her lush form; he didn't miss the way her breasts pushed against her shirtfront and reconsidered. Well, no weapons that could kill a man, at least.

"We're going to have to get a few things straight."

"Go to hell."

"You'll be coming with me."

"Drop dead."

Hawk smiled. "Abby, I know you're anxious to find your sister, and I promise I'll help you, but first I have business to attend to."

"It can't wait. I have to find her now."

"It has to wait. I can't let you wander through this forest alone."

"Then come with me."

"I will, once I find the men who murdered my father."

"I'll stay with Robert then. Once he can travel . . ."

"No good."

"Why?"

"I need you." God, but that was an understatement.

"For what?"

"You saw the men, didn't you? At least one of them? I'm going to need you to identify them." That wasn't entirely true, of course. She might be able to identify one of them, but that wasn't the real reason he wanted her with him. The truth was, he had no intention of ever letting her go again. Hawk figured, for the present at least, it would be a wise move on his part to keep that bit of information to himself.

"It was dark. I didn't get a good look."

Hawk ignored her comment.

"I'm not going with you."

Still, he said nothing.

Abigail shook her head, came to her feet, and re-mounted her horse. She tugged on the reins. Hawk refused to let them go. Instead he tied them to his saddle.

Abigail shot him a hate-filled glare that promised untold suffering if he didn't allow her instant freedom.

Hawk merely shook his head. "I'm sorry, Abby."

"You're going to be a lot sorrier," she said as she dismounted and started to walk.

Hawk jumped from his horse and followed. "Abby, I'm trying to be fair. After I finish with those men, I swear I'll help you find your sister."

Abigail said nothing.

"Are you listening to me?" he asked, ducking a branch she had purposely let go, hoping it would hit his face.

Again nothing.

Hawk grabbed her shoulder and forced her to face him. "We're wasting time."

"Not me."

Hawk figured she was right about that. She might not have made much progress, but at least she was heading in the right direction. "Are you going to listen to me?" he asked one more time, and when the question brought nothing but sneering silence, he swung her over his shoulder and started back to where he'd left the horses, ignoring the punches she delivered to his back and the curses that flowed freely over the all but silent forest.

Suddenly he swung her back to her feet. She was

241

obviously dizzy and staggered a bit, but Hawk forced himself to show her no compassion lest she take his concern for weakness. She had to know, as of right now, that he wasn't about to take any more of her nonsense. "Don't confuse me with your boyfriend, Abby." He gave a short nod toward the cave above them. "I'm a man. And no woman is ever going to control me."

"Oh, so you're a man, are you? Well, I wouldn't be so proud of the fact if I were you."

Hawk laughed. "You've got a thing or two to learn about men, I think."

"Taking for granted, of course, that I'm interested in learning about them."

Knowing she wouldn't admit interest under the threat of death, Hawk changed the subject. "You have two options. I tie you to your horse, or you ride with me."

"My horse," she said, knowing anything would be preferable to being forced to share a saddle with him. She'd done that before, and the last thing she wanted was to feel his body pressed tightly to hers again. Then she realized her mistake. She'd never get away once he tied her. She should have said she'd ride with him, at least then she might have found the opportunity to run. Still, she said nothing as he bound her hands together and then tied them to her saddle.

It wasn't until he had mounted his horse that she said, "If I fall and kill myself, it will be your fault."

Hawk glanced at her and realized the very real possibility of her words coming true. Tied to a horse she wouldn't be able to escape if the animal should take a fall. Hawk said nothing, but simply leaned over and pulled the ropes free. A second later she was sitting in front of him, his arm securely around her waist as both animals began a steady pace through the woods, the sun at their backs.

Amanda placed the platter before the man and smiled at his "Thank you, miss."

"You're welcome, sir," she said as she had a dozen times in the last hour.

She would have moved away from the table then, but for the sudden wave of dizziness that assaulted. It was the heat and the smell of food. For the last few days, the combination had caused her stomach to roll sickeningly.

Amanda thought she had kept her secret well, for she imagined Mr. Cassidy had not noticed her quick trips to the privy, nor her white complexion upon her return. She didn't want him to know about the baby. She wasn't at all sure she could keep her job if he found out.

Amanda felt again the sudden lurching nausea. She had to get to the back, and she had to be quick about it. She took two steps, wondering if she hadn't waited just a moment too long, when an arm circled her and a hand squeezed roughly at her breast. A low, supposedly sensuous, voice whispered near her ear. "You're a ripe little piece, aren't you? I could make it worth your while if you joined me for a toss upstairs."

Amanda struggled to free herself of his hold. She couldn't tell him of her distress. There simply wasn't time.

As it turned out, he found out without a word spoken on her part.

Amanda tried to fight him, but she was a small woman and her strength was no match for a man. He turned her into his arms and then jumped away as she was suddenly heaving all over the front of his shirt.

The man simply stood there. It was his friend's laughter that snapped him from his shock. He cursed and raised his hand to strike her, as if she'd had the ability to throw up on command and had done it on purpose. His hand was still in the air, high above his head when he landed face first on the floor.

Amanda only blinked her surprise. She hadn't realized Mr. Cassidy had left the bar and was standing at her side. A moment later she felt the room swing dizzily around her as Mr. Cassidy brought her into his arms and headed for the kitchen.

"I'm sorry. Oh, Lord, I'm so sorry," she moaned as he sat her upon a chair just outside the back door.

"It's all right, Amanda. Don't worry yourself about it." He handed her a clean towel and she wiped her face and the front of her dress clean. "Maybe the next time Parker will ask before he touches."

Amanda shot her employer a look of gratitude. "He was going to hit me." She shivered at the thought of being abused again. "Thank you."

"How do you feel?"

"Oh, I always feel better after I . . ." her voice dwindled down to silence when she realized what she'd just said. Now he'd know that this was a common occurrence. That she got sick most every night.

"I thought so," Bill Cassidy said. "How far along are you?"

Amanda gasped. She'd thought she'd kept her secret so well. How did he know? "Mr. Cassidy, please. I need the work. I—"

"How far, Amanda?"

"I'm not sure." She sighed, disheartened at his insistence. This was the end, of course. She couldn't expect him to keep on a serving girl who was with child. "Almost three months, I think."

"And your husband? Where is he?"

Amanda bit her lips, unable to face this kind man, while saying what must be said. For some reason, that he should think well of her was terribly important. She didn't want to see the disillusionment he'd surely know once she told him the truth. Still, she had little choice but to say, "I have no husband."

Bill Cassidy knew a deep sense of relief and then sadness for her plight. She had no husband. Most would look down on her. Most would hold her in disgrace, but he couldn't find it in himself to do as much. There was something about this girl that was sweet and innocent, no matter her present circumstances. She'd been here more than a week, and as each day passed it became harder to think of anything but her. He knew, of course, that he was in love. Knowing now that she was going to have a baby didn't lessen the emotion. If anything, it only seemed to intensify it and this need to care for her.

He wanted most of all to take her into his arms and soothe away her fears. He wanted to tell her everything was going to be all right. But he couldn't. Not yet. She'd be afraid if she knew the things he felt. Perhaps she'd even run away.

Bill Cassidy suffered under no delusion that he was

in any way a special man. Perhaps that was exactly why he was most special of all. To his way of thinking, he was too big, too brawny, too ugly, too stupid, and probably too soft. Women didn't seem to like a man who was gentle. Still, he was what he was and couldn't do much about that. Maybe, just maybe, she was different. Maybe she could grow to, if not love him, at least like him a little. And for that to happen he'd have to make sure she stayed on for a while.

"Are you completely alone?"

"No. I have a sister, but she lives far from here." Amanda had no idea that home was little more than a three-day ride away.

Bill nodded. "Have you seen a doctor?"

She shook her head.

"You will tomorrow."

Amanda looked at him then, surprised to find his gaze filled with concern. "But, I have no . . ."

"I'll take care of it." He watched her for a long moment before he added, "Go to bed now."

"But—"

"Go to bed, Amanda. You'll feel better in the morning."

Amanda did feel better the following morning, but she could have told Mr. Cassidy that she would. She always felt good in the morning. It was only at night, especially when faced with heat and the smell of food, that she found herself less than well.

She washed, dressed, and brushed her hair, pinning it neatly to the nape of her neck before pulling on a lacy cap. She left her room, her intent to clean the tavern room thoroughly. She hadn't worked last night and felt she owed her employer at least that much.

The chairs were piled upon otherwise empty tables, and she was on her hands and knees scrubbing the floor when Bill Cassidy entered the room. "What are you doing?"

Amanda smiled at the work she'd already accomplished. "Don't walk over there. The floor is wet."

"You didn't answer me."

"Is something wrong?"

"No, nothing is wrong. I just don't want you scrubbing floors."

"But I didn't work last night. I thought I would—"

He cut her off with, "Amanda, you know I have a boy who comes in here to do that."

"Yes, but—"

"Come over here. It's time we had a talk."

Amanda dropped the brush back into the pail and followed her employer to a table. He removed the chairs and sat, motioning for her to do the same.

Amanda knew he was going to ask her to leave. She steeled herself, awaiting the words, and knew no little surprise when she heard instead, "Have you eaten?"

Amanda raised her wide-eyed gaze from the table. "Not yet."

"You should take better care of yourself."

She smiled but said nothing.

A long moment of silence went by before he surprised both of them by asking, "What happened to him?"

Amanda knew he was asking about the baby's

father. She worried her bottom lip, refusing to look at him again and almost whispered, "He died."

Bill Cassidy knew there was more to it than the simple fact that the man had died. He'd never in his life seen a woman more afraid, more . . . What? Guilty? "How?"

Amanda didn't know how he had done it, but she knew he knew. She couldn't have been more wrong, for Bill Cassidy had no idea he was about to hear a confession. "Mr. Cassidy, I swear I didn't mean to—"

"Bill," he interrupted. "Call me Bill."

She nodded. "Bill, I didn't mean to do it. He just fell."

"What do you mean?"

"He was hitting me. I was trying to get away. I kicked him. At least I think I kicked him, and he fell. He hit his head."

"You mean you killed him?" Christ, he hadn't expected to hear this.

"Oh, please don't tell." Her blue eyes pleaded as she twisted her hands in anguish. "They'll put me in prison and take my baby if they find out."

Bill reached for her hands and held them firmly in his grasp. His eyes were warm and gentle when he said, "Tell me the whole story."

It took the good part of a half hour, but Amanda told him everything. Even the part about the man in Memphis. The man called Max Dallas. What he had tried to do to her and how he, too, had died.

Bill figured the baby's father deserved to die but was probably alive and well. Amanda didn't know much about the male anatomy. Kicking a man as he stood over you could easily result in watching him crumple to the floor. Hitting his head had probably only knocked him out. The bastard in Memphis was probably dead. A fall like that would surely do a man in. Bill wished him all his just rewards.

He'd known, of course, right from the first, that she'd been hiding something, but he hadn't expected a woman like her to have been through so much. "What are you going to do now?"

"I don't know. Are you going to send for the constable?"

"No."

"Why not?"

"Because you shouldn't have to suffer for what two men tried to do to you."

It took a long moment before she finally said, "Oh, God, I can't believe it. Really? You're not going to tell?"

Bill smiled. She looked so hopeful, almost childlike. He wanted more than anything to wrap his arms around her and tell her everything would be all right. He shook his head. "No. I'll never say a word about it again."

Amanda frowned. It couldn't be this easy. Even the man who had loved her had wanted something from her. Would a stranger do this simply out of the kindness of his heart? "What do you want?" she suddenly asked.

And without thinking, Bill returned, "To take care of you."

"What?" she asked, obviously startled by the admission. "Why?"

Bill shrugged. It was too soon to tell her he loved

her. Much too soon. He didn't want to scare her away, so he said, "I'm alone. I have no one. You have no one as well. I could take care of you and your baby if you let me."

"Why would you want to do that?" She looked like a frightened child, and Bill vowed if she gave him the chance, she'd never have to be afraid again.

"Amanda, there's no need to be afraid of me. I'd never hurt you."

"But—"

"If you want to leave, I'll advance you the money. But if you decide to stay, we'll have to get married." Bill came from his chair and reached a huge hand to her shoulder. "You don't have to decide right now. Think about it for a few days."

"Wait a minute," she said as he started from the room. "What do you mean, we'll have to get married?"

"I mean you're in a family way. You need a man's protection. I'd have to kill the first man who said anything about you. If you were my wife, no one would dare."

Amanda felt completely dazed. He'd have to *kill* a man for *me!?* She couldn't fathom the possibility. No one had ever said anything like that before. No one had ever . . . She couldn't think and yet she knew she must.

Amanda left the tavern and walked toward the woods behind the inn. She spent most of the morning there, trying to decide what to do.

Hours later she realized it was almost time for the noon coach to arrive. People would be wanting to eat before starting again on their way. She'd have to go back.

Amanda slid inside the kitchen and almost laughed aloud as Mrs. Washington slapped Bill's hand. They both turned at the sound of her muffled laughter. Bill grinned at the laughter she couldn't hide. "I told you to keep your hands out of that pie."

"Now don't go fussin' on me. I just wanted a little taste."

"It tastes just like it always does. Leave it alone."

"I'm hungry."

"You're always hungry. Get out of my kitchen."

"It's my kitchen."

"Not while I'm working in it. Go on, now. Get going."

Amanda grinned as Bill gave a helpless shrug and obeyed the woman's command.

Amanda tied an apron around a minuscule waist that had not yet begun to thicken and poured a cup of coffee from the pot. A moment later a meat pie came from the oven. She cut a large piece and took both coffee and pie into the tavern room. She placed them before a surprised Bill.

"What's this for?"

"You."

"Why?"

"Because you said you were hungry."

He was standing behind the bar, Amanda sitting on one of the stools facing him. They smiled at one another, at least one of them seeing, for the first time, the other in a new and not altogether displeasing light. Neither had a chance to do or say more before

251

the door to the inn opened and six hungry travelers entered.

Late that night a very tired Amanda sat alone in the tavern room. She'd been thinking all day about Bill's proposal. It would have been easy to say yes, for she'd never need more the title of Mrs., as well as a father for her baby, if it weren't for one thing. One very scary fact. If she married him, she'd have to sleep with him. Amanda was positive she wasn't ready for that.

She should go home, she thought. But if she did, Abigail would have to share her shame. A woman could expect only brutal treatment if she found herself in Amanda's condition without a husband. Could she bring that kind of shame on her own sister?

She wished she knew what to do.

"Why are you still up?"

Amanda glanced at the man who had caused her so much confusion today and smiled at his gentle expression. "I was thinking."

He sat opposite her. "About our conversation this morning?"

"Yes."

"Have you decided?"

"Not yet."

"Good. I wanted to tell you something before you did."

Amanda said nothing but waited for him to go on.

"Well, it's . . . I don't know how to say it exactly . . . but . . ."

He seemed to be having quite a bit of trouble saying anything at all. Amanda couldn't imagine why. "What?"

"If you marry me, you can keep the same room," he said in a rush.

"What?"

"I mean, you don't have to . . . you know—" He shrugged and then amazed Amanda by turning a bright red. "—Sleep with me. You can keep the same room."

"Ever?" Amanda couldn't have been more astonished. She'd never heard of such a thing.

"Not until you're ready. I mean, not until you want . . . I mean, not until you get used to me."

She said nothing but simply stared at him.

"Do you understand?"

"I think so. It's just that I've never heard of a husband and wife sleeping in separate rooms."

"Oh, well, we could sleep in the same room if you want, but I swear I wouldn't touch you."

"Why?"

"Because I don't want you to be afraid."

Amanda nodded in understanding even as a frown creased her forehead.

"What's the matter?"

"I don't think I've ever met a man like you before."

Bill thought he rather liked that notion and couldn't stop himself from asking, "What do you mean?"

"I mean you're so kind."

"Oh, that," Bill said, his voice sounding oddly disappointed. He knew for a fact that women didn't much like men who were kind. Women equated kindness with weakness. He'd lost his first wife because of that, hadn't he? She had told him he was a weakling, and he probably was. He hadn't done a thing when she'd told him she was leaving him for another man, except watch her walk out of his life.

Bill's mind was on his first wife and the pain he had known because of a weakness he couldn't seem to control, therefore he knew nothing but shock when Amanda said, "I think I will marry you, Bill."

She laughed at what could only be called a shocked expression. "It's what you wanted, isn't it?"

Bill couldn't find his voice. His face turned red again. He'd never been so embarrassed in his life. Imagine a man not being able to respond to a woman who just consented to marry him.

All he could do for the moment was nod.

"Good. Should we do it soon?"

"Get married, you mean?"

She smiled again. "Have I given you the wrong answer? Did you want me to refuse?"

"No! No, definitely not. I'll talk to the minister tomorrow."

She nodded as he came from his chair and left the room, only to suddenly return. "I don't want to scare you, but I think we should act like we love each other. At least when we talk to Reverend Stone."

She nodded. "Of course."

"Well, you can act like you always do. I'll act like I'm in love."

Amanda nodded again and found it impossible to stop smiling.

Chapter Twelve

Abigail had no notion of course that the very day she'd been kidnapped by this aggravating beast, her sister was very well protected, very well loved, in fact, even if it wasn't common knowledge just yet.

She sat on a rock as she watched him make a fire. "How the hell did you stay warm at night."

Abigail frowned at the question. "When?"

"When you were traveling with Robert."

"With a fire, of course."

"Really? Did you buy that, too?" Hawk was aware that they had not lived off the land but bought their supplies at farmhouses and inns passed along the way.

"No, as a matter of fact, I made it."

"I thought you said you couldn't make a fire."

"I said I wouldn't make a fire. I'm not about to do one thing to help you."

"Oh, you won't? Fine, then I won't do one thing to feed you."

"Fine."

"Fine."

Abigail came to her feet.

"Where do you think you're going?"

She turned around, ready to deliver yet another snide remark and gasped. He was standing right behind her. Actually he was standing now right in front of her. "You scared me."

Hawk offered no apology. "Where were you going?"

"To get my blanket. Since I won't be eating, I might as well go to sleep."

"You could make things easier on yourself by cooperating."

"With *you?*" She shot him a look that told clearly her low regard. "I don't think so."

"Abby, you're only spiting yourself."

"Well, you won't be suffering for it, so what do you care?"

Hawk watched her settle down beside the fire. Wrapped inside the blanket, she turned her back to both him and the fire. The fact was, he hadn't needed her help. So why had he insisted on it or deny her food? Hawk shook his head. The woman forced him to say things he never would have dreamed of saying. "Stubborn woman," he mumbled as he prepared a pot of coffee. It didn't matter that he was equally as stubborn, or maybe it was best that he was. A woman like Abby would take advantage of a weaker man. He'd seen how she treated Robert. Well, she could think again if she planned to treat him the same.

The truth was, Abby wasn't planning on treating him one way or another. What she was planning on was escape.

She lay there a long time waiting for him to finish

256

his meal, waiting for him to settle down for the night, waiting for her chance.

She didn't realize until he rolled from her side the next morning that she'd fallen asleep. Worse yet, he had joined her beneath her blanket and she had been snuggled against his warmth. She shivered now in the early morning chill and scowled at his naked back.

Why in the world did the man refuse to wear a shirt? Wasn't he cold? Granted she'd heard that Indians often went without shirts, but the only time she had seen Indians at all was in town, and while there they had dressed appropriately.

She wondered why Hawk had so drastically changed his mode of dress. He couldn't look more different than the man she'd known in New Orleans. Except perhaps for the fact that his trousers were still too tight.

Hawk, unaware of her scrutiny, slid his gun belt around his narrow hips and pulled his leather vest over his shoulders. He turned, and thinking she was still asleep, glanced in her direction. He knew some surprise as he watched her gaze travel up his length. "What's the matter?"

Abigail hadn't realized he was watching her watch him. "Nothing."

Hawk grinned. He didn't think it was nothing. He knew admiration in a woman's eyes when he saw it. Only he figured it would be a long time before she admitted to it.

He wondered for just a second what she would say if he told her the truth. If he told her how he really felt about her. Hawk gave a quick shake of his head. He hadn't a doubt she'd sneer her contempt and ridicule those feelings. Probably wouldn't believe him, in any case. No, it was best, he thought, to wait on that for a spell.

He made a pot of coffee and watched as she came from the blanket and disappeared behind a thick bush. A few moments later she walked toward the stream, some ten yards away. She washed her face, rubbed at her teeth with powder taken from her saddlebags, and brushed her hair.

"Breakfast is ready," he said.

"How nice for you," she remarked as she replaced both her brush and tooth powder in her bags.

"I meant *our* breakfast is ready," he said.

"You mean you're offering me food? Why?"

"Because there's no sense in your getting sick. It would only slow us down."

Abigail sneered at his words. So what had she expected? Kindness? Hardly.

They ate in silence, Hawk glancing now and then at a face devoid of all emotion, her rigid shoulders and stiff back. She was still furious with him. He didn't mind her anger so much as her silence. God, even her sneering contempt was preferable to being ignored.

Hawk, hardly a man to prattle on about nothing, tried twice to initiate conversation, once remarking on the weather and next on the succulent bacon, only to receive a stony glare of silence for an answer.

He sighed and then decided it wouldn't hurt things any to make sure she knew what might lie ahead for them. "Abby . . ."

"What?" She kept her gaze to her plate of bacon and beans.

"I'm going to give you a gun. In case anything happens to me, I want you to save the last bullet for yourself." Hawk had every confidence that things would never come to that point. Still, it wouldn't hurt if she knew there was some danger involved. It also wouldn't hurt if she came to depend on him a bit more either. Maybe even grow a little afraid for him.

Abigail raised her gaze to his, and Hawk felt his chest squeeze with emotion. She hadn't thought to hide her concern. "What? What do you mean—if something should happen to you?"

"The men I'm after are murderers. There's no telling what might happen."

She shivered at the thought of facing those men again. All she could think to do was run in the opposite direction, and yet this man insisted on following them. "Then why are we out here alone? Why haven't you gotten some men together to hunt them down?"

"Because *I'm* going to kill them."

"You're going to kill them?" she repeated. "Just like that?"

"Exactly like that."

"But I thought lawmen didn't . . . I . . . I mean, I thought you would arrest them."

"They killed my father."

Abigail had been aware of that fact, but she hadn't suspected until this moment how very deeply this man suffered over the fact. She didn't want to ask. She didn't want to know, and yet despite her silent insistence, she heard the words, "You were close to your father?"

Hawk shrugged. "I guess."

Abigail was positive that shrug was meant to hide

259

the depth of his feelings. But it was his eyes that told of an intensity of emotion so profound it nearly took her breath away. She wondered for just a fleeting moment if anyone would ever love her with that kind of fervor. And then almost groaned knowing she'd made a serious mistake. She didn't want to know this man. She didn't want to understand the reasons behind his actions. And most of all, she didn't want to feel anything. Not anything at all.

Abigail vowed it made no difference. She understood that this man was driven to find those responsible for his father's death, but she was driven as well—to find a sister who might be in desperate need.

The second night they made camp, Abigail was still awake when Hawk settled down at her side. She had expected this. She knew the only reason he slept so close was to make sure she did not escape. That was all right with her. Soon she'd hear the steady rhythm of his breathing and know he slept. Then she would ease herself away. With any kind of luck at all, he wouldn't even know she was gone until the morning sun came to wake him up.

Please, God.

She lay there for the longest time. He was breathing regularly. He was sleeping, but it wasn't enough. He had to be deeply asleep before she dared to make her move.

The thought came that it was too bad that he didn't sleep with his gun. If she could have gotten her hands on the weapon, it wouldn't have mattered if he were awake or not. She would have simply aimed it in his direction and kept it pointed at him until she was out of sight.

She waited. It felt like for hours and then finally, breathlessly, she eased herself away from him. She'd moved only an inch or two, and his arm came suddenly over her hip.

Oh, God, please!

Abigail groaned out a silent curse as he shifted, groaned and settled down again. She should have moved before. Now she had to come from beneath his arm. Lord, it would be nothing less than a miracle if she could do it. She almost groaned in despair as his leg came over hers.

It took something like the better part of an hour. At least it felt as if it had, but she was finally free of his hold. Abigail lay upon the ground, exhausted from the patience, energy, and self-control so far expended. Sliding from under his weight, and doing it without awakening him, had been the hardest thing she'd ever done in her life.

She came silently to her feet. A moment later she was untying her horse from a tree branch. There was no time to saddle the animal. She couldn't take the time or chance discovery.

Abigail had ridden bareback before. It hadn't been a pleasant or easy chore, but she'd do it again now. She'd ride a buffalo if it meant getting away from this man.

"Going somewhere?"

Abigail jumped at the sound of his voice, the words whispered close to her ear. And that's all she did. A second later she dropped the horse's reins and without saying a word, walked back to the blankets. Deep inside the covering, she was almost asleep by the time Hawk joined her. She never even noticed that she moved to accommodate him, nor that she snuggled her rear very comfortably into the front of his thighs.

The next night the events repeated themselves, but her subsequent recapture was hardly taken with the same degree of cool and calm composure.

Just as she had the night before, she again crept from the warmth of their shared blankets, only this time she kept looking at where he slept. Again and again she glanced behind her, thanking God every time she found him still there, still obviously asleep. Apparently he thought that last night's fiasco had cured her of any further attempts. Abigail almost snorted a laugh, catching herself just in time.

Gently, hardly daring to breathe, she backed the horse into the darkness, away from the camp light.

Abigail shivered at the thought of riding into the forest alone at night. She knew danger awaited her at every turn, but what choice had she? Every day that passed took her farther away from her sister.

Tonight, because both horses stood tied in the shadows, away from the light of the fire, she took the time to saddle it. She was in the midst of mounting, actually had her left foot in the stirrup and her right leg high, about to place it over the animal's back, when the saddle simply, and for no apparent reason, fell from his back. Abigail grunted at the fall and now lay sprawled upon the ground, unable for a second to understand what had happened. And then she saw moccasin feet before her and knew he had somehow sneaked up on her and released the saddle. How in the world he had done it? She couldn't have ventured a guess—and to have done it without making a sound was, to her way of thinking, nothing less than eerie. But Abigail was hardly of the mind to dwell on such matters. The fact was, it took only the sight of his feet to bring about a burning rage that would not soon be equaled.

"You bastard!"

She came to her feet, with arms swinging and lunged at him.

Hawk blocked one punch and then another. A moment later he pulled her hands behind her back and gave her a hard shake. "You're going to hurt yourself."

"Maybe," she sneered, "but I'm going to kill you first."

"Don't make me tie you, Abby."

"You slime!" She wiggled from his hold, but instead of running when she had the chance, she charged at him again, contacting with two blows, one to each side of his face, before he had the chance to stop her.

Hawk knew some surprise and instantly decided he'd been too easy with her. He couldn't let her go. There was absolutely no way, and if it took a little rough treatment on his part before she saw the error of her ways, so be it.

He shoved her to the ground.

Abigail landed with a bounce that rattled her teeth. Her mouth twisted into a sneer. "You bastard. You—"

"Shut up," he said, suddenly flinging himself upon her. Abigail blinked her surprise as he put a hand over her mouth, an arm around her waist, and rolled

263

them both farther into the protection of the woods.

A moment later Abigail realized what he was about as she heard a voice call out, "Hello? Anybody here?"

Sweet Mother of God. Abigail felt her entire body go slack with relief. Her prayers had been answered. Someone had come. She was going to get away from this madman.

Abigail shot her abuser a look of gloating, missed of course, since his attention was at the moment on their visitor. It didn't matter. He'd be sure to see it later. She almost couldn't wait. She watched with a giddy sense of anticipation as a man rode into the camp. His clothes were torn and dirty, his hat having seen better days, his mustache and beard long and unkempt. He looked tired, and considering the long look he shot toward a pan that held the remains of their supper, was probably hungry—but what caught Abigail's full attention was the fact that the campfire reflected upon the badge pinned to his chest. It sparkled with light. And Abigail knew all the jewels in the world couldn't have offered half so brilliant a sight. Oh, thank you, God.

She almost laughed aloud her joy and actually did a tiny little jig the moment Hawk helped her to her feet, her happiness knowing no bounds, until the vile monster started to speak. She caught only a word or two, her shock being so great, she couldn't seem to find the words to deny.

He saw her stiffen and back away, but Hawk grabbed her shoulder, holding her at his side.

Abigail glanced at her abductor, her mouth open with shock at his incredible gall, as she heard the beast calmly tell the lawman that she was his prisoner.

"Don't believe him. He's lying." Abigail tried to shake him off; her actions only seemed to prove his words.

Hawk threw the man his identification.

"What's she wanted for?"

"Bank robbery. She's part of the Olster gang. Married to one of them, I think."

Abigail couldn't believe how easily this man lied. She said again, this time forcing herself to remain calm, "He's lying. My name is Abigail Pennyworth, and I'm being kidnapped."

Sheriff Johnson frowned, never once glancing in her direction.

It was obvious to her that the sheriff was ignoring her. For just a second she wondered if she hadn't suddenly grown invisible. Couldn't he hear her? Didn't the man have the least bit of sense? Why didn't he, at the very least, question her claim?

"I didn't know the Olsters had a woman riding with them."

Abigail breathed a sigh of relief at the doubt in his voice. She could have kissed him—dirty, sweaty beard and all.

"Yeah. A lot of people didn't know. Dressed like a man, you can't always tell the difference at first."

Sheriff Johnson looked curiously at her then. Long, thick blond hair, obviously unkempt, fell from dislodged pins and almost cloaked a dirty face. She wore men's clothes, all right, and they were mostly covered with twigs and leaves. She looked like she'd just been rolling over the ground. The sheriff hadn't often seen a woman who cared so little about her looks.

Still, with the way her chest filled out that shirt, a man would have to be blind not to know the difference, and Sheriff Johnson figured this deputy not only dressed peculiar, but probably was peculiar if he hadn't instantly known a good-looking woman from a man.

He'd never met one, until now, maybe, but he'd heard about those kinds of men. Still, looking at him, one would never have guessed.

In a burst of inspiration, Abigail said, "I'll give myself up to you. Take me to jail." She offered her unbound hands for his shackles as she shot Hawk a sneering look of victory.

From the look on his face, Sheriff Johnson seemed to like that idea. It certainly wouldn't be a mark against his record if he brought in an outlaw single-handed. It didn't matter any that she was a woman. An outlaw was an outlaw, after all.

"Sorry," Hawk said reading correctly the man's thoughts. "But I picked her up out of your jurisdiction."

"You don't know that," Abigail snapped in Hawk's direction, and then to the sheriff she said, "Tell him where your jurisdiction is."

The two men discussed where the lawman's authority lay, and Abigail knew, before they were half-way finished, that it was a lost cause. The villain simply lied. She should have said it the other way around. She should have made Hawk tell the sheriff where he found her first and then asked for boundaries. Lord, how easily he was managing this.

Hawk shot his "prisoner" a grin, the gleam in his eyes silently promising she was going to pay for this later. He had known that she was an intelligent woman but hadn't until now realized just how clever. He'd have to stay on his toes if he wanted to keep this one.

"Ask him for his warrant," she next directed. "He doesn't have one." The last was said with some gloating. She had him now.

The sheriff glanced at Hawk awaiting his answer.

"I don't have one because, like you said, no one knew a woman was riding with the gang."

The sheriff nodded, and Abigail groaned in frustration. It was easy enough to see the sheriff believed Hawk, flimsy excuses and all. It was too much. It was just too much. How could she be expected to keep calm when her entire future, and perhaps Amanda's as well, lay in the outcome of this ridiculous confrontation? "Oh, my God. How could you believe him? Don't you see he's making a fool out of you?"

"That's enough, girl," the sheriff said, none too happy about being called a fool.

Abigail instantly realized her mistake. "I didn't mean that. I meant he's trying to fool you."

"You telling me he ain't no deputy?" The sheriff realized there was always the possibility that the man was an impostor.

"No. He is a deputy, but—"

Hawk almost burst out laughing. One lie on her part might have turned things completely around. She might even have convinced the man that Hawk had stolen his own identification and he was, in fact, the bad guy.

267

But Abigail was not one to lie. It was not a habit she had acquired. She realized her mistake the moment she saw Hawk's grin. "Forget it," she said as she walked back to the fire and sat down on her blanket.

Hawk offered the sheriff coffee and what was left of their meal, before riding on, and the two men spoke for some time, while Abigail settled down to sleep.

Hawk found out that there had been two reports of robberies and one of murder in the vicinity. The vicinity taking in some fifty or so miles. Still, Hawk knew he was on the right track. He told the sheriff about the murder of his father and two young girls in his community and warned him to be on the alert for three men.

"You should keep her tied," the sheriff said, nodding toward a sleeping Abigail, as he came to his feet.

Hawk glanced toward her as well. "I was just about to do that when you showed up."

He fell asleep with Abigail in his arms, knowing their journey would soon be at an end. They were closing in. The men couldn't hide forever. Sooner or later he'd find them and when he did . . . Hawk allowed himself the luxury of imagining the deadly scenario.

He'd find her sister for her then. Hawk almost couldn't wait, for his mind began to imagine all the delicious ways she could go about showing her appreciation.

* * *

The next night and the next, Hawk tied the two of them together. She fought him madly the first night.

"What do you think you're doing?" she asked as he attempted to slip a rope around her waist.

"Tying you up."

"What?" She shoved his hands away, to no avail. "I can't sleep tied up," she said, struggling to get out of his hold. The rope slipped and Abigail wasted no time. She ran. But she'd soon realize that running from an Indian was a wasted effort. He had to have seen her, although she couldn't understand how anyone could see into the dark. Did he hear her? Did he hear the pounding of her heart? Probably. What else could explain his ease in finding her?

She dove with a muffled grunt of pain under the low-lying branches of a tree. Totally still, totally silent, and yet he was suddenly there. God, how had he done it?

Hawk dragged her, none too gently, especially since she refused to stand up, back to their camp and just about threw her on the blankets. He didn't hurt her, but she figured if he'd had a mind, he could have been more gentle. By the time they finished this trip, she was going to be one giant black and blue.

He tied their waists together and settled down beside her, apparently perfectly comfortable and ready for sleep. The beast!

Abigail rolled to her side, moving as far from him as the rope allowed, maybe an inch, which wasn't nearly far enough. China wouldn't have been far enough.

How could he sleep when she was so furious she could only think to kick and punch something? She blinked at her thoughts, for that particular some-thing just happened to be lying at her side. What was she waiting for?

Abigail couldn't resist. Without any warning she swung around and landed a punch to his face. She almost smiled at his grunt of pain. He'd have a black eye tomorrow if she wasn't mistaken.

An instant later, with her hands suddenly pinned over her head, he almost crushed her flat with his weight. His dark eyes narrowed with warning. "Do that again and I'll tie your hands behind your back. See if you can sleep like that?"

Her teeth clamped together, and she gritted, "I hate you."

"Hate me all you want tomorrow. Now go to sleep."

Abigail bucked her hips, trying to dislodge his weight. "Get off me."

It took a long moment before Hawk even heard her demand. The movement of her hips, the softness of her body, her womanly scent, all three slammed into him, leaving him breathless and aching for more. He took a deep breath as if to steel himself of her allure and muttered a low curse as her scent filled his senses. His mind reeled against the temptation. God Almighty, how was he going to find the strength to resist?

One kiss. Please, God, just *one* kiss. I won't ask for more. But he would. He knew he would. One kiss could never be enough.

Despite the raging silent arguments, his head dipped, his mouth lowered, coming closer, closer to the magic. Inches separated them when he saw the flicker of fear in her eyes.

Hawk knew he could soon quiet that fear. A kiss, a touch would, within seconds, have her begging for more. But no. He didn't want it that way. This woman was going to be his forever. She had to know that. To come to understand that even forever wouldn't be long enough. She had to turn to him, to want him at least half as much as he wanted her.

Hawk forced aside his need and, despite his throbbing eye, glared an anger he was far from feeling. "Remember what I said."

Abigail breathed a sigh as he rolled from her, not at all sure if it was relief or sadness she felt. All she knew for sure was something had just passed between them. Something she couldn't, or perhaps wouldn't, name. His silent look had asked something of her and she was afraid, for the emotion he seemed to demand promised to be too powerful, too all-consuming. It almost terrified her, leaving her breathless in its aching sad aftermath. She shook her head, disallowing the thought. She was tired. More tired than she'd known to imagine such nonsense. He hadn't looked at her in any particular way. It had merely been a trick of the light and nothing more. Yes, he had been about to kiss her and for some unknown reason had changed his mind. For that she could only thank God. She found herself grunting a sound, having no real comeback to his warning, but stubbornly refused to let him have the last word.

Just before she fell asleep, she asked, "How did you do it?"

"Find you, you mean?"

Abigail nodded.

"I almost tripped over your foot. You forgot to roll into a ball."

Abigail almost groaned at so simple an answer. "I'll remember the next time."

"I'll find you anyway." His arm circled her waist and drew her back against him. "I'll always find you."

Abigail lay awake for a long time, wondering what he meant by that . . .

Chapter Thirteen

It was three mornings later when he shoved her shoulder yet again.

The sun was just creeping toward the treetops, marking yet another day's beginning. Abigail groaned and rolled to her stomach, upon hard unforgiving ground. Lord, but she was sore. Everything ached: her hips, her back, even her elbows. Not only was she sore, she was bone-weary tired. Once she was back home, no one was going to drag her from her bed for a month.

God in heaven, how much longer would she be forced to stay with him? To ride from dawn to dusk, until every muscle and joint screamed for relief, until she thought they'd never stop. "Go away. I'm tired."

"It's time to get up."

"I don't care. Leave me alone." She made another grunting sound of pain as she shifted, trying to find a comfortable spot on ground as hard as rock. If she hadn't been so tired, Abigail might have smiled at that thought, since the ground was indeed mostly rock, and digging out one only brought another to the surface.

As if her uncomfortable bed wasn't bad enough, she also had to contend with her abductor and his unasked-for and definitely unwanted proximity. God, but the man nearly crushed her to death every night. He spread out comfortably at her side and fell almost instantly asleep, as if he hadn't a care in the world. Apparently he never realized the fact that he nearly squashed her flat, what with his body half upon hers, his leg thrown over her hips, his arms around her waist.

Abigail wasn't sure she could stand even one more night of his mauling. And to her mind there was no other word for it but mauling.

Yesterday she had awakened to find her shirt open and his hand boldly cupping her breast, as if it were naught but an everyday occurrence. Gathering her wits about her, she had managed to roll to her side, shove away his hand, and rebutton her clothing.

She supposed he had been asleep when he'd touched her, but she couldn't be sure, of course. Still, yesterday had brought no sign that he'd known what had taken place. There had been no confident or gloating glances, no secret smiles to hint that he was aware of these most intimate touchings. The happening had not been repeated last night. At least she couldn't remember that it had.

Abigail came to her elbows and glanced at her shirt, just to be sure. The sight brought a gasp, for the buttons lay open yet again.

She couldn't have done it. Surely she would have remembered opening her shirt. Abigail shot his back a glare and then frowned. Hawk was already tending to the fire, about to prepare their morning meal.

As she again closed her shirt, she watched him at work. Apparently her first supposition was correct. She nodded as she silently convinced herself of it. The phenomena happened while both were asleep. He hadn't purposely touched her. No doubt he never even remembered the intimacy.

The fact was, Hawk remembered every second of the last two nights. Especially last night, for her softness had nearly driven him wild. He'd come from sleep to find his hand inside her shirt. And at his gentle caress, she had turned to him, sighing her pleasure, and he hadn't been able to resist just a small sampling. She'd tasted so good, so warm, so soft. It had taken more strength than he'd known he possessed to stop. He almost couldn't wait for tonight and another, perhaps more generous, tasting.

And the only thing he regretted about the intimacy was not thinking to tie her to him sooner.

It was late the following day, somewhere around the dinner hour, if the growling of his stomach meant anything. Most often, by this time of day Abigail dozed, exhausted in his arms. Today proved to be no exception. He held her against him as he maneuvered the horses between thickly grown trees, his sharp gaze ever observant of obvious signs. Three horses had passed this way a while back. Maybe a week, maybe a day or so more.

Hawk was sure it was them. He was just as sure that they had no idea that they were being followed.

They'd come upon a town soon. Hawk would lose the trail for a time, but it wouldn't take him long to find it again.

One day soon he'd face the men who had shot down his father. On that day they'd know his own personal form of justice. They'd know what it was to suffer as had their victims. They'd know what it meant to look death in the eye and welcome the coming oblivion.

Abigail, in her sleep, made a sound of discomfort at a particularly jarring step. She was uncomfortable, he knew, and tired as well. Hawk silently promised that once his business was complete, she could stay in bed a week. A slow wicked grin curved the corners of his mouth at the thought, for a week in bed, especially if he joined her there—and he most certainly had every intention of doing just that—promised even less rest.

He cuddled her against him, trying to ease, even temporarily, the hardship of this constant riding. Her head fell back against his arm, exposing her throat, and Hawk never thought to resist.

Often during the later part of the day, when she slept, he would allow himself the pleasure of nuzzling his face to hers. Now as he did so again, he breathed in her scent, while wishing he could lose himself in the soft silkiness of her warm skin.

Dusk had already fallen, and he should have made camp by now, but the feel of her in his arms was too good. He didn't want to stop. He didn't want to disturb this moment.

Her face snuggled to his throat. He watched her breasts rise and fall with every breath, and then his hand reached for her. He hadn't realized he was going to do it. Hadn't known it was even in his mind. Suddenly her softness filled his hand.

She squirmed just a bit, as if in her sleep she felt the pleasure and the need for more.

Hawk opened two buttons and reached inside, almost groaning aloud at the warm giving flesh encountered.

She moaned a low sleepy sound of pleasure, and Hawk cursed the fact that he hadn't waited until tonight. That he hadn't been able to control this need for her. There wasn't a doubt in his mind that should she suddenly awaken, this luxurious moment would find itself at an end. That once he brought her from the saddle, she'd turn cool again.

Hawk almost jumped at the feel of her lips. *She kissed him!* His heart slammed against the walls of his chest. She'd kissed him, and even as she did, her hand had come to cover his, holding him fast against her breast.

Hawk had been in a semihard state of lusting almost from the first day of this journey. It had been impossible to hide, impossible to control, what with the way her bottom rubbed against him with every jouncing step of the horse. Now his arousal was full and tight, threatening to burst as she cuddled against him. Damn, but he was sure to suffer throughout the night as a result of this stolen moment of enchantment.

She rubbed her face against him, her lips drifting lower, over his bare chest, gliding lower still with the haunting promise of madness. Hawk couldn't hold back his groan.

It was the pounding of his heart and that groan which brought her from the edge of yet another delicious dream. Abigail pulled her face from his chest and blinked her surprise to find it so positioned. She watched as his hand fell from her. She watched for an endless minute the longing in his dark hungry eyes. A moment later she turned and straightened in the saddle.

Abigail's heart pounded. Lord, how could she—even in sleep—have done that? And Abigail suffered under no misgivings that she had participated fully in this intimacy. Her face grew warm at the thought, warmer still as she imagined the outcome had they not been sitting astride a horse.

She was aware of his excitement. How could she not be aware? She leaned forward a bit, trying to create some space between their bodies, knowing even as she did so, space between them was impossible. No matter her movement, their bodies touched where they couldn't help but touch. Abigail stopped trying to avoid the unavoidable. And her voice held hardly a tremor as she asked, "Will we be stopping soon?"

"Soon," he returned, amazed that he had the strength to say even that much.

Abigail stared straight ahead, her mind filled with confusion. She'd thought it had been a dream. Had all the dreams been real? Had he often kissed her neck, nuzzled her cheek, breathed in the scent of her hair? Had it been no accident then that he'd fondled her breast? Abigail couldn't understand why that thought should prove so exciting. She didn't want these intimacies, did she? Of course, she didn't. Then why did the thought of them suddenly prove to be so appealing?

It came to her then that she knew no anger. Odd, she reasoned. She would have thought that she'd be ranting at his daring conduct, and yet she hadn't. Why? Abigail couldn't come up with a reasonable answer. Not until the truth suddenly dawned. She did want them. She wanted his touch more than she'd wanted anything in her life.

Abigail thought it possible, even as she tried to understand how that could be. She'd hated him for days. There were times when, had she the opportunity, she might have done him some serious harm. How then had this bizarre relationship—and she admitted there *was* a relationship of sorts—evolved from rage to acceptance? No, not acceptance exactly. It was more than that. Only she couldn't as yet name precisely what it was. Lord, how terribly confusing.

They rode in silence for a time. Hawk couldn't help but wonder why she hadn't said anything. Was she pretending it hadn't happened? Was she storing up her hatred, waiting for the right moment to attack, perhaps when he least expected it? Or was she growing accustomed to him? Accustomed to the idea of being his woman. Was he slowly breaking down the barrier between them?

The surrounding forest was dark and still. A clearing ahead offered a bit of light. Hawk drew his horse to a stop, his eyes narrowing with suspicion as he peered through the leafy growth. Ahead, in the midst of the clearing, like a dozen others they had passed, stood a farmhouse.

The place appeared quiet and still. Hawk frowned.

Too quiet and still. He supposed the man had finished working his fields for the day. If so, why did everything look so deserted? Where was his wife? Why hadn't the simmering scents of supper come to greet them? Why was there no smoke coming from the chimney?

He frowned again as he realized the reason behind the quiet stillness. There were no animals. No cat lazed away the last of the day upon the front porch. No dog barked. No chickens strutted their jerky steps within the small yard.

Hawk dismounted and helped Abigail to do the same.

"I want you to stay here."

"Why?" she asked, instantly alert to possible danger. "What's the matter?"

"I don't know. The place is too quiet. Something's wrong."

Abigail followed the direction of his gaze, noticing as he had the strange sight of an all too quiet farm. "Maybe it's been abandoned?"

"Maybe," he said as he gave a small nod. He placed her behind a thick tree. "Promise me you'll stay here."

She nodded.

"If anything happens, get on the horse and get out of here."

Abigail gasped at the order. She gave a slight shake of her head, her hands reaching for him. "I can't leave you."

Hawk didn't ask why. He figured she probably wouldn't know why herself and couldn't have answered if asked. He did know, however, what lay

280

behind those words. She cared for him. She might not be aware of the fact as yet, but she did.

He looked at her for a long moment before they were suddenly in each other's arms. Neither could have said who moved first. It was enough to know that both greedily accepted the feel of the other, knowing safety only now, at this moment, each in the other's arms.

Abigail couldn't shake a terrible feeling of foreboding. "Don't go." She clung tighter to his shoulders. "Let's just pass this place."

His mouth was on hers then, telling her without words the depth of his feelings. God, but he never knew he could feel so much.

"Abby," he groaned as he tore his mouth from hers. He crushed her to him and then was suddenly gone.

Abigail watched, her fingertips upon her lips, hardly daring to breathe as he ran forward, bent almost in half, stopping only when he reached the side of the house. She never thought this was her opportunity to escape. For the first time in weeks, leaving this man never entered her mind.

Half hidden behind a bush, he pressed his back against the building and tried to peer into a window. It was dark inside. He saw nothing and heard even less.

Perhaps Abby was right. Perhaps this place had been abandoned.

Hawk ducked beneath the window and moved along the side of the house to the front porch. Silently he climbed over the railing and moved to the door. A touch and the door swung open.

He glanced inside and almost gagged at the stench of death. It was darker in than out, but the fading light from the doorway and window illuminated the room enough. It enabled Hawk to take in the destruction.

A man and woman lay side by side. Both had died horrible deaths, apparently in the midst of screams, for their faces were contorted, frozen for all time in pain, jaws wide, teeth exposed.

She was naked, but for a few torn scraps of material at her shoulders, and even in this light obviously abused. Her husband had been disemboweled.

Hawk shuddered at the horror, praying they had both died before the worst of their abuse.

Animals had done this, for human beings couldn't have brought this kind of destruction upon one of their own. Hawk's soul filled with rage. They were nothing but animals. Soon, he promised himself. Soon, he'd have them in his sights.

And then it came to him. Good God, what could he be thinking to bring the woman he loved into this kind of danger? He broke out in a cold sweat. Nothing like this could happen to her. And he was going to make damn sure of it. He was putting her on the very next stage they happened on. She might not know it yet, but Abigail Pennyworth was going home.

Hawk turned at the sudden gasp behind him.

Abigail hadn't been able to stand waiting another minute. She had had to see what was happening—to make sure Jeremiah was all right.

She came to the front porch and frowned at the sight of him just standing there at the doorway. What in the world was he doing? Why hadn't he come back for her? Silently she came to his side.

A moment later the stench of decaying bodies reached her and she saw for herself the cause. She had gasped, then gagged just before Hawk dragged her to a corner of the porch, pushing her face to his chest, enabling her to breathe his scent alone.

She clung to him desperately, willing her mind to forget the unforgettable. How could anyone have done that? "I'm sorry," she murmured into his chest. "I'm so sorry."

Hawk understood that she realized at last what was behind his need to find these men. He nodded against her hair, drinking in the clean scent, willing away the stench that had closed over him.

She gagged again. Would she ever forget that smell?

"Are you going to be sick?"

"No." She fought down the bile. "I don't think so," she said and then realized she couldn't manage the chore. Her stomach was going to empty itself no matter her objections. "Maybe."

A second later he leaned her over the railing as her stomach did exactly what she had sworn it would never do again.

"Oh, God," she said as he wiped her mouth with a handkerchief.

"Are you all right now?"

"If you don't count my pride. This is the second time I've done this."

"Anyone would be sick after seeing that."

"You weren't." She pulled back and glared at him.

"And don't you dare say that's because you're a man and I'm only a woman."

Hawk smiled and guided her against him again as he said, "I wouldn't dare."

Despite what lay inside the house, or perhaps because of it, Hawk felt an almost overpowering need to take her, to make her his forever, to feel her against him, to blot out the death and destruction, to clean his very soul, even if the cleansing lasted only for a moment. He'd never need her more. Never know again this nearly uncontrollable need to reaffirm life. He crushed her against him but forced aside this most basic instinct. This wasn't the time or the place—and to give in to the emotion would have been almost obscene.

"How they must have suffered," she said and shuddered yet again.

"They won't suffer anymore, Abby. It's all over."

They stood there for a long moment trembling against the horror, each greedily taking of the other's warmth, revelling in the very fact that they had been left untouched, that they breathed, that they lived. "I feel . . . I feel so . . ."

"Don't think about it now, sweetheart."

She pulled back just enough to see his face. "Jeremiah, we have to get help. They're so evil."

"I know, honey," he soothed. "I know."

"Promise me you'll get help. We can't do this alone."

"We won't be doing this at all. I'm putting you on the next stage we come across. You're going home."

Abigail pulled from his arms. Her shock couldn't have been greater. She'd thought him so brave, so fearless. Could she have been wrong? "What are you saying? You can't let them get away with this."

"They won't be getting away with it, but you won't be getting hurt either. You're going home. This is too dangerous for—"

"I'm going home? Alone?"

Hawk could see her shock was growing into anger. "What's the matter now? That's what you wanted all along, wasn't it?"

"No, it wasn't! What I wanted was to find my sister."

"I told you I'd help—"

"I know what you told me. I'm talking about now. What are you doing now?"

"I'm putting you on a stage," he repeated.

"And if I don't want to go?"

"There are no options here, Abby. I couldn't stand it if anything happened to . . . You're going."

"I won't and you can't make me."

"We'll see."

"I'll get off the stage and follow you."

"You little fool." Hawk shook her shoulders and then crushed her against him again. He couldn't believe it. For the longest time she'd fought him because she wanted to leave. Now she fought him because she wanted to stay. He shook his head and forced back a smile.

"Don't call me a fool, you bully." What was wrong with her? Why did she want to stay with him? Most likely she was a fool, for only one of little or no intelligence would put up with this man and the aggravating way he had of ordering her about. She

285

pressed her face into his warmth. "I can't leave you. You might need me."

Hawk sighed, knowing he'd never need her more than he did at this very moment.

"All right, let's not argue about it now."

"There's no way I can wait to fight about this. It has to be now."

Hawk laughed.

"I'm happy you think this is funny."

"I think you're adorable."

"Thank you, but—"

"Let me cover them for the night. Tomorrow, when it's light, will be soon enough to bury them. Make us a bed in the barn, will you sweetheart?"

Abigail nodded and left him to his grisly chore. The inside of the barn was cold and getting darker by the minute. She found a lantern and, on a shelf beside it, matches. Soon the interior took on a golden glow.

No animals lent their warmth to the building. The place was empty. Straw littered the dirt floor. Abigail climbed to the loft and smiled at the abundance of hay there. For the first time in weeks, she was going to enjoy a soft bed.

Moments later Hawk entered the barn with their horses in tow. While he brushed the animals, allowed them some feed and water and put them into stalls for the night, Abigail retrieved their blankets, water, and what was left of their food supplies. They'd have to stop soon, she reasoned, unless they were content to live solely on his hunting. In the loft again, she made a cozy bed of soft loose hay.

Hawk came up behind her. His arms circling her waist, he pulled her against him. The second sight of those bodies had been no better than the first. He'd be happy to leave here tomorrow.

"Are you hungry?"

"No." He guided her toward the blankets. "Let's go to bed."

They didn't speak again, for the happenings on this night went beyond conversation. Instead they sought out comfort in each other. For the first time she came willingly into his arms and snuggled tightly to his strength. Clinging close, each absorbing the other's warmth until the cold fear that had settled around their hearts began to melt away.

He buried them the next day, while Abigail braved the stench of rotting corpses and said a few words of prayer. Before they left, Hawk took the needed supplies from the dead woman's kitchen. There was no need to explain that they might as well be put to some use or go bad. Abigail knew he was right. Still, she offered him no help, for she couldn't have stepped one foot into that house if her life had depended on it.

Chapter Fourteen

The next night, as they sat before a fire, Abigail asked, "Are we still following them?"

Hawk nodded. He knew what she was up to. He knew she wanted to know if he'd changed his mind. The fact was, he hadn't—but he wasn't willing to argue about his decision. He was, no matter her objections, putting her on a stage for home. He simply hadn't mentioned it again.

"How do you know they came this way?"

"One of the horses has a crack in his shoe." Hawk didn't mention the other obvious signs. The horse droppings, the broken branches and overturned ground, or the occasional thread found among the shrubbery. "I've been following it since I left the reservation."

"Suppose the horse goes lame?"

"I figure it will, eventually. That will slow them down some." He took a sip of his coffee. "What they should have done was exchange their horses for those at the farm. Instead they probably let them go."

"Maybe there weren't any."

"There were until recently. There was feed, remember?"

Abigail nodded. She would have liked to have mentioned the insanity of allowing a horse to live, but not the animal's owners. Only she didn't want to bring up the subject again. She knew it would only remind him that he was sending her back.

He glanced at the small lake across from the fire. Whenever possible Hawk camped by water. Tonight moonlight glistened on the still black surface. He watched the gentle sight for a long time before he heard, "It's beautiful, isn't it?"

She was asking the wrong man. The only thing he knew of beauty was her. His gaze moved to hers then, dark and hungry. God, he wanted her so badly. How much longer would he have to wait?

Abigail swallowed, feeling again that strange and powerful wanting. Only she wasn't exactly sure what it was she wanted. Lord, but that was a lie, wasn't it? She knew what she wanted, all right. She'd known despite her anger, since almost the beginning of this trip. She couldn't forget the night when he'd showed her the pleasure possible only in a man's arms. No matter how she might sometimes deny it, she wanted that pleasure again. She wanted that and more. She wanted all he could show her. Abigail shivered at the enormity of that wanting.

Hawk saw the involuntary movement and asked, "Are you cold?"

"No."

Hawk wondered what was behind that shiver, and decided it was long past the time to find out. He'd waited long enough. Tonight might be their last

289

chance. He couldn't wait any longer. He came to his feet, his rifle in his hand, his blanket tucked under one arm. "I want to take a bath. Come with me?"

Abigail almost moaned aloud at the softly spoken request. He was asking, not ordering, and she knew she didn't have the will to resist.

His hand reached for hers, and Abigail found hers closed in his as he helped her to her feet. They walked together from the small fire to the seclusion and privacy of darkness.

No light shone here. None but the moon's silvery glow. The forest spread almost to the water's edge, allowing them only a narrow patch of grass. He propped his rifle against a tree and slid his vest from his shoulders.

The dark skin of his chest and shoulders glowed smooth and beckoning. He stood before her like a pagan god, like a man born to a primitive culture. His long hair flowed in the gentle breeze, long, beyond his shoulders, thick and black. His body was sleek, smooth, and hard. Abigail trembled at the sight of a man perched on the edge of civilization. He looked savage, untamed, wild, one with nature. He almost frightened her, for she'd never seen anyone more deserving of the title *man*. Hunger glittered in his eyes, and yet there was a gentleness there that eased her fears and promised only pleasure.

Abigail never thought but to give in to the need to touch him. She reached out a hand to rediscover his silky warmth. A moment later her other hand joined the first, and Hawk stood there dying a little with the pleasure, a willing subject of her sweet investigation.

She glanced up into eyes darker than the night and

yet glowing with need. "Do you mind if I touch you?"

Hawk smiled at the question. The flash of white teeth caused an unexplainable tightening in Abigail's chest. "I'd only mind if you stopped."

"You feel different."

"Than what?"

"Than me."

"And thank God for that," he teased. "I don't think I'd want to touch you half so badly if we felt the same."

"And you do?"

Hawk smiled again, but Abigail wasn't watching his mouth. Her gaze was following the movement of her hands.

"Want to touch you?" He laughed a soft silky sound. "You might be safe in assuming that."

A long silent moment went by as Abigail continued her study. It was getting harder with every passing moment to restrain his need, to keep his hands at his sides. "Shall I open your shirt?"

Abigail might have felt at ease in his company, at ease in touching him, but she wasn't so accustomed to a man that she could actually answer a question like that. As it turned out, she didn't have to. She raised her gaze to his. It was all the permission he needed. Within seconds her shirt lay open.

He breathed a sigh of delight as he exposed her to his view. "You're right. We are different."

Abigail laughed a low and, if he wasn't mistaken, wicked sound. God, how he loved it. How he loved her. He pushed the shirt from her shoulders. "Come closer, I want to feel you against me."

Without a moment's hesitation or a word of objection, Abigail stepped into his arms.

Hawk thought he must have done something very good, at least once, for he couldn't imagine himself deserving of this special piece of heaven. He held her against him for a long minute before he realized this wasn't nearly enough. He had to feel more, he had to know all of her.

"Sit," he said. "I'll help you with your boots."

Abigail did as he asked, and Hawk took further delight in the fact that her breasts swayed with every jerk and pull. He couldn't take his eyes off her and almost breathed a sigh of relief as he finished the chore. He didn't know how much longer he could have stood the sight of that.

A moment later she was standing again in his arms. He was trying to go slow, but God, it was the hardest thing he'd ever done in his life. Still, he'd do it if it killed him. First, she had to feel comfortable in her nakedness, then comfortable in his. After he was sure of it, they'd swim and play like children. Hawk almost laughed at the thought. Well, perhaps not like children, exactly. Then they'd come from the water and finally, finally, he'd know what it was to love her.

"If I didn't know better, I'd think you like me with no clothes."

"No!" Hawk gasped, feigning shock even as his hand reached between them and opened her trousers. A second later both trousers and drawers slid down her legs.

Abigail gave another wicked laugh at his muttered, "I'm shocked that you would think such a thing." He hesitated for only as long as it took him to take a breath. "And stop laughing like that. It's driving me crazy."

"Sorry," she said, and then unable to help herself she laughed again.

"I should keep you like this all night just to show you the error of your thoughts."

"Oh, that would do it all right."

"I will admit there was a time or two that I might have inadvertently—"

"Inadvertently?" she asked with more than a little doubt.

"Of course. You couldn't have imagined that I'd purposely—"

"What about the night I picked up the snake, while I was bathing?" she asked, interrupting him again.

"Oh that," he said as if discounting the entire happening.

"Yes, that. You didn't want me to get dressed. Remember?"

"Ah, now that you mention it, I might have said something like that."

"You might have?"

"All right, I did."

Abigail nodded and then drew in a deep breath as he asked, "Do you remember the things I did to you that night?"

Abigail buried her face in his neck, feeling her cheeks grow warm at the thought. "No. I forgot everything."

Hawk ignored her denial. "Did you like them?"

"What?"

"The things I did."

"I might have, if I remembered them."

293

"Should I—"

"Oh, please stop talking about it. You're not supposed to ask a lady these kinds of questions."

Hawk chuckled a low husky sound. Apparently it was all right to do it, but not to talk about doing it. He breathed deeply of her scent, his lips nuzzling the warmth of her neck. "I am, if the lady is mine."

Abigail didn't know what to say. She couldn't deny she felt something special for this man. Despite the aggravation he had caused her, her heart pounded every time he stood near. Maybe she loved him. She wasn't sure. All she knew for a fact was, she couldn't leave him. She had to be there, to protect, to comfort. She couldn't allow him to get hurt. Was that love?

She felt a wave of guilt at the thought. She should be longing for her freedom, desperate to find Amanda, but she wasn't. And she didn't know why.

He felt her stiffen against him and knew he'd said too much. It didn't matter. She might have a hard time taking to the notion right now, but she soon would. Of that he had no doubt.

"What's the matter?" Hawk figured they might as well get everything out in the open. It was best if each knew where the other stood.

"I have to find Amanda first."

"Before you can be my woman, you mean?"

She nodded.

"I've promised to help you."

Abigail raised beseeching eyes to his. "I know, but until I know she's safe, I can't promise anything."

"For tonight then, Abby. Be my woman for tonight?" Hawk didn't say the rest. He didn't tell her that there was no way that he could ever let her go, especially after tonight.

"For tonight," she whispered in return.

He stepped away from her and shoved his buck-skins down thickly muscled thighs. He heard her soft intake of breath and knew she was watching him. He was half afraid to look, lest he find revulsion in her eyes.

He knew Abigail had never seen a naked man before. Would she feel disgust? Would she know fear?

Hawk was right. Abigail had never seen a naked man before, but the emotion she knew at the sight of him had nothing to do with disgust or fear. Her gaze was all admiration as it ran over the length of him, taking in his wide chest, flat belly, narrow hips, muscular thighs and lingering for endless moments at the blossoming promise of pleasure nestled in a triangle of dark curling hair.

Her throat went dry. He was so big. Were all men like this? Should she be afraid? No, she decided. He wouldn't hurt her. No matter what happened between them, she could count on the fact that he'd never hurt her.

Her gaze moved to his, and Hawk saw more than acceptance in her gaze. He saw love.

"You're beautiful." She said the words in a rush of breath, her eyes wide, as if she couldn't believe it.

He smiled. "You're not supposed to tell a man he's beautiful."

"All right, you're ugly."

Hawk grinned at the way she bit her lip and the mischievous twinkle in her eyes. He reached a hand

295

to the back of her head and dug his fingers into the silkiness of her hair. The slightest pull brought her gaze from his body to his smiling eyes. "Brat."

Abigail giggled. "Turn around. Let me see you."

He gathered her into his arms, bringing her high on his chest. He started for the water. "Later. You can look at me all you want. Later."

"Ahhhh," Abigail's teeth chattered as he lowered her to the water. "It's cold."

"Move around, you'll get used to it in a minute."

"I'm staying in for only a minute."

That wasn't at all what Hawk had planned. "Do you want me to make you warm?"

She shot him a glance of disbelief just before she dove under the water and then came up shivering a second later. "All right. Go get me a coat."

"A coat wasn't exactly what I had in mind."

"No? You mean you have the power to heat this water? Can I watch?"

"You can do more than watch. You can help me."

"What should I do?"

"Kiss me."

"I should have known you'd be leaning toward those kinds of thoughts."

"Yes, you should have." His gaze dropped to her gleaming breasts.

"Wicked man," she said as her hand skimmed across the surface of the water, splashing him well, just before she dove away again.

He caught her within seconds and pulled her slippery body against his. She laughed, but her laughter was suddenly stilled as his mouth took hers in a kiss that caused a searing of her soul. God, she hadn't remembered that it felt this good.

Her arms circled his neck and the buoyancy of the water helped her to slide up and down his length. He felt so good against her. She hadn't imagined that a man could feel so good.

He was right. The water was beginning to grow warm. Either that or her mind had sort of forgotten about water and was thinking on other things to feel.

His hands moved over her back and down to her bottom, cupping her fullness as he pulled her gently against him. And then his fingers slid farther down to her lovely thighs, and around her body, coming up her body now, closer, closer to where she wanted his touch most.

She made a soft sound of pleasure as he touched her at last.

Hawk was drowning in her taste, her scent. If he wanted to prolong this moment, he'd have to create some distance between them, and yet he couldn't stop touching her. What he had to do was stop kissing her. He tore his mouth from hers and smiled as she moaned a low greedy sound of need. Her eyes opened very slowly, and she watched him for a long moment before she said, "Oh, it's you."

Hawk bit his bottom lip, unable to stop the grin. "Is that your way of telling me you kiss all men like that?"

"Actually, Mr. Hawk—" She cleared her throat and tried to get her thoughts together, not an easy chore considering where his fingers touched her and the things that touching was doing to her senses. "I wasn't kissing you at all. You were kissing me."

Hawk wondered how she could act so prim and proper standing naked almost against him, her arms still around his neck, his hand under the water, doing all the things he'd dreamed of doing for the last month or more. He loved it. He loved everything about this woman. A fire raged here. A fire she thought to keep at bay with her teasing. He wondered how far he'd have to push before she gave up the last of her control?

His finger dipped gently inside. Not far, just enough to make her conscious of the fact, lest she forget, that he was there. Her head fell back a bit, her eyes half closed. She moaned.

"And you played no part in it?"

"What?" Her hips moved forward a bit. It was more than obvious that she was enjoying the things he was doing to her. Still, she managed some control. "Oh, you mean the kiss?" And at his nod she said, "Minimal, at best."

"Interesting."

"Is it? Why?"

"If that was minimal, I can't help but wonder what you could do if you set your mind to it."

"What?" she asked again.

"Are you having a hard time thinking right now?"

"Not at all, why?" The words were dragged out as if she were drugged.

"You keep saying, 'What?' "

"I'm hard of hearing."

Hawk chuckled a low, terribly wicked sound. "Are you? Would you like me to stop?"

"Why? You're not touching my ears, are you?"

He laughed again, bringing her close against him

for a tight hug. "Not yet. But perhaps I should." He breathed against her ear and allowed his tongue to gently investigate the small shell-like object.

"Oh Lord," Abigail moaned. "That's very good, isn't it?"

"What else do you like?"

"I haven't done much of this before, you know."

"I know," he breathed, his mouth dipping lower, his intent obvious. "But you've done enough to tell me what you like."

"I like you." Lord, but that was an understatement.

"Then touch me."

"I can't. If I let go, I'll fall."

"I think we should finish this on the blanket."

Abigail knew some real disappointment as he brought her again into his arms and started for the shore. Her disappointment didn't last long, though, for the moment she lay at his side, his fingers returned to further thrill her throbbing need.

Like the first time his hands drifted over her, only this time he had the added delight in being able to see what he touched.

Within seconds she was straining toward him again, her urgency, her need to find appeasement not to be denied. She squirmed, aching for more of this pleasure. Her belly grew tight and she welcomed the ache, knowing the pleasure that lay ahead this time.

A minute more. Please, God—just a minute more. Her body strained upward, and then his fingers were gone. "No," she cried out. "Don't stop!"

But he hadn't stopped.

Abigail had never imagined such a thing. Her mind

couldn't fully comprehend. All she knew for a fact was the feel of his hot tongue against her brought about the most extraordinary sensations. She'd never felt anything like it in her life.

This time she wasn't afraid. This time she tried to hold back the coming bliss because this felt too good. She wanted it to last longer. She wanted this to last forever. Only nothing lasts forever, and she had no strength to insist. With a cry torn from deep within, she gave in at last to the need.

Hawk felt the bursting waves of pleasure, imagining himself deeply inside, but still he held back, waiting for her pleasure to ease, for the bliss to fade before he'd start yet again.

Only he didn't.

Abigail stretched out before him, her needs temporarily appeased. She felt a delicious sense of well-being. Relaxed now, her body soft again, pliable to his touch, but somehow longing for more. The sweet euphoria she suffered still allowed her a sense of daring. She reached for him.

Hawk gasped and thought to pull back, knowing to permit her touch would bring to an end this luscious moment. He tried, but he had no will against her gentle inquisitive fingers.

She seemed to be measuring his length, his thickness, and he arched his hips forward so she might see what it was she touched, his head thrown back, his mouth tight, his body helpless but to silently beg for more.

She pushed him to his back and came to her knees. Hawk realized they had reversed positions. He realized as well, there wasn't a thing he could do to stop her.

She touched him as if in adoration. Her hands moved over his chest and his hard belly to his stomach and thighs, edging up again to settle with devastating accuracy at his sex.

Hawk groaned as she measured him again. Thickness was judged, length appraised, and Hawk moaned in near delirium at her gentle study. Suddenly it was her mouth, not her hands he felt against him. His entire body jerked, in an instant ready to explode. It was too much. He couldn't make it if she did what he wanted most for her to do.

"Don't do that," he said as he rolled her to her back and leaned over her.

"Why? You did as much." If the truth be told, he did more. Much more.

"Because it's too good, and I won't be able to hold back."

"Do I want you to hold back?"

"It would be better for you if I did."

"Better than what you've already done?"

"Much better."

She looked at him in disbelief.

Hawk laughed. "Maybe I'm even better than I thought I was."

She frowned at his cockiness. "You're obnoxious in any case."

A low rumble of laughter slipped from his throat. "Kiss me."

"I don't kiss obnoxious men."

"Man," he corrected. "And yes, you do," he said

301

as he teased her mouth with a gentle brushing of his lips.

"Well, if I do, it's only because he won't stop nagging."

"He wouldn't have to nag if you were more generous with your kisses."

"Maybe he wouldn't want them so much if I were generous."

"He would. Take my word for it. He would."

Abigail kissed him then, and Hawk swore he'd never know more pleasure than when her mouth came willingly to his.

He was wrong.

There was more pleasure and then more again. Her touch drove him nearly mad and increased the pleasure tenfold. He wasn't going to make it if he allowed this moment to go on much longer.

Gently he eased her thighs apart and settled himself upon her. His mouth never left the sweetness of hers as he gently pushed forward. He knew she'd be tight and he'd have to go slow lest he hurt her, but she was wild in her need and Hawk couldn't hold back.

He inched forward, more and then more, enclosing himself into the tightness, into the luxury. And then he pushed through the last obstacle, claiming her as his forever.

He felt her stiffen, but she soon relaxed again under his gentle soothing words and caresses. Relaxed enough to begin to feel again the wanting, the pleasure, the need to find still more in this man's arms.

He waited a long moment for her body to accept him and then, to their mutual delight, he began to move. Gently he guided her hips, showing her how to achieve the most pleasure. And she did. Her cries of delight sounded twice before he gave in to his own need at last.

"Abby," he breathed against her neck. "I can't hold back." And he didn't. He came to his knees, pulling her body closer to his and then his body surged forward again and again and yet again. His head flung back, his features tight as if he suffered unbearable pain and then he shuddered and groaned, knowing nothing had ever been like this. The woman was magic, pure and simple. He'd never known this degree of pleasure before. He slumped forward, covering her body with his.

"My God, you almost killed me. I've never waited so long in my life."

"What were you waiting for?" she asked, her breathing still shaky and uneven. "We were together for weeks."

"No, I mean tonight. I've never . . ." He hesitated, careful not to say too much, lest he destroy this moment. "I just waited too long."

"You mean it's not supposed to last this long?"

Hawk laughed, falling to her side in only slightly exaggerated weakness. "Hardly."

"But I like it long."

"Do you?" And then with obvious interest, he asked, "What else do you like long?"

Abigail glanced at his expression. Just as she imagined, from the humor she thought she heard in his voice, he was smiling. A very wicked smile, indeed.

"Your hair."

"Hardly worth mentioning. What else?"

"You mean there are parts of you that are worth mentioning and parts that are not?"

"Uh-huh."

"Parts that are long, you mean?"

"Uh-huh," he said again.

"Well, your feet are long. As a matter of fact, they're probably the biggest feet I've ever seen."

Hawk only shook his head.

"How about your legs? They're long."

He laughed. "You're getting closer."

Abigail rolled to her side, her hand held her head as she looked down at his grin. "I'll never say it. So you might as well give up."

He laughed as he grabbed her and pulled her atop him. "What would you say if I told you I loved you?" Hawk hadn't meant to say that. He hadn't meant to actually bare his soul. At least not quite yet, but the words just sort of slipped out.

Abigail thought her heart would burst with happiness. She couldn't believe that a man like this could love her. "In the past tense?"

"No." The damage was done. There was no sense in denying it now. "The present. What would you say?"

She touched his hair, remembering the silkiness of it against her face when he kissed her, when he loved her. "I'd say I love you, too, of course."

"Oh, of course." He nodded and then asked with a hint of sarcasm, "Was I supposed to take that for granted?"

"You mean you didn't know?"

Hawk shook his head as he watched her force back her laughter. "You are a brat." A moment went by before he asked, "So what is it you love about me?"

"Oh, that's easy. You're the most beautiful man I've ever seen, and I don't care if I'm supposed to say that or not."

"Is that it?"

"No," she said, smiling at his disappointment. "You're also kind." She shrugged and corrected, "Well, you are sometimes and ah . ⌄" She rolled her eyes upward as if having a time of it finding more to say. "Let's see, you're . . . brave and strong and . . . loyal." Abigail threw that last one in, not at all sure of the fact, but she was running out of compliments.

"Like a dog?"

Abigail laughed. "Except you don't come when you're called."

Hawk growled against her throat, delighting in her laughter. "I'm going to get you for that."

"When?" she asked, all eager anticipation.

"Not tonight," he returned, knowing exactly what she meant. "You'll be sore if we do it again."

"No, I won't."

"Sweetheart, we can't. The first time is—" He sucked in his breath as her hand reached between their bodies, flowing over and then cupping his now soft sex. "Abby, I'll hurt you."

"All right, we won't do anything. I'll just touch you."

Just touch him? Just drive him crazy, she meant.

He made a moaning sound as if he suffered terrible pain, even as his hips strained toward her hand. "Abby, God, I don't think . . ."

"I'll give you a penny," she said in a singsong

voice, as she had a hundred times to her sister to bribe the young girl into doing something she wanted done.

Hawk blinked his surprise. Surprise because at the moment, a penny sounded damn good. "All right, a penny."

She laughed. "I never realized you were so cheap."

"Cheap, but firm." And getting more so, they both realized, as she continued her gentle ministrations.

She bit her lip. "The trouble is, I haven't got a penny."

"You can owe it to me." His voice was beginning to take on a slightly desperate tone.

She seemed to think on that for a minute before she asked, "Do you think I could owe you a dollar?"

Hawk knew he was done in, by a woman half his size. He had no means of fighting her and found he couldn't say anything more but "God!"

Chapter Fifteen

Margaret Boyle watched her baby gurgle and coo in his small bed. A soft smile curved her pretty lips as she allowed the memories to come again. In her mind she saw her husband slide the present across the table once more. She opened the paper-wrapped package with a cry of delight and had almost jumped upon her husband's lap. "I knew I made the right decision when I married you."

Mike Boyle had laughed. "You mean I haven't given you a reason to be sorry yet?"

"Not yet."

"It's too late, you know. You're going to be married to me forever." His arms squeezed her tightly against him.

Margaret grinned. "Then I'll just have to tell my many beaus there's no hope."

Margaret rested her head against his strong throat and breathed a sigh of contentment. She had made the right decision, all right. Mike was a good man, and she couldn't have chosen better. Somehow, and without her knowledge, he had managed a few hours out of each of the last few weeks to work for Mr. Cummings. He had taken the money earned and bought her a new coat and boots for her birthday. She smiled again as she remembered the luxurious thickness of the coat and the fur that lined her new boots. She'd been anxious then for the cold to come so she could wear them.

That day was her twentieth birthday. The best birthday she'd ever had.

Margaret had never had much. The truth was, coming from a family of eight daughters and four brothers, she hadn't had anything at all. Not until she met Mike. Not until he'd asked her to marry him.

Margaret blinked back the tears as she undressed for yet another night's stay in a cold lonely bed. For a short time she'd been truly blessed. A year ago she could claim a husband who was loving, kind, and pleasant even when he didn't have to be, a pretty little home, and more happiness than most could find in an entire lifetime. Before he had died, Mike had given her the most precious gift of all: her own baby to love.

A year ago today Mike had given her those most luxurious gifts. Margaret hadn't been able to stop smiling the entire day. Not until she began to worry, that is. Not until it grew dark and Mike still hadn't come in from the fields. Not until she left the house to look for him. Not until she found his body lying facedown in a field of newly plowed ground.

Margaret shivered. The old plowing horse had kicked him in the head, they said. No one knew, of course, exactly how or why. It was enough that Mike was dead. Nothing else mattered.

Mike hadn't known he was going to be a father. He hadn't lived to see his son. Mike junior was three months old, and Margaret could forget the pain of her loss only when she held the baby in her arms.

Everyone had told her it would get better. The pain wouldn't be so bad as time went on, only they lied. It was easily as bad. Sometimes it was even worse.

The sound of a horse approaching brought her from her reverie. She didn't get much company, especially not at this late hour. Yes, now and then one of the men in town took a ride out to the farm, but she always sent them packing. They came to court her, she supposed, but she didn't want courting. All she wanted was to be left alone.

Margaret turned the sleepy baby onto his stomach and came to the door. She held a rifle in her hand as she stepped outside. "What do you want?"

Thomas Hill had taken what he could for the paintings and left New Orleans with something like ten dollars, after buying his horse and a few supplies. The supplies had long since been used and the money as well. He didn't have anything left, and if this woman didn't take pity on him, he would probably die. He couldn't remember ever feeling so ill, so weak, and even though the night was warm, so chilled. "Lady, please," he said swaying a bit in his saddle.

It wasn't beyond Hill to pretend an affliction in order to see his ends met. During his poorly spent twenty-eight years, he'd done at least that and more, but he didn't have to pretend this time. He could hardly talk, his throat was so dry. When had he last filled his canteen?

"What's the matter, mister? You sick?"

"Lady," he managed, although he wasn't sure how, and then it was beyond his power to manage anything more. He stopped trying to fight the blackness and slid from the saddle to land with a hard thud, in a crumpled unconscious heap upon the ground.

Margaret gasped in shock as she watched the stranger succumb to his weakness. He needed help, but did she dare go to him? Did she dare touch him? Suppose he carried a disease? Suppose she caught it—or worse yet—suppose the illness was transferred to her son?

Margaret stood for a long moment watching the man, waiting for him to come again to his senses. She bit her lip, straining for the courage to go to him. Finally she could wait no longer. The man would surely die if left unattended, and she couldn't live knowing she might have helped a fellow human being and had not.

A cool, trembling hand pressed against a burning forehead. Margaret whispered a prayer that she was doing the right thing, that she wouldn't, in the end, suffer for this charitable act.

It took most of her strength, but she somehow managed to drag him to the barn. No matter how desperate his situation appeared, she couldn't allow the man entrance to her home. After all, she had a baby to see to and her first concern would always be her son.

A half hour later, Hill was settled, as comfortably as was possible. A blanket covered a bed of soft hay in one of the barn's stalls. Blankets were heaped upon

310

his shivering form; warm liquids were soon forced down his throat.

For two days he hovered close to death, alternating between burning fever and bone-jarring chills. On the third day the fever broke, and Hill reentered the world of the living.

Hill opened dull eyes to the dimness of a barn and wondered where he was and how he had gotten here. The questions had barely come to mind when a beautiful lady suddenly appeared at his side.

She reached a cool hand to his damp forehead and asked, "How do you feel?"

Margaret was happy to see this man in control of his senses again. Perhaps, after another day or so of rest, he would be well enough to continue on with his journey. Because she was a woman alone, and because it was hardly proper for a man to stay, even though he'd yet to step foot into her home, she felt a great anxiousness for the moment of his departure.

"Better, I think. Was I very ill?"

"You had a fever."

"And you took care of me?"

Margaret nodded.

"Thank you, ma'am." Thomas eyed the lovely lady kneeling at his side. If he worked things right, he just might find this one easy pickings. He'd done it countless times before and knew it would take no great effort to sweet talk a lady as pretty as this one.

His body might be weakened from the fever. Still, he felt a surge of lust as he watched her come to her feet and smooth her skirts into place.

She nodded again, dismissing her ministrations as

nothing beyond the norm. "You must be hungry. Would you like to come to the house and eat?"

"Yes, ma'am, thank you."

"Do you think you can make it on your own?"

Hill thought it obvious that this lady hoped he could and was wise enough not to push her hospitality, at least not just yet. He figured she was the skittish sort. Still, he had every confidence that within a few days he'd be sharing her bed. The fact was, he had plenty of time.

Only he didn't.

Ten miles east of Margaret Boyle's small farm, three men awakened cold, damp, and uncomfortable. Each glared with disgust at the damp smoldering fire that had offered not a moment's warmth throughout an endless night. It had rained, and they had had no choice but to endure the discomfort, for protection from the elements had not presented itself for close to a week. They grunted unhappily as they saddled their horses. Willie knew they couldn't be far from Memphis. Maybe less than five days. He knew as well there had to be a farm around here somewhere. He didn't want to spend another night like the last one. They'd find a place to stay for a while and a real bed to sleep in for a change.

Mike was sick but dared not complain. The bullet that bitch had put into his arm had passed clean through, but the injury it had left behind was festering. The stink was enough to gag him. If he didn't get some doctoring soon, he'd probably lose it. He was hot. He didn't tell the others that he had a fever.

312

They'd leave him behind to fend for himself. Out here alone, he'd surely die.

Willie brought his horse to a stop at the sight of the little house. Smoke was coming from the chimney. His stomach growled at the thought of food. His body longed for a warm dry bed.

The thought came that there might be a woman here. Willie grinned as his gaze took in the front of the house. There was a woman here. No man would plant flowers to each side of his front door.

Good. Mike needed some doctoring, and they all needed food. After they ate—well . . . after they ate, they'd just have themselves a little fun. This time maybe they'd let the woman live for a while. At least until they reached Memphis.

Willie signaled for the other two to dismount. Three men ran to the wall of the house and listened to sounds of cooking inside. A baby fussed. Willie grinned, for the sound only confirmed his suspicions.

Someone knocked on the door. All three men stiffened at the sound. They hadn't seen or heard a rider coming. Who would knock? A hand, Willie guessed. A hand had come for breakfast.

The sound of conversation was muffled as chairs were pushed into place around a table.

"How are you, sir?" Margaret asked as she poured Hill a cup of coffee.

"Thomas Hill, ma'am," Hill said and then nodded at her question. "I'm better. I don't know how I'm ever going to thank you for all you did."

Margaret placed a plate before him piled high with fresh eggs, bacon, and fried corn bread. Hill glanced at the plate and then at the woman before him. He smiled, but never got a chance to say anything more than "Thank—" before the door was wrenched open and three armed men charged into the room. Before he could blink Thomas Hill lay dead upon the floor, half his face shot away, and the sleeping baby brought abruptly awake screamed, terrified at the sounds of discharging guns.

"Kill the brat," Willie said.

"Nooo!" Margaret screamed as she watched one of the three move toward the back of the one-room house. She charged after the man. It took only a few steps to pull the baby into her arms. She pressed him tightly to her chest and begged, "No, don't kill him. I'll do anything if you don't kill him . . . please."

Not one of the three were affected by her pleas. The only reason they didn't kill the baby was because they were hungry, and pulling the baby away from her and flinging it out the door, or quieting it permanently, would have caused them too much trouble.

Willie instantly saw to the wisdom of keeping the kid alive. The woman would be sure to do them all up fine if they held the threat over her head. "All right, leave the brat alone," Willie said to Josh, reversing his order. And then to the terrified woman he said, "Just make sure he stays quiet. I ain't in no mood to listen to squalling."

Hill's body was shoved to the wall, and three men sat down, ready to be served their meal.

Margaret soon quieted her son. Now that he was awake, he would soon need a few moments of care. She hurried to fill the plates, thanking God that she'd made enough. She trembled at the thought that Mike junior might make noise before she could get to him again.

Margaret left the three to eat and as they did so, she changed and fed her son.

There was no privacy here. The house consisted of one room—and as she went about this most normal happening, Margaret was conscious of the fact that all three men watched.

She turned from them but was instantly ordered to turn back. She did as she was told. Her face grew warm, knowing three pairs of eyes watched. Their appetite for food was being appeased even as an appetite for other things began to grow in the pit of each man's stomach.

Margaret was conscious of the fact. She'd been married and knew the look in a man's eyes when he wanted a woman. She trembled at the thought, wondering how she was going to live through the next few hours. It didn't matter. All she cared about was her baby. She'd do anything if the two of them could be allowed to live.

She didn't have to wonder for long.

No sooner had she finished with the baby, did she hear, "Forget about buttoning that dress. You won't find no need for it. Just take it off."

Margaret placed her sleeping baby back in his bed and turned to the three still sitting at her table. One of the men pulled his gun from his holster, and Margaret never thought to refuse. Her dress dropped to the floor, and she stood before them in shift, petticoats, and drawers.

"All of it," came the next order. "Take everything off."

Again she obeyed.

Margaret knew some amazement here. She would have thought that she'd be mortified to stand before three gawking men completely naked, but the fact was, she felt no shame, no degradation. She felt nothing at all. Nothing . . . if you didn't count her terror.

Willie was enjoying this. Actually all three enjoyed it. For the first time they wouldn't be forced to hold a woman down.

"Get me more coffee," Willie said and then grinned as she obediently went about his bidding stark naked, save for her stockings and shoes.

Margaret continued to serve the men. Again she reminded herself that it didn't matter. That they couldn't do anything to her that mattered. That she would do anything to make sure her son lived.

Soon enough the three grew tired of watching her. They wanted more. Much more.

"Get on the bed," Willie ordered, and again Margaret did as she was told.

They did terrible things to her. Unmentionable things, but she never once denied them their wants. Never once did she hesitate, nor cry out her pain, or shudder her horror as two mounted her at once. She did as ordered when the third pressed his member to her mouth. Her mind had shut down; feeling did not exist. She moved automatically, obeying every command, knowing none of this mattered.

Margaret said the Lord's Prayer again and again, never noticing the sweaty men crawling upon her, touching her, thrusting into her. She never heard their curses. She never smelled their odors, never felt their touch.

316

It was over faster than she would have imagined. Satisfied for the time being, two of the three slept, while the other returned to the table and ordered her to serve him even more food. And after he ate, she was told to fix his arm. Margaret went about the chore in silence. After cleaning and bandaging the injury, she was told to kneel between his legs and service him again.

It wasn't until the morning of the third day that she was finally allowed to dress. Margaret seemed to come out of her stupor a bit then. Her eyes grew wary as she watched each man go about the chore of loading up supplies. They were leaving. She had no hope that they would let her stay behind. All she could do was pray that they wouldn't hurt the baby. Please, God, *please*—don't let them hurt my baby!

Abigail moaned a low sound of discomfort as she mounted her horse. But not low enough. Hawk had watched her closely since awakening. Despite his objections, they had made love last night again and again. Hawk cursed. He knew she would be stiff and sore this morning. He wished he had shown better control.

"Are you in pain?"

Abigail glanced at his concerned expression and smiled. "Not at all. Why?"

"I thought you might be suffering from last night."

The truth of it was, she did suffer, but not terribly. She was sore and more than a little tired. They probably hadn't had three hours of sleep. Still, she wouldn't have given up last night for anything. "I love you," she said in a burst of heartfelt happiness.

Hawk grinned. "Who do you love?"

"You," she said with a small frown.

He swung himself into the saddle. A wicked light danced in his eyes. "What's my name?"

One look at that delicious smile and Abigail understood. Hadn't he asked her to say it a dozen times last night? And each time she said it hadn't he given her further cause for delight. "Let's see, what's your name?" she murmured as if thinking on the matter. "Could it be Horace? No, no, no, Horace wasn't even there last night, was he? Now let's see."

Hawk shot her a sideways grin as he started forward. "You're a wicked lady, Abigail Pennyworth."

Abigail laughed. "Not nearly as wicked as you, Jeremiah."

"The minute we find a preacher, we're getting married."

Abigail laughed her delight. God, was there ever a woman so happy? "Are we? I don't remember hearing you ask."

"That's because I didn't ask. I'm telling you."

Abigail said nothing. Her silence made him distinctly uneasy.

Hawk shot her a glance. "What's the matter now?"

"Nothing."

"You didn't answer me."

"You didn't ask me anything."

"Are you going to marry me?"

"Perhaps."

"What the hell does perhaps mean?"

"It means if you ask me right, I might."

"Witch," he grumbled as he reached an arm

around her waist and lifted her from her saddle to his lap. She gasped and wrapped her arms tightly around his neck. "You're strangling me."

"Too bad. I might fall."

"You won't fall; I have you. Let go."

Abigail did as he asked and smiled as he repeated his question. "So . . . are you going to marry me?"

"Stop the horse and I'll tell you."

It was Jeremiah's turn to do as he was told. Abigail slid to her feet and grinned. "Get down."

Again he obeyed.

"Dust off that tree, so I can sit."

Hawk shot her a look that told clearly of the absurdity. "That's ridiculous."

"Jeremiah," she said in a warning tone.

"All right." He sat upon the fallen tree, wiggled his backside a bit, hoping for no splinters, and stood again. "Is that better?"

"It will do." Abigail sat in the exact same spot. Hawk blinked at her show of elegance. If he hadn't known better, he might have thought she wore a skirt, for she appeared to be smoothing the material over her lap. A moment later she dabbed at her forehead with an imaginary handkerchief and fluttered her eyelashes in a demure but artificial and exaggerated fashion.

Hawk only blinked in amazement. "What are you doing?"

"I'm waiting for a certain man to propose, of course."

Hawk heaved a great sigh. "Oh, of course."

Abigail giggled.

"I suppose you want me to get down on my knee?"

Abigail's cough went far toward hiding her laughter, but not far enough. "I wouldn't want you to do anything you don't want to do."

Hawk scowled. "Right." He knelt, feeling every inch the fool. "All right, here goes. Marry me," he said with all the feeling of ordering a tankard of ale.

"That's it? That's the best you can do? After all the time and trouble I went to getting dressed and having my hair fixed properly?" She touched her hat, pretending it was an artfully arranged hairdo.

"You didn't have to get dressed. I like you naked."

She shot him a glare. "I didn't hear that."

Hawk laughed. "You heard it all right. Stop fooling around and give me your answer."

"My answer is yes."

"Good, now get back on your horse."

Abigail stood. "I can't remember when a man has ever been so romantic while proposing to me."

"You won't remember any of them for long."

Abigail chuckled a low wicked sound. "I'll forget them as soon as you forget Lydia."

"Lydia who?"

"Beast."

"Brat." He reached for her and pulled her willing body tightly to his. His face was buried in her throat as he murmured, "God, I love you."

They didn't find a preacher that day or the next, but what Hawk did find was a stagecoach heading east.

Abigail watched in growing trepidation as he hailed the coach. She knew what he was going to say before the words were spoken.

"Where are you going?"

"Liberty," one of the two men aboard returned.

"Do you have room for another passenger?" It hadn't taken Hawk a minute before coming to this decision. The moment he saw the stage, he knew exactly what he was going to do. He loved Abigail too much to allow her to come to harm. Too much to chance anything happening to her.

"We have no passengers this trip."

Hawk nodded, dug two fingers into a tiny pocket, and threw the man a coin. "I'll tie her horse to the back."

"I won't go."

Hawk shot her a warning glare. "You're going."

"I won't," she returned stubbornly.

"Abby, if you give me any trouble, I'll—"

She cut him off with, "I'm going to give you nothing but trouble if you—"

It was his turn to cut her off. "Get on that stage!"

"No!"

"Is something wrong?" This came from the driver. The man beside him was shooting both Hawk and Abigail some strange looks. If that woman was his lady, he wouldn't be half so determined to get rid of her.

"My prisoner is giving me a bit of trouble."

Abigail moaned. She'd been through this before and knew the chances of convincing these men of the truth of the matter. She didn't try.

"Your prisoner?" Neither man could have looked more astonished. The woman was dressed like a man—but a prisoner? A woman prisoner?

Hawk grabbed her hands and, as fast as she could blink, tied them together. "Jeremiah, stop it!" she demanded to a deaf ear. A moment later he dismounted and was at her side. Despite her struggles he pulled her from the horse and into his arms.

"Jeremiah, please," she said, even as she tried to kick him away.

"I'm doing this for your own good." Hawk steeled himself against any emotion, against the look of hurt in her eyes. It was too important that she be safe. He couldn't allow her pleas to influence his judgment. She was inside the coach, sprawled upon the floor before she had a chance to say anything more.

"Jeremiah, please. Don't."

"As soon as I'm finished, I'll come for you," he said in a whisper, just before he slammed the door shut.

Hawk flashed both men his identification and said, "Tell your sheriff I'd be obliged if he'd keep her for a bit. I'll be along directly to pick her up."

Both men nodded, but the stage remained still until Hawk shot the driver a long stern, silent glare, along with a nod pointing out their intended direction. Seconds later they were on their way again.

"I'm going to get you for this, Mr. Hawk," she swore as the man atop the coach swung the whip and brought the stage into motion again. She didn't know how exactly, but she swore she would.

Hawk sat upon his horse, in the middle of the road, for a long time before turning back to continue on his journey once again. The three he trailed were more than two days ahead. He'd come upon them soon. Without Abby, and the care and precautions he was forced to take with her, he'd only find them sooner. Hawk was searching for a sign of the cracked horseshoe when the thought occurred. Before a moment passed, the thought became an absolute certainty. The moment she got over her shock at what he'd done, she'd find a way to escape. Hawk was positive of it. Damn her to hell. If he didn't go back, she'd be sure to get herself lost or hurt or possibly killed.

Abigail spent most of an hour biting at the ropes that tied her hands together. Loose at last, she rubbed at her wrists and laid every curse word she could find upon the villain's head. Her eyes narrowed as she judged the moving ground outside the coach. They were going too fast for her to jump. Could she climb from the door to the roof? Could she then untie her horse and leap into the saddle? Abigail sighed. She could if she were a heroine of a penny novel.

She punched the seat in her frustration. If she had a weapon of some sort, a rifle in particular, she could have forced them to stop.

Abigail glanced outside and then forward. An instant later she almost laughed aloud as she leaned farther out and saw what lay ahead. The road was little more than a mud-slick path between heavy forest. Hard and rutted at the moment, it stretched up a long, high incline. All she had to do was wait for the coach to start up the hill. Abigail laughed softly. The day will *never* come when you'll beat me, Mr. Hawk. We might as well get that settled right off.

Abigail checked the stagecoach's progress. As she assumed, they started off fast, but soon enough the stage would slow. And she'd take the opportunity offered and jump free the moment it did.

Abigail opened the door and stood bent in half,

perched upon the edge. The horses strained, the whip whistled through the air, sounding again and again across the animals' backs. She could hear the two men above her curse, the horses whinnied their reluctance, the turn of the wheels, the grating against hard earth. And then all sound was pushed into the background as she watched and waited and waited.

Her opportunity came some ten yards from the summit. The coach moved slowly now. Abigail took a deep breath, praying for courage. It didn't seem to matter that her jump wouldn't be more than four feet, or that they were moving slow enough for a runner to keep up. She was still afraid.

She glanced ahead, assuring herself that no trees stood nearby and, with eyes then closed, she flung herself from the coach into a soft—well, almost soft—bush.

"Ow," she moaned as her elbow hit hard against the ground. She rolled into the brush, lest the two men notice her leap and stop to search for her.

Abigail lay in place for a long moment, waiting for any signs of pain. Nothing appeared to be broken, thank the Lord. She tested her legs, her arms. Nothing. Abigail smiled and came slowly to her feet.

A moment later, with the sounds of the stage fading, she was walking back to where she had boarded the coach.

The odd thing was, she hadn't thought they had traveled so far. It was growing dark, and she wasn't anywhere near where she had started off. At least she didn't think she was. Abigail breathed a sigh of disgust. She should have tried to climb the coach. She should have tried to reach her horse. An owl sounded its creepy "Whoo, whoo, whoo," and Abigail knew she had made a serious mistake.

She had two alternatives. Either to try to find Hawk, which she realized all too late would be something like trying to find a particular snowflake, or turn around and head on home. Neither possibility offered her much in the way of security. If she stayed in the forest alone, she'd probably die, if not from man or beast then from exposure. And if she started back toward home, she'd never make it. She was probably a hundred miles or more away. She'd never be able to walk that distance.

She had no money, thank you, Mr. Hawk, for her bags, which held her purse, were on the horse and the horse was attached to the coach. She had no weapon—her rifle, like her bags, were on their way home. She had no food, no water. She was going to kill that man with her bare hands.

Abigail tried to think. The first thing she had to do was make her decision and stick with it. It didn't take long for her to realize she was better off on the road, no matter what or who she might come upon. At least there she had something of a chance.

Hawk cursed as he watched the lone figure come to a stop. She hadn't realized it, but she'd been trailing him for the last two hours. It was getting dark now. She'd head off into the woods for protection, maybe find herself a tree to sleep against. Damn fool. He should wring her neck.

Hawk backtracked until he figured he was no more than a few yards from wherever she'd stopped for the night. He made camp. A bright fire soon brought warmth from the night's chill and boiling coffee wafted its aroma a good hundred feet into the forest. The scent of frying bacon soon joined the coffee, and Hawk figured he'd give her ten minutes to find him. If these scents didn't flush her out soon, he'd have to go search her out himself.

He crouched on his haunches by the fire and hid a smile along with a sigh of relief as he listened to the rustling of underbrush. She was out there, behind him, hesitating. Only Hawk wasn't in any mood to wait for her to show herself. He said, "You might as well come in, Abigail. The bacon is done, the coffee is hot."

Abigail walked toward the fire and sat near it. She reached her hands out to its warmth. "All you managed to do was lose a good horse and all of my money. I hope you're satisfied."

Chapter Sixteen

"Why did you do it?" he said with what Abigail thought was amazing calm. She had expected anger. At the very least a sharp word or glare.

Abigail wasn't destined for disappointment.

"Why did *you* do it?" she returned, more than a little defensively and with none of Hawk's control.

"I wanted to keep you safe, damn it!" He suddenly shouted and watched with satisfaction as she jumped a half foot off the ground. He'd started off almost amused at her tenacity, but it took only a glance in her direction for the truth to come crashing upon him. She was a small woman, unprotected, out of her element. How would she have survived alone in the forest? He knew a sickening wave of despair as he imagined all the horrible things that could have happened to her, if he hadn't suspected her of this absurd act and turned back.

He cursed, unable to remember when he'd last known such anger.

"Well, I want the same for you," she returned equally as loud.

"And you're going to do it?" he roared almost in ridicule. "You'll keep *me* safe?"

"Don't make it sound impossible. You're not infallible."

"Oh, God." Hawk shook his head, knowing exasperation in the extreme. "I don't know if I should throttle you or kiss you."

Abigail laughed at that. After a moment she asked, "Do you still want to marry me?"

"Of course I want to marry you. Why do you think I wanted you safe?"

"Then I think you should kiss me."

Hawk shook his head, even as a smile came to tease his lips. "Come over here, brat."

"Yes, master."

Hawk only groaned, knowing the fallacy of that title. He sat back as she came to his side. "Master, my ass. If I were your master, you would have obeyed me."

Abigail snuggled against him. She sat opposite him so that they were able to face each other. She took off her hat and shook her hair free. It floated over her shoulders in a mass of loose curls, like spun gold. She looked into his dark eyes for a long moment and then with all seriousness asked, "Jeremiah, how does one master one's ass?"

Hawk laughed. By the serious look of her, he had taken for granted that she was about to apologize, perhaps even offer a profession of love. He should have known better. This woman would never do the expected. His hands wrapped around her throat. "On second thought, I think I will throttle you."

"No, you won't, darling," she said, her voice sweeter than he'd ever heard it before.

"Won't I?" Hawk could hardly keep his laughter at bay. God, how he loved this woman. "And how would you stop me if I set my mind to it?"

"You love me," she said flippantly—as if that simple sentence were all the answer he needed. She smiled but said nothing more.

"You're right about one thing, brat. I do love you. I probably love you more than I've ever loved anyone in my life."

Abigail's blue eyes narrowed. One eyebrow raised threateningly. "What do you mean, probably?"

He laughed again, knowing this woman was bound to keep him smiling for the rest of his life. He almost couldn't wait to live in peace with her, although he didn't know how much peace he was likely to get, with this one as his wife. "No probablies. I love you more than anything or anyone, period."

"And you're glad I escaped and came back to you?"

"Don't push it, Abby," he said suddenly stern again.

Abigail laughed. "And Lydia?" she couldn't help but tease.

Hawk frowned. "What about her?"

"Do you love me more than you loved her?"

"I never loved Lydia," he said with a touch of amazement that she had believed such a thing.

"You slept with her."

"So?"

Abigail made a face. "God, men are such dogs. I should hate you for that."

He smiled. "But you don't."

She glanced up at the dark sky. "I don't know. Maybe I do."

He leaned back, flat upon the ground and brought her with him. "Would you have preferred that I remained a virgin?"

"Actually, I wouldn't have been greatly upset about it."

"Are you upset because I didn't?"

Abigail shot him a wicked smile. She didn't care about the others. He was hers and he was going to stay hers forever. "Just make sure I'm your last."

"You're my first, last, and always. I swear. Now kiss me."

She deposited a tiny peck upon his lips.

Hawk's forehead creased, his eyes narrowed. "What was that?"

"A kiss. Didn't you just tell me to kiss you?"

"That wasn't a kiss."

"How about this one?" She kissed him again, allowing their mouths slightly longer contact.

"Better, but not quite what I had in mind."

"No? Maybe you had better show me what you had in mind."

"No. Try it again."

"All right. Tell me how you like this one." Abigail brushed her lips across his mouth with slow and purposeful seduction. She pulled back the moment his lips parted. "How was that?"

"Definitely better. But maybe you should work on it some more."

"To get it perfect, you mean?"

"Stop talking and kiss me again."

"Tell me you're glad I came back."

"I'm glad."

"And that you need me to protect you."

"That's it," Hawk said as he nearly threw her off and came to his feet. Moments later he spread out their one blanket, shook off his vest, pants, and moccasins. He wrapped himself in the blanket and raised one side in welcome. "Get in here."

Abigail chuckled a low sound of happiness as she kicked off her boots and flung aside trousers, drawers, and shirt. "I'm going to freeze tonight."

"Are you cold?"

"Not yet," she said, snuggling her naked body to his.

"You won't be," he said in all confidence.

"I think you're right. You're very warm."

"I'm burning up," he said as he pressed his hips forward, showing her exactly why.

"Now where were we?"

"You were about to kiss me."

"Was I? Oh yes, like this, right?" Her kiss was wet and hot, long, luxurious, eager, and daring as she used all her newly gained expertise. She put into that kiss every ounce of love she felt for this man and used her lips, teeth, and tongue to make clear the fact. The kiss was warm, delicious, and told of love and building urgency that Hawk found himself only too willing to see appeased.

Bill Cassidy laughed as he watched Amanda's expression. "Close your mouth before something flies in it."

"Oh, Bill. He's so beautiful." Amanda hadn't expected that Bill would think to give her a puppy. The furry, lively little thing squirmed in her arms. "How did you know I wanted . . . ?"

"You look the puppy type," he said as he touched a finger to her small nose. "Besides, we've been married three weeks today, and I had to give you something."

Amanda laughed.

"We have time before the next stage. Why don't we take the little beggar outside?"

Bill couldn't have been more surprised if a piece of the moon had fallen at his feet when Amanda laughed again and then reached up on her toes to kiss him smack on the mouth. He felt his heart twist with longing, and then she hugged him tightly with one arm, squashing the puppy between their bodies. The puppy yelped, and Bill alternated between an intense dislike of the creature and gratitude for his very existence, for had he not given her the little beast, she never would have shown him this affection.

They went outside and the two of them smiled as they watched the dog run here and there, only to return and growl ferociously as he tugged at his new mistress's skirts. Bill snaked an arm around her waist. Not an altogether uncommon happening. He displayed much affection while in the company of others. But this was the first time he'd touched her while they were alone. He felt his heart triple its beat when he realized she was not only allowing the possessive gesture, but was leaning into him just a little bit.

To all they appeared a happily married couple. Only Bill knew different. Only Bill knew of the endless nights spent at her side. Only Bill knew of the pain of loving her and never bringing her into his arms.

Amanda reached down for the small dog and snuggled her face to his fur. "If you're going to sleep in my room, you'll have to bathe."

"Is that where he's sleeping?"

Amanda turned to face her husband. "Do you mind?"

Bill shrugged. He didn't mind. Not really. What he minded was all the attention the puppy was getting while he, as usual, got none.

Amanda put the puppy down again and, once more to his absolute astonishment, kissed him right on the mouth. "You are the most perfect man."

Bill colored at the compliment, not believing her for a minute. She was teasing him. Making fun of his ugliness, his awkwardness, his size. Jane, his first wife, had done as much and more at every opportunity.

Amanda stepped out of his arms as every bit of happiness seemed to drain from his face. "What's the matter?"

"I'm ugly." Bill felt his heart squeeze in pain. He wished he could be better for her. He wished she could be proud to be his wife.

Bill sighed. He had imagined Amanda to be better than most, far above all, in fact. Only he'd been wrong. His eyes were downcast. He hadn't the strength to watch her as she ridiculed. It was bad enough to hear the words. He was a weak man, he knew. All he could do was stand there and accept her abuse.

Amanda frowned. Her voice held none of her usual sweetness. The truth was, she sounded just a little annoyed. "That's a ridiculous thing to say."

Bill couldn't fathom her reaction to his statement of fact. Could it be she hadn't noticed? "But I am. My ears are too big and they stick out."

Amanda laughed. "You're being very silly."

"What about my nose?"

"What about it?"

"It's too big."

"No, it's not. You have a lovely nose."

It was Bill's turn to grin. "A lovely nose?" he repeated, somewhat dazzled by the compliment.

"Very. As a matter of fact, your nose was one of the first things I noticed about you. After your eyes."

"You noticed my eyes?" Bill couldn't believe it. In his entire life he'd never received a compliment. The only thing he'd ever known was to be the butt of jokes. It was astonishing to say the least. He wondered if his pretty wife weren't in need of spectacles.

Amanda nodded. "They're very blue."

"When did you notice them?"

"Why, the first moment I saw you, of course."

"Did you? And what did you think?"

"I thought, this man has the most beautiful eyes. There's kindness there. I hope he'll give me a job." She laughed at the last of it.

"It's a good thing I did, or I'd never know how beautiful I am," he said with a tender smile.

"You don't believe me?" she asked in all seriousness.

"I think you're the one who's kind."

The stage pulled into the courtyard at that moment

and brought to an immediate end any chance for furthering their conversation.

That same night Amanda blew a stray wisp of hair from her forehead. It was late, but the tavern room was still hot. The inn's kitchen was not separated from the rest of the building as often was the case in most inns. And although the ovens had been working all day to produce the most delicious fare, leaving the air heavy with the scent of juicy roast beef and hot corn bread, it produced as well an almost suffocating heat. The harsh winters were somewhat tempered because of the added warmth, but during the spring and summer months, one was forced to withstand almost unbearable heat. Amanda could only imagine how she would suffer this summer.

There were only a few patrons left, for most had sought their beds at least an hour earlier. Bill was as usual behind the bar. Amanda—after delivering a tankard of ale to the last customer—stopped to say, "I'm going to step out back for a minute."

Her skin glistened with perspiration. Wisps of golden hair had escaped her lace cap and clung to her neck. There was no need to say more. Bill could see at one glance that she was uncomfortable. Ever conscious of her condition, he asked, "Are you all right?"

"I'm fine." She shot him a brilliant smile. Both were aware that her nightly nausea had ceased some two weeks back. "I'll be back in a few minutes."

Amanda stood at the back door and wiped at her damp face and neck with the edge of her apron. Lord, but it was hot.

"Excuse me, ma'am."

Amanda hadn't heard the stranger's approach and jumped just a bit at the sudden sound of his voice. Especially since it sounded so very close to her ear. She stepped forward and to one side, allowing him total access to the kitchen door. Apparently the man was in need of the privy. The back door went unused, except for that purpose. "Sir," she returned with a nod of her head.

Clyde Baker was a tall man. He had to duck his head as he exited the building. Clyde was a regular patron of the tavern room. He lived ten minutes down the road in a ramshackle house upon land that had proven to be more unproductive as each year went by. Growing poorer each year, he'd long ago stopped trying to work the nearly barren land and had changed his profession from farmer to conman/gambler/thief. Clyde had to his credit a nagging wife and a passel of youngsters. None of which brought him a minute of joy.

Clyde and Jane Cassidy, Bill's first wife, had been lovers until that city slicker had come along and she had gone off with him, ruining their little arrangement. That had been a long time ago. Clyde hadn't as yet found a woman to replace her. The truth was, with what he had to choose from around these parts, he hadn't expected to. Not until three weeks ago, when he'd come for his usual Friday night card game in the far corner of the tavern room and found the most beautiful woman he'd ever seen serving the tables.

He'd returned to the inn every night since, but the little lady hadn't once glanced in his direction. He'd been watching her all night, as he did every night, and had been aware of the fact that she'd gone out back alone.

This was his chance. Her stupid, ugly husband never let her out of his sight. If he wanted a little fun—and Clyde couldn't remember the last time he'd wanted it more—he had to make his move.

Clyde had every confidence that he could, with only a little persuasion, convince her to see to the wisdom of his way of thinking. After all, she couldn't possibly love the big, ugly buffoon she had taken as her husband. What harm could there be if the two of them enjoyed one another for a bit?

"It's a warm night."

"Yes, sir, it is."

Well, she wasn't the talkative sort, was she? Clyde grinned at that bit of knowledge, for he was one man who believed silence a virtue in a woman. Any man married to a woman like his wife would believe it. The harpy never shut up.

Amanda glanced at the man who stood beside her. She frowned. What was he doing here? If he needed the use of the privy, why hadn't he gone and used it? Amanda felt the need to run and then almost smiled in ridicule at her thoughts. There was nothing to be afraid of. A man had stepped outside for a breath of air. He had no ulterior motives. She had to forget her past. Forget the men who would have seen her harmed.

"You're a lovely lady, Mrs. Cassidy."

Amanda didn't know what to make of that. Most men did not indulge in such talk with a woman who was not of their acquaintance, and yet he had used her married name while doing so. Perhaps he was simply the sort who gave compliments to every woman he met. "Thank you, sir."

"I do enjoy looking at a lovely woman."

Amanda felt again the need to run. Her first feelings of alarm had proven correct. The moment she first saw him, she should have immediately returned to the inn. "Thank you, sir," she said again. "I have to go in now."

Amanda turned to do just that but was brought up short by an arm around her waist. Suddenly she was flung up against the back wall of the inn, the man's hand over her mouth. "Don't scream, little girl. I just want a little fun. You won't get hurt."

Amanda's eyes grew huge with fright. She shook her head, or at least tried. His hand, pressed hard across her mouth, had disallowed movement. She screamed with all her might, but the scream came out as a low muffled sound that couldn't be heard beyond their ears.

His hips held her tightly to the wall. His free hand came to fondle her full breasts. He tore at her bodice. It wasn't enough to feel material. He wanted to touch her, not her dress.

Amanda cringed and her muffled screams turned to faint sobs of pleading. She tried to fight Clyde off, for he had not thought to hold her arms, but a punch against his chest and a slap to his cheek did nothing but bring a horribly evil smile to his lips and a tightening of his hand on her naked breast.

"Easy, pretty one. No one needs to get hurt here."

Amanda's head buzzed. In her fright she hadn't at first realized that he held not only her mouth but her nose as well. She couldn't breathe.

338

Bill, concerned for his wife, stepped outside only seconds after Clyde pinned her to the wall. It was dark. He couldn't see much except for the fact that his wife was in another's arms, that his hands were all over her body.

The pain crashed upon him like a living breathing thing. It was happening all over again. He'd thought they were growing close. He'd prayed that they would grow close, and to find her in another's arms was simply too much. He couldn't go through this again.

Amanda had stopped struggling. Her heart continued to pound violently, but the world grew fuzzy as each second ticked by without air. She felt somehow oddly relaxed. Her knees buckled and blackness swam around the edges of her consciousness.

And then—thank you, sweet blessed Lord—he let her go. Amanda didn't have the strength to run. All she could do was sink to the ground, sobbing softly in her relief.

Amanda wasn't at first conscious of the reason why Clyde Baker had let her go. She never realized her husband was there. She heard the vaguely familiar sounds of flesh hitting against flesh, but never put the sounds to reality.

It was over within seconds. Clyde never had a chance. He was suddenly swung around to face Bill Cassidy's rage. Had he the time he might have cowered in the face of such fury, for Bill Cassidy was a big man, a massive man. Mild mannered, perhaps, but he possessed uncommon power and strength. And when it came to protecting his own, it seemed Bill could be as vicious as any.

Bill breathed deeply as he watched, without a flicker of emotion, as the man fell unconscious to the ground. A moment later he turned to his wife, who oddly enough remained exactly where she had fallen. Bill frowned. He would have thought that she might have run from the sight of violence, for Amanda had appeared such a peaceful gentle lady. He knew better now, of course. She was no better than the rest. No better than Jane.

He took her by the arm and pulled her to her feet.

"Don't touch me, sir. Please, don't do this."

Bill hardly heard his wife's mutterings. Within seconds he had her inside and on the way up the back stairs to their room. It was only when he reached the door of their room that he realized something was wrong.

Amanda never called him sir. She was begging someone not to touch her.

He got her into the room and lit a candle. It was only then that he noticed the blue marks already forming around her mouth. Her cap was gone, her hair half fallen from its pins, and the bodice of her dress was torn, exposing one gleaming smooth breast. Jesus, she'd been abused, and he hadn't even realized it. He'd thought she stood willingly in another's arms.

Bill felt another bout of almost uncontrollable rage. He wished he would have known the truth of the matter, for he would have gone on beating the man long after the bastard had lost consciousness.

"Mandy, sweetheart," he said as she continued to beg for her freedom. "You're safe now, darling. Can you hear me?"

The words that tumbled from her lips came to a sudden stop, and Amanda looked into the gentle blue eyes of her husband. He knelt before her, his hands on the arms of the chair in which she sat. Her blue eyes filled with tears, and huge drops rolled over soft cheeks. She shuddered. "Oh, Bill. He almost . . ." She couldn't finish but shuddered again. A moment later she almost knocked him back as she flung herself into his arms. Her hands reached around his neck, and she clung tightly as she pressed her body against his.

Amanda had no idea of Bill's first supposition. He vowed she never would as his arms came to cradle her against him. "Don't cry, sweetheart. You're all right now."

He shifted so that he could lean his back against the chair, and he held her in his lap, pressed close against him, long after she slept.

The candle was nearly burned out by the time he came to his feet and brought her to their bed. Gently he pulled away her torn clothing and covered her with a clean nightdress. It was only after she was sound asleep again that he removed his clothes, pulled on his own nightshirt, and lay down beside her.

Bill Cassidy lay stiffly beside his wife of three weeks. God, how much longer would he be forced to bear this? He loved Amanda with all his heart, but she seemed to feel nothing but fondness for him. The truth being, she treated him more like a brother than a friend or lover.

True to his promise he had yet to touch her as a husband touches his wife. Undressing her tonight, he had not allowed his gaze, nor his hands, to linger

341

. . . and it had cost him. He lay next to her now, trembling with a need that might never find its ease. And Amanda seemed not to notice at all the oddity of sleeping beside a man who kept at least six inches between them at all times.

Minutes ticked by. The old clock in the hall sounded the hour of one. He almost jumped—for he had supposed her to be asleep—when from out of the darkness came, "Bill, are you sleeping?"

"No."

"Bill, he was trying to—" Her voice choked up with tears as she tried to speak and found it an impossible chore.

He turned to her then. His thick arms reached for her slim form and pulled her against him. Gently he nestled her face to his neck, and his big hands moved over her back in a comforting gesture.

"It's over, Amanda. Don't think of it. He won't touch you again."

"I have to tell you. Please."

Bill realized her need to talk about it and nodded, waiting for her to go on. He smiled into the dark when she remained silent. Finally he asked, "Did he have his hand over your mouth?"

She nodded. "How did you know?"

"I saw the marks."

She sniffed. "It was awful. He was going to—"

"I know."

"How did you know I needed you?"

"You were gone for a long time. I came to see if you were all right."

"You saved me again, Bill. How will I ever thank you."

"There's no need. You're my wife. It's my job, my pleasure to protect you."

"I love you, Bill. You're the most wonderful man I've ever known."

Bill knew she spoke of her appreciation for his help tonight. He knew she didn't really love him, not in the same way that most wives loved their husbands.

"Better even than my father."

"Thank you." He gave her a little squeeze, careful that he didn't use much strength.

It was very dark. Amanda couldn't see more than shadows. No doubt that was why she found the courage to ask, "Do you love me, Bill. Maybe just a little?"

Bill found he suddenly couldn't hold back. It had been only three weeks, but he loved her beyond imagining, more so every day. He poured out his heart with a gentle laugh. "Do I love you? Only with my whole heart and soul. I'll never love another the way I love you."

"Is that true?" she asked, coming to lean upon her elbow, trying to see into his eyes.

"It's true."

"Then why haven't you said anything? Why didn't you tell me?"

"I was afraid."

Amanda laughed. "You? Afraid? Of what?"

"I'm ugly, big, and stupid. I thought you'd feel disgust if you knew."

"Don't ever say that you're ugly again. I won't have it, do you hear?"

"Yes, ma'am," Bill agreed, unable to hold back his smile.

"And you're not stupid, either. Do you understand me?" Her voice was very stern. Bill half expected to see her shaking a finger in his face.

"Yes, Amanda."

"And what's wrong with being big? I wish I were a little bigger."

"Do all tiny people want to be big?"

She smiled at his question. "Probably. Or at least a little bigger." She was silent for a moment. "If I were bigger, I would have given that man a beating he wouldn't have soon forgotten."

"Don't worry. I did it for you."

"I remember now. Thank you." She kissed him. It was dark, so she missed most of his mouth, but Bill didn't mind. He didn't care where she kissed him so long as she did it again and again. And blessed be God, she did.

Bill wished his body felt as good as his heart did. His heart had never felt lighter, his body more heavy with pain. He wanted her so badly, it was just about killing him. And all he allowed himself to do was lie there and accept her sweet gentle kisses.

When she rested her head again in the crook of his neck, he asked, "Are you tired, Amanda?"

"No, I'm too happy to be tired."

"I love you."

"I know. That's why I'm so happy."

"Amanda?"

"What?"

"I want to touch you. If you don't want me to, I'll understand."

There was a long moment of silence where Bill's spirits sank lower than any pit in the earth. He took a deep breath and said, "It's all right, sweetheart. Just go to sleep."

And then, like a shining miracle, came the sound of her voice. "I want you to touch me, Bill. You're my husband. It's not wrong for a husband to touch his wife."

And then she found his hand in the dark and directed it to her body. He muttered a low wordless sound as he touched her, ever so gently, and then unable to hold back any longer buried his face against her breasts with an aching groan.

It had taken a long time. Thirty years of waiting— but he had finally found the one woman who could love Bill Cassidy. And he was never going to let her go.

Chapter Seventeen

After three days the body was beginning to smell, the odor not in the least pleasant. But unpleasant odors, and the possible unhealthy circumstances that were sure to develop, weren't paramount in Margaret's concern. Her worry was, as always, for her baby. The men were packing up, obviously readying themselves to leave. She had no hope, since they'd told her to get dressed, that she'd be allowed to stay behind. What would become of her son?

Would they simply kill the baby as a casual parting gesture that proved nothing but their capacity for inhumanity? Or would they leave him behind, knowing he faced certain death by starvation?

She had to think, and yet no matter how hard she tried she could come up with no plan. There had to be something she could do. Something!

"Let's go," Willie said as he walked toward the door.

"What about—?"

"Take her," he said before Josh finished his sentence.

"Wait. Let me put the baby in the cellar." She nodded toward Hill's body. "The body will draw animals. Please."

Willie gave her a hard look, obviously annoyed at the simple request. He nodded toward the man with the injured arm. (Margaret had yet to learn any of their names.) "Kill it."

"No! Please, don't kill my baby," she screamed, showing more emotion in one sentence than she had shown in all of the last three days combined. She ran to the child and clutched him to her chest. Her eyes were wild with fear, her body trembled violently. The baby began to cry, picking up on his mother's terror. "I'll do anything. Please, don't kill him."

"You say that now, but what about after he's left behind?"

"It won't matter. I swear, it won't matter. I promise I'll do anything you say. Just let him live."

"That's right, 'cause I can always come back and kill him, can't I?"

Willie grunted as he watched her shiver in fear. "All right. Let her put the kid in the cellar. And hurry up about it." The last he directed at Margaret.

Margaret did as she was told. She took hardly a minute. After wrapping him tightly in a thick quilt to guard against the chill, she placed him in an empty crate. There was a chance. A very good chance that someone would come by and hear his cries. It had been almost a week since any of her neighbors had come. One or another would be sure to stop in soon, and they would hear the baby cry. Please, God, let them hear it.

They rode that day from early morning until dusk,

but Margaret knew her chores were far from over once they stopped for the night. One of the men made a fire, the rest sat around and talked while she prepared a pot of coffee and a meal of bacon and beans.

Once they were finished, Margaret was allowed to eat. She did so automatically, knowing she had to keep up her strength or lose her chance of ever seeing her son again.

When she was done, she was ordered to collect more wood for the fire and clean up. She did.

By the time she was finished, it was time to service each man. Two of them ordered it done twice. It was only when they were satisfied that she was allowed to rest.

Margaret curled herself into her blanket as the men sat around the fire and talked. The next thing she knew, she was being shaken awake. "Get up, bitch. Make a fire. I want coffee."

Margaret was stiff and sore, for she'd slept through the night without ever moving. The overall mistreatment she'd received so far only added to her aches. Still, she ignored the pain. Her mind was a blank— she performed her duties as if a puppet. There was nothing she wouldn't do, and each man knew it and took complete advantage. She harbored no thoughts of disobedience. These men were bad, very bad. She knew they would carry through on their threat if she dared to disobey. She lived for one purpose only: to see her son alive and well. It didn't matter what became of her in the process.

Quickly she did their bidding. The day became a repeat of the day before. The night as well. And through it all Margaret prayed.

It was the third night. A small fire glowed. Supper was cooked and eaten. Margaret was again on her back. Willie, most always the first, had done his evil deed. Josh was grunting and sweating as he thrust his body between her legs. Her mind was, as always, far away. Suddenly she was brought back to the present with a powerful blow to her cheek. She saw stars and thought perhaps she might black out, but no . . . he hadn't hit her hard enough. "Don't just lie there like a dead cow. Put something into it."

"I wonder if she'd be so calm if she knew about the fire." Willie said, with an insinuating evil grin twisting his hard features into a grotesque smile.

The fact was, Willie hadn't ordered a fire. It wasn't that he was too kindhearted to have burned her house down, thereby killing her son. It was simply that he hadn't thought of it. Still, it didn't hurt none to let her think he had. He'd never seen a woman so damn calm. She was almost creepy. It didn't matter what anyone did to her, all she did was roll over and silently take even more. Sometimes she looked like the walking dead. The thought of her dull vacant eyes sent chills up his spine. He couldn't look into her face while atop her.

"What?" Margaret blinked as his words finally penetrated the protective haze of apathy. "What about a fire?"

Willie chuckled a low evil sound of pleasure. Well, he got a reaction at least. "Oh, nothing much. It's just that I ordered Josh here to burn the place to the ground."

"There was no fire."

"None that you could see. It didn't catch real good

until we were a few miles away." His eyes darted to her horrified expression and back to the piece of wood he whittled. "I reckon that boy you were so anxious to protect got toasted up real nice and warm. What do you figure he looks like about now?"

His words brought instantly to mind her baby and the pain and fear he would have suffered in a fire. Whimpering sounds slid from her dry cracked lips. And then instantly her mind shut down. She couldn't think, for to imagine her baby engulfed in flames would drive her insane.

The rage began somewhere in the pit of her soul. And then it was suddenly more than rage. It was hatred. It was loathing. It was revenge. Together they grew into hysteria, a silent hysteria, so strong her body trembled as if palsied. She welcomed the strength, for she knew exactly what had to be done.

The man above her laughed, but she never heard it. The steady growing emotion was foreign to her nature. She didn't recognize it, nor did she ponder what was happening to her. All she knew was that these men would die. Somehow she'd see to it that they died.

The change in her was sudden and extreme. It had taken only a few seconds, but docile obedient Margaret was suddenly wild. The only word that truly fit was berserk. Nothing mattered anymore. She didn't care if she died. Uncaring of the consequences she attacked with the power and strength of three men.

Josh's body jerked, ramming hard into hers, as the first of his seed emptied itself into her body. He was far from finished when she suddenly shoved him off and kicked his still hard, still emptying, sex with a booted foot.

His eyes grew puzzled, for it took a few seconds for the pain in his groin to catch up with his brain, and then the pain was so intense it left him momentarily stunned. Stunned until it grew greater and then greater still.

A cry of torment was torn from his throat. He screamed his agony and thought he probably died, for he couldn't imagine pain to equal this.

Josh rolled over the ground, moaning in breathless mind-stealing agony as she came to her feet and charged the monster who had brought this suffering upon her. The son of a bitch who had killed her son.

Willie grinned as he watched her come for him. He was ready for a little fun. What he wasn't ready for was the heel of her boot smashing into his cheekbone. The force knocked him back. And then the camp site erupted with curses and movement. Mike—his arm healing, but still hardly as strong as it could have been—tried to grab her. He held her with his good arm, but Margaret tore at that arm like a wild animal. Nails and finally teeth ravaged the bandage and the injury beneath. Margaret was clearly out of her mind. She didn't have even the wherewithal to feel satisfaction as the man howled his pain and then roughly shoved her away.

Her hair was wild, her eyes more so, but as she saw the three filthy animals writhe in pain, she found the presence of mind to take this chance and run.

Margaret didn't take ten steps before she was brought up short with a bullet to her head.

Minutes later the three men stood around her

body, each in varying degrees of pain. Willie cursed as he watched the blood form a small puddle to one side of her head. They'd have to make their own camp from now on, and do without the fun afterward as well, unless he could find them another woman.

"What the fuck did you go and tell her we killed her kid for?"

"Shut up. I was just having some fun. How was I supposed to know she'd go crazy?"

"Are we going to bury her?"

Willie looked at Mike as if he'd lost what little sense he had. "What for?"

"Well, kick her under the brush then. Suppose someone comes along?"

Willie laughed. "What the hell difference does that make?" he added with a shrug of disinterest. "If someone comes, we'll just kill him."

All three grinned and turned back to the fire. They left her exactly where they had shot her down and made up their beds for the night.

It began to rain early the next morning, just as all three men gained their saddles. They were close to Memphis. Willie figured maybe a few days more and they would have themselves a time of it. Mostly careless of his personal hygiene, Willie was nevertheless anxious to sit himself in a tub of hot water and allow any one of the city's perfumed whores to work their charms over him. A woman and a bottle of whiskey—life didn't come better than that.

Their pockets bulged with coin, taken from every small farm, every lone traveler, every place they had stopped to pillage, rape, and murder. They had enough for a while. Maybe for a long while.

Three days and still the rain continued on in an unrelenting downpour. It caused narrow streams to grow into rushing white-capped water, and Hawk's horse to sink at least six inches into sucking mud with every step it took. They had to stop or chance the horse some real injury. They had to find a place to stay until the worst of it was over. "Oh, God, not again."

Hawk and Abigail stood just inside the dark protection of the woods. Their gazes took in the small muddy clearing, the pretty little house, the empty front yard, the cold chimney, and the deadly quiet.

She didn't want to see another massacre. She didn't want to see another couple horribly mutilated, their agony frozen forever in death. "Let's just pass this one by," she said as she touched his arm.

"We can't, Abby. Someone might need our help." Hawk shrugged, figuring that possibility remote. The three he trailed had come this way, he knew. He was equally sure they wouldn't have left anyone alive. Still, there was always a chance, unlikely perhaps, but a chance that someone lived. He couldn't bypass this house and never know for sure.

Besides, he and Abby might never be in more desperate need of shelter. They had no choice. They had to stop.

"Stay here until I call you."

"No. I'm not letting you go in there alone."

Hawk breathed a sigh. "Why do you have to argue with everything I say?"

"I'm not arguing. You are."

He shot her a hard look. "Stay behind me then."

Abigail was perfectly happy to obey him on this score.

Hawk started forward, while muttering something about women not having the sense to know their place. Abigail ignored him and, with a rifle in her hand, followed close behind.

"Don't slip in the mud. You'll probably shoot me if you fall."

"Don't worry. My finger's not on the trigger."

"Wonderful," he said with a touch of sarcasm. "That should work out just fine if someone starts shooting."

Abigail shot his back a nasty look but said nothing.

As he had before, Hawk peered through a window. It was dark inside, but not so dark that he couldn't make out the room. The hearth was black, obviously cold. All was still. The house appeared empty. Perhaps the owners had gone off to visit someone. Maybe, just this once, he wouldn't come across further remnants of death and destruction.

Hawk moved around the side of the house and opened the front door. The moment he did, he knew the chances of finding the place empty were nil. There was no mistaking the odor of death. Someone had died and had been left inside.

He motioned for Abigail to remain outside. Abigail ignored the gesture and followed him into the house.

She, too, noticed the odor and knew there was a body here. But it wasn't until her eyes grew accustomed to the dimness that she found the body. A second later she realized who it was. Her rifle clattered to the floor, causing Hawk to jump, spin around, and then curse. Damn woman! She'd just scared him half to death.

Hawk had barely the time to reholster his gun when Abigail was suddenly in his arms, sobbing out her terror. "It's Hill. My God, Hawk, they have Amanda!"

"What are you talking about?"

"Hill! That's Thomas Hill," she said impatiently.

Hawk frowned. Her identifying the body made nothing clear. Who the hell was Hill?

"What about Amanda?"

"They've got her." She trembled violently and was suddenly racked with sobs. He could hardly understand her as she accused, "I told you I had to find her. I told you."

Hawk was finally beginning to piece it all together. He remembered now that Amanda had been with a man named Hill. "Wait a minute. I thought you said Amanda left New Orleans alone. You said she boarded the *Princess,* remember? Didn't you tell me the man she was with left his room a week later without paying his rent?"

Abigail felt her knees weaken. She'd forgotten. Amanda had left days before Hill. They hadn't been together. Oh, God! Please, don't let them have been together.

Abigail was terrified to look. Just in case there was another body, her sister's body, she couldn't— wouldn't—look.

Hawk guided her to a chair and sat her at the table as he searched the place. Moments later he returned, holding a baby in his arms. "Look at what I found," he said, not in the least happy about the discovery.

There had been a woman here. And now that woman was gone. God only knew, if the woman still lived, what she must be suffering.

"A baby!" Abigail came instantly to her feet. She couldn't have been more surprised, nor more relieved. She looked the little child over and realized he was at least a few months old. Amanda had not been with child. At least not so anyone had noticed. The baby couldn't be Amanda's. The baby belonged to the woman who lived here.

Abigail's smile was tempered with sadness. Her sister was safe, at least she prayed she was safe, but the poor lady who lived in this house was not.

Abigail glanced at the body against the wall. "What do you think happened? How did Hill get here?"

Hawk shrugged. He could only guess. "Maybe Hill was looking for Amanda. In any case he stopped here long enough to die. The lady who owns this place is gone. The bastards must have taken her."

"What about her husband?"

"He's either dead or took off long ago."

Abigail frowned. "How . . . ?"

"No shaving gear, no clothes." Hawk glanced at the pegs to the right of the front door. A woman's cape, hat, and apron hung there. "Only a woman and a baby lived here."

Abigail followed his gaze toward the back of the house and the bed. Beside the bed, along the wall, hung two dresses. A pair of boots sat neatly beneath them. On a shelf nearby baby clothes were folded. Hawk was right. The house held no trace of man.

Hawk did not mention the possibility that Amanda might have been here and was gone as well. Hill might have been looking for her. Perhaps had found her. They might have been traveling together. Hawk figured Abigail was better off not imagining the horrors that could have befallen her sister.

"Take care of the baby, and I'll see to him." Hawk nodded toward Hill's body. A moment later he was dragging the corpse outside.

Abigail opened all the windows and then, on the rumpled bed, changed and cleaned the baby. Lord, what a mess. It had to have been days since the poor little thing had been cleaned.

The baby fussed some but appeared more sleepy than anything else. Abigail thought that not a very good sign. After days of being without his mother, he should have been screaming for food.

He didn't seem overly warm. Abigail wondered if he wasn't ill.

Hawk returned and immediately made a fire.

"Something is wrong with the baby."

"What do you mean?"

"He just lies there. He doesn't cry, he doesn't move, and his eyes are half closed."

"Give him something."

"What? I don't know how to take care of a baby."

"You're a woman, aren't you?"

"That's the stupidest thing you've said so far. What has being a woman to do with anything?"

"Women are supposed to know about babies."

"Mothers know about babies."

"Well, you'll be a mother someday, won't you?"

"God." Abigail groaned at his last statement. The man was unbelievably dense. Abigail tried to think. The baby hadn't had any care in days. He needed to eat. Perhaps after he ate, he'd show some improvement.

There was one real problem here. How was she supposed to feed him? Water. That was it. She'd give him water, at least until she could think of something else.

"Get me some water. Maybe he's thirsty."

"He's hungry, probably."

Abigail shot him a nasty glance. "You want to feed him?"

"Funny," Hawk said as he left the house with a pitcher in his hands.

From a spoon Abigail dribbled a few drops of water into the baby's mouth. The poor little thing had a time of swallowing even that much. Still, he managed. And she dribbled a few more drops and then more and then more again.

"You'd better stop for a while. He won't be able to hold it down if you give him too much at once."

The baby took just that moment to show Abigail the truth of Hawk's words. She snarled at Hawk's chuckle even as she went about the chore of cleaning both of them.

Before an hour had gone by, the baby appeared to be recovering. He no longer lay there completely listless. He was beginning to fuss. Abigail knew he was coming out of his lethargy.

"I think he's coming around."

"Good," Hawk said as he cleaned the table and

started a huge pot of water to boil for a bath. He hadn't missed noticing the tub leaning against the side of the house.

"How are we going to feed him?"

"Maybe there's a cow. I'll look after I make us something to eat."

The baby cried—for the first time a good strong howl. Both adults smiled. Abigail said, "Maybe you'd better look now."

Abigail began to pace, all the while patting the exhausted, hungry baby on his back, while Hawk went in search of a cow. He found one in one of the barn's stalls. Ten minutes later he returned to the house with a pail of milk and almost dropped it at the sight of her with the baby at her breast.

"What the hell are you doing?"

"Keeping him quiet."

"He's not getting anything, is he?"

"No. And he isn't the least bit happy about it either."

Abigail left the rocking chair and moved again to the table. She took the fussing baby from her breast and covered herself before she began to dribble warm milk from a spoon into his quivering mouth. It took more than half a cup before the baby grew content and drifted off to sleep.

Both adults breathed a sigh of relief.

Abigail placed the baby on his stomach in his bed. "Do you think the lady would mind if I used one of her dresses?"

"Take a bath first. You're shivering."

Abigail realized she was. She'd been so intent on seeing to the baby's care that she'd forgotten that she

359

was still wet and now growing cold from her damp clothes.

Hawk tried not to look. An impossible chore. He burned his hand twice as he worked over the hot stove, while watching her strip off her wet clothes. She wrapped herself in a sheet as she waited for him to bring in the tub.

Hawk cursed as she turned her back to him, dropped the sheet, and got into the tub. She heard the muttering. "What's the matter?"

"Nothing," he said a bit sulkily. Didn't she know he'd seen just about all there was to see of her? What the hell did she think she was hiding?

Having no idea of Hawk's sudden change of mood, Abigail sighed with pleasure. "This feels good."

Hawk forced aside a response. Anything he said right now would only make her angry. He was rewarded for his silence moments later when she came from the tub and began to dry herself with the sheet. Either she felt perfectly at ease in his company or had forgotten he was there. Hawk didn't ask her which. He was happy enough to simply watch.

Their eyes met as she finished, and both smiled. Abigail felt a surge of warmth at the tenderness in his eyes. "I feel better. Thank you."

Hawk nodded. "Get dressed." God, he'd never thought he'd be saying something like that.

She slid the dress over her head. It was too big, but it didn't matter. It was dry, and she was comfortable again.

Hawk stripped off his clothes and bathed as Abigail put together a meal of sorts. There wasn't much to work with here. Still, she managed.

They ate fried corn bread and bacon. Hawk was sipping at his third cup of coffee when he said, "You know, I've been thinking."

"About what?"

"Your idea to keep the baby quiet."

Abigail frowned. At first she couldn't imagine what the man was leading up to. And then one look in his eyes and she knew. "What about it?"

"Do you think it would work on a man?"

Abigail smiled. "What man?"

"Me."

"You're quiet enough."

Hawk grinned. "I could get very talkative."

"The baby wasn't talking. He was crying."

He shrugged. "I could cry."

Abigail laughed. "You'll wake the baby if you do."

"I could cry quietly."

"You're a little old for that kind of soothing, don't you think?"

"It's better when you're old."

"I wouldn't be able to hold you."

"No, but I could hold you. Get over here."

Abigail giggled. "Now? With the baby here?"

Hawk smiled, got up and barred the door. He sat again opposite her and pushed his plate and cup across the table. "Come here."

Abigail was happy to do as she was told.

He positioned her before him, on the table. Abigail had expected to sit on his lap and asked, "What are you doing?"

"I'll show you in a minute."

Slowly he opened the buttons of the dress. Opened them clear to her waist and made a sound of pleasure as he exposed her to his view. Next both his hands slid beneath the material at her ankles. Abigail took a deep breath as warm fingers began to drift up the inside of her thighs. Both were aware of the fact that she wore nothing under the dress, since her drawers, as well as the rest of her things, were even now hanging before the fire. "I like you in dresses."

"Really?" Her breathing was growing a bit choppy. "I never would have guessed."

"But I like you best with nothing on at all."

He was almost touching her. His fingers were so close, all she had to do was shift and he'd be where she wanted him most. But Abigail was enjoying the teasing and forced her hips to remain still. She leaned back, supported by her hands behind her. "I think I knew that."

"Do you like this?"

"You might say I like it."

Hawk chuckled a low sound of enjoyment. He loved to see her like this, with her eyes half closed, her head thrown back, holding on as best she could to her senses. He knew after a few more minutes, no matter how she tried, she wouldn't be able to keep up her end of the conversation.

He leaned forward and took the tip of one breast into his mouth. She breathed a sigh of pleasure as he rolled his tongue over her sensitive flesh. "Tell me what you feel."

"Like I'm floating. This is too good."

"Tell me what you want."

362

"I want you to touch me," she said with no hesitation.

"Like this?"

Abigail groaned as his finger slid against her moisture, over the tiny bud of her building desire, teasing it into full bloom. "Yes, like that."

"More?"

"Mmm, more."

He touched her again and again until the room swam around her, until her moans filled the house, until she was nothing more than a mindless, throbbing creature intent on finding release from the torment he had imposed.

And then his mouth was there, taking from her the waves of pleasure, the ripples of ecstasy, the aftershocks that would ease at last into contentment.

When he heard her sigh, he pulled back and smiled. "I can't tell you how delicious you taste."

"Thank you."

"No, thank you."

Abigail laughed as he raised and lowered his eyebrows. "It seems I've taken up with a very wicked man."

"Are you sorry?"

"Not likely."

"Tell me why," he said as he brought her from the table. Her legs, still parted, were guided over his as he lowered her against his throbbing sex.

"Because a man who wasn't wicked wouldn't be able to think of such wonderful things."

"Oh, I think all men think of them."

"Really? How amazing. One wouldn't know by looking at them."

"We keep some things a secret."

"Until you get a lady alone, you mean?"

"Exactly."

"Do you have any more secrets to show me?"

Hawk smiled. "I might be able to come up with something."

She rubbed herself against him. "Mmm. It looks like you've come up with something already."

Hawk laughed. "I'm brilliant. What can I say?"

"Don't say anything. Just show me."

And to both their pleasure, he did.

Chapter Eighteen

"What in the world . . . ?" Abigail couldn't understand what was causing that racket. Who was making all that noise?

"The baby's crying," Hawk murmured near her ear as he cuddled her against him.

What baby? came the question, and then she remembered.

"Abby, honey, wake up."

"No." God, she felt like she'd only just closed her eyes. She and Hawk had made love again and again. It couldn't be time to feed the baby already.

"I'll go get the milk," he said as he left the bed, only to return a minute later with the bundle of crying need. "Here, hold him."

Abigail was exhausted. She cuddled the baby close to her side and sighed with relief as he drifted off to sleep again. It didn't last long. Cuddling wasn't all the baby needed. He was wet and hungry. Abigail groaned as she rolled from the bed to change him.

Moments later Hawk was back with milk. Abigail

threw the dress over herself and sat again at the table. A half hour later the baby slept again.

"You're getting very good at that."

"Thank you," she said as she crawled back into bed.

The following morning the baby cried again. Hawk did as he had the night before. Abigail as well, only this time the baby ate, threw up, and ate again. He cried, obviously in some pain. Abigail glanced at a concerned Hawk. "What's the matter with him?"

"I don't know. Maybe he needs to be burped."

Abigail had never been around babies before. She had no idea that it was necessary to make sure any bubbles did not remain in his stomach. Therefore she had not once during any of his feedings thought to burp him.

It took her an hour to calm him down, and the rest of the day before he slept for more than fifteen minutes at a time.

The baby cried and the rain continued. The baby cried, and still the rain went on. Abigail was growing visibly exhausted and edgy, while Hawk felt his share of irritation, along with the sensation of being trapped. He would have fared better to spend most of his time in the barn.

The fact was, there was no way that he could leave even if the weather cleared. He couldn't take a baby with them, and he couldn't leave Abby alone. And every day that passed the men he was after might be farther away. To top it all off, the baby wouldn't stop crying. Hawk knew the baby couldn't help it. Still, it wasn't easy to listen to his screams. He never entered the house that the kid was quiet. "Can't you do anything with him?"

"As a matter of fact, I can."

An instant later the baby was in his hands, and Abigail was storming out the door. The slamming of the door behind her only caused the baby to jump and cry all the more.

Hawk shot the door a hard glance and cursed.

Margaret groaned as she tried to turn her head away from the muddy water, although she didn't know it was muddy water at the time. All she knew was that she was having a problem breathing.

It took some effort, but she managed to roll onto her back. A moment later she realized it was raining. She couldn't imagine how she had fallen asleep outside.

And what had happened to her head? Why did it hurt so?

Moments later the horror she had sustained came rushing back, and she remembered. She'd been running, trying to escape, and had somehow sustained a blow to her head. Probably she'd been shot. She couldn't be sure and was afraid to touch her head and find out.

Where were they? Were they sitting as usual around a fire, waiting for her to recover enough to see to their wants again? Oh, God, how was she to bear more?

Margaret lay there for a long moment, listening to the sounds of rain falling upon the forest. She listened for their step, for their low evil laughter, for the sounds of a horse, for the rustle of movement as they ate or drank, for a snore, for a snort of their horses. Nothing. All she could hear was rain.

Could it be that after days of constant prayer, God had finally answered her?

Margaret fought against the fear of what she might find and opened her eyes at last. Either it was growing dark or the rain caused the day to appear so. She glanced to her right, her left. Nothing. Beyond her feet lay an abandoned camp site. They were gone. No men, no horses were in sight. Margaret began to cry with relief. Tears of joy mingled with the rain to wash away the worst of her horror. As the tears came so did a new knowledge. They had told her they killed Mike junior in a fire, but she didn't believe it. At first she had, but now that she had time to think she knew they lied. They wouldn't have waited so long to tell her. They would have been thrilled at her horror and couldn't have waited. Besides, she would have noticed the smoke.

No. Her baby was at home. Still in the cellar, awaiting his mother's return. She had to get up. Her baby needed her. She had to go home.

How long had she been gone, she wondered? Three days at least. Perhaps four. And by the time she got back, maybe another four, maybe five. Would he make it? Would he live that long without her?

She knew he wouldn't. No baby could go a week or more without food and care. He might be dead already. Margaret shook the thought aside. Somehow she knew he wasn't dead. He couldn't be. She couldn't have suffered the things she had for God to take him anyway. Someone had come by. Her neighbors had found him. They *had* to have found him.

Margaret moaned as she rolled to her knees. She was terribly dizzy, but she couldn't allow the dizziness to stop her. She had to get back.

Four days later she burned with fever as she reached the clearing and smiled. Her house was there, just as she'd left it. She knew they had lied.

It was growing dark, but a lamp was lit inside. A lamp and a fire. Someone was there. Margaret felt so suddenly weak, she wondered how she would manage the last hundred feet.

Hawk and Abigail had suffered through four days of rain and baby. Neither knew what to do next. If the weather didn't break, they'd soon be at each other's throats—not that they hadn't been once or twice already.

Abigail bounced the baby against her as she tried to eat. She and Hawk had stopped talking to one another three days ago. Abigail put down her fork and then jumped as Hawk yelled, "What's the matter now?"

"Nothing." The more the baby cried, the more Abigail felt like crying herself. She left the table and started to pace again. She was exhausted, having slept not more than an hour straight in days.

"Then why aren't you eating?"

"I'm not hungry." She blinked away the tears that threatened.

"How much longer do you figure he can cry like that?"

"I don't know." Abigail snuggled her face into a tiny neck and moaned, "Please, baby, stop crying."

The baby seemed to quiet some. He hiccupped a sob and then another. His tiny body trembled as he drifted off to sleep. Abigail knew it wouldn't last. He slept, yes—but only for a few minutes at a time.

"Abby."

"What?" She wiped at her eyes with her free hand.

"Are you crying?"

"No."

"You sound like you are."

"I'm not."

"Turn around."

"No."

Hawk was suddenly behind her. His arms reached around both her and the baby in her arms. "I'm sorry."

"For what?"

"For yelling at you, for the baby crying, for everything."

"It's not your fault."

"It's not yours either, but that didn't stop me from yelling."

Abigail breathed a watery sigh and leaned back against him.

"I wish you would fight with me. I feel like I've been kicking a kitten. What good is my yelling when you won't yell back?" She chuckled softly. "I haven't heard a nasty word in days." He held her a bit more firmly, his chin upon the top of her head. "And I never thought I'd ever say this, but I miss them."

Abigail smiled. "I can't. I'm too tired."

"Give me the baby. I'll hold him while you get some sleep."

She smiled and turned in his arms. "And when I wake up, we'll fight?"

He kissed the tip of her nose. "Only if you're ready."

He kissed her mouth softly sweetly and then jumped back, shoving her behind him as the door slammed against the wall behind it.

The first thing Margaret saw upon entering her home was an Indian. It was the last thing she'd expected. The combination of fear, anxiety, and fever—and now shock—was a bit too much for her to handle. She cried out and then crumpled to the floor in an unconscious heap.

Hawk had drawn his gun at the sound of her entrance. He had yet to replace it when he shoved Abigail against a far wall, out of the direct line of whomever might still be outside.

He stepped over the woman's body and made a quick search of the area outside. There were only her muddy footprints. He breathed a sigh of relief, knowing she'd been alone. Perhaps she lived here. If so, she had apparently escaped the men who had taken her.

Hawk stepped over the woman at the doorway and nodded. "No one is out there. It looks like she was alone."

"Maybe she's Margaret." Abigail knew a Margaret Boyle lived here. She'd read the name in the small Bible they had found flung to the floor.

Hawk gathered the woman into his arms and placed her on the bed. "Do you think you can undress her? I'll hold the baby."

Abigail went about the chore of seeing to the woman. She undressed her and then helped her into one of the two soft cotton nightdresses found in the top dresser drawer. Once she was under the heavy quilt, Hawk came to stand at the bottom of the bed.

"She's been terribly abused. There are black and blues everywhere. And I think she was shot." Abigail pointed to a spot just above her left ear. "It's healing, but her hair is still full of blood."

Hawk nodded but said nothing. The woman had been awake most of the time that Abigail helped her out of her dress and into clean nightclothes. She managed to get her senses about her at one point and asked, "Mike junior. Where is my baby?"

"Your baby is fine. Let me help you dress, and I'll bring him to you."

But once she'd gotten into bed, Margaret had fallen deeply asleep.

Still, Hawk knew an untold sense of relief. Now that his mother had returned, the baby would stop crying. No doubt he yearned for his mother's breast, for the cow's milk, although filling, seemed only to bring the little thing pain.

An hour later the baby began to cry. Both Abigail and Hawk sat at the kitchen table, talking low as they sipped at cups of coffee. They watched in some amazement as the woman, weak and burning with fever, came from the bed and then hurried beneath the quilt with the child in her arms. Moments later came the hungry sounds of sucking and then blissful silence. Both Abigail and Hawk smiled.

They made a pallet on the floor that night, and both slept soundly for the first night in almost a week. They never heard the baby stir and fuss again a few hours later. All they knew was the comfort and bliss of sleep at last.

It was another two days before Margaret Boyle left the bed. Terribly shaken, she nevertheless insisted on coming to the table to eat. Wrapped in a robe, she began to tell them what had happened. She didn't tell them everything, of course, but both Abigail and Hawk could imagine the parts she left out.

"And Mr. Hill?" Abigail reminded.

Margaret looked puzzled for a moment, and then her gray eyes filled with sadness as she remembered. "Oh, yes, Mr. Hill. You knew him?"

Abigail nodded.

"He came a week or so before those men. He was ill with fever. The sad thing was, the first day he was better, he came into the house. He was just about to eat when the men came." Margaret shook her head. "Poor thing."

Poor thing indeed, Abigail might have returned. Hawk had only to look at her to know the way of her thoughts, but she'd clamped her lips together instead. Only Hawk realized the effort it had taken to keep quiet. He smiled at his lady.

"And he was alone?" Abigail asked. She had to be sure. Only then could she know some relief from these fears.

Hawk shot her a look of surprise. She hadn't said a word. He hadn't imagined that she'd been thinking along the same lines as he.

"Oh, yes. He was quite alone."

Abigail breathed a sigh and then came from the table to busy herself with tidying an already clean sink and stove. Hawk knew she needed a moment to compose herself, to realize the truth of the matter, to understand that her sister was not with those men. He nodded and left the table as well. "I'll be in the barn."

There was little for Margaret to do but rest. Abigail—now that she was no longer forced to care for the baby—managed the cooking and straightening up. Margaret did not argue, for her fever had yet to completely disappear, and the wound she had taken to the side of her head still caused her some dizziness. She returned to her bed and was soon fast asleep.

Abigail followed Hawk to the barn. She didn't say anything as she watched him brush down his horse and then feed both the horse and the cow in the last stall.

He finished the chores and leaned his back against a stall door. "You feeling better?"

Abigail smiled weakly. His horse stuck his head outside the stall between them. He looked from one to the other and then whinnied for attention. Hawk obliged without thought. "Some."

"You thought your sister was with him, didn't you?"

Abigail shrugged. "The thought occurred to me."

"You should have talked about it."

"It wouldn't have made any difference." Her gaze followed a cat as it jumped from the barn's floor to the wall of one stall. It balanced itself upon the wall and then stood perfectly still as it studied a small mound of hay. Abigail frowned. "What's the matter with that cat?"

Hawk followed the direction of her gaze. "She's waiting for a mouse to come out, probably."

"Mouse? You mean there are mice in here?" Abigail shuddered at the thought and knew only relief that she had taken to wearing her own clothes again. She didn't want to think what might have happened if a mouse ever climbed up her skirt.

Hawk smiled. "Don't you have a barn at home?"

"Of course, but there are no—"

"You just didn't see them. I never heard of a barn that didn't have any."

She shuddered again. "Oh, God."

Hawk grinned. "They won't bother you."

"Just knowing they exist bothers me."

Hawk figured if a mouse could bring about that kind of reaction, she was better off ignorant of the animals that lurked in the forest, no doubt watching them from the cover of underbrush, each and every time they had made camp.

"We'll be leaving here soon. The rain can't last much longer."

Abigail nodded. "Do you think the rain forced them to stop?"

"I think they probably made Memphis before the worst of it." He'd told her days back that they were heading for the city. "And while we were taking care of a baby, they were probably drinking and whoring to their hearts' content."

Abigail laughed as she joined him in petting the horse. "You sound jealous."

"I am. I wouldn't mind a drink and a good cigar."

"But not a woman?"

"A woman?" He looked surprised. "What would I do with her?"

"You mean you've forgotten what to do with a woman?"

He smiled at her teasing, while a definite hungry gleam entered his eyes. "It appears that I have, but you could refresh my memory. It's been a while."

Abigail's glance told clearly that she thought his remark absurd. She reminded, "It's been exactly . . ." She counted back and then realized she couldn't say exactly how many days had gone by since they'd last made love. They hadn't dared touch one another while sleeping in the same house with Margaret, not that the thought had even come to mind, what with the exhaustion both had known. And before that the baby had fussed so. "A few days."

"Exactly a few days?" Hawk returned, repeating her less than precise accounting. "Exactly eight days, you mean."

"Eight days." Abigail shook her head, her voice droll, her eyes wide with feigned amazement. "One can only marvel at your control."

"I know. I was thinking the same thing."

Abigail laughed. "Exactly how often do you think of that?"

"Making love to you?"

She nodded, unable to hold back her smile.

"Not often. Only about once every few minutes."

"You do not," she countered, unable to believe such a preposterous notion.

"All right. How often *do* I think about it?"

"Do you really . . . ? Every few minutes?" He'd left her with no option but to believe.

"Especially when you wear pants." His gaze moved over her rounded hips.

"Or a skirt?" she reminded.

"Or a skirt," he agreed.

"Or nothing at all?"

"Especially when you're wearing nothing at all."

"That doesn't leave much time for anything else, does it?"

"There isn't much else."

Abigail frowned, not at all happy with his comment. "But there is. There has to be more. What about companionship? What about working together? Sometimes fighting, sometimes laughing, everyday chores, having children. Just living. There's a lot besides making love. You even said you missed my nasty remarks."

"Nasty remarks only make me want to kiss you. And you know where kissing leads."

"Oh," she said with some real disappointment. She seemed to think about that for a moment and then asked, "You mean all a man wants from a woman is . . ." She couldn't seem to bring herself to say the word. "Is that all you want from me?" She appeared oddly unhappy at the thought. Hawk realized she misunderstood.

"No. I'd be lying if I told you sex wasn't part of it. A very large part. But it wasn't until I met you that I thought about it all the time. And I think about it all the time because I love you."

His confession appeased some. Still, she asked, "And if for some reason you couldn't make love to me, what would you . . . ?"

"It wouldn't matter, Abby. If I couldn't make love to you, I'd manage somehow."

She seemed to find satisfaction in his last statement.

Hawk pushed his horse farther into the stall and came to stand before her. "But since I can make love to you, and since we appear to be alone, and since we're not likely to be interrupted, take off your clothes." The last was said a bit firmly.

She giggled at his order. "I'd look pretty silly standing here naked, don't you think?"

"I think you'd look beautiful, and you wouldn't be standing there for long."

"There are mice in here." She wasn't happy about that fact.

"Not in the loft." Hawk felt not a twinge of guilt at the lie. Sometimes a lie was simply and absolutely necessary. He reached for her shirt and began to undo the buttons.

"Are you sure?"

He cupped her breasts, delighting in her softness, marveling again at how easily he could bring the tips to rigid points of pleasure. He pushed the soft flesh together and then allowed them to part, while wondering if he'd ever get enough of touching her. "Do you think a little mouse could climb a ladder?"

That seemed to ease her worries some. Abigail didn't bother to tell him that she knew for a fact that a mouse could climb just about anything.

As it turned out, if there were a family of mice in the loft—if there were more than a family, in fact—Abigail never noticed. The truth was, she stopped thinking about mice only moments after they climbed the ladder. And at more than one point, if a dozen had made themselves known, she simply wouldn't have cared.

Chapter Nineteen

The rain came to an end at last, and Abigail and Hawk prepared to leave. Margaret, who had more courage than most, took no delight in the fact that she would soon be alone again. Because of her dreadful experiences, she jumped at every sound and trembled at the very thought of braving the endless days and nights with no protection. Most likely the men would not return. Still, the woman was loathe to take the chance. It was decided that Margaret would spend a few days in town, looking for men who would help her run the place. Only then, with one or two armed men in evidence, would she know a measure of safety in her own home.

Abigail and Hawk had brought Margaret to the small town some ten miles from her farm. They left her there to begin again their search for the three outlaws.

It took almost a week before they entered the city of Memphis. Tired, hungry, in need of a bath and a soft bed, they entered a small hotel far from the city's center.

After asking for a room, Abigail stood in stunned silence as the clerk's eyes narrowed with disgust and his fat lips twisted into an ugly sneer.

No one was more surprised than Abigail at what happened next. She never knew what came over her. One minute she was standing there, allowing the man's abuse, and the next she was reaching across the counter. Her fingers dug into the sweaty fat around his neck, her hand closing over his collar and bow tie, before either she or Hawk realized what she was about. Hawk blinked in astonishment as she yanked the man forward, almost slamming his face into the desk that stood between them. "Obviously I did not hear you correctly. Would you mind saying that again?"

Donald Rutherford couldn't believe what was happening—that a little thing like this one possessed so much strength. That she was, no matter how he protested, yanking at his tie, strangling the breath out of him. That he saw not a flicker of fear or, for that matter, softness in her cold blue eyes. Thank God no one else was in the small lobby, or he'd never be able to live down the disgrace of it.

Of course, he could have used a bit more effort and fought her off. He had no doubt that he'd win out against what was, for a woman, amazing strength. Still, he was a man after all. But fighting her might have caused her some injury. The man behind her had taken the abuse directed his way in stony silence, but Donald didn't trust the look in that Indian's eyes at the moment. He looked ready to kill should a hand dare to be raised against his woman.

381

"Lady," he choked. "Please. I'll lose my job. I don't make the rules."

Abigail released him, surprised at herself, embarrassed at her show of violence, and yet somehow proud of the surge of protectiveness that had caused her to act so out of character. "Abby," Hawk said softly, no longer behind her, lest the man believe it his right to retaliate. He hovered close by, almost between the two. "Let's go."

Hawk was no stranger to injustice, and injustice in the particular form of prejudice, least of all. He'd known it all his life. In a city of color like New Orleans, there had been considerably less of it, perhaps, but it had still come into play now and again. There were many who, for one reason or another, did not take kindly to an Indian in their midst, and had he not been the deputy marshal, Hawk had no doubt he would have known many indignities.

Hawk had long ago come to the realization that he couldn't change the world. Prejudice would always exist. That had been part of the reason, besides their mode of dress, why he had chosen a hotel far from the city's main streets.

"We're not going anywhere," Abby said, sidestepping her protector and then directing her comment to the man who struggled still to gain a full easy breath. "Mister . . . Excuse me, what was your name?"

"Rutherford," the man managed with some obvious effort as he reached a stubby finger into his collar to loosen his tie.

"Mr. Rutherford was just going to show us to our

382

room." Her eyes hardened into blue chucks of ice. "Weren't you?"

"Yes, ma'am."

"Abby, it's just as easy to find someplace else."

Abby turned to Hawk. "No." She shook her head. "It's not as easy. We'll stay here for the night." Silently she pledged to buy this place the first chance she got. She couldn't wait to boot this surly bastard out of a job. First thing tomorrow she'd wire her man of business and solicitor of her intent.

On the second floor of the less than first-class hotel, Hawk and Abigail stood at the doorway as the man went into the room, opened a window, and pulled down the coverlet upon the bed. He fluffed a pillow, obviously nervous and trying to make amends. Too late. "Will there be anything else?"

Abigail folded her arms over her chest. She was having a time of it remaining civil—the truth being she could hardly look at the man. "Yes, have someone bring up a tub, soap, towels, and lots of hot water." The man nodded. "And food. We want two steaks." She glanced at Hawk. She had been with him for more than two months and was surprised to realize she'd yet to discover his preferences. "Rare?" She waited for his nod before going on. "Fried potatoes, bread, and fruit. An apple and whatever else you can find. Also, a bottle of good whiskey and another of wine. And a cigar."

The door closed behind them. The man couldn't wait to get out of there. He only hoped he could remember everything.

Hawk locked the door behind him. "Remind me never to upset you," he said as he threw his saddlebag to the floor near the bottom of the bed and leaned his rifle against the wall.

Abigail shot him a hard look and began to pace. "I can't believe he had the nerve to say that. And right in front of you."

Hawk shrugged. "I've been called worse."

Worse than a dirty, sneakin' Injun? Abigail could hardly believe it. "Have you? And what did you do?"

"When I was a kid, I used to beat them up. Later I learned to ignore it."

"Well, I'll never ignore it. No one had better ever, ever . . ." She was so angry she couldn't finish. So angry that tears of frustration misted her eyes. Hawk took her in his arms and rocked her gently against him. "I'm afraid you'll hear that and more. You'll get used to it."

Abigail laughed at what she considered an impossibility. "Used to it? I doubt it."

"You're the first person who ever fought for me." Hawk grinned as he remembered the clerk's shock at being pulled across the counter by a woman half his size. Like the clerk, he, too, had been frozen with shock. "If you could have seen his face."

Abigail grunted. "I don't know what happened. All of a sudden I was grabbing at him. I've never done anything like that before."

Hawk chuckled a low sound of enjoyment into her hair.

"Don't think he would have let me get away with it if you weren't standing there with a rifle in your hand."

"It doesn't matter. It matters only that you did it and that I love you."

384

A knock sounded moments later. Their dinner arrived soon after a woman entered with towels and soap. While they ate, the tub and water came as well. As he swallowed the last bite, Hawk nodded toward the tub. "Take your bath before the water gets cold. I'll be right back."

He left immediately and with no further explanation. Abigail was in the midst of swallowing and could only stare at the now closed door. It wasn't until she stepped into the tub that she realized he had gone about the business of looking for those men. She knew he'd be asking questions of whatever form of law presented itself in this city. After all they'd been through together, she felt slightly annoyed that he hadn't included her.

"No trouble at all?" Hawk frowned. He knew the men had come here. Even if he hadn't picked up their trail again, there was little chance that they would have purposely avoided a city. A city filled with whiskey and women.

"Well, there were the usual fights. A stabbing. Brownings got his big toe shot off while a bunch of cowboys from the Douglas place and the Remingtons were going at it last Saturday night." The sheriff shrugged. "You know, the usual."

Hawk nodded. So they were minding their own business for the time being. The problem was, how the hell was he supposed to find them in a city of hundreds, maybe thousands of people?

"There are three of them, you said?"

"Three." Hawk nodded in agreement. "Very dangerous. Cold-blooded murderers." Hawk told of the trail of vicious murders he'd uncovered while searching for these men.

"And you don't know what they look like?"

Hawk could only go by Margaret's accounting—the woman, to his knowledge, being the only survivor. "An ugly dirty bunch is all I know. One fella is blond, the other two have brown hair. Willie, Josh, and Mike are their names. And Mike has a serious injury to his arm."

"I know Doc Martins. I'll ask him to keep an eye out." A moment later the sheriff shook his head. "Fact is, we have a half dozen doctors here." He hesitated again and then said, "I'll see what I can do. Is that it?"

"One of them rides a horse with a cracked shoe."

"Maybe if we find the horse . . ."

Hawk nodded. "I'll ask at the livery. Got to go there anyway."

The problem was, a city the size of Memphis was bound to have more than one stable and blacksmith. Tomorrow he'd search out the others.

Hawk picked out a horse for Abby and paid the blacksmith before he mentioned the horse with the cracked shoe.

The dark burly man shook his head. "Haven't seen any lately. He won't be riding it long though. The animal's bound to go lame."

Hawk shook his head. "The crack is on the end of the shoe. He'll last for a while."

Hawk left the man the name of his hotel and room

number. "I'll be around for a few days. Let me know if you hear of anything."

The man promised he would, and Hawk left.

Hawk stepped into the hotel room, threw his packages on the bed, and smiled at the lady reclining in a tub of water and quickly evaporating suds. "You look comfortable."

Abigail breathed a sigh and opened one eye. "I just might never get out.

"And that was a dirty trick."

"What was?"

"Running out of here like you did. Before I had a chance to say anything."

Hawk grinned. "You would have missed your bath. How's the wine?"

"Delicious—and don't change the subject."

Hawk grinned. "You sound like you're ready to fall asleep."

"I am."

"Your bubbles are bursting."

"The water is getting cold."

"You want to get married tomorrow?" Hawk figured this was probably the last chance they'd have for a while. One didn't come across a preacher as a common everyday occurrence.

"I want Amanda to be at my wedding."

"We might not find her for another couple of months. Suppose you're having a baby?"

"I'm not," she lied, for she was positive she was. She hadn't come into her monthly flow since their first time together, and she should have, at the mo-

ment, been in the midst of it for the second time. She
was having a baby, all right. She only hoped to keep
that information to herself for a time.

"Abby," he said, his voice a low warning.

Abigail glanced in his direction and then away.
Her cheeks warmed slightly as she realized it was
already too late. Hawk was apparently well aware of
the situation. "All right, maybe I am, a little."

Hawk grinned at that, knowing a rush of happiness so intense it nearly stole his breath. "You know,
of course, that this puts a whole new light on everything."

Abigail sat up straight; the movement caused
water to splash. She reached for a towel and, to
Hawk's delight, stepped from the tub. "Don't even
think it. You're not going anywhere without me."

"What about the baby?"

She glared in his direction. "What about the
baby's father?"

"I've done this before. I'll be all right."

"I know. I'll be there to make sure of it."

Hawk couldn't hold back his grin of pleasure.
He'd never had anyone besides his mother and father
love him before. That love he, like most offspring,
had taken for granted. This was a totally new and
exhilarating experience. "What are you doing?" he
asked as she tied the towel at her breasts, effectively
covering everything he wanted to see uncovered.

"We're going to talk."

Hawk shrugged and stripped off his clothes just
before he slid into the water. "About what?"

"About you going off without me again."

Hawk only glanced at her and then dunked himself

beneath the surface. He blew out, wiped his face with his hands, and pushed his long hair back as he sat again.

"You're going to have to promise me that you won't," she said the moment he resurfaced.

"I promise."

She shook her head. "Not good enough. You'll have to mean it when you say it."

He smiled at that. "When did I ever lie to you?"

"You lied about the mouse in the barn, for one."

Hawk laughed a deliciously wicked sound. He shook his head. "If you knew I was lying, it didn't count."

"That's ridiculous. Of course it counted. You still said the words. It doesn't matter that I knew better."

"Sure it does. If—"

"We're getting off the subject. Promise me."

"No."

There was a long moment of silence before she spoke again. "Promise me and I'll make it worth your while," she said, her voice suddenly very soft and, if he wasn't mistaken, downright seductive.

That got his attention, all right. Hawk looked at her for a long moment before he heard himself ask, "How?" He swallowed over the sudden pounding in his throat as he watched her hands open the towel. "How would you make it worth my while?"

The towel dropped to the floor at her feet. "I'm sure I'll think of something." She knelt at the side of the tub and reached toward the small table nearby. A cigar was placed between her lips, and Hawk grinned at the face she made after lighting it. She slid the lit cigar between his teeth. Next she poured two fingers

389

of golden liquid into a small glass and pressed the glass into his hand.

Hawk hated to see this moment end. He'd never been the recipient of such luxurious treatment before. Still, now that he was sure about her condition, there was no way that he was going to allow her to put herself in danger. It didn't matter how she tried to convince him.

"What did you find out?"

"No one has seen them."

Abigail nodded at this piece of news. "But you know they're here."

"I know they came here. I don't know if they stayed."

"Tomorrow you'll ask around?"

Hawk nodded as he watched her soap a rag and then sighed as she ran that rag over his neck and shoulders.

"How long will you look?"

"A few days."

"And then we'll try to find their trail again?"

"Then *I'll* try to find their trail again," he corrected.

"I'm not staying here without you."

He said nothing.

"Jeremiah?"

"Mmm," he returned as she massaged the slippery suds into his shoulders.

"Did you hear what I said?"

"Would you put the baby in jeopardy?"

At the moment the baby was only a distant promise. Abigail's first thought was of the baby's father. "Neither the baby nor I will come to harm."

"You're staying."

"I'll follow you."

"No, you won't. The last time I looked, I was the man and the one in charge. You'll do as I say, and that's the end of it."

The problem was, it was the end of other things as well. Hawk realized too late that he should have spoken a bit more gently, or simply allowed her to believe what she would. He realized it the moment she threw the sopping wet rag at his face. He glared at her, a wet cigar hanging limply from his teeth, soap bubbles coating his whiskey.

"So you're a man. If I were you, I wouldn't be so proud of that fact."

He squinted through the soap burning his eyes. "What do you think you're doing?"

"What does it look like? I'm getting dressed."

Hawk emerged from the tub and used Abigail's discarded towel to dry off. "You're wasting your time. You'll only have to get undressed again."

Abigail snorted but made no further reply.

"Don't even think about it," he said as she shoved her feet into her boots.

"Think about what?"

"Leaving."

"Oh, so it's all right if you leave me, but I'm not allowed to do the same? God, I hate men."

"It's not the same, and you know it."

"You don't own me, Mr. Hawk. And I'll do as please, thank you."

"You'll do as I say. Get over here."

Abigail ignored him as she walked toward the door. A second later she yelped to find herself suddenly in the air and flung upon the bed. She landed with a bounce. "Oh, I can see you're very worried about the baby."

"I didn't hurt you."

"You could have."

"Abigail, you might as well get this straight. Nothing is going to happen to you or our baby, and I'm going to make sure if it."

"It's not your baby."

Hawk grinned as he knelt on the bed. He leaned over her, all power and might. His long damp hair fell forward, framing his handsome features. His smile held a touch of menace. Abigail trembled at the savage look of him and then frowned as excitement filled her being. His voice was a low whisper of warning. "Unless you've had an immaculate conception, it's my baby, all right."

"All right, so it's your baby. Satisfied?"

"No, but I intend to be." With no further warning than those words, he yanked at her shirt and instantly tore the material apart. Buttons popped in every direction. Abigail shoved him, but she might as well have shoved a mountain for all the good it did. A second later her arms were pinned to her sides, and his mouth took her breast deep into a blast of heat. She gasped at the shock of his touch, at the fire of his mouth, surprised at his sudden aggression, and then cursed her unwanted reaction to it.

He'd never been anything but gentle before. At one point that gentleness had been her undoing, but this . . . This was more than she'd ever dreamed possible. The feelings he instilled frightened her and at the same time excited her beyond bearing. She struggled against his strength, against her own need that bubbled so closely to the surface. "I hate you."

"I love you," he returned.

Her pants were open and his mouth slid to her midriff and then to her still flat belly. "I love you, and I'm going to love this baby."

He released her but only for the time it took to tear away the rest of her clothes. Her boots were flung across the small room. She lay there naked but for a torn useless shirt—and more than a little surprised to realize, aching for more of this mastery.

He knelt between her thighs. Gently he reached for her hips and pulled her to meet his engorged throbbing flesh. A moment later, and with no further words spoken, he entered her body with a devastating, mind-boggling thrust. Abigail groaned at the pleasure, the power, the might she felt in his hard body.

He held her in place for an endless moment as he strove for control. This felt too good. God, nothing had ever felt this good. He never wanted it to end. "Can you feel how much I want you?"

"Yes."

"Do you know I love you?"

"Yes." Tears streamed down her face. Not of pain, but of fear. She couldn't win out against him. She loved him desperately. There was nothing she wouldn't do for him, nothing she wouldn't give him. She was terrified that he'd win in this instance. She couldn't bear the thought.

He guided her to a sitting position and removed her shirt. She clung to his neck, her mouth and tongue tasting of his flesh, her legs twisting around his hips. And then with a groan, he buried his face in her neck. "I'm never going to lose you." His arms crushed her against him. "Never!"

Later she lay cuddled against him, their bodies damp, cooling, exhausted, replete. It was an effort to talk. For Hawk it was more than an effort. It was damn near impossible.

Her foot touched one of the packages he had earlier thrown on the bed. "What did you buy?"

"Something for you to wear," he returned drowsily.

"It's a good thing, after what you did to my clothes."

Hawk chuckled a low sound of laughter. "And you hated every minute of it."

She snuggled her face into his neck. "I love you."

He murmured a low sound of happiness, more than half asleep.

"When are you going to leave?"

Hawk groaned. He didn't want to talk. He didn't want to think. He wanted to sleep. "I don't know."

"You're not going to tell me, right?"

"Probably not."

"You'll just be here one day and then gone the next."

"Maybe." Hawk figured the less she knew, the better. He didn't want her to get it into her head to follow him.

"Fine."

Hawk grew suddenly alert and a lot more awake than he would have liked. He glanced down to see only the top of her head. "What does that mean?"

"Nothing."

"You're planning something, aren't you?"

"No."

"Yes, you are. Damn it, Abby, why can't you be like other women?"

Abigail came up on her elbow at that. She glared into his worried expression. "Don't ever confuse me with the others you've known."

"Little chance of that ever happening," he said unhappily.

"I'm not one of your women."

"There are no others. You're my only woman."

"And I'll never sit by and watch you go off to face danger, waiting like a good little mindless idiot for your return."

"What does that mean?"

"It means just what I said. I won't wait for you."

"Are you going to tell me what the hell you're talking about?"

"I'm leaving tomorrow."

"For where?"

"Paris."

It took Hawk a minute to digest this information. He hadn't a doubt that she meant every word she said. The worst of it was, there were no guarantees that she'd be safe in Paris. And worst of all it might take him a year or longer to find her again. There was no way he was going to allow that. "God damn it, Abby. You're crazy if you think I'll just let you go."

"Fine," she said as she dropped to her back and pulled the coverlet over herself.

He came to his elbow and leaned over her. "Fine again? Now what does that mean?"

"Fine means fine. Shall I buy you a dictionary?"

His dark eyes narrowed as he glared at her. "You're wasting your time, shooting me evil looks. I'm not afraid of you."

Hawk was well aware that this woman wasn't afraid of anyone. That fact alone scared him half to death. "I suppose you'll leave right after I do, right?"

"Right."

"All right, you win."

"Say it clear, Jeremiah."

"You're coming with me. And I don't want to hear another word about it."

Abigail grinned. She should have thought of this before. She laughed softly at his scowl. No, if she had thought of it sooner she would have missed this last hour of exquisite pleasure. "I love you."

Hawk grunted in disbelief as he lay at her side again. "If you loved me, you'd do as I say."

Abigail couldn't have looked more amazed if he'd just sprouted wings and begun to fly around the room. "How does one have anything to do with the other?"

Hawk groaned and pulled her against him. "Go to sleep."

She was beautiful. Her features small and perfect. Her lips were red and inviting. Dark, mysterious, her hair a glorious confection of gleaming black curls beneath a gorgeous hat. Her red dress tightly emphasized lush charms, and Abigail knew a moment of jealousy. Well, not jealousy exactly—her feelings ran more toward murder as she watched the woman throw herself into Hawk's arms. "Chéri," the woman said just before she kissed him right on the mouth. No tiny peck of greeting here, but a real kiss. Abigail's eyes widened, for she hadn't missed the fact that the woman's tongue slid back into her mouth as their lips parted. Wide eyes suddenly narrowed. Abigail was going to kill one of them, perhaps both. Especially that stupid oaf who just stood there and allowed this shameless hussy the opportunity to rub herself all over the front of him.

Apparently she had made a sound, a gasp no doubt, for Hawk finally noticed she was still at his side. He shot her a stony expression, a weak smile, and then cursed, knowing he was in for a time of it. Why the hell had Kit happened along at this particular moment? Damn.

"Abigail, this is Kit, Catherine Du Maurier. Kit, Abigail—the lady I'm going to marry."

Well, that was something at least, Abigail supposed. He had made his intentions clear. The only problem was, it seemed to make not the slightest bit of difference to the woman facing them. She smiled at Abigail, all but dismissing her with one glance. Even though one of them had moved—Abigail didn't know which—creating some space between their bodies, Kit kept both hands upon Hawk's chest. And all Abigail could think was, thank God he'd changed back into city clothes. She didn't know what she'd do if this bold woman were caressing his bare skin.

"Have you seen my sister and the rest lately?"

"A couple of months back," Hawk returned, apparently unaware that the woman continued to touch him. "Everyone is fine."

Kit smiled at this bit of news, showing some obvious relief, and Abigail wondered why she had had to ask Hawk about her family. Why wasn't she in contact with them herself? But mostly she wondered if Hawk was so used to being touched by ladies that he never noticed Kit's hands all over him. Abigail's gaze narrowed further as her hands itched to strike out. The problem was, she wasn't sure which one she wanted to hit first.

"Kit is Cole's sister-in-law." Hawk saw the look in Abigail's eyes and figured he was in for it. She was going to kill him and maybe, for the first time in his life, he was innocent.

"*Oui.* We're old friends." Kit shot Abigail yet another dismissing glance and then to Hawk she finished with, "Are we not?" The question told Abigail clearly their relationship had been very friendly indeed. It also told her that Kit was ready to take up where they had left off. The last thing she wanted to do was stand here and watch this tasteless spectacle.

"Well, I've some shopping to do," Abigail said as well as stiff lips allowed. "Why don't the two of you get caught up on—"

Hawk's arm was suddenly around her waist. He squeezed her close to his side, his arm a steel band, impossible to break. The sudden intensity of his hold cut off her words.

"We could have a drink," Kit suggested in her most seductive tone. She pointed behind her and said proudly, "This is my place."

It took only one glance to know that she was the owner of a brothel. A high-class brothel, Hawk thought, considering the carriages parked nearby and the obviously rich men that entered the place.

Hawk knew it would be the last drink he'd ever have if he dared to say yes. The truth of it was, he didn't want to say yes, even if Abigail wasn't standing there, stiff and angry, ready to give him hell. "Ah, thank you, but we have an appointment. Maybe we'll see you later."

"Will you be staying long?"

"No."

"How long?"

He shook his head. "We're leaving tonight."

Abigail frowned and wondered if that were true. He hadn't mentioned leaving tonight. A moment later she was being half dragged down the busy sidewalk. "What are you doing?"

"Trying to get away from her. Hurry up, before she decides to follow us."

"She'd be following you, not us."

He came to a sudden stop and looked into her eyes. "It's the same thing, Abby."

Hawk pulled her into a coffee shop and sat them in the back of the room, far from any doors or windows. "Are you hiding from her?" Abigail, despite her annoyance, thought that idea amusing.

"You don't know what I had to go through when she lived in New Orleans."

"Beat down your door, did she?" Abigail laughed.

"It's not funny. She was part of Cole's family. Emy's sister, for God's sake." Hawk shook his head. "I couldn't."

"Not that you didn't want to."

Hawk said nothing, and Abigail realized she couldn't fault him on that score. The woman was beautiful and obviously anxious, and he'd been a single man, after all, with no one to answer to. "I'm sorry. That wasn't fair."

A moment later she smiled again. "I imagine she was a mite disappointed with your decision."

"The woman practically hounded me."

"Poor baby." She dragged out the words in false sympathy.

"I'm happy to see you're enjoying yourself."

"You seemed to be enjoying yourself before."

He frowned. What was she talking about now? "When?"

"When you were talking to her. She kissed you with her tongue." Just the thought of it caused her to be angry all over again.

Hawk frowned, looked quickly around and hissed, "Lower your voice."

"She kissed you with her tongue," Abigail repeated, this time more softly, "and then rubbed herself all over the front of you. And you allowed it."

"I didn't even notice."

Abigail gave him a disparaging and most unladylike snort.

"I was so worried that you were going to get mad at me, I don't even remember what I said. I couldn't get the hell out of there fast enough."

Abigail remembered how his arm had tightened around her. She remembered feeling him grow stiffer by the second at her side. He was telling her the truth. She allowed a small smile. A very small smile. "The next time we come across one of your ladies, tell her to keep her hands to herself."

Hawk had every confidence that should that occur, a lady of his former acquaintance would show a hell of a lot more discretion. He doubted that the woman would do more than smile a greeting from afar and go about her business, never creating a scene. "Kit was never my lady." A moment passed before he said, "Let's forget about her."

She shook her head. "Tell me about her."

"Abby, she's not important."

"Go ahead. I won't be upset. Tell me."

Hawk breathed a sigh, knowing he had no real choice. Not to speak of it would only cause Abby to grow more suspicious. And especially, in this instance, she had nothing to be suspicious about. "She was wild. Not at all like Emy, her sister. Although they look alike, they're as different as night and day."

Abigail nodded.

"She wanted me to . . ."

"Make love to her?" Abigail offered when his hesitation became obvious.

"No." He shook his head. "What she wanted from me had nothing to do with love. She wanted sex."

Abigail's cheeks grew warm. Was she actually embarrassed for the woman? Abigail was surprised to realize she was.

"And when I wouldn't, couldn't do it, she took up with a man who would. The two of them were a perfect pair. Neither cared for anyone but themselves. In the end he almost killed her sister."

Abigail gasped.

"And then Cole almost killed Kit, trying to get information out of her." He shook his head. "It was a scary few hours.

"Finally she left the city. No one has heard from her since." Hawk felt confused. He hadn't done a damn thing, and yet he found himself wanting to beg for her forgiveness.

A few moments of silence passed between them before Abigail said, "I can see why she wanted you."

"Can you?"

"Of course. You're a very attractive man."

"Am I?" He breathed easy for the first time since meeting Kit again, knowing Abigail had every right to be angry at Kit's unentitled and definitely unasked-for display and yet had put aside the emotion. A moment later he frowned as he asked, "What happened to beautiful?"

"You're beautiful when you take your clothes off. She couldn't have known that."

Hawk breathed a sigh of relief as he leaned back. "I didn't know until today how scared I am of you."

Abigail giggled at what she believed to be a jest and opened her menu. "What are we going to do next?"

Hawk consulted the list he had taken from his pocket. "We have five more stables. And then we'll start on the doctors."

Chapter Twenty

"Yeah, I noticed the cracked shoe."

"Did you tell the owner about it?"

The man shook his head. "Never got a chance. I don't work on Thursdays."

"And?" Hawk prompted.

"Yesterday was Thursday."

"Tell me something I didn't know."

"He came in yesterday, paid up his bill, and left."

"Who works on Thursdays?"

"Eddie."

"Where is Eddie now?" Damn, but the man didn't offer a bit of information without being asked.

"He's out back."

Eddie was exercising the horses. One by one he took them from their stalls and walked them around the paddock a few times before bringing them back.

Eddie was on his way back to the barn, a horse in tow, when he caught sight of the tall dark man and the small beautiful lady who stood at his side. The lady was about his height. Eddie wished he had a lady like her. If he did, he could get married and start a family of his own. His mom wouldn't live forever, and when she died he was going to be alone. Eddie didn't like that idea much.

Considering that he was only a stable hand, maybe he'd never find someone that pretty. The pretty ones were usually taken by men who had more money. Maybe he'd have to settle for less. All he knew was he was going to have to find a lady soon.

"Eddie?" the man said as he started on by the couple.

"Yeah?" Eddie brought the horse to a stop.

"Can I ask you a few questions?"

"Sure. What do you want to know?"

She was even better up close. For a long minute Eddie couldn't tear his eyes away from her face.

Hawk almost smiled at the open admiration he saw in the boy's eyes. The fact was, he couldn't really blame him. Abigail was a beautiful lady, and Hawk supposed he'd see many an admiring glance shot her way in the future. It was Hawk's question that brought Eddie's gaze from Abigail. "There was a horse here with a cracked shoe. Can you tell me anything about the man who owns him?"

"Just that he didn't talk much. I told him about the shoe. Said he could come back today and get it fixed. He said it don't matter none. The next place he stopped, he'd get another."

Hawk's heart began to pick up its pace. "He didn't say where that would be?"

"Nope. But his friend said something about New Orleans. The other guy said, 'Forget New Orleans. We're going east.' The other two didn't look happy about it."

404

"Did you see which road they took?"

Eddie nodded and then pointed away from the barn toward the road. "That one."

"When did they pick up the horses?"

"Yesterday, about two o'clock, I guess. It was right after I finished eating."

Hawk nodded. That meant they had a full day's head start. He'd have to hurry if he wanted to find their trail again. "You didn't notice what they were wearing, did you?"

"Yeah, ragged clothes, mostly." He glanced at his own clothes. "Worse than mine. They looked pretty bad and didn't smell much better than these horses, 'cept for the perfume."

Hawk grinned. Abigail looked confused.

Hawk knew that meant one of two things. They had either just come from visiting perfumed whores, or had splashed something on themselves in lieu of bathing.

Neither possibility entered Abigail's mind, for she never used perfume without bathing first. She mentioned the oddity of smelling like perfume and horses at the same time the moment they left the stable. "That's odd, don't you think?"

"If a man were with a certain lady who smelled of flowers, it's likely that the scent would attach itself to him."

"Oh," she said, feeling a bit foolish at her naivete.

Hawk smiled. "You didn't think they came to Memphis to attend church meetings, did you?"

"Hardly."

"Then you shouldn't be so surprised to find out where they spent their time."

"I'm not surprised. It's just that I didn't think of it."

Hawk gave his lady a tender smile. No, she wouldn't have thought of it.

"When are we leaving?"

"We might as well wait until morning. By the time we have everything ready, there'll be only a few hours of light left."

They shopped that afternoon for their supplies, packed two sets of saddlebags, picked up Abigail's horse, and left the hotel before light the next morning.

Amanda looked at the wire and frowned. She had tried to reach her sister a number of times, both in New Orleans and since coming to Bill's inn. All to no avail. Finally she had contacted the family's solicitor. Mr. Carver had wired back. It was that wire she held.

"Mr. Carver says she's in New Orleans. She must have gone looking for me."

"Don't worry, sweetheart. Once she finds out that you're no longer in the city, she'll be back."

"She's been gone a very long time. Do you think she's all right?"

"I'm sure she is. She's not traveling alone, is she?"

"Mr. Carver says Robert went with her."

"There, you see?" Amanda had already mentioned the man telling him he and Abigail would soon be married. "Robert will take care of her. She'll be fine."

Amanda nodded, even though she didn't seem all that convinced. "Do you think we could take a trip to Chelsy once Abigail returns?"

"You want to show me off?" he teased.

"Of course."

Bill laughed. Damn, if the woman didn't think he was something. That fact alone was astonishing. Bill knew well enough the truth of the matter. He was an awkward, far too often bumbling, oaf. That Amanda seemed never to notice the obvious kept him in a constant state of awe.

That love shone from her wide blue eyes whenever she looked his way left him practically speechless. That she was going to have a baby only filled him with gladness. Had it been his child, he couldn't have known more fulfillment, more happiness.

His life was rich and full because of her, and if she wanted to take a trip home, to show off her funny-looking husband, Bill would grant her at least that much. He only wished he could give her more.

Some hundred or so miles west of the inn, three men sat around the campfire reminiscing about the week spent in the big city. A week of good whiskey instead of the rotgut they usually came across, and pleasure. Damn, but they hadn't known that kind of pleasure in a long time. Not since before they'd gotten sent up. Not since they'd been released from the pen. They'd enjoyed themselves all right, until their money ran out.

"Damn, but she was good, wasn't she? I never saw anyone move like that. She'd squeeze a man's—"

Josh felt his sex come to life at the thought of the whore and the tricks she'd been able to perform. He interrupted with, "We should have stayed."

407

"Yeah, I can see her playing with your dick just for the fun of it," Willie said with no little sarcasm.

"So? Why didn't we just get some more money? The city was full of—"

"Deputies," Willie said cutting him off. "Or didn't you notice?"

Josh laughed. "It's hard to notice much of anything when a woman's mouth is that good."

Willie sighed, wishing they had taken one of the whores with them, but he knew, of course, the impossibility of that. Any one of the bitches would have screamed their heads off. And the giant hulk that guarded them all would have cut them down if they had even hinted at trying.

No, they'd just have to find themselves another woman to share. "We'd better stop talking about it," Willie suggested, glancing at the bulge in his pants.

Both Mike and Josh laughed, for their conversation had left them easily as hungry and not one of the three was thinking about food.

Mike didn't feel good. His arm, which mostly hung useless at his side, was hurting again. Now that it was too late, he knew he should have gone to the doctor while in Memphis. But it hadn't hurt that much then. Of course, he'd been drunk or close to it most of the time, and nothing had hurt.

Mike figured he'd come across a doctor sooner or later. Once he did, he'd get himself fixed up.

Mike never knew his "friend" was thinking about his arm as well. Willie didn't need to look to know Mike was nearby. His arm stunk. Willie had hired out as a mercenary once. He knew how a wound could rot if left uncared for. He knew the scent of gangrene.

Mike was done for, only he didn't know it yet. Willie wouldn't be sorry to see Mike die. He wasn't pulling his own weight anymore. Besides, everyone had to die. Most just didn't know when it was coming.

Willie, on the other hand, knew exactly when Mike was going to die. Tomorrow.

The next day the three leaned over the young man they had ambushed and picked his pockets clean. The man was shot up pretty bad, but he wasn't dead. He'd die of course, but not one of the men thought to put him out of his misery. Not one of them showed even that mercy. Bullets cost money, after all.

"Take his horse, Josh. I don't want that cracked shoe to show which way we went."

Josh did as he was told. Moments later he was adding his own supplies to those already in the stranger's saddlebags. And then without any warning, Willie took the man's gun and shot Mike in the head.

"What the hell!" Josh gasped as he spun around and reached for his own gun. He relaxed a second later, after realizing Willie had no apparent intention of turning the gun on him. "What did you do that for?"

"He was going to die anyway. He couldn't do nothing with that arm."

Josh watched the blood squirting from Mike's head. Mike had fallen across the man they had shot. Blood covered everything. It was disgusting. He looked away.

Moments later the two mounted their horses

again. Willie counted the coins in his hand. A dollar and ten cents. It had almost not been worth the effort. Almost.

They'd gotten themselves another gun and a new horse. That was something, after all. Maybe they'd have better luck with the next one.

Hawk drew his horse to a stop. It was early. The sun wouldn't set for a few more hours. Abigail glanced in his direction, a frown creasing her smooth forehead. "What's the matter? Why are we stopping?"

"I'm tired."

"You are not. Don't lie."

"How do you know I'm not?"

"Because I've seen you ride from dawn to almost dusk and then hunt for our supper, make camp, and—"

"Well, I'm tired today. Maybe I'm coming down with something."

"Yeah, you're coming down with a case of the ridiculous."

"Abigail . . ." Abigail ignored the warning in his voice. She knew why he had stopped. She knew as well that it was unnecessary. She felt wonderful. Apparently having a baby agreed with her, for she'd never felt stronger or better in her life.

"Let's go. It's too early to stop."

"We're stopping."

"You'll never catch them like this."

"I'll catch them." He was loosening his saddle as he spoke.

"Jeremiah, stop treating me as if I were infirmed. For God's sake, I'm only having a baby."

"You're only having *my* baby," he said with some emphasis. "And nothing is going to happen to either of you."

"If you want me to ever have another, you'd better start treating me better than this."

"What's the matter with the way I'm treating you?"

Abigail didn't answer him but stalked into the woods looking for a bit of privacy. A second later she was back at his side, her face white with fear. "There's two dead men over there."

"Stay here," Hawk said as he rushed toward where she pointed.

Abigail, of course, followed him. There was no way that she was going to stay by herself. The shadows caused by trees and brush suddenly appeared eerie and ominous. Hawk, of course, had no idea why she had once again disobeyed him. All he knew was she had, and he was angry.

Angry at being forced to take her with him, to involve her in this danger. Angry that he couldn't push himself to the limit, lest she suffer the consequences. Angry that yet another had fallen victim to these monsters.

"Get the hell out of here."

"But—"

"Did you hear what I said? Get going!"

Abigail did as she was told. Jeremiah took a while, but he finally returned to where their horses stood. By that time she was furious. What right did he have to talk to her like that! Just who did he think he was?

411

She turned her face from his the moment she saw him coming. Abigail couldn't deny the rush of comfort she knew, just having him nearby. Still, she wasn't about to speak to him until he apologized. She didn't know it just yet, but she had a bit of a wait in store.

"Let's go," Hawk said as he retightened the cinch around his horse's belly.

Abigail said nothing. Apparently the beast had changed his mind. Well, that was fine with her. If he kept dawdling like this, they'd never find those men and never get on with finding Amanda. At this rate the baby she carried would be a few years old before they got married. Abigail glared at his back. It was one thing to ignore him and another thing entirely to be ignored, she suddenly realized. Maybe she should think over this marriage business. Maybe she wouldn't marry him after all.

Two hours later it was almost dark when they came upon a crowded inn.

Abigail was careful that her sigh of relief was released in silence. She didn't want him to know just how tired she suddenly was. They had ridden hard today and covered a lot of ground, especially in these last few hours. She couldn't wait to slide into a warm tub and a soft bed.

Jeremiah didn't know which of them upset him more. His lady or himself. He shouldn't have done it. He shouldn't have pushed like that, but damn it, she made him so angry. All he could think of was the possibility that she could be hurt. He'd wanted to protect her from a gruesome sight, and she had ignored him yet again. Damn, when was he going to get some control over this situation? This woman?

What she needed, of course, was a real man. Someone who had the strength to go up against her and win. At the moment Hawk didn't feel he fit the requirements. He was too soft, too willing to give in to her demands. He'd once ridiculed Robert for that very thing and yet had somehow found himself in much the same predicament.

Well, as of tonight all that would end. It was too late to leave her behind, but, damn her, she was going to listen to every word he said and obey him instantly or feel the consequences of his wrath on that sweet little backside. Hawk figured a good spanking was what she needed most, and God, he'd never been more tempted in his life.

If she said one word, just one word, he'd give in to the temptation and damn the aftermath.

Hawk entered the inn, with Abigail close behind him. He ordered a room from the man behind the bar, a man who knew murder when he saw it in another's eyes and didn't dare utter a word of objection. The fact was, Ben Stevens wouldn't have objected in any case. He never questioned a man who rented his rooms. As long as a man could pay, he could have what he wanted.

"We're hungry. When do you serve . . . ?"

"Anytime. Just sit down and one of the girls will bring it to you."

Hawk shook his head. Abigail was wearing her trousers again. There would be trouble for sure if they stayed downstairs. Some fool would be sure to say or try something. "Upstairs. Bring us something there."

Ben nodded.

Hawk led the way, carrying both sets of saddlebags on one arm and his rifle and hers under the other. Abigail opened the door and continued to ignore him.

She kicked off her boots and twisted this way and that as she stretched her back, trying to relieve the stiffness. Soon enough a knock sounded, and two young boys brought in enough food for four men. Hawk figured this was going to cost him some but said nothing.

They ate thick stew, rich with meat and chunks of vegetables, in silence. The moment he was finished, Hawk left the room. He ordered a tub for Abigail from a passing maid, and then went to the bar, ready to pick a fight.

He didn't have to wait long. Three drinks and a half hour later, he was beginning to lose some of his earlier rage.

It was then that he noticed the hovering barmaid. Apparently she had once shown some interest in the fellow who sat across the room, if his loud comments about never trusting a woman and her reciprocating glares meant anything. What was also apparent was tonight she had turned that interest on Hawk.

She bent low as she wiped the already clean table, allowing the too loose neckline of her blouse to fall forward. Hawk could see all the way to her waist. Pretty, he silently thought. Swaying pink-tipped breasts might have brought about some reaction, had it not been for a particularly aggravating woman upstairs, probably sitting in a tub of water at this very moment, who had fuller, pinker-tipped, and far more attractive assets.

Hawk looked his fill and then allowed his gaze to return to his glass and the bottle that sat before him. "Can I get you anything else?" the woman asked as she obviously and boldly eyed his crotch. And all the while the man across the room continued his comments about women being nothing but whores, especially ones that took up with dirty Injuns.

Hawk stopped drinking. He didn't want to feel mellow. He was going to need all his anger and need it very soon.

Tired of getting no response to his comments, the man staggered from his seat and came toward Hawk's table. He grabbed the woman around her waist and suddenly pulled her blouse low, exposing her breasts for all the clientele to see.

"You get your fill, Injun? You want to see more?"

"Charlie, damn you. Get your hands off me." The woman shot the man a hard glare as she yanked her blouse back into place.

"You were showing him everything you got."

"What's it your business?" she asked, never bothering to deny the obvious.

"I don't want you after an Injun has a go at you."

"Well, maybe I don't want you after you have a go at your wife." That comment brought a round of chuckles from the men watching.

Charlie thought, and rightly so, that they were laughing at him. "Shut up," he said and then reached out and backhanded her. The woman fell to the floor, a trickle of blood oozing from the corner of her mouth.

Hawk was itching for a fight. He didn't want anything more than to sink his fists into this man's belly and jaw. It wasn't so much to protect the woman, but he figured that was as good an excuse as any.

"You're a big man, Charlie. It takes a big man to hit a woman, doesn't it?" Hawk couldn't ignore the fact that he might have done as much to Abigail had he been given half a chance. No, that wasn't completely true. He would have liked to have given her the spanking she deserved. He'd never backhanded a woman. He'd never hit a woman, period. And he wasn't about to start anytime soon.

"I'm big enough to take care of you, little Injun."

Hawk came slowly to his feet. It wasn't until he reached his full height that he realized why the man had called him little. Funny he hadn't noticed until now that the man was huge.

Hawk shrugged aside the thought. It wouldn't have mattered any. He'd been longing for a good fight. If he got his ass kicked in the process, that didn't matter either.

"There's more room outside."

"I ain't gonna need much room to take care of you."

The man came close to telling the truth. Hawk never saw the punch coming. It sat him down in his chair faster than he could blink. If the chair wasn't already leaning against the wall, it would have toppled over.

Hawk knew in an instant—well, the minute his brain stopped throbbing, at least—that there was no

416

way he could win out against this man's brute strength. He couldn't match him blow for blow or come out the loser here.

Charlie began to grin as he realized he'd dazed the Indian with one blow, but his grin turned into a gasp of surprise as all of Hawk's two hundred pounds suddenly crushed into his stomach. Hawk came from the chair and lunged forward, shouldering the burly man backward.

The man staggered but a moment later came at him again. Hawk ducked, danced to his side, and coming low, reached up and smashed his fist into the man's oncoming chin. The blow popped his head back, despite the fact that his body was going forward. Charlie staggered again.

He leaned heavily against the wall for a minute before he lunged toward Hawk and swung again. Again his meaty fist found no mark as Hawk moved aside. Charlie almost found himself on the floor with the force of missing again. The momentum carried him into the table behind Hawk and sent two men scurrying for safety.

Charlie roared his frustration as he charged again and again felt the results of his less than brilliant fight. Hawk landed a solid blow to the man's gut, effectively weakening his legs. Another blow caught Charlie just below his left eye. There was a definite wobble to his step now. Were it not for the wall, the man would have fallen.

"Enough," he said, his hand raised, as Hawk stepped in for the kill.

Hawk cursed. He hadn't wanted it to end so soon. He would have liked to get a few more blows in, but he wouldn't hit a man who raised his hand in surrender.

"You're a tough little fella, Injun," Charlie said as he reached out an offered hand.

Hawk didn't want to shake the man's hand. He didn't like men who hit women. Still, he figured it wasn't up to him to judge a man. He had no real choice but to reluctantly shake the man's hand.

Hawk knew the minute he did it, it was a mistake. He couldn't get the hell away from him as one blow hit after another. He took three blows before his knee came in contact with the man's groin.

Instantly his hand was released. The man was almost out on his feet. He couldn't have fought off a fly and won. But Hawk wasn't about to let the sneaking bastard off that easy. Before he hit the floor, Hawk delivered two punishing blows to Charlie's jaw. He knew some satisfaction as he heard the last blow crack a bone.

Charlie might lose a little weight before his next fight. Hawk figured he wouldn't be eating much in the way of solids for a while.

It took three men to drag Charlie outside. Hawk straightened his chair and sat again. He finished off three fingers of whiskey in one gulp and welcomed the warmth as it slid into his stomach. He was going to need that and more. Much more once the pain in his face made itself known.

The barmaid was suddenly at his side, wiping his face with a clean damp rag. Hawk breathed a sigh of disgust. The truth was, he didn't want to be bothered. Didn't he have enough trouble with one woman? He'd have to be out of his mind to start with another.

"Thanks, lady. You don't have to bother with that."

"It's no bother," the woman returned. She leaned down again, drawing Hawk's gaze to her swinging breasts. Hawk thought they looked better than the first time. Maybe because they were a lot closer. And then he turned away, feeling not the slightest bit of temptation, thinking nothing more of the matter.

The entire encounter took all of maybe five seconds. Just long enough for Abigail to catch him at it. God damn. Why the hell did she have to choose just that minute to show up? There she was, standing opposite from where he sat, and the damn woman had yet to stop fussing over him. By the look in Abigail's eyes, there was no sense in denying that he had been looking where he probably shouldn't have been looking. Hawk gave a mental shrug. It was no big deal, really. Men saw that kind of thing all the time. It wasn't anything to get upset about.

The problem was, Abigail had never seen it before. And she thought it exactly the right thing to get upset about. She never said a word but simply turned on her heel and headed up the stairs again.

Hawk watched her departure with growing anger, knowing there'd be a confrontation. Hawk, being like most men, found no delight in the prospect. Now he'd have to try and explain. Why the hell couldn't she have just ignored the whole thing? Everything would have been all right if she'd just stayed upstairs in the first place.

He took another swallow of whiskey, stood and followed.

The door was locked. He'd expected that. He

didn't knock. She wouldn't have answered the knock at any rate. The wood splintered around the bolt as he kicked the door open.

Abigail sat in the room's only chair, ignoring his entrance, ignoring his presence. Hawk shut the door behind him and scowled as it swung open half an inch. Now he'd have to pay for the door and get them another room—if they had another room.

He walked to the bed and sat. A long silent moment went by before she glanced in his direction. When she did, she couldn't hold back. Her voice was soft, low—and damn her—more enticing than it had ever been before. "What are you doing here?"

"If you're going to start in about the woman downstairs, don't bother."

"Why?"

"Because that kind of thing happens all the time. It means nothing."

"Really? The way you were looking down her blouse didn't look like nothing." She might have been discussing a grocery list for all the emotion she allowed.

"She was bending over me. What did you expect me to do, close my eyes?"

"You maggoty piece of horse manure."

Hawk's eyes widened a bit. She said that far too calmly. "I'm a man, Abby." Somehow it made him feel better to say it, even if he didn't feel much like a man at the moment.

Abigail leaned back and gave him a cool smile, just as if he'd been a stranger. "Perhaps the problem here is, I thought you were better than most."

"She practically shoved them in my face. What man wouldn't look?"

"You know how tired I am of hearing that you're a man? Apparently you think because your body has one certain protruding part, you have rights others don't have." She smiled again, sending a chill up his spine. "You couldn't be more wrong."

"What the hell does that mean?"

"It means, I'm leaving you."

Hawk laughed a soft low sound. He'd allow this woman anything, anything but that. "Not a chance."

Abigail smiled. "We'll see."

"You're not going anywhere," he said more strongly and perhaps with just a trace of fear.

Abigail just sat there, saying nothing, not looking at him, not listening as he swore she wouldn't leave.

It was her calm, cool determination that did it. He lost some of his usual control when faced with that icy resolve. He had no doubt that she'd try to leave him, try it, in fact, again and again, until the day came when she finally managed it.

Abigail had not been watching him, so she knew some surprise to find herself suddenly pulled from the chair and held out before him, suspended by her upper arms from the floor. It was a mistake Hawk would never make again.

The fact of the matter was, she didn't kick him so she might watch him fall to the floor and moan in tormented agony. She hadn't expected that. She'd kicked him trying to escape his hold, and it had brought about instant results.

Still, she couldn't deny the fact that he was moaning. Moaning most pitifully, if the truth were told.

She almost felt sorry for him. If she didn't hate him quite so much, she might have.

"What's the matter with you?"

Truthfully Abigail had no idea. Despite her experience with this one particular man, she was still an innocent in regard to the male anatomy. It couldn't be that her kick had done this, she silently reasoned. She hadn't kicked him that hard, had she? Abigail shook her head. No. She had hit him a number of times both in play and otherwise and had never seen him react like this. One minute he was holding her, the next she had slipped from his grip and he was rolling upon the floor as if demented.

"Abby, Jesus," he finally managed through a tight throat.

"Are you hurt?" Stupid question. Obviously he was hurt, only she couldn't understand how or why. Now that she looked a bit more closely, she could see his face appeared to have taken some punishment. And then she realized he'd obviously been at least part of the reason for all that shouting downstairs. He'd been fighting. Was the swelling beneath his eye causing him this much pain? It couldn't be. Was he having an attack of some sort? Abigail thought that might be the case and was about to call for help when he seemed to quiet some.

He lay there for a long silent moment, staring at the ceiling, gasping for breath, before he said, "I give up." God, what was the use? He'd been a fool to go looking for a fight. It had accomplished nothing but, in the end, to have the one woman he loved most in the world furious with him.

Hawk winced as he came to a sitting position.

"What are you talking about?"

"I'm talking about us. You and me. I give up. You win."

"Wonderful. Exactly what did I win? And why were you fighting?"

He took a deep, if shaky, breath. "I was fighting because I wanted to hit someone."

"Why?"

He didn't answer her but asked instead, "You know what I thought the first time I saw you, Abby?"

Abigail frowned. "What?"

"I said to myself, 'This beautiful woman needs a real man.'" Hawk's laugh was wry and directed at himself. "Like an idiot, I imagined that I was strong enough to be that man."

"I really don't know what—"

"All Robert did was simper, 'Yes, dear. Yes, dear.' I thought, God . . . this man needs a pair of balls."

Abigail imagined correctly his meaning. She was beginning to get a vague picture. "You thought I had unmanned him?"

Hawk glanced at her wide-eyed expression and shrugged. "All I knew was, I'd never take orders from a woman."

"And I've been ordering you about?"

He shrugged again. "Mostly you just haven't been obeying mine."

Abigail nodded. Her arms were folded across her chest, and she began to pace the small room. "Let me see if I have this straight. You were afraid that I would unman you, since it looked as if I had done as much to Robert. So, in order to prove to yourself that you're still a man, you took up with another woman."

She walked up to him and then delivered a powerful kick to his thigh. "Ow! God damn it!" Hawk grabbed his newest injury and then lunged for her legs. There was no way that he was going to let her kick him for the third time.

Abigail knew some surprise to find herself suddenly tackled to the floor, flat on her back, with the man she despised most in the world upon her.

"If you kick me again, I swear I'll . . ." Hawk couldn't finish because he didn't know what he'd do.

"Fine." She slapped him instead, quite hard actually. Between clenched teeth she grated out, "I won't kick you, I'll just—" Her hands were pinned instantly to the floor.

She squirmed beneath him, trying to throw him off.

"Abby, listen to me." He put a bit more pressure on her, trying to keep from getting hurt again. "I think you're partly right, but it wasn't the woman. I had no interest in her. It was Charlie."

"What?" Abigail couldn't have known more confusion. What in the world did he mean by that?

"I mean I wanted to fight Charlie."

"Why?"

"Because you never once listen to me. And I wasn't man enough to give you the spanking you deserved."

"Oh, now there's a good reason," she said, her voice heavy with sarcasm. "I don't listen to you, so you beat up men and look down lady's blouses. Next you'll be kicking dogs. It makes perfect sense."

"She's no lady."

Her eyes narrowed with rage at the thought of him looking at another and then she realized his comment. "The spanking I deserved? Try hitting me and I'll put a bullet between your eyes."

Hawk sighed and looked straight into her eyes as the last wall of self-preservation crumbled away and he spoke from the depths of his soul. "This has never happened to me before. I was always in total control. I never cared what a woman thought, what she felt. Loving you has done me in, I think." He breathed a long sigh as he gathered his thoughts. "I have no control, especially none over you. You ignore me at every turn and I let it happen because I'm afraid you'll get angry with me." He sighed again. "It doesn't make a man feel much like a man when he can't control the woman he loves."

"Are we in a contest for strength here?"

"Sometimes I feel like we are. And the fact is, I can't win against you."

A low chuckle escaped her throat. God, men were such babies. What difference did it make who was strong and who was not? The only thing that should have been important was that they loved each other. "Would you love me more if I were weak?"

"I couldn't love you more. Your strength is part of you." It had taken a bit of soul searching, but he thought he was beginning to understand. Now and then her strength and determination made him feel inadequate. And yet he loved her because she was strong. It was his failing, not hers. The fact of the matter was, he was no less a man for loving her, but more a man because of that love. Why had it taken him so long to understand?

Abigail frowned. "You're very confusing."

Hawk laughed. "If you think you're confused, imagine how I felt."

Abigail giggled, and then her laughter suddenly dried up as she remembered again. "Why did you look at her? I hate you for looking at her."

"Abby, I swear, I didn't even know I was looking."

Her eyes narrowed in disbelief.

"All right, maybe I did know, but I only looked because—" His words came to a sudden stop, for he was unable to come up with an answer. Why did men look at women? Much of the time it was done without thought, and he couldn't think what to tell her. "Because I don't know why. But I swear I'll never look again. God, I never thought it would get you so upset."

"You mean, you never thought I'd catch you at it."

"That too," he answered, perhaps a bit too honestly. The trouble was, his confession seemed not to soften her heart one iota. A moment went by before he asked, "Abby, what would you do if you saw a naked man? Would you look?"

Abigail watched him for a long moment before a smile began to soften her tight lips. She laughed, knowing the truth of it.

"There, you see? You'd do as much. And it would mean nothing to you."

Abigail nodded in agreement.

He brushed a curl from her face, his gaze tender with love and asked, "Do you think we could pretend that I'm the boss when there are others around?" His eyes narrowed some in thought. "I'll settle for that."

Abigail laughed at the request. "If it's so important to you, you can be the boss all the time." Instantly she reconsidered. "Well, perhaps not all of the time." She thought again and then nodded in agreement. "When others are around."

Hawk laughed, rolled to his back, and brought her with him. "There's no one around now."

"Does that mean I'm the boss?"

"It does."

"Does being the boss give me the right to tell you what to do?"

"It does."

"Mmm, I think I like this." She raised herself, leaning an elbow upon his chest. "What shall I tell you to do?"

"I could offer a suggestion."

Abigail nodded. "You could, but since I'm the boss, I don't have to take it, right?"

"Oh, I think you'll take this one," he said as his fingers reached for the buttons of her shirt. And then a moment later, "Damn, I forgot about the door."

"Pull the dresser in front of it."

Hawk grinned and did as he was told. He returned to find her sitting on the bed, her shirt open, and she was kicking off her boots. He pushed her gently to her back and helped with the rest of her clothing. It wasn't until she was naked and he was discarding his own things that he said, "It was very wise of me to make you the boss."

She laughed at the obvious hunger in his eyes. "I thought so."

Chapter Twenty-One

Abigail was exhausted. She'd somehow lost count of the hours she'd spent in the saddle and the days as well. It didn't matter at any rate. The only thing that mattered was that they find these men before they killed again. And then making sure that Amanda was safe.

They rode across Tennessee again, this time by the southern route.

Hawk figured they were less than a day behind. He knew as well, they followed only two. Apparently there had been a falling out, and one of the two dead men they'd found three days back had been part of the gang. Following wasn't as easy now that the horse with the cracked shoe had been left behind. Still, the men ahead had no idea they were being trailed and did not try to cover their tracks. Following was easy enough.

Hawk pulled his horse to a stop and studied the overturned ground. Two hours at the most. He shot Abigail a worried look and wished he could put her somewhere just for a short time.

"What's the matter?"

"We're close. No more than two hours."

Abigail felt a chill of fear race down her spine. It was one thing to plan and carry out this necessary trailing and final capture and quite another to actually come face to face with these monstrous men. She worried less for herself than her man, for she knew Jeremiah would never allow her to come to harm. If only she could be equally as confident of his welfare. She offered a quick silent prayer for his safety. At least it would be over soon. "Good."

"Abby, I want you to listen carefully to everything I say."

"I will." She agreed far too quickly and easily as far as Hawk was concerned.

"First of all, I want you to ride behind me from now on."

She frowned. "Jeremiah, I—"

"Behind me," he said. His tone offered her no option.

"All right," she returned, obviously unhappy at the thought. "It's just that I don't want you to get hurt."

"I won't be getting hurt if I can keep my mind on what I'm doing. Which means trusting you to listen."

She nodded. "You can trust me."

Hawk watched her for a long moment before he breathed a sigh, remounted his horse, and said, "All right, let's go."

Less than two hours later, somewhere between the noon hour and dinner, they came upon the inn. The place looked empty. Hawk's skin crawled. He had a bad feeling about this one. Damn, if he had to look upon one more massacre, one more mutilated body, he just might get as sick as Abigail looked. "Again?" she asked, even as her eyes begged him to tell her no, not this time.

Hawk shook his head. "I don't know. Maybe not."

Chickens scurried over the backyard with their usual jerky step, pecking at the ground; a cow mooed somewhere behind the barn; a horse whinnied from inside. At least the place wasn't deserted. It was quiet, yes, but that could mean the folks inside were busy preparing for the next stagecoach. It didn't have to mean anyone was dead.

Together Abigail and Hawk circled the building, careful to keep themselves hidden in the surrounding shrubbery. And then they came to the front yard.

Hawk breathed a sigh of relief at first. Patrons visited. The place wasn't empty at all.

Two horses were tied to the hitching post. Two horses meant . . . Hawk knew a moment of anxiety, for it was two horses that he followed, and his heart began to pound again.

They dismounted and moved closer to the edge of the woods so they might see more clearly. Hawk's dark careful gaze took it all in.

A young woman took just that moment to step outside. She walked to the pump and filled a bucket with water. "Oh, my God—" Abigail began, only to be instantly cut off as Hawk's hand pressed tightly against her mouth.

"Quiet," he whispered.

Abigail shook his hand loose. "You don't understand. It's Amanda!"

She was about to run toward the woman when she was suddenly lifted off her feet and yanked back. She turned her head, her eyes puzzled as she glanced at Hawk, who had again closed his hand over her mouth, as well as placed an arm around her waist, securing her against him. Slowly he released her mouth, while his other arm kept her tightly against him. "What's the matter with you? What are you doing?"

"Be quiet and listen to me." He spoke directly into her ear, his voice lower than a whisper. "Look at her dress. Look at her hair. The mark on her arm. Do you see it?"

Abigail nodded.

"Something is wrong."

"But—"

"The two horses. They've been ridden hard and through thick woods. Look at the scratches. They haven't been cared for, they haven't been fed or watered."

Abigail frowned and looked up at him. How could he possibly know that?

She might as well have asked the question aloud.

"Because they hear the water. They're trying to get to it. See?"

Abigail watched as the two horses strained against their ropes. She nodded.

"If they were fed, they would have been watered as well. Only their riders were in a hurry to get inside."

He hesitated a moment, hating to tell her. "What could have caused them to hurry?"

431

Abigail closed her eyes and made a soft moaning sound. "No." the word was more a whisper of breath than sound. It couldn't be. The men they followed were inside. God in heaven, no.

Amanda pumped the water. It overflowed the bucket and still she pumped, as if her mind were anywhere but on water.

Abigail screamed in silence: Don't just stand there. *Run!* Run while you've got the chance!

A man stepped out to the inn's porch and leaned his back against the door frame. He had a gun in his hand. The gun was pointed at Amanda. "Come on, missy. Let's move it along."

Abigail's knees collapsed and she moaned again, knowing why her sister had not escaped, knowing the man had had his gun aimed at her the entire time. "What are we going to do? Oh, my God, what are we going to do?" Abigail couldn't think. She'd never known such panic, such fear.

She turned in Hawk's arms and grabbed his shoulders, never knowing her nails bit deeply into his flesh. "Tell me what to do!"

"First of all, calm down. We can't help her if we panic."

It took some effort and many deep breaths, but Abigail finally managed a sort of calm.

"What now?" she asked briskly. "Tell me. Tell me what to do." She was anxious to be about this business, anxious to see this horror done at last.

"Be quiet. I'm thinking."

Abigail watched him closely, waiting for him to say something. And when he did, she only frowned. "All right. Stay here. I'll be right back."

"What does that mean? What do you want me to do?"

"Nothing. Stay here. Stay calm, and I'll take care of it."

"What are you going to do?"

"I'll go in a back window and take them out. There's only two of them. It won't be hard."

"Only two of them with guns."

Hawk smiled. "I'll be fine. Don't worry."

She grabbed his arm. "Wait a minute. I have an idea. I'll walk up the front steps. They're probably watching. They'll be so surprised they won't hear you coming in the back, and you can get the drop on them."

"Get the drop on them?" Hawk grinned. "Where did you hear that?"

"Penny novels." She dismissed his tender smile with a wave of her hand. "I'll hold a gun behind my back and when one comes out, I'll shoot him."

"Terrific," Hawk breathed on a sigh. "For just a minute there, I thought you were going to say something stupid."

"And that's your gentle way of telling me I just did?"

"Have you ever shot a man before?"

"I've shot rabbits."

"And, of course, man or rabbit, it's all the same to you."

"All right, maybe I won't shoot him. I'll just hold the gun on him until you take care of his friend inside."

"And you think that I'll allow you to put yourself in that kind of danger."

433

"What could happen?"

"You could get killed, for one."

"Jeremiah, I'll have a gun."

"And that will make a difference to them?" he asked in ridicule. And then answered the question himself. "They'd kill you faster than you can blink."

"All right, then what should I do? I can't leave my sister in there with them."

"Just stay here."

He waited for an answer and when it didn't come, he gave her a little shake. "Do you hear me?"

"All right."

Her response left him less than satisfied. "If I have to worry about you, I'll probably get myself killed."

"I won't do anything."

"I should tie you to a tree."

"I told you, I'm not going to do anything."

Hawk watched her for a long moment before he nodded and slipped away so silently that had she not been watching, she wouldn't have realized he'd gone.

Abigail began to pace a four-foot stretch of grass as she waited for something to happen. She was terrified to hear gunshots and then terrified not to. She couldn't stand not knowing. How long had he been gone? How much longer would she be forced to wait?

Hawk slid inside the building by a back window and almost stepped on the big man slumped beneath it. Jesus! Hawk shuddered at the thought of stepping on him, for the man was not dead and would surely have made some sort of sound. Hawk knelt at his side. The man had been shot, but the bullet had only caused a deep groove in his side. Apparently it had happened only a short time ago, for he bled still.

He was in the kitchen. A black woman lay dead just a few feet from the stove. A towel hung from a nearby table. Hawk reached for it and pressed it to the man's side. The man instantly opened his eyes. Apparently he'd been pretending unconsciousness, for he instantly had Hawk in a headlock, a headlock impossible to break. Thank God, neither made a sound while doing it. "Who the hell are you?"

"Amanda's brother-in-law," Hawk did his best to whisper. Not an easy chore with Bill's fingers closing around his neck.

Bill let him go. "Abigail got married?"

Hawk didn't bother to explain that he wasn't exactly Amanda's brother-in-law but soon would be. "You know her?"

"No. I'm married to her sister."

Hawk nodded at this information. "Where are they?"

Bill didn't bother to ask what the man was doing climbing in his window, or how he knew there were intruders. He said simply, "In the front room."

"Can you walk?"

Bill nodded and came to his feet unassisted.

Hawk handed him his rifle.

Together they moved toward the front room.

Inside the room Amanda sat on one man's lap while both men pinched, grabbed, squeezed, and fondled her body at will. Amanda automatically pushed their hands away, but her objection to their touch was more a reflex action than an actual complaint. Had she her senses about her, she might have been terribly afraid, but the fact of the matter was, the horror she'd just witnessed could never compare with the meager abuse now imposed upon her. All she could think of was Bill and how these awful men had callously shot him dead. She'd screamed when it had happened and tried to run to him, but one of the men had, with one blow, knocked her to the floor and ordered her to get them something to eat.

Tears filled her eyes as she remembered his look of surprise and how he had fallen. She hadn't been able to touch him, hold him in her arms, cradle his head to her breast during his last few minutes on earth— and she had so wanted to bring him just a touch of the comfort, of the love, he had shown her.

He was so good, so tender, so sweet. She'd never expected to find a man that good. How could God have taken him from her so soon? A low sob slipped from her throat. If either man heard it, they ignored it.

Oddly enough, Amanda knew no fear. Nothing much had been done to her as yet. The men appeared more interested in their food than in abusing her. Still, she knew the abuse would come. At the moment she could garner no horror for what lay in store. It didn't matter what was done to her. It mattered only that her Bill was gone.

Amanda whimpered. Both men laughed, believing she was thinking on what was to come. Josh reached for her dress and tore both bodice and chemise apart, exposing her breasts to their view, to their cruel touch. It didn't register on either man that Amanda seemed not to notice this latest violation. They only laughed again as they reached greedy hands to her softness.

Bill had heard the tearing cloth and knew a moment of utter insanity. He made to crash into the room, but Hawk grabbed him with both hands and pulled him back. He whispered soothing unheard words and shook his head. Unless one of them were willing to die, perhaps all three, Hawk had to keep the man calm. "Take it easy. If they have a gun on her you'll get her killed."

Bill knew, if that were the case, she'd die the second he charged into the room. For the first time in his life Bill knew a cool, calm, murderous rage, but along with that rage came the sense that everything would be all right. At the moment he was helpless but to allow his wife some suffering at their hands, but not for long. In the end he'd have his sweet Amanda back, and these bastards would suffer more. Much more.

They waited, knowing the men were eating by the slurping sloppy sounds they made. Inching closer, Hawk glanced around the doorway, slid back, and cursed. Amanda—her dress torn, her lace cap askew, her hair fallen half in her face—was sitting on one man's lap as another fondled her breast. If Hawk fired his gun, she might easily get hurt. No, he had to wait for her to move. And as hard as it might be, he had to keep her husband calm in the process.

Hawk could only imagine his own rage had Abigail been in Amanda's place. It would take almost no effort on his part to kill the men with his bare hands.

Meanwhile, a dozen or so yards from the inn, Abigail continued to pace. Finally after what seemed like an hour, she figured she'd had just about all she could take of this waiting. Hawk was in the building, perhaps hurt, or already dead. She shivered at the thought. No, he wasn't dead. He couldn't be dead, and she was going to make sure of it.

Abigail flung her hat aside and shook her hair free. It fell in tangled curls almost to her waist. She opened four buttons of her shirt and allowed the material to part. She nodded as she looked down, knowing more than enough flesh showed to entice. The two men inside had to look at her with lust. Lust would be their undoing. If there was any justice, lust would see them dead.

Abigail pulled her gun from its holster as she dropped her belt to the ground.

Moments later she was walking toward the inn, the gun held behind her back.

Willie happened to glance toward the window as Abigail moved up the long brick walkway. "Look at that, will ya'. A woman in pants." He'd never seen such a thing. "Don't that beat all?"

Josh followed his partner's gaze. "Damn, the place is crawling with them. Look at the tits on that one."

Hawk leaned up against the wall just outside the room and gritted his teeth as he swore a long stream of silent curses. The first chance he got, he was going to wring her neck. He hadn't a doubt that the two men were ogling his wife, that the damn woman had exposed herself to danger, no matter his insistence that she stay safely hidden away.

A chair scraped against the floor as one of the men came to his feet. "Why don't we invite her in? I ain't never had a woman in pants before."

Josh held Amanda still in his lap. Hawk cursed as he looked around the corner again. It hadn't worked. Abigail had put herself in danger for nothing.

As he spoke, Willie was already at the door, his gun drawn as he waited for her to come closer. She seemed to hesitate, as if she knew something were wrong. Willie figured it best to issue his invite about right now.

He opened the door and stood there with an evil smile and a gun pointed at her heart. "You lookin' for somethin', missy?"

Abigail shivered at the sight of a gun pointed in her direction. It was a terrifying experience to know a man could snuff out your life with the simple pulling of a trigger, and this man was more likely than most to do the evil deed.

Abigail knew she was as good as dead if she didn't finish what she'd started. She forced a grin as she came to a stop not ten feet from the man and ran the fingertips of one hand up and down the opening of her shirt. In doing so, the material parted.

Willie couldn't tear his gaze away. Every time she moved her hand, the shirt opened just a little bit more. The little one inside promised to be fun, but this one promised more.

"Maybe." Abigail forced another smile. God, she hoped he didn't see how she trembled, or if he did, she hoped he'd believe her trembling was excitement, not fear. "You got something to offer a lady?" Thank God she had somehow managed to force her voice into a low seductive tone.

Willie laughed, holstered his gun and looked down at the bulge at his crotch. "I reckon I could find somethin'."

Abigail was more than nervous, she was terrified. She took a deep breath and continued to play with her opened shirt. She was so scared that she never noticed the soft breeze that parted the shirt even more. She never knew that Willie caught a glimpse of a very full breast and rosy nipple. Abigail would never know he'd seen quite so much, nor would she know that a breast was just the thing to totally relax his guard.

Willie licked his lip and called out behind him, "Hey Josh, look at this."

Josh dumped Amanda to the floor and came to his feet. Hawk issued a quick prayer of thanks as he came around the doorway into the room. Josh never knew what hit him. One second he was looking toward the door, and the next he knew nothing as a bullet entered his left eye and flung him back. Glass broke as the force knocked him into the front window, and he lay there limp, obviously dead, partially suspended from the floor, half in and half outside.

Abigail had been waiting to hear a gunshot. The instant she did, she jumped for the protection of the porch and rolled out of sight beneath the spider-infested damp wood. She was already under its thick protection before the glass shattered.

Abigail had been faster than Willie, for she had expected the gunfire. It took Willie a moment longer. First he had to come out of his lusting state before he could realize something was wrong. In truth, it took only a second but it was a second too long.

He turned, crouched low, and fired. As he pulled the trigger, he saw the two men. A frown creased his forehead as he tried to understand how a dead man was standing there shooting at him. A dead man with an Injun at his side. Willie didn't think on it for long. He didn't have the time.

The rifle's bullet hit him in the shoulder and knocked him back to the wall. He slumped to the floor, his arm instantly numb. Along the way he had dropped his gun.

Amanda—crouched beneath the table during the shooting—came to her feet and ran to her husband with a cry. Her arms went around him. Bill closed his eyes and thanked the Lord for this blessing. He never felt the discomfort in his side. If he had, he wouldn't have cared. He didn't care about anything but taking this woman in his arms, but holding her tightly, reassuring himself that she was truly all right.

Willie had inflicted his share of pain and fear. More than his share if the truth be told. Still, he wasn't much for withstanding pain himself. He blubbered in fear as Hawk slowly aimed his gun at the Willie's gut. "Injun, no, please. I didn't do nothin'."

Bill touched Hawk's arm. Hawk shook him off. "I want him; he killed my father."

Bill said simply, "He touched my wife."

Hawk glanced in Bill's direction and sighed. Either way the man was already dead.

Hawk understood justice. The man was due his revenge. He knew he'd want as much had Abigail been subjected to their merciless treatment. He nodded but kept his gun aimed at the man.

"Are you all right, honey?" Bill asked his weeping wife.

"I thought they killed you," she sobbed into his chest. "Oh, God, I can't believe you're here."

441

"I'm fine, sweetheart. Why don't you go upstairs and change."

Amanda hesitated. She didn't want to leave him just yet.

"Go ahead," Bill urged. "I'll be right here."

It was then that Amanda realized her dress offered her no protection. She nodded and gave him one more squeeze before she clutched the edges of her bodice together. While wiping at her tears, with her free hand, she hurried from the room.

Bill grabbed the man by his injury, never hearing the groan of pain, nor his pleas for mercy, as he dragged him outside and into the barn. What he had in store was not for anyone's eyes but his. Willie was to suffer greatly, but as far as both Hawk and Bill were concerned, it could never be enough.

Bill had disappeared into the barn when Hawk yelled out, "Abigail, get in here immediately!"

Abigail breathed a sigh of relief. She'd heard the guns fire, but hadn't known until this minute that her man had not been hurt during the foray. It wasn't until this very second that she realized she'd been holding her breath. She gasped now, feeling a relief so intense that she started shaking all over again. Still, she knew she was in for a time of it. From the anger in Hawk's voice—and the fact that he called her by her full name, something he rarely did—she figured he wasn't about to go easy on her.

Lying huddled beneath the porch, she had forgotten about her shirt. It was only when she stepped inside and noticed the direction of Hawk's dark scowl that she remembered and quickly did up her buttons again.

442

No one had to tell him what she'd been about. Hawk had imagined as much. He wondered only how far she might have gone trying to gain the attention of both men. And the thought brought about a fresh bout of rage. A rage he had some time controlling. How had she dared to put herself in danger like that?

"Are you all right?" Her anxious gaze searched his face, his chest, and then she breathed a sigh at finding no obvious injury. He was furious with her. It took only one glance to know that. Abigail wanted to go to him, but instinctively knew any demonstration of concern or tenderness on her part would not be welcomed.

Hawk watched her for a long moment before he found the strength to speak at all. He'd never come closer in his life to striking a woman. He didn't trust himself in her company. "Go up to your sister. She needs you." He nodded toward the stairs.

Abigail fairly flew and gained the last step with no knowledge of having taken the first.

Hawk poured himself a drink and then another as the two women upstairs cried and consoled one another. He sank to a chair, his body trembling with the delayed reaction of fear. He didn't want to think how close he'd come to losing her. He didn't want to think at all.

It was almost ten minutes later when Hawk heard the shots. He knew it was over. The men, all four, were dead. His father could rest easy now.

He only wished he could. With Abigail as his wife, he'd probably never know a day of rest again.

Bill came into the inn at the exact same moment that the two sisters walked down the stairs.

Hawk had his leg stretched out before him, another drink in his hand.

It was only then that Abigail saw the blood. Her eyes widened with shock. "You said you were all right!" The fact of the matter was, Hawk hadn't answered her at all. He scowled again and emptied his glass once more. "If you remember, I never answered you."

"Get a doctor. Bring him upstairs." Abigail looked about ready to go mad as everyone stayed in place, staring at her. Suddenly she shouted, "Somebody help him!"

Bill never thought to disobey. He brought Hawk upstairs and sat him on the bed and then left for the doctor. Abigail was right behind him, pulling away Hawk's pants the moment the door closed. She couldn't bear to see the injury, but not knowing the extent of the damage done was infinitely worse.

"You said you'd be all right," she accused.

"And I would have been if you would have kept out of it." Hawk wondered how much of his statement was true. Had she not diverted their attention, things might have turned out quite a bit differently. But he wasn't about to let her know that.

Hawk leaned back on fluffed pillows as Abigail moved to the dry sink and poured water into a bowl. The water was placed at his side as she began to clean around the wound with the edge of a towel. The wound wasn't nearly as bad as she had first supposed. The bullet had gone wide and only grazed him, leaving half an inch of flesh missing. The injury

444

had already stopped bleeding. Abigail figured he'd end up with little more than a neat little scar on the outside of his thigh. It didn't seem to matter. Abigail knew only horror at the thought of Hawk being shot. She shuddered at the fact that this could have been so much worse. "You said you could take care of yourself. I could kill you for lying to me."

"I didn't lie. If you hadn't come out of the woods, I would have been fine."

She glared at him. "Oh, right. Try to blame this on me."

She fussed over him, obviously upset, obviously angry. "I hate you for doing this to me."

"What the hell did I do? Except to tell you to stay in the woods? Which you conveniently forgot to do."

"You took too long. I knew something was wrong."

"So like the cavalry you thought to come to my rescue? Lady, you do wonders for a man's ego."

"Well that's too bad, isn't it? Your poor masculinity must have suffered a terrible trauma. Maybe I should have let you die. At least it would have saved your miserable manhood."

There was more than manhood involved here, and both knew it. Abigail had put both her life and the baby's on the line. The slightest error could have easily brought about disaster.

"I promised myself that I'd wring your neck the first chance I got."

"And?" she dared.

Hawk didn't bother to mention the fact that he was so relieved that she was all right that he didn't know what had happened to most of his anger. Instead he said, "The next time you disobey me, I'm going to beat you."

"Go ahead and try it," she sneered as she wrapped a dry clean towel around his leg and glared at his threat.

"So—are you going to marry me or not? We found your sister."

"Absolutely!" she said with some real emphasis. "I'm not finished with you yet."

"What does that mean?"

"It means that I can't think of a better way to get even. If I marry you, I'll have years to nag and argue and pay you back for all the aggravation you've—" She shrieked her surprise as he suddenly pulled her over him and onto the bed at his side.

The bowl tipped. Water soaked the mattress, but Hawk didn't care as his mouth sought out the deliciousness of hers.

"I want you to know that the only reason I'm not fighting you is because you're hurt," she breathed on a sigh.

Hawk grinned down into the eyes of the stubborn woman at his side, knowing a love and tenderness beyond compare. "That's very considerate of you."

Abigail moaned a sweet sound of delight as he nuzzled his lips against her throat. "I thought so."

Her eyes suddenly misted with tears. Hawk felt some amazement. He hadn't ever seen her cry before.

"What's the matter?"

"Promise me you'll never do it again."

"What?"

"Put yourself in that kind of danger. I couldn't bear it if I lost you."

Hawk could have asked at least as much of her, but as it turned out, neither had the chance to make their vows.

It would be months before Abigail could remember what happened next without her cheeks turning cherry red. The doctor she had demanded Bill to fetch chose just that moment to step into the room, only to find his very naked patient hardly in need of his care and otherwise occupied.

If you enjoyed reading NIGHTS OF PASSION *and would like a bookmark, write to Zebra Books.*